THE SECRETS OF
WILLOWRA

Visit us at www.boldstrokesbooks.com

THE SECRETS OF WILLOWRA

by

Kadyan

2021

ISBN 13: 978-1-63679-064-0

This Trade Paperback Original Is Published By
Bold Strokes Books, Inc.
P.O. Box 249
Valley Falls, NY 12185

First Published in French as *Willowra* in 2007
First BSB Edition: October 2021

Credits
Translator: Joan Lagache
Editor: Shelley Thrasher
Production Design: Stacia Seaman
Cover Design by Tammy Seidick

Acknowledgments

I want to thank the whole BSB team for their dedication and their help, especially Shelley for her patience and her willingness to understand this book and my way of writing.

Thanks to Len for giving me this wonderful opportunity.

I hope you enjoy this book.

Thanks to MP. Without her, I would not be the author I am today.

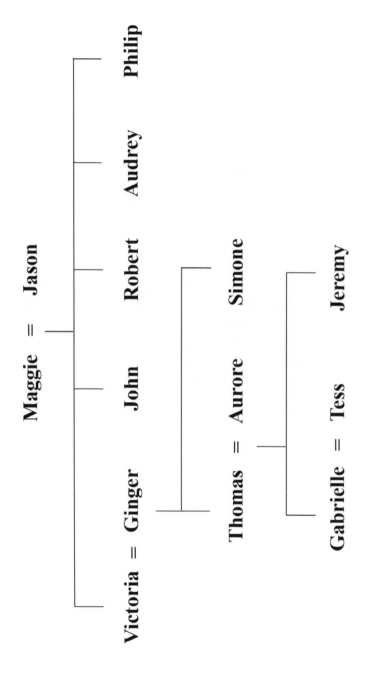

PART I: GABRIELLE

CHAPTER ONE

Sydney, New South Wales, 2006

When Gabrielle heard her mobile's ringtone, she sighed and put the *Sydney Morning Herald*, which she had been trying to read since the ferry had cast off, down on the empty seat next to her. She was late and knew very well who was calling. As she rummaged through her little backpack searching for the blasted phone, she mentally prepared herself for the reproof she knew she was about to receive. She glanced at the screen to check who was calling and reluctantly answered.

"Gab, where are you?"

"I'm late, I know. I'm still on the ferry. We just left Cremorne Point. I'll be home in ten minutes max."

"We were supposed to eat out..."

"I know."

A sigh, then silence on the other end of the line. Guilt swept through Gabrielle. "Tess."

Gabrielle couldn't find the words. What excuse could she have given to justify being late, again? None, her conscience whispered. Tess knew perfectly well that Gabrielle didn't see any patients after five p.m. unless it was an emergency, and emergencies didn't exactly come up every day. If she wanted to be honest with herself, she had to face up to the situation once and for all. But how?

"Tess, we need...to talk," Gabrielle said, firmer but still hesitant.

"I never thought such simple words could be so upsetting, and at the same time such a relief," murmured Tess with tears in her voice. "Hurry. I'm waiting for you."

Hearing the dial tone, Gabrielle realised that Tess had hung up, but as though anesthetized, she kept the phone pressed to her ear. Did she really just tell Tess they needed to talk things over? That meant she'd have to explain why for the last two months she'd been coming home later and later. Explain why, with the exception of her work, she'd been dragging her feet to do anything, especially with Tess? She stared out at the stretch of water, taking a deep breath to try to calm her pounding heart.

She already regretted having left Cremorne Point and the security of her office. Finally reacting to the monotonous dial tone, she mechanically turned off the phone before putting it away in her bag. Ten minutes. In no more than ten minutes she would have to face Tess. She could already feel the ferry's powerful propellers slowing down. Soon, the entire hull would vibrate as the captain reversed the vessel's engines to prepare for docking. Then would come the thud against the pier and the stampede toward the exit, although describing the handful of commuters left at this late hour as a "stampede" would be an exaggeration.

Tess had been crying on the telephone. Gabrielle felt a tug at her heartstrings. She didn't want to make her cry. Tess was the love of her life. Meeting her at a party when Gabrielle was a fourth-year medical student had changed her entire existence. A flirt, who could never get herself to settle down with just one woman, Gab had by the end of the evening irrevocably fallen in love eight years ago.

While getting off the boat, she reminisced about that time. She had been immediately attracted to this tall, slim redhead with her svelte, feline gait. Gabrielle had never seen her before on campus; she had been sure of it. Without a moment's hesitation, as if attracted by a magnet, she had headed straight for this forlorn-looking woman standing alone in a corner, whose green eyes and beautiful smile had entirely melted Gabrielle's heart. Tess, however, had resisted.

Grinning, Gabrielle left the pier and walked down the little road that led to their house. Six months. It had taken her six long months to convince Tess of the sincerity of her feelings. They'd moved in together the year after they met, and since then, everything had been perfect. Except for these last two months.

What is wrong with me? I have a gorgeous woman, an interesting career, a beautiful home, and friends. What more do I want? Why do I need to make the woman I love cry because I'm incapable of assuming the responsibility of a decision we've made together…?

8:58 p.m. Standing before the entrance to the house they'd bought just the year before, Gabrielle stalled for time. The tall trees and bushes planted around their home had made it a peaceful haven then, but now they had since taken on a sinister appearance, tormenting her and reflecting her fears every single evening before she had to walk through that door. How would she explain it all to Tess? Seeing the beautiful face through the glass pane in the front door prompted Gabrielle to take the last few steps inside.

They stood facing each other. When she saw Tess's puffy red eyes she felt like she was being stabbed in the heart. Staring into them, she softly raised her hand to caress Tess's freckled cheek, but Tess immediately took a step back, as if she had been slapped. Gabrielle looked down and closed her eyes, the pain of rejection seeping through her. She was getting what she deserved, but it still hurt.

"I cancelled the restaurant," Tess said curtly, turning her back on Gabrielle and walking outside onto the wooden deck.

Driven by habit, Gabrielle put away her satchel and bag in the tiny front hall closet. She leaned her head against the exotic wood of the doorframe, thinking how she would like to bang it against all the walls to chase her fears away, to force her lips to utter an explanation. She hated the way she always needed to be in control, unable to talk about her weaknesses. She had to try for Tess, for their relationship. She knew that. Taking a deep breath, she went over to Tess and joined her on the deck. Tess was already seated in a wicker chair.

Although slightly hidden by the trees, the view of the Bay of Sydney once again took her breath away. This view had convinced them to buy this unpretentious house on Mosman Bay, despite the price. When they had visited the property, they hadn't noticed the kookaburras that lived in the eucalyptus trees. Gabrielle stoically put up with these birds that made it difficult to sleep late because Tess loved their mocking laughter so much.

Gabrielle served herself a big glass of tamarind juice from the carafe resting on the coffee table before sitting down in an armchair next to Tess.

"You're leaving me…Is that it?"

Gabrielle opened her eyes wide in surprise at Tess's words. The tears that ran down the face of the woman she loved choked her up so much she couldn't speak. Panic. Where could Tess possibly have gotten this idea? She shook her head to refute her words.

"What's her name? No. Don't say anything. How could you do this to me? And now, of all times?"

As if trying to protect the baby, Tess put her hand on her belly. Gabrielle was incapable of uttering a sound despite the thoughts screaming in her head.

She took Tess's hand, but Tess abruptly recoiled. "It's our baby, a baby we both wanted, and now you want to leave me!"

Tess's voice was filled with despair. Tears welled up in Gabrielle's eyes. Shaking her head, she once again tried to take Tess's hand. How could Tess think there was someone else? That would never happen!

Gabrielle knelt before Tess, grasped her hand, and squeezed it tight so she wouldn't escape. This soft hand in hers anchored her, gave her strength. Gazing deeply into Tess's green eyes, she forced herself to speak. "Tess. Stop. Listen to me."

Tess froze when she saw Gabrielle's serious expression. She could no longer breathe. Waiting for the inevitable, she wanted to shield herself. She had rarely seen tears in Gabrielle's eyes—another clue that her world was falling apart. Gab had been coming home later and later these last two months, giving increasingly pathetic excuses. Tess had readily understood: Gab was going to abandon her.

"Tess…there's no one else but you. There's never been anyone else these eight years we've been together. Don't you understand that I love you, and I will always love you until I die? I swear it on everything nearest and dearest to me."

Tess was totally surprised. What had Gab just said? That there was no one else? She closed her eyes. Relief swelled in her heart. No one else…Gab wasn't leaving her. Had it possibly all just been a bad dream? Gabrielle quickly wiped away the tears running down Tess's face, already softly brushing her cheek. Tess put her hands around Gab's shoulders, pulling her toward her. Gabrielle rested her head on Tess's belly as they huddled together, crying all the tears they had kept locked up inside.

"Then why have you been coming home later and later each day, when I know office hours are over? Why have you stopped making love to me? Why have you stopped speaking to me? You never joke or laugh anymore."

"I'm sorry. I…"

The words were stuck in Gabrielle's throat, and her tears started again. She never could have imagined that Tess would believe she had met someone else. She hated herself for having made the love of her life suffer. For two months she had obstinately shouldered her fears and doubts alone—the two longest months of her life—ever since the tests had come back confirming that the artificial insemination had been successful.

"Shh. Hold me tight, Gab. I need to feel you against me."

Slowly, the minutes passed, accompanied by the growing silence of night falling, interrupted from time to time by the sound of a car or a boat hurrying to be moored.

Unable to hold off any longer, Tess sat back. She needed to see Gab's eyes to be completely reassured. Gab's eyes never lied. Gently, she forced Gab's face, nestled against her stomach, to turn up toward hers. Tess gazed deeply into her big, dark eyes, though under the deck lamp's soft light it was difficult to make them out. Overcome with emotion, she ran her fingers over the outline of Gab's beautiful face: her prominent cheekbones, fine nose, and full lips...and tears welled up again in her eyes.

"You're so beautiful, and I thought I'd lost you."

"Please don't cry, Tess. I'm sorry."

Gabrielle closed her eyes as Tess brushed her lips against hers, at first softly. And then, with increasing passion, she responded to Tess's insistent kisses. She hadn't touched her for two months, hadn't felt the softness of her skin, hadn't tasted the flavour of her lips...

Gabrielle lifted Tess's T-shirt and stroked her full breasts, making her moan from this joint adoration of her lips and breasts. She then broke away from Tess's lips to take her right breast fully in her mouth while she sensually played with the other. Though they were out on the deck where they might be seen despite the heavy vegetation, Tess, her breathing shallow, closed her eyes and laid her head against the back of the chair.

Gabrielle explored Tess's silky-soft skin with her free hand before sliding down toward Tess's shorts, which she expertly unbuttoned. She tenderly let go of Tess's erect nipple to taste her other breast. Tess's moaning increased Gabrielle's desire, pushing her to go faster, but she resisted the impulse. She wanted to take her time. Only Tess counted. Oh, how she had missed this silky, supple body! She then grabbed Tess's shorts to pull them down, and Tess lifted her hips to help, her pelvis brushing against Gab's chest. Moans of pleasure.

Gabrielle gazed directly into Tess's green eyes burning with desire. Their mouths met again, their tongues duelling until Gab finally gave in to the fire running through her veins. She began a trail of tiny kisses from Tess's mouth down farther and farther...Sliding her hands under Tess's backside, she pulled her to the edge of the chair, inciting Tess to open her legs. Unable to resist any longer, Gab immediately tasted the sweetness offered her, provoking an immediate groan of pleasure from Tess. She was close to coming…very close…

❖

Tess lovingly observed the woman sleeping by her side. The first time they'd met, she'd known this woman could own her heart and her life if she let her. The young woman who had approached her that first evening was so beautiful! Intense, dark, almond-shaped eyes and a determined look on her face lit with a smile that anyone would sell their soul for another chance to see. Tess hadn't had the strength to resist the temptation of running her hands through Gab's thick, wavy, black hair, despite her reputation as a ruthless womanizer. And this woman who was now the light of her life was still so beautiful. She had been so afraid of losing her these last months!

Once again, a wave of doubt engulfed Tess. Were their troubles really over? Tess flinched. Gabrielle had apologized, but she hadn't given any reason for her behaviour. Now that she knew Gab wasn't cheating on her, Tess had an inkling of what was bothering Gab, but in order to solve the problem they would have to communicate. Tess stifled a joyless chuckle. Communicate? With Gabrielle? Pulling a tooth without anaesthesia would be less painful.

Tess brushed her hand against Gabrielle's thick mane of hair while planting a peck on her shoulder blade. Smiling, she contemplated the perfect body stretched out beside her. Yes, they had to talk. Not tomorrow or this evening, but right now, this morning. Gab's hand inched across the bed, clearly searching for Tess's warmth; she then cuddled up against her.

"What are you doing already awake?" Gabrielle whispered, nuzzling Tess's neck.

Tess smiled. They had fallen asleep very late last night, or rather early this morning. She wouldn't have given up this night of lovemaking for anything. Since she'd become pregnant, her libido had magnified, and satisfying herself was so much less gratifying.

"I wanted to watch you sleep, but after a while I couldn't resist touching you. I've been so scared recently, Gab. I truly thought you were seeing somebody else…"

Gabrielle, perfectly awake now, squeezed Tess in her arms. "I'm sorry…" Gab hugged her tightly, but still didn't say another word.

"I need you so much, Gab. My emotions are all over the place. My hormones are out of control. I can't deal with another situation like the one I've had to handle these past months. It was destroying me," Tess whispered.

Gabrielle swallowed with difficulty. How could she explain herself, her awful behaviour? "You know how hard it is for me to speak about my feelings. The way I was brought up…"

"I know, but I need you to try for me…please."

Gabrielle let go of Tess and sat on the edge of the bed with her back to her. Staring into space, she tried to force the words to come out.

"Tess, I'm afraid…what am I saying? In fact, I'm terrified. I think about it night and day. The baby…I'm afraid I won't be good enough. I'm afraid we did something stupid when…"

Tess would have liked to take Gabrielle in her arms, but she placed her hand warmly on her back. "Why haven't you said anything? You're very much aware that a child will be an enormous change in our lives. You see couples every day in this kind of situation."

"I didn't want you to think I was…weak."

No longer able to resist, Tess wrapped her arms around Gabrielle. "It would never occur to me that you were a weak person, Gab. Don't you think I can see your empathy? The way you constantly try to hide how sensitive you actually are? Others may be blind, but I'm not. You will be a fantastic mother. You'll see. I'm sure you've observed often enough in your practice that fathers always go through this period of doubt, but when the child arrives, everything falls into place."

"You know I'll never be a father, Tess. Isn't it obvious that I'm one member short?" Gabrielle joked to mask her emotions.

"That all depends…" whispered Tess, with a tease in her voice now that she was reassured of Gab's sincerity, "but you're right to point out it isn't a flesh-and-blood member."

"Tess!"

Tess grinned as she grabbed Gab's face with both hands and pulled it closer to slowly kiss her lips before resting her cheek against her chest.

She was annoyed with herself for not having understood Gabrielle's fears and apprehensions about raising a child. Gab was always so strong and brave, always ready to flag homophobia or racism across every layer of Australian society. Tess never would have imagined that their decision to have a child together could shake up their relationship. Now that she thought about it, she realised that if she had actually studied the early signs, she would have been able to understand Gabrielle's angst. But she was so indescribably happy to be pregnant that she'd been blind to anything else.

"I can't get over it," Gabrielle whispered. "The baby is such a shock. I know we discussed it beforehand, that we both wanted this child, and that's why it was so important for me to be the one to do the insemination. But knowing that in six months it'll be here, I...I feel lost, crushed by all the responsibility. And what if we're not good enough?"

Tess leaned back to better observe Gabrielle's face. A gleam of uncertainty was reflected in her dark eyes. "We will be good enough. I know it. And you know why?"

Gabrielle shook her head.

"Because you're asking yourself all these questions. I have faith in us, Gab. If you love me, our child will be happy. Just promise me one thing. The next time you have doubts, talk to me, immediately."

Gabrielle sighed without looking away. "It's so hard for me. No one in my family ever spoke about emotions. They are personal, private, and should stay that way."

"That's all bullshit, Gab! You know it as well as I do. How many of life's precious moments have you missed because of this silence? Why don't you see your brother or your parents anymore—and I'm not talking about the two yearly phone calls you dutifully make, but about real visits, Gab, for the pleasure of sharing something with your family. You go to lunch with my mother once a month. You know my sister, and you met my father when we were on vacation in Scotland, even though I can't stand his new wife. In the eight years we've been together, I haven't met a single member of your family. It's like you're ashamed of me, of you, or of what you are, whereas you should be proud, proud of your personal and professional success."

Gabrielle slipped out of Tess's embrace and lay back down, staring at the white ceiling. How many times had they had this conversation? Gabrielle sighed.

"You know why, Tess. They're incorrigible homophobes."

"Why do you say that? Because you once heard your brother and his friends, when they were kids, making fun of homosexuals? Who hasn't heard that kind of joke?"

"My father heard them also, and he didn't react. He just let it go. And of course my mother didn't say a word. She rarely does. From that moment on, I thought of only one thing: leaving Willowra. Yet God knows how much I loved that place. My only real regret was leaving my grandmother, Victoria, and her outspokenness. How could my father, who was raised by her, turn out that way? They're complete opposites. And nobody ever talks about my Aunt Simone, whom I've never met. Do you think she's a lesbian, and they chased her from the family? That would explain it all."

Gabrielle warmed as she recalled her grandmother, Nan Victoria. How she had loved to listen to her grandmother's stories about sheep farming. Those had been the good old days in Willowra.

"Didn't you tell me Victoria isn't really your grandmother? If she lived with another woman, who knows? Maybe she is a lesbian and your father knew?"

Gabrielle stared at Tess. "Yeah, right. They became friends during the war. They must have served together in the AWAS, and when my grandfather died just after it ended, she gave shelter to her friend and her children."

"The whatsas?"

"The AWAS! The Australian Women's Army Service. You're a typical Brit, Tess, who knows nothing about Australian history. They served in Australia to replace the soldiers who left to fight the Japanese."

"And I prefer to believe that they were having a torrid affair and conveniently disposed of the husband."

Still lying on her back, Gabrielle burst out in laughter. Imagining Nan Victoria and Grandma Ginger getting rid of a burdensome husband was surreal. She shook her head.

"You wouldn't say that if you had ever seen the photos in Victoria's room. Ginger couldn't have been more than one-metre fifty and weighed all of forty kilos, and I think Victoria was in love with a soldier who died during the war and never got over him."

"How do you know that? Did she tell you?"

"No. But she has two photos hanging on the wall in her room. One shows a group of soldiers in the jungle armed to the teeth, and the second is a portrait of a dashing young man in uniform who has to be her lost love."

Gabrielle grew pensive. The photos in Victoria's bedroom recounted the history of someone's life. When she thought about it, she realised she knew the history of Willowra, but very little of her own family's story.

"So what if we went there for a vacation?" Tess said. "You might find some answers about your two grandmothers, and you could introduce me to your family."

Gabrielle immediately sat up, accidentally letting the sheet that covered her slip, revealing all for Tess to see. "Are you crazy? You want to go to that country of backward bigots so we can get lynched?"

Ignoring her outburst, Tess slowly massaged Gabrielle's forearm, working her way up to her shoulder.

Gabrielle grabbed the exploring fingers. "I thought you wanted to talk," she whispered, her voice husky.

"I thought you didn't want to," Tess replied. A naughty smile appeared on her face as she gently pinched Gab's nipple.

"Hey!"

Without hesitating, Gabrielle reached out hands first and threw herself on Tess, who tried to escape the tickles.

"No, Gab. Think about the baby. Tickling isn't good for the baby."

Bursting out with laughter, Tess blocked Gab's hands, but the sheet wrapped around her prevented her from making a clean escape. Taking advantage of the fact that she weighed more, Tess pushed Gab back onto the bed with all her strength, Gab finding herself on her back with Tess straddling her.

"And now who's going to be a good girl?" Tess asked, firmly holding Gab's wrists down as she wriggled to try to get away.

As Gabrielle was trying to catch her breath to strike back, her cell phone, left somewhere in the living room, started to ring. Damn phone! Tess grimaced but let go of Gab, who jumped off the bed.

"Are you on call?"

"No."

"Let it ring then."

Tess's husky voice stopped Gabrielle, persuading her that she had better things to do than answer her phone.

"You're so beautiful like that. I should take a picture."

Gabrielle traced Tess's glance back to herself, noticing that she was standing in the middle of their bedroom completely naked, her hands on her hips. Her lack of dignity and Tess's mocking eyes made her realize how absurd the whole situation seemed. She stretched her lips into a grin, but just as she was about to jump back into bed, Tess, with a dignified air, got up.

"Where are you going?" Gabrielle asked, disappointed.

"To have breakfast. I'm starving and incapable of thinking or reasoning with you."

"Hungry? Already? You're a walking stomach. We just ate late last night. You'd think you could wait. I was considering a brunch at the Rock before meeting up with the girls, but it's still a bit early. And why do you need to reason with me anyway? I thought we were done talking."

"Gabrielle Abbot! A scrawny cheese sandwich at eleven p.m. does not constitute a meal. Do I need to remind you that I am eating for two? And both of us, at this very instant, are starving. Incidentally, it's your turn this weekend to make breakfast. So get your fabulous ass out of this room and into the kitchen to prepare us something delicious while I take a shower."

Gabrielle contemplated Tess, who, arms crossed over her chest, was waiting for an answer. "How could I possibly refuse anything you ask me while you're wearing your birthday suit? If you could keep it on just a while longer, I can assure you that the chef would be inspired."

"Oh, you and your dirty mind!" Tess said as she walked to the bathroom.

"That's not what you were saying last night," Gabrielle yelled as the door closed.

❖

Showered and replete, they finished sipping their tea on the back deck. It promised to be a beautiful day, and Gabrielle, holding her mug, watched the sailboats leave their mooring.

"Have you thought about it?" Tess asked.

Gabrielle was puzzled. Had she missed something in the conversation? "About what?"

"Spending our next vacation at Willowra."

Gabrielle was so surprised she almost dropped her cup. "I thought we'd decided not to go."

"*You* decided we weren't going. I'd like us to make a mutual decision, Gab."

Uncomfortable, Gabrielle avoided the soft green eyes staring at her. Her tendency to decide for both of them had caused more than one argument between them, especially at the beginning of their relationship. Gabrielle grinned.

"What?"

"Nothing. I was just thinking that it's been a long time since we fought about this."

"I hadn't noticed we were fighting."

"You know what I mean..."

"Yes." Tess conceded with a smile. "You've made great strides in that area, and now I more often hear you say 'we' rather than 'I.' But in reference to Willowra..."

"Tess..."

The determination in Tess's green eyes made Gabrielle sigh inwardly. She wasn't going to drop the subject.

"Your parents have the right to know their future grandchild, don't you think?"

Gabrielle bit her lower lip before answering in a hushed voice. "They may not see it that way."

Tess frowned, so Gabrielle explained. "Even if it's our baby, it won't be their flesh and blood. I'm not entirely certain they'll ever be capable of seeing the baby as their grandson or granddaughter."

"I thought you told me Victoria wasn't your real grandmother?"

"So?"

"Unless I'm mistaken, you and your brother call her 'Nan,' don't you?"

"It's not the same thing."

"How is it different?"

Gabrielle opened her mouth to explain but had no words. She perfectly remembered the conversations and interactions between her father and Nan Victoria, and with her mother also. As a child, she'd thought Victoria was really her grandmother, until the day her father spoke about his mother. What a shock it had been for Gabrielle and her brother Jeremy to learn that Victoria was in fact the best friend of their actual grandmother, Ginger, who had died shortly after Jeremy's birth in 1972. Gabrielle now realised that deep in her heart of hearts, this discovery hadn't changed anything: Victoria was indeed her grandmother.

"I grew up believing Victoria was my grandmother, but I'm not sure my parents will ever get over their daughter being a lesbian, who on top of it got another woman pregnant through artificial means."

"You think Victoria didn't love your father like her own son because he wasn't her own blood? Or you and your brother like her own grandchildren?" Tess asked.

"She loves us, of that I'm certain…Well, at least I think so."
Doubt crept into Gabrielle's mind as she noticed the tiny victorious smirk on Tess's lips.

"I'd really like to go to Willowra."

"I don't think you'd like it. It's very hot, and there's dust everywhere, hardly any trees, and…"

And you're scared to death.

Tess's smirk grew as Gabrielle enumerated all the reasons they shouldn't go.

CHAPTER TWO

When Tess heard the front door, she opened it, filled with joy. It was barely six p.m. and Gabrielle was already home! She looked up from her medical journal, which had arrived that very morning. Gabrielle was holding a beautiful bouquet of red roses, which, to Tess's embarrassment, immediately brought tears to her eyes. Blasted hormones.

"Something smells good."

Gabrielle knew her words were trite, but Tess's reaction to her gift embarrassed her, and she couldn't think of anything else to say. It had been far too long since she'd given her flowers. She lightly kissed Tess's forehead, and all the day's stress melted away.

"Tandoori chicken and salad," Tess said before pointing at the bouquet of roses. "For me?"

"Who else?" Gab joked. "I saw them just before getting on the ferry, and they made me think of you. They were too beautiful to leave on the pier."

Tess's eyes shone even more brightly, and she wiped away the tears that were threatening to overflow. "Quite the charmer, aren't you, with your intense dark eyes and tender smile?" She threw herself into Gabrielle's arms, holding on tight and obviously overwhelmed by the emotion of the last few days.

Gab could feel Tess's heart beating wildly and would have slapped herself if she could.

She'd already berated herself hundreds of times since Friday evening. How could she have been so engrossed in her own fears that she couldn't see the ones gnawing at Tess? Stroking her soft hair, she murmured reassuring words of love that she felt deep inside, even if she had difficulty expressing them.

"Give me the flowers so I can put them in water," Tess said, seeming to try to get a hold on her emotions.

"The flowers can wait," Gab whispered, her face nestled in Tess's neck.

Tess felt Gabrielle's lips make a trail of kisses along her throat with the tip of her tongue. She closed her eyes and put her hand on Gab's black mane to keep her head in place. She could have almost cried from the joy of feeling desired again. She responded instantly, and every coherent thought faded away.

Suddenly, the telephone's ring invaded the room. Tess opened her eyes, and Gabrielle jerked her head up.

"I'm going to throw that goddamn phone into the bay," Gabrielle muttered.

"Don't answer."

"I'm on call."

Gabrielle grabbed her phone. "My father." She sighed and answered. "Dad?"

Tess watched Gab's expression transform from annoyance to surprise. Removing her arm from Tess's waist, she took a few steps toward the picture window.

"What's wrong with her? At her age? But she's crazy! Okay. I'm coming, Dad, but I have to get organized. I can't cancel all my patients' appointments in two seconds. I'll call you back to let you know which flight I'm taking."

Was Gabrielle going to Willowra? Tess's mind was churning. There must have been an accident. Who? Her mother? Her grandmother? Was this the right time for her to go with Gab? Not really.

"Yes. What message?"

Gabrielle's mouth dropped open, but no sound came out. Speechless for a few seconds, she stared at Tess. "Yes. I'm here. I don't know, Dad. I...Yes. We'll talk about it, and I'll get back to you."

Gabrielle hung up, feeling completely dazed.

"Gab? Are you all right?"

"Nan Victoria had a horse-riding accident two days ago. She refuses to go to the hospital, and the doctor thinks she won't get better if she doesn't. But she's as stubborn as a mule and now wants the whole family to come see her one last time...including you."

"Me? She doesn't even know I exist."

"Her message was, and I quote, 'Gabrielle must bring the person she lives with, and I'm not accepting any phony excuses.'"

Gabrielle nervously passed her hand through her hair. "Darn it. How does she even know I live with someone?"

"It's an easy assumption to make about someone your age."

Tess became very excited. To finally get to go to Willowra and discover where Gabrielle grew up and meet her family! She could have kissed Victoria for giving her this opportunity. It was the perfect chance. "I don't know, Tess. I don't want to risk your being poorly accepted. What a crazy idea to go horseback riding at her age! She's eighty-six years old. Why couldn't she just peacefully stay put in her armchair? And why does she want to meet the person I live with?"

"Your grandmother, who is on her deathbed, has asked you to come with your companion. You can't deny her that."

"She doesn't know you're a woman. Otherwise, she never would have asked," Gabrielle grumbled between her teeth.

"Oh, for goodness' sake. If you were a man I'd say you didn't have any balls. Muster up some courage and face your family for once. At least you'll know where you stand. Apart from refusing to see you again, what else could they do? It's not like we live in a village and are dependent on self-righteous customers to earn our living."

Tess's outburst was followed by a deafening silence.

"You're right," Gabrielle conceded with a sigh.

Tess smiled, victorious—she was finally going to discover Willowra! "I'll tend to the flowers and our meal. You take care of the tickets."

CHAPTER THREE

Kalgoorlie-Boulder, Western Australia, 2006

"Calm down, Gab. At worst they'll reject you, and we'll return to Sydney earlier than planned. But at least you'll know."

Gabrielle was barely listening to Tess's words as they walked off the tarmac toward the small building that served as a terminal for the Kalgoorlie-Boulder airport. She shouldn't have brought Tess along, but how could she ignore her grandmother's last wishes? Her stomach had been in knots since early morning. Her parents would be waiting for them at arrivals. *If they make even the slightest remark, we're jumping on the next plane back.* Tess's hand brushed against hers.

"Breathe. No matter what happens, we're together. And see this glorious blue sky? That alone is worth making the trip."

Despite the crowd behind her, Gabrielle stopped to turn and face her. After she considered her words for a few seconds, she glanced at the sky, and for the first time since her father's phone call, she smiled slightly. Tess was right. Her life was in Sydney with Tess and the baby, and the sky here was a blue that existed only in the outback. If worse came to worse and things were really awful, she'd go alone to see Victoria, and then she and Tess would return home.

"You're right. Ready to face the pettiness of the Australian outback?"

Tess smiled, and Gabrielle's heart swelled. That very smile, radiating across Tess's face and lighting up her beautiful green eyes, had made Gabrielle fall in love with her. Gab couldn't refuse her anything. She looked around but saw no one. All the passengers had gone into the terminal to pick up their luggage.

"Let's go. The faster we throw ourselves into the lion's jaws, the faster we'll know where we stand."

Once inside the terminal and when her eyes had adjusted to the change in light, she nervously searched the small trickle of people waiting for arriving passengers. Were her parents late? That would be unlike them.

"Gabrielle!" a soft voice called out.

She would have recognised her mother's gentle, patient tone anywhere. A grin came to Gabrielle's lips before she even saw her mother's face, as smooth and young as it had ever been. Without hesitating, Gabrielle hugged her tightly.

How had she not seen them? It was hard to miss the tall, well-built man with the fair complexion standing next to her mother. Her father and she cautiously stared at each other before they awkwardly reached out to exchange enthusiastic hugs and kisses.

"We're so happy to see you, Gab. We've missed you! It's been such a long time. Your mother and I were wondering if we shouldn't just pick up and go to Sydney so we could finally see you. You're still so beautiful. Just like your mother."

A tiny cough interrupted Gabrielle as she was about to stammer out a lame excuse. Her parents both glanced over her shoulder toward the woman standing slightly behind her.

When she turned around, Gabrielle couldn't help noticing that Tess's smile was restrained, her eyes filled with tension. Despite wanting to come, Tess was obviously nervous. She hesitantly glanced from Gabrielle to her parents, silently but clearly indicating that Gab should introduce them, but Gabrielle had lost her nerve.

"Hello. I'm Aurore, Gabrielle's mom," her mother kindly said, her hand held out. "Welcome to Western Australia." Tess shook her hand and beamed at this little woman with dark eyes and jet-black hair. Her ever-so-slightly Asian features were a bit more noticeable than Gabrielle's.

"Tess. Tess McCartney. Pleased to meet you, Mrs Abbott."

"This is my husband, Thomas."

While walking over to Tess, Thomas couldn't help throwing a knowing glance at his wife. Only yesterday they had discussed and concluded—despite Victoria's arguments to the contrary—that if Gabrielle had really been a lesbian, she would have told them a long time ago. They knew that their daughter, with her strong personality, would never have hidden such an important part of who she was. Yet, seeing the beautiful young woman standing next to her, they were now sure that Victoria was right. Thinking about all the senselessly lost years made Thomas's smile fade for a moment. When he shook Tess's hand, he felt it tense in his, and seeing the doubt in her green eyes, he immediately grinned widely.

"Tess, you are more than welcome in our family. And that's sincere, believe me."

Turning to Gabrielle, he added sternly, "You and I need to have a talk."

She tensed up all over. "If it's to criticise my lifestyle, we're leaving right away!" she replied, immediately on the defensive.

"I'm sorry." Her aggressive answer made Thomas realise what he hadn't seen: her fear and uncertainty. He wanted to kick himself for being so harsh in his choice of words. How could he explain to her that he was disappointed and hurt only by her lack of trust in him, not by her lifestyle?

"Gab. Calm down! Give them a little time, and if we have to talk, we'll talk." Tess gently lifted Gab's chin, forcing her to look into her eyes.

Gabrielle was still angry, but then Aurore came to the rescue. "We'll talk later, Gabrielle, but, like your father said, not to criticise your lifestyle, though we did have an inkling about it. What your father was trying to express in his awkward way is that he doesn't understand why you never spoke to us about it. What have we ever done to make you afraid to tell us that you share your life with a woman? Or that made you never come to visit us with her?"

Surprised, Gabrielle turned to her mother. Overcome with emotion, she couldn't speak up. Her mother's calm voice was neither critical nor accusatory, just terribly sad. Gabrielle felt guilty that she'd never given them a chance.

"Aurore, leave her be. This isn't the time or the place for this type of discussion. We'll talk once we're back at Willowra. Do you two have any luggage?"

Without even finishing his sentence, Thomas had walked over to the baggage carrousel to grab the two big suitcases that remained. The bags weren't light, but Thomas lifted them easily and then calmly walked away toward the exit.

"Your father is both strapping and handsome," Tess whispered to Gabrielle as they stood to one side and watched him leave. "Now I see who you take after. His smile must have made more than one young girl swoon. He and your mother make a beautiful couple. Now I'm looking forward to meeting your brother."

"How's Nan holding up?" Gabrielle asked her mother, who had stepped aside while she and Tess whispered together.

"You'll see for yourself."

As they were leaving the airport parking lot, Thomas struck up a conversation with Tess.

"Your accent leads me to believe you're British."

"Yes. Scottish, to be precise. I was born in Inverness."

"Victoria will love that," Aurore softly commented, and then turning to Tess, she added, "Gab's Nan, Victoria, well, her father Jason was born in Inverness. He immigrated to Australia just before the First World War."

"How long have you lived here?" Thomas asked.

Gabrielle sighed at the thought of the interrogation Tess was going to have to endure, but after all, she was old enough to defend herself.

"About nine years. My mother is Australian. She returned home after she divorced my father. I decided to come see what the other side of the world looked like, so I finished my studies here, and after I met Gabrielle, I decided to stay."

"Are you a doctor like Gab?"

"Yes, but my speciality is dermatology, not gynaecology."

"We're leaving Kal, the city of gold mines, to take the Coolgardie-Esperance highway to Norseman," Thomas said. "It should take us two hours, and it will give you an idea of the landscape and local colour. Then we'll have about an hour to go from Norseman to Willowra. The road isn't in great shape. You'll see that this entire part of Australia is quite flat, but not nearly as flat as the Nullarbor Plain that borders Willowra on the east. I imagine Gab will take you there. More and more tourists are interested in the place. In fact, we've been thinking about building a few bungalows for holiday rentals."

"Bungalows for tourists? In Willowra? I can't believe my ears," Gabrielle said. "Who would want to spend their vacation here?"

"Victoria said the same thing, but one's got to make a living, my girl, and the more we vary our sources of income, the less we'll be dependent upon the rain to survive. We've already converted half the livestock into meat these last few years. They require less manual labour since they don't have to be sheared. Export prices for mutton have become quite favourable."

Tess swept her gaze across the semi-deserted landscape. When they'd gotten out of the plane, and despite the 4x4's air conditioning, it was even hotter where they were now.

"How many sheep do you have?" Tess asked, interested in this new aspect of Australian life, of which Gabrielle had hardly ever spoken.

"Right now, about 30,000 head."

"30,000 sheep?! That many?"

"That's not a lot for a surface of 1,700,000 acres. On good years, we've had as many as 40,000. It all depends on the rain and the water sources."

In the course of the trip, Thomas pointed out here and there sites and places of interest while giving short explanations. Gabrielle was stunned that her father knew so much about the region's history. The landscape of her childhood unfolded before her eyes, and much to her surprise, she realized that she had missed the bush. Yet although she'd initially been eager to show this place to Tess, she had quickly succumbed to her misgivings. She was afraid Tess would hate it all, just as she had predicted.

As soon as Thomas drove onto the trail that led to Willowra, Gabrielle grew nervous, and Tess, reassuring, took her hand.

"It's very beautiful, Gab. Nothing at all like Scotland or New South Wales. I hope we'll have a little time to visit."

Gabrielle didn't answer. From the beginning, Tess had always been able to read her with ease.

After an hour's drive down the dusty road, Thomas pointed to a grove of trees in the distance. "Willowra."

Gradually, as they got closer, a few details came into sight: the windmill, the house, several other buildings, pens. All the rooftops, as almost everywhere in Australia, were made of sheet metal, and most of the buildings were also built of sheet metal or of wood.

"It seems you added a building near the house?" Gabrielle asked.

"Jeremy wanted some space and independence, so we built him a small one with two bedrooms and a living-room/office area," Thomas said. "You'll sleep in his old room, the one Jason added on for me all those years back."

"Jeremy still isn't married?"

"He dates a lot, a little too much if you ask me, and not always particularly nice people. He claims he's waiting to meet his soul mate."

"Thomas!" Aurore softly but firmly interrupted.

"Your mother says to leave him be, but he's thirty-four, and we have very few available women in the area."

Gabrielle felt a bit guilty for cutting ties with her brother. They didn't have much to say to one another because their lives were so different. What common interests could a gynaecologist and a sheep farmer share? Especially when the farmer was homophobic. But was he really? The question started to gnaw away at her. Could she have been mistaken about her entire family?

Thomas had just turned off the 4x4's engine when Gabrielle suddenly heard the sound of a horse galloping toward them. She was getting out of the car, followed by Tess and her parents, when the rider rode past the workers' quarters. Her jaw almost hit the ground in disbelief when she recognised the rider.

"Yeah. When Pa explained Nan's plot to me, I told him that would be your reaction," someone said from behind them. "Hi, Gab."

Gabrielle swiftly turned around to greet Jeremy, who had come out onto the porch to welcome them, before proceeding with a firm step over to the woman who was getting off the horse, which she had halted near the car. Now fully aware of how she had been tricked, Gabrielle was angry. Her hands on her hips, she planted herself squarely in front of this woman decked out in bush horseman's gear, who calmly took off her hat and rested it on the saddle, revealing a shock of short white hair. Her wide, contented smile enhanced the wrinkles on her face. However, Gabrielle's anger merely increased a notch when she noticed the twinkle of joy in her grandmother's sparkling blue eyes.

"How dare you, Nan! How dare you make me think you were on the brink of death?"

"Hello, Gabrielle. I'm happy you could make it to see your poor grandmother on her deathbed."

With an amused expression, Victoria glanced over Gabrielle's shoulder and skirted around her, stopping right in front of Tess with a huge grin. Victoria's appreciative once-over—as if she were drinking Tess in—surprised Gabrielle, made her feel slightly jealous. She didn't want anyone, even her grandmother, to scrutinize her wife like that.

"Hello. I'm Victoria McKellig, Gabrielle's grandmother."

"Tess McCartney."

"Why?" Gabrielle, fuming, asked from behind her.

Victoria's face froze when she turned around to address Gabrielle. "My brother John died last year. His children and grandchildren came to the funeral. I wanted to see my children and grandchildren while

I'm still alive. I wanted to meet your partner, and if I hadn't forced your father to put this charade together, you simply wouldn't have come. Now the only one still missing is Simone, but once she arrives tomorrow, everyone will be here except Robert."

Victoria's smile returned when she asked Tess, "When are you due?"

"August."

"Boy or girl?"

"We don't know yet."

"Artificial insemination or natural?"

"Nan!" Gabrielle intervened in reaction to this very private question.

Tess chuckled. "Artificial insemination."

"I would have bet my life on it. If Gabrielle is anything at all like me, then she is very possessive. Now if you'll excuse me, I need to go shower and make myself presentable."

Gabrielle, astounded, watched her grandmother walk into the house as Tess laughed softly. "Now I know who you take after. She's as sharp as a tack and has quite a personality. Everything you've said about her, or rather the little you've imparted about her, hardly does justice to the living picture."

Gabrielle didn't have a chance to reply because her tall, tan brother Jeremy, who'd had no qualms about listening in on the encounter, said, "I don't know what she's like now, but you should have seen her when we were growing up—the local terror."

"Since you seem so amused, Jeremy, make yourself useful by taking our suitcases to our room," Gabrielle said.

"Ah, just as charming as ever. I'm glad to see some things never change."

Without waiting for a reply, Jeremy, with his thick, black hair and dark-brown eyes so similar to hers, took her in his arms and gave her a manly hug.

"You!" Gabrielle pulled away and pointed at Jeremy with an accusatory air. "Traitor!"

He shook his head. "Don't waste your time blaming me, Gab. I had nothing to do with it. Pa only told me about it this morning when he set out to pick you up. I don't know why they cooked up this whole scheme, but I'm mighty happy you're here…and your girlfriend too, by the way. I'm so glad to get to know the prettiest woman in

Willowra," he said, leering at Tess appreciatively. "You know I'm still single."

Although Gabrielle was astonished by her brother's immediate acceptance of the situation, she remained sceptical.

"As long as you keep your hands off," she warned him.

"Nan is right. You're so possessive."

"You just try me—"

"Children! What is Tess going to think about your behaviour?" Aurore interrupted the playful squabbling with her calm but commanding voice as quickly as someone else would have with loud reprimands.

Tess sniggered slightly, and Gab winced.

"Jeremy, make yourself useful and take these suitcases to the back bedroom," Aurore said. "Tess, you shouldn't be standing for too long in this heat, given your condition. Come in for afternoon tea. We have to find you a hat. The sun here is treacherous."

In just a few seconds, Gabrielle found herself alone with her father, who was leaning against the car waiting. As she turned to follow everyone into the house, he placed his hand on her forearm to hold her back.

"Do you want to see the horses? We've acquired a few more, including a particularly beautiful stallion."

Gabrielle couldn't suppress a smile. She had loved riding when she was young, but since Tess was afraid of horses, she had taken up sailing instead.

Gabrielle followed her father, who was walking toward the stables. The scattered trees, mainly eucalyptus and acacia, which had been meticulously cared for over the years, still couldn't hide the expanse of barren land that spread out into the distance. She took a deep breath, filling her lungs with this hot, dry air that smelled of warm dust and sand. She noticed an outbuilding a few hundred metres away, with its shiny new sheet metal glistening in the sun.

"A new shearing shed?" she asked, pointing to the enclosures located farther behind.

"I had it built last year. The old one was falling apart, and the machines needed to be replaced. Come on. Have a look at this beautiful animal."

Thomas pointed to a stallion with a shining coat trotting over in their direction. Gabrielle and her father stopped before a paddock fence, stepping up onto the lower rung and resting their elbows on the top rail. The stallion, a few metres short of reaching them, pirouetted briskly.

"He's still young and quite mischievous. Nothing nasty, but if you try to saddle him, you'll see what I mean."

Gabrielle watched the handsome animal join the three mares that were sharing his paddock. She didn't dare take her eyes off the horses. Her heart rate quickened in anticipation of having a serious conversation with her father.

"Gab, why didn't you say anything?" whispered Thomas, as he stared at the horses. "On top of it, you're expecting a baby...Were you that much afraid of us?"

"You and mum never did or said anything that would have led me to believe my sexual orientation would be acceptable. Admit it," Gabrielle dryly told him. "When Jeremy and our cousin spoke degradingly about homosexuals, you never said a word to stop them, as far as I know."

"Oh. I remember, but that was a long time ago, Gab. At least fifteen years. Your brother was young and stupid, like all boys his age. He wanted to impress your cousin who lived in Perth—"

"He wasn't that young. He was nineteen."

Thomas turned to watch his daughter, who was staring at the horizon. He noticed her hands balled up in tight fists, her delicate profile, thick head of hair, and beige-coloured masculine shirt. He was dying to ask a question, but he hesitated to probe this young woman who, in fact, he no longer knew anything about. His son always came to him for counsel when it had to do with affairs of the heart, but Gabrielle had locked herself up in her solitude because of one single unchecked moment of idiotic banter. "You already knew back then?"

Gabrielle finally turned her head toward him before softly replying. "Yes."

"I'm sorry, Gab. Stupid things adolescent boys say didn't seem important to me at that particular time, although I believe your mother pulled them aside to say something, because I haven't heard any other homophobic comments pass their lips since...She's very pretty."

"Who?"

"Tess. Who do you think I'm talking about—the mare over there?"

Gabrielle blushed. "I'm lucky. I know."

"Have you been together for a long time?"

"A while...eight years."

"Eight years? Sweet Jesus! And you've never even mentioned her?"

Thomas's anger flashed in his light-coloured eyes, though he made a clear effort to control himself. "Do you know her family?"

Slightly ashamed now that it seemed that everyone accepted them naturally, Gabrielle lowered her eyes. "Yes. Her mother lives in Sydney, and last summer we went for a vacation in Scotland to meet her father and sister."

Thomas was clenching the top of the fence so tightly his knuckles turned white. Gabrielle saw him take several deep breaths.

"You think we're some kind of ignorant monsters, don't you?"

"I was afraid, Pa. Afraid of being rejected for something I can't change. I know so many gays whose families have disowned them. Some thrown out like they meant nothing to them."

Thomas awkwardly wrapped his arm around his daughter's shoulders, who, for once, let him. He remembered the kid who used to follow him around everywhere like his shadow, who constantly bickered with her brother. How did they get to this place? How did they sink so far into this lack of communication and trust?

"If only…" Thomas murmured to himself. "I should have said something. Come on. Tea must be ready. I think you're up to discover quite a few surprising things during your stay."

Puzzled, Gabrielle broke away from his arm. "What's that supposed to mean?"

Thomas shook his head. "It's your grandmother's show. She planned this reunion, and I don't intend to spoil her pleasure."

Together, under the hot afternoon sun, Gabrielle and her father walked across the dusty courtyard whose earth was as hard as cement after having been trodden for countless years.

❖

Following afternoon tea and a visit of the house and its surrounding grounds in Aurore's company, Tess and Gabrielle went to their large, classically decorated room, with whitewashed wooden walls. Yellow flowers in a vase near the window brought in a touch of colour. The minute they shut the bedroom door, Tess smiled tenderly at Gabrielle.

"Visibly, you were wrong about them."

"Visibly, you are right."

Gabrielle walked over to Tess and wrapped her arms around her. "I still can't believe Nan put this scheme together," Gabrielle whispered while softly kissing Tess's neck.

They let their embrace linger, the sweetness of being in each other's arms calming Gab's ruffled feelings. Three light knocks at the door followed by "Time for dinner!" made them jump.

Gab let go of Tess, who asked, "This early? When your mother said we'd be eating soon, I didn't think it meant at five thirty p.m."

"My father and Jeremy go back to work when it gets cooler in the evenings. They're already behind schedule. It's a light meal. The big meal is at eleven thirty, before their naps, in order to avoid being outside during the hottest part of the day. After spending some time here, you'll understand why."

Gabrielle planted a peck on Tess's lips and then headed directly for the door.

In the narrow hallway, Tess pointed to several black-and-white photos hanging outside their bedroom. "I noticed these photos earlier. Is this Willowra?"

"Yes."

"What year was it?"

"I guess the beginning of the century, the twentieth, I mean."

"It was 1930," someone behind them said. "They were a gift to my parents from an itinerant photographer in return for room and board. During the Great Depression, a lot of people came through here, and some left souvenirs."

Victoria pointed out two children among the group in the photograph. "Aubrey and Philip had just joined our family. You can see that they don't look as though they fully fit in with the rest of us."

Tess leaned toward the wall to better see the photograph. Indeed, two of the five children weren't happy at all. They stood slightly apart from the others. She then pointed to two adults standing as straight as could be in the shadow of the porch.

"My parents, Maggie and Jason. You don't find those kinds of people anymore: courageous, honest, hard-working, and generous."

Surprised by the emotion in Victoria's voice, Tess turned toward her. "Audrey and Philip 'joined' the family? Did their parents abandon them here?"

"It's a little more complicated than that. But yes. Essentially they came one day and stayed. Every time a child showed up, John and I were a little jealous, but then we got on with it. We just had to remember where we came from as well."

Tess frowned and glanced at Gab for an explanation, but she shook her head with incomprehension written on her face.

"We were all adopted as children," Victoria explained. "Robert was the only one adopted as a baby. I so wanted him to come be with us for the next few days, but he's been too busy with aboriginal-rights issues lately."

Victoria pointed to the only black child in the photograph. "Having him here was a scandal at the time. I was just six, but I'll never forget the looks people gave Maggie when they learned she and Jason had adopted an aboriginal baby. I still admire their courage."

"You never told me you had an aboriginal great-uncle."

Still struck by the fresh knowledge that her great-grandparents had adopted all their children, Gabrielle shrugged. "I must have seen him once or twice, at most, when I was little. It didn't seem important to me. I didn't even realise that you were all adopted—"

"Dinner…" Victoria said. "Your mother will skin us alive if we don't hot-foot it into the kitchen." She nudged them along.

Gabrielle and Tess sat down on the side of the table with free seats, while Victoria settled in at the head of the table, facing Thomas.

"I know you're probably not used to eating so early, Tess," Aurore said, "but the men have to get back to work as soon as the temperature becomes bearable."

Gabrielle cleared her throat to attract the attention of Tess, who was busy smiling at her mother. "Help yourself."

When Tess finally seemed to realise everybody was waiting for her to begin eating, she blushed.

"You're the guest of honour," Victoria said. "It took Gabrielle one heck of a long time to bring you home, but now that you're here, we're going to make the most of it."

"I'm already making the most of the view," added Jeremy, sitting across from Tess.

Tess blushed all the way to her ears. Obviously embarrassed but not wanting to show it, she thanked Jeremy for his compliment, then served herself salad and cold mutton.

Thomas's voice cut through the amused silence. "Hey, Gab. Do you want to help us after we're done eating?"

"Why not? I guess you're aiming to wear me out when I've only just gotten here?"

Thomas raised his eyebrows questioningly. "You used to love horseback riding. When you were a little girl, getting you off the saddle was an impossible task."

"I rarely ride in Sydney," Gabrielle explained. "We go sailing instead."

"They've got horses there though, don't they?" Jeremy asked.

"Yes, dear brother, but I don't take time to go riding. Tess prefers water sports."

Jeremy smiled ironically while Victoria seemed quite entertained. Gab frowned.

"I'm afraid of horses," Tess said. "Gab did try to get me to ride when we first met, but I couldn't overcome my fear. I do admire them from afar, but getting up on one is out of the question."

During the course of the meal, while Jeremy was joking around with Gabrielle and Tess, Victoria silently observed how they interacted with one another. Each woman tried to protect the other and came to her defence if necessary. Her granddaughter hadn't changed much—still willful and stubborn, ready to fight back blow for blow. Instinctively, watching her grow up, Victoria had known Gab leaned toward women. She regretted not having done anything to help her at the time. Jason wouldn't exactly have been proud of her for that omission. Victoria then scrutinized Tess.

She and Gabrielle truly made a beautiful couple. Her thoughts strayed toward Ginger, the love of her life, for a moment, then toward the arrival of Thomas's sister, Simone, the next day, which was likely to shake things up. They had parted in anger the last time they'd seen each other, and Victoria wondered how Simone would react when she learned the truth about her father. Yes, the next day was bound to be a very difficult one, but she didn't want the truth to die with her. She owed it to Jason and Maggie. She owed it to Ginger.

While Thomas, Gabrielle, and Jeremy rode off on horseback, Victoria watched them nostalgically as she sat out on the porch as Aurore and Tess—who wouldn't be talked out of helping—cleared the table and cleaned up the kitchen.

Aurore wasn't quite sure what to say to this highly educated, sweet woman who was at least a head taller than she. So she just smiled.

"Gabrielle resembles you a lot," Tess said.

"Feature-wise, yes, but we're nothing alike." Aurore closed the fridge. "Incidentally, the generator stops automatically at ten p.m. and starts working again at five thirty a.m. I hope it won't bother you. We're used to it."

"I can hardly hear it. Do you have any photos of Gabrielle to show me? I'd love to see what she looked like as a child."

Joy spread through Aurore, and she nodded. Browsing her photos this evening would be a true pleasure. How many times these last years had she leafed through the albums with a heavy heart? These childhood photos and the occasional phone call had been her only link with Gabrielle.

Thomas had taken her aside to tell her about the conversation he'd had with Gabrielle, and she hated herself for having wasted so many years because of a simple misunderstanding. She and Tess settled into the living room and let themselves get lost in the photograph albums. Time seemed to stand still.

CHAPTER FOUR

When Tess, feeling refreshed from a good night's sleep, came into the kitchen, she wasn't surprised to find it empty. Gab had awoken very early, and the morning noises she had overheard from their bedroom made her assume that everyone had already gone to work, far off from the house. Victoria was most likely too old to spend her day in the saddle, although the amount of energy this woman exuded was truly impressive. It didn't require much imagination for Tess to see that Victoria couldn't have been easy as a child. Although in the autumn of her years, she had a strength of character still highly visible in her features and the way she moved about. Her piercing blue eyes, which seemed capable of looking through you to the very depths of your soul, could be unsettling. What a character, Tess thought as she poured herself the one cup of coffee she was allowed to have per day, which was quite a challenge for the coffee addict she was.

"There's bread in the pantry."

Tess turned around and saw Victoria walk in and take off her wide-brimmed hat. Her blue denim shirt was sweat-soaked; it was already a very hot day. Thanking her, Tess grabbed the bread while Victoria took the butter and jam from the refrigerator. From the corner of her eye, Tess observed Victoria's slender figure. She hoped she would have a body as muscle-toned as Victoria's at her age. The day before she had noticed Victoria's slight limp and wondered if a horse-riding accident had caused it. Both of them sat down at the table. While Victoria drank her coffee, Tess spread butter and jam on several pieces of bread and ate with a hearty appetite.

"Gabrielle should be back soon," Victoria commented. "Thomas has to go pick up Simone from the Norseman train. He'll drop off Gabrielle on his way there."

"Have you always lived in Willowra?" Tess asked, between two bites.

"Almost always. I landed here when I was five, and except for one part of my life, I've never lived anywhere else. Thomas said you came from Scotland. What is it like?"

"Green," Tess exclaimed, "and mountainous."

"That's what my father Jason said. Before travelling to Queensland, I certainly had no idea what the words 'lush vegetation' really meant. It was beautiful there, but I only really feel at home here. My mother Maggie never left Willowra. She was born here, raised here, and she died here. You can see her tomb and her parents' tomb from the living-room window. Her parents bought the property in 1892, after having found a vein of gold ore in Coolgardie. They were wiser than most. Others squandered it all."

After a long moment of silence, Victoria suddenly asked, "Would you like to see how a shearing shed works?"

"Everything about Willowra interests me."

"Well, then, Tess. You and I are going to become fast friends. Come along."

❖

"How dare you let me believe that you were dying, and get Thomas involved on top of it! You're nothing more than a—"

The sound of a slap interrupted the screaming. Gabrielle and Tess exchanged a glance, and in answer to Tess's silent question, Gabrielle shook her head. The intimate moment they had started was going to have to wait. Gabrielle was overcome with curiosity. With so few distractions in Willowra, anything out of the ordinary was interesting.

"Will you listen to me now, Simone, or do I have to slap some more sense into you?!" Victoria asked.

"I don't intend to listen to anything. Thomas will take me right back to town and—"

Gabrielle opened their bedroom door and found herself face-to-face with a woman she had never met, but whose photos she remembered seeing in the family picture albums. This little shrew with grey-blond hair and entirely dressed in denim had to be Simone. She didn't resemble her brother Thomas one bit.

"Thomas will not be taking you back to town," Victoria said. "If you want to go, you'll have to walk."

"If that's the way it's going to be, I will!"

Ignoring Gabrielle and Tess, Simone whirled around, grabbed her bag, and planted herself right in front of Thomas.

"She still has you wrapped 'round her little finger, doesn't she, Tommy? Now take me back."

Thomas looked at his sister, then at the person he'd always considered his second mother, Victoria. He really didn't know what to do. His sister, who had adored Victoria when she was a child, had drastically changed when she grew up. Her obsession with finding her father had eaten away at her to the point of embittering her. He glanced at Victoria, silently begging her to do something, before turning to his wife, who had placed a calming hand on his arm. Simone's anger didn't really surprise him. As long as he could remember, since adolescence, she'd always been angry at someone or something.

Victoria's voice broke the silence. "I thought you wanted answers, Simone?"

Clearly surprised, Simone spun around, glaring at her. "Answers?"

Victoria drew closer to this tiny blond woman, whose petite figure was so reminiscent of Ginger's. "Isn't that what you asked me at your mother's funeral, although the dust on her coffin hadn't yet settled, and I was still mourning her?" Victoria asked. "You demanded answers. You, who, whenever my back was turned harassed her with questions every time you came to Willowra. You couldn't even respect her the day she died."

Simone calmed down slightly. "I've always searched for information about my father. You know that. Neither you nor she ever wanted to give it to me. Thomas might have been content to live that way, but I certainly wasn't."

"Maybe Thomas remembers your father beating your mother," Victoria replied, the memories still saddening her. "If you want answers, Simone, then stay until tomorrow."

"Maybe you don't really know anything," Simone spit out in return.

"Your father is dead. If you want to know more, I advise you to be patient and opt for a different tone."

"How do you know he's dead? Did my mother receive a letter? I want to see it…"

Victoria sighed, weary. "Stay until tomorrow, and you'll find out. After all these years, I've decided to talk about the past, to bring back to life, if only for a day, all those I loved so dearly, and incidentally clear the closets of a few skeletons. I'll tell you everything after lunch. Thomas, put your sister's things in her room."

Gabrielle and Tess watched Victoria peacefully head for the front door and walk out of the house. A few seconds later, they were alone in the hallway.

"This promises to be a very interesting weekend," Tess murmured.

Gabrielle rolled her eyes in exasperation. "I'm going to speak to Jeremy before lunch to see if he knows a bit more than I do. You don't mind if I leave you alone for a moment?"

Tess's eyes twinkled. She was happy that Gabrielle wasn't being stubborn. "Don't worry. I'll see if I can help out in the kitchen and get a few childhood stories out of your mother."

Gab threw Tess an indignant look, which Tess returned with a mischievous grin. Gabrielle then kissed Tess on the forehead and left, shaking her head, much to Tess's amusement.

CHAPTER FIVE

"Jason was never again the same man after Maggie died. He spent his last days in his rocking chair reading these notebooks…"

Without taking her eyes off her attentive audience sitting around the family dining table, Victoria lifted a bunch of old, faded notebooks, bound together with a wide, discoloured ribbon that must have once been bright blue. She stared hard at each member of the family, one by one, and for the first time, she fully grasped that she was the only remaining link between them and these incredible people she had known and loved. Apart from her, not a single soul knew their story—a story of which she was very proud, one that should make them all proud. If it weren't for Jason and Maggie, they wouldn't be there, right now, around this table, fed and sated.

"These are Maggie's notebooks. How very often, while hidden behind the screen door, I peered through and saw Jason wipe his eyes as he read these pages. He outlived her by only two years, and during that time, I could do nothing but witness the slow decline of this man I loved so much. I saw him become withdrawn and lose the will to live, despite the presence of his family and grandchildren. No, Simone. I won't allow you to object to this gathering, because in his eyes you were as much his grandchild as I was his daughter. Jason loved his children and grandchildren with all his heart."

Simone kept her mouth shut, clearly stifling the words she'd been about to pronounce.

"You have to remember the good, kind fellow you called 'Pappy,' who spent all his time in his armchair contemplating the horizon, these very notebooks resting on his lap. You were only eight when he died, but surely you've never forgotten his sad blue eyes that would sometimes rest on you, or the sorrowful smile that never left his lips after Maggie's death."

Simone squirmed as Victoria's words evidently rang true.

"The night before he died, Jason, who'd no longer had the strength to leave his bed for several days, gave me these notebooks and asked me to read them. He said that inside I would discover the history of Willowra, as well as his and Maggie's story. I once again tried to inspire him with the will to live, but in vain."

Victoria paused, brushing her fingertips across the cover of the first notebook. Lowering her head, she gathered her thoughts.

"He also entrusted me with a secret that day, and I promised never to speak of it. Yet I couldn't keep this secret to myself. It was too tremendous. My brother John had been my best friend and my confidant. He had always been. Together we decided to honour Jason's wish, until today. Jason and Maggie's story deserves to be told. I've contacted several publishing houses and finally found one interested in it."

Simone sarcastically cut in. "What kind of 'big' secret could possibly be hidden in this godforsaken hole?"

Victoria didn't answer. She just stared at Simone and then at everyone present around the table. The silence lingered. Victoria looked down at the notebooks sitting on the table before her, stroking them again. When she raised her head, she gazed at Tess. "Green eyes, green like Scotland," she murmured.

"Oh, Victoria. Please continue. I'm impatient to learn Jason's secret." Aurore's gentle voice cut through the silence.

Victoria nodded. "Jason McKellig, my adoptive father, was born on May eighth, 1893, in a small Scottish village near Inverness. The name he was given at birth was Laura McKellig. Jason was a woman."

Silence. Thomas shook his head as if to clear it. And then, in a voice filled with disbelief, he said, "No. I knew Jason. I was ten when he died. He wasn't a woman. That's impossible."

"I was thirty-four when Jason died, and I learned my father was a woman only the night before he passed away," Victoria said. "I can confirm to you that after John and I prepared his body for burial, we no longer had any doubts. Do you want to know the story of your grandfather and great-grandfather? Without him…without her, none of you would be here today, and I would surely have been dead already. Dead a very long time."

"Okay, but I think I need a little pick-me-up to face what follows," Jeremy said, and Gabrielle shook her head as if awakening from a dream. "And I bet I'm not the only one," he said. "Brandy for everyone?"

"Not for me, thank you," Tess said.

Hearing the sound of a photo being pushed across the table toward her got Gabrielle's attention. It was a black-and-white photo of a handsome man with short blond hair and pale eyes. He seemed so serious in his dark suit, but what was most remarkable about him was the utter gentleness he exuded.

"Jason..." Victoria spoke almost in a whisper now. "If we are to believe what is written on the back of the photo, Jason was twenty-one. It was taken in Bourke in 1914. Jason had just arrived in Australia."

Another photo.

"Jason and Maggie, their wedding photo in 1923."

Then a third.

"Jason and Maggie, and their family—John, Audrey, Philip, Robert, and me. It was taken in the summer of 1930, like the others in the hallway. Times were hard. The stock markets had gone bust, causing the Great Depression. All we had to eat was what we managed to cultivate on our land...Thank you, Jeremy."

Victoria took the glass of brandy from his hand and stood up. "I would like to make a toast. To Jason."

Everyone around the table raised their glasses and toasted him. Even Simone followed suit, albeit halfheartedly.

"As I was saying, Jason was born in Scotland in..."

PART II: JASON

CHAPTER SIX

London, England, 1913

Jason elbowed her way through the crowd with a determined step. Nothing was better after an exhausting day's work than to raise a glass with her fellow dock workers, with whom she had spent the day carting along and carrying crates and sacks. A bagpipe's insistent music added to the surrounding hubbub of the men's voices. It felt good to be amongst one's own, reminding her of home. She couldn't make out the words through the awful din, but they were all accented with her native Scottish brogue. She could see only a few yards ahead through the dim light and cigarette smoke, but they always met at the same corner table at the back of the room. It had become a ritual. For the past year, every evening after work, Jason would wash up and go meet her countrymen and peers.

The only difference between them and Jason was a well-kept secret, but every day, while getting dressed, she pushed away her fear of being found out. She knew that things would go awry if her workmates suddenly learnt the truth about her gender. But did she have any other choice if she wanted to live in a man's world? Nature had given her a slender but powerful body. Her muscles, already much more developed and visible than most women's, had only become more well-chiselled and prominent from months of working on the docks. Here, for everyone, in her grey coarse canvas pants and worn white shirt that had seen better days, she was Jason McKellig from Inverness, Scotland, respected for her cool-headed seriousness.

An accident on the docks the other day had more than proved it. When a crate fell from high atop a pile and knocked over a fellow worker, Jason, who was the closest to him, kept calm and had the presence of mind to organise the men in order to lift the crate together and tend to him. Unfortunately, it had been too late, and he couldn't be saved, but the foreman had congratulated Jason on his level-headedness. He'd even added that if Jason continued this way, he could become a foreman himself in a few years. Although shocked by the man's death, Jason had stood straight and tall with pride at the compliment.

As Jason approached the bar, she just avoided a staggering man who almost knocked right into her. As soon as the bar owner caught her eye, Jason raised one finger. It was impossible to be heard over the noise at this hour, so she didn't try. The bartender immediately handed over a draught beer. The first sip was like nectar to her throat, parched by the pub's smothering heat. From the corner of her eye, she saw someone waving in her direction. Her workmates were already there. Her beer in hand, she slowly made her way over to them.

"Hits the spot!" yelled Allan, to be heard above the noise.

Jason lifted her glass and smiled, so as not to have to shout. Although she could easily disguise the feminine curves of her body, she couldn't disguise the high pitch of her voice when shouting and had to speak as quietly as possible. However, her low voice only reinforced the impression of her serious, calm character. The whole group raised their glasses to her greeting and drank a sip of the well-deserved golden liquid. Ernest's cheeks were already beet red; sweat was streaming down his face. He appeared to be well beyond his first beer. In fact, everyone was drenched in sweat, and Jason started to feel the perspiration gathering under her arms and dripping down her chest, absorbed by the thick cotton bandage she used to hide her breasts. Should she sweat too much, the bandage under her shirt would be visible, and she'd have to cut the night short.

"Hotter than hell in here," Peter, who was sitting next to Ernest, commented. He wiped his forehead and then his thickly bearded cheeks with the back of his hand. His washed-out grey shirt still had a dry patch here and there, but a half hour from now the whole thing would be drenched.

Even with the windows and doors open, it was too warm, in this exceptionally hot August, to beat the heat in this establishment filled with dozens of men in the prime of life. Jason was accustomed to the noise, the smoke, and the sweat, but she couldn't risk raising any suspicion among her mates.

"Just the one and then I'll head back," she said in Allan's ear. "Got things to attend to."

Allan started laughing. "Who is the young lady who has once again fallen under your charm, Jason? Kathryn is going to be disappointed." Allan pointed to the waitress walking toward them with an empty tray as he pronounced these words. A woman in the midst of all these men might have seemed incongruous, especially such a young one, but McLeod, the pub owner, was her father, and not a single man present would ever have dared show her anything but total respect. Furthermore, as Peter often said, "It would be far easier to climb the northeast face of Ben Nevis than to face McLeod," whose body was a mountain of pure muscle.

Kathryn, despite the hoots that greeted her, stopped right next to Jason. She shamelessly smiled directly at him before bending closer.

In her eyes, Jason was the most handsome young man she had ever seen. She ached to stroke his golden-blond hair, and his pale blue eyes reminded her of winter skies she had seen in the Highlands when visiting her grandparents. When she'd told her father about her feelings for Jason, he had pointed out to her that Jason was still a very young man, seventeen or eighteen at most. Indeed, he visibly still wasn't old enough to shave.

Exactly, Kathryn had thought. *How I'd like to caress that silky looking skin.*

Kathryn gave Jason a look filled with so much innuendo, Jason almost choked as she swallowed a sip of her beer. She knew what that meant.

"Hi, Kathryn," Allan hollered. "Jason was just leaving."

Kathryn was no longer smiling. She felt distraught. Suddenly she leaned over to Jason. "You can't leave so early. I've been waiting all night to show you something interesting. Come!"

Kathryn turned away from the table and started retracing her steps to the door at the back of the pub that opened onto a courtyard. Jason hesitated. She knew the place well, as Kathryn and she had often kissed there in a dark corner. But they were not really sheltered from prying eyes, as the urinal was in the courtyard, and the later the hour, the more often it was used. Also, how could she explain to Kathryn that their stolen kisses were becoming increasingly frustrating, that she wanted more, even if she really wasn't sure what "more" implied exactly.

"What are you waiting for?" Allan pushed Jason in Kathryn's direction with a friendly slap on the back. "I can go in your place if you like," he joked.

Throwing him a dark look, Jason put her almost-emptied beer mug down on the table and followed Kathryn to the back door that was already closing on her. She couldn't risk having her workmates ridicule her and didn't want to be on the receiving end of an earful of their distasteful comments.

Besides, even though it was difficult to snake her way through this increasingly agitated crowd of men, Jason wouldn't have been able to do otherwise but follow her. From the very first time she had stepped foot in this pub, she couldn't resist this hazelnut-eyed, brown-haired girl who tried to hide her curvaceous figure under an oversized dress. The attraction had been mutual, and it hadn't taken much time before they had exchanged their first kiss.

Jason's throat was dry as she pushed open the door onto the courtyard. Someone immediately reached out and grabbed her wrist, leading her to a darker corner, far from the urinal's putrid odour. Despite the knot in her throat, Jason asked Kathryn in a falsely innocent-sounding tone, "What did you want to show me?"

"This…"

Kathryn's hand brushed across the nape of Jason's neck, pulling it toward her and provoking pleasurable shivers throughout Jason. Once again, Kathryn's cool, soft lips made her forget all her fears. Blinded by pleasure, she devoured the lips offered her, until, breathless, she had to break away from this sweet embrace.

Kathryn's heart was beating wildly, and she snuggled up in the arms of this young man who hugged her tenderly and reassuringly. Kathryn knew she wasn't the first girl Jason had ever held in his arms—she had heard the other men's comments—but she didn't care. Jason was attracted to her, and this evening, she was with him.

"Kathryn…"

Kathryn lifted her head in response to Jason's soft voice, trying to make out his expression despite the darkness.

Overflowing with emotion, Jason decided to speak. "Kathryn…I want you so badly."

"Me too, Jason. I want you. I'd like to lie with you…like man and wife," she said breathlessly.

At these words, Jason—her heart pounding madly—hugged Kathryn, kissed her neck, stroked her hair, and tasted her lips one more time.

"I'd so much like to go further," Jason said, "but I've never…you know…and then your father would kill me if he caught us."

Although surprised by this unexpected admission, Kathryn gently ran her finger across Jason's cheek. This beautiful young man would be hers, she solemnly vowed to herself. "I've wanted you for so many months. I can't wait any longer."

At these words, Jason once again tasted the lips offered her, prolonging the kiss until, panting, she broke their embrace. "Somebody could catch us," she murmured.

"Meet me Sunday. In front of the church at two p.m."

"And your father?"

"That's my problem. Go back in first. I'm gonna fetch some whiskey bottles so my father doesn't see us walk in together."

Joy in her heart, mixed with the apprehension of having to confront McLeod if he did notice them, Jason returned back inside the pub. No one called out for her, and she was surprised to step into the same noisy, agitated pub. Her world had just changed drastically in a few seconds. Unsteady on her feet, she forgot her workmates and headed for the exit. A friendly slap landed on her back as soon as she walked out the front door.

"You old devil! If McLeod ever catches you flirting with his daughter, I wouldn't put my money down on ya. But I must confess, if a little number as cute as Kathryn was interested in me, I'd chance it too."

Jason sighed. What should she say to Allan? After all, he was her best friend. He had already confided his heartaches to her, while she had remained quite discreet on the subject. Despite the dusky light outside the pub, Jason gave him the once-over. They could have been brothers if people only looked at their hair and eye colour. Although Jason could carry any load as heavy as Allan could, she knew she appeared small and fragile next to his more impressive figure. If she had been attracted to men, she would have chosen one as loyal and sensible as Allan.

"Kathryn wants us to…go further," Jason stammered as she walked.

"You really are a lucky devil. First the little laundry girl, and now Kathryn. You have them all for yourself. I'm beginning to get jealous, but if you want my advice, keep your hands off Kathryn. There's no joking around for McLeod when it comes to his daughter."

Jason nodded. She knew that, but her desire for Kathryn made her ready to face any danger. "The problem isn't McLeod." She blushed.

In the darkness, even if Allan couldn't see her red cheeks, he would be able to hear her voice shaking.

With a mocking grin, he teased her. "Don't tell me you've never…"

Jason's cheek flamed when she saw Allan sticking his middle finger into a hole he made with his left hand. She shook her head no, and Allan almost stopped in place. "With all those girls running after you, you've really never…"

"No," she whispered, embarrassed.

"You're a virgin? How do ya like that?!"

"Why don't you shout it louder?" she squeaked. "If you're my friend you'll keep that to yourself and give me some advice so I won't be too clumsy with Kathryn…provided you have more experience than me, of course."

Jason's mocking tone hit its target. Allan straightened himself up before answering between his teeth. "I've got tons of experience. I'm not all talk and no action. Ask me anything, and you'll see."

Jason, happy, knew she would learn a lot tonight. She would need it.

CHAPTER SEVEN

"Hurry up. Come in before somebody sees you!"

Kathryn grabbed Jason by the front of his shirt and pulled him inside the pub. Once the door was closed behind them, she led Jason to a steep, narrow staircase. Jason, who had already been upstairs one day when McLeod wasn't home, knew there were two tiny bedrooms up there. That first and last time Kathryn had ever taken her up there, she had teased and aroused her to such a point she'd thought she'd gone mad.

"If your father catches us…"

"He won't be back until it's time to open the pub. He forgets the time when he's with his friends. We have three whole hours, and I intend to take full advantage of them. I love you, Jason. I want you to be my first."

"Kathryn. It isn't reasonable, your father. And I don't want to risk getting you pregnant."

Jason wasn't sure how to get herself out of this impossible situation. Now that Allan had explained all the details and mechanics, she knew she couldn't hide her true nature. She had thought about it from every possible angle these last two days and had realised she could never replace what she didn't have. If Kathryn learned she was a woman, and if she told anyone, her career on the docks was over.

Kathryn crossed her arms over her generous bosom and stood as tall as could be. Jason smiled at this slip of a woman, despite the anger she could see in her blazing eyes.

"Jason McKellig, are you a Scotsman or a coward?"

What other choice did Jason have? Trying to hide her rising fear, she could only give one answer. "A pure Scotsman."

Joy beamed from Kathryn's face, and she instantly grabbed Jason's hand, leading the way to the bedroom.

Jason's senses soared when she felt Kathryn's lips on hers, and she took possession of the tender mouth being offered. Kathryn stroked her back, pulling the bottom of her shirt out of her pants.

Jason grabbed her inquisitive hands. "Help me undo your dress. I won't be able to do it alone." While Kathryn hurried to unbutton her dress, Jason continued kissing her, travelling from her lips to her long neck, and then, with her tongue, leaving a moist trace from her cheekbone to her forehead. Jason's blood was pumping so hard she couldn't hear or see anything else. She could only perceive Kathryn's skin and her warm, supple body under her callused hands. All the blood rushing between her legs was starting to make her ache with desire. She could think only of releasing this tension, but, above all, she wanted to touch Kathryn. Not bothering to unfasten her clips, she drew back Kathryn's petticoat and bodice, and then she froze, unable to look away from Kathryn's creamy bosom.

Jason licked her lips. "You are so beautiful…"

Slowly, with her fingertips, she lightly touched a breast. A wave of shyness overcame her, and she immediately felt lost. But Kathryn grabbed her wrist, forcing her, crazy with desire, to take her breast. The round, supple form in the hollow of her hand, Jason finally raised her head, falling prisoner to Kathryn's dark eyes, veiled with hunger.

She swallowed with difficulty. "Kathryn…I told you…I never…I have never lain with a woman."

Kathryn smiled recklessly. "Me neither. But I don't think you'll have any problems."

Kathryn slipped her hand under Jason's shirt, stopping at the bandage. "Your torn muscle still isn't healed?"

Jason desperately shook her head. "It's not that."

Tears suddenly came to her eyes, and Kathryn frowned. Their entwined hands froze. "Explain yourself."

Jason took a deep breath before jumping in the deep end. If Kathryn rejected her, she would lose everything. "It's to hide my breasts. I'm a woman."

Kathryn's eyes immediately filled with doubt. After a moment, she slid her hand down between Jason's legs and grabbed her, a bit roughly.

Jason shivered. This simple touch brought her to the edge. "Kathryn, please…"

Kathryn, quickly recovering from her surprise at finding a piece of cloth where she'd expected to find a piece of flesh, smiled and started softly rubbing her hand against the seam of Jason's pants. Seeing desire in Jason's eyes gave her a feeling of infinite power. Jason's hands dug into her shoulder, holding her fast, but Kathryn didn't feel any pain. The power of being able to excite Jason made her own desire soar beyond anything she had ever imagined. Jason ended up on the ground on her knees panting.

Kathryn, who had also fallen to her knees, finally let go. "Touch me!"

Still kneeling, gazing at Kathryn, Jason melted. She had never come like this before. "Kathryn…"

"Look at the bright side. You can't get me pregnant. Touch me, Jason."

Kathryn abruptly grabbed Jason's hand and put it between her legs. And with this touch, all the air left Jason's lungs.

"If McLeod learns what you're up to with his daughter, you're a dead man."

"Who said I'm up to something with her?"

"People aren't blind, Jason. Everyone has eyes. Don't think your little game has gone unnoticed. She leaves to get something in the courtyard, and in the minute that follows, you go after her."

"Allan…I'm in love. Kathryn is…"

"A beaut. But McLeod has greater ambitions for his daughter than a dockhand. You're too young and poor. Even if your intentions are honourable, McLeod will turn a deaf ear to you. I just hope that, despite our conversation the other day, you and she haven't done anything beyond repair."

"Do you think I'm stupid? I'm careful. She won't end up with child. But she's so beautiful…If only I had a little money, McLeod might accept me courting her."

"Sweet Jesus. You want to marry her? And our plans to go live in Australia and search for gold? What about them? I need you, lad. The two of us are going to wallow in mountains of gold. You'll see. And the girls will fall into our arms by the dozens. You can't do this to me!" Allan got off the narrow stool and raised his arms, touching the low ceiling in Jason's bedroom.

"I haven't given up on our dream, Allan. Kathryn could come with us."

"And with what money are you going to pay for another person over there, let alone setting up a household? We barely have enough money for ourselves, but with a woman on top of it..."

"You always say it would be easier with a woman."

"No. I say that if we were women, it would be easier. They don't have enough women in Australia, as opposed to men. Women don't even have to pay their passage."

"Listen. I'll talk to Kathryn about it. Maybe she has some money put aside. She'll probably be interested, especially if her father is opposed to our marriage. Australia would be a new beginning for us. Think of how rich we're gonna be. I heard it's as easy to find gold as picking flowers. You just have to rake it up. After that, imagine us, well-dressed in a big house, landowners, our wives and children, our herds of sheep. If you're with me, I'm sure we'll succeed. We'll make a fortune off the wool. Just because I'm in love doesn't mean I will walk out on my best friend. Anyway, while we're busy collecting gold, Kathryn will cook and mind our cabin. What do you say?"

Allan stared at him and sighed. "All right. Discuss it with Kathryn, but discreetly, and wait until we've saved all the money for the boat trip before asking McLeod for her hand. That way, if he refuses, you can always escape on the next boat."

And that will give me the time to try to convince this stubborn mule that a woman can only get in the way.

CHAPTER EIGHT

At the sound of the door abruptly opening, Jason immediately jumped to her feet. McLeod was standing in the doorframe, making the worst of her fears come true. She frantically buttoned up her pants, as Kathryn, drawing her dress around herself to hide her bare breasts, tried to calm her father with cajoling words.

McLeod didn't budge. His eyes, creased in anger, shot Jason a look filled with rage, which was also reflected on his flushed-red face. Jason already felt pinned down by the threat of the enormous fists that were opening and closing threateningly in front of her. She was stuck in this tiny room, her only exit, aside from the tiny dormer window, blocked by this mountain of muscle called McLeod. Jason had no chance. She might have been tall and strappingly strong for a woman, but McLeod was way over six feet tall and must have been at least twice her weight.

"Trollop!" he screamed at Kathryn. "If my friends hadn't warned me about your carrying on…"

He was choking on his anger. "I'll kill both of you for making a fool of me. Who will want Kathryn now that you've dishonoured her?" He heaved a deep breath and glared at Jason. "I'll kill this angel-faced young man, Kathryn. Then I'll figure out what to do with you later."

"McLeod, I want to marry your daughter. She was afraid you would say no. I love her."

Jason's voice was shaking with fear. She could read murder in McLeod's eyes as he slowly but inexorably moved toward her. The punch she received straight in the face sent her flying into a small wardrobe. Her back smashed into the bed frame as she was trying to dodge the second one. All the air rushed from her lungs; she felt as though she had broken in half, her hands on her stomach. She then fell over on her side, collapsing to the floor. Stars danced before her eyes as she tried to crawl to the door. She cried out in pain when his kick landed in her ribs. She continued crawling across the floor. *Escape McLeod. Get yourself out.* Those were her only thoughts.

"Pa, stop! You're going to kill her! Pa!"

Kathryn threw herself against her father's arm to try and stop him from hitting Jason again, and the slap she received in return sent her flying onto her bed. In a daze, she watched Jason as she attempted to crawl toward the door under a rain of punches. Ignoring her nudity, Kathryn gathered her courage and threw herself at her father again, who, despite his weight, was pushed off balance just as he was about to kick Jason.

"Pa, stop! My virtue is intact. Jason is a woman!" Kathryn screeched.

McLeod, whose hand was raised to slap her again, froze and opened his eyes wide.

"Jason is a woman," Kathryn repeated, sobbing.

She was crying for herself, and for Jason. She was crying because she knew she had betrayed Jason's secret and that she would never see her again. But she couldn't let her love die. Her father would have killed Jason.

Jason was still crawling, inching her way toward the door, blood flowing in her eyes. Kathryn's father felt between Jason's legs to make sure the truth had been told.

"Daughter, this is appallin'. It's against nature," he muttered angrily.

Although obviously still madder than hell, he seemed much calmer now that he knew Jason was a woman. At least his dear daughter, the apple of his eye, was still a virgin.

"We weren't doing anything wrong, Pa."

Kathryn had to convince her father. Her future depended on it.

"You were naked with her."

"Pa, she and me, we just wanted to know what to do with boys. Jason is a virgin like me. We didn't want to be ignorant on our wedding night."

Her father creased his eyes as if wondering if he should believe her. Kathryn, who knew her father well, could read what he was thinking, wondering whether he could believe her and why Jason dressed like a man and did a man's job. She feared the suspicion growing in his eyes. "Jason is in love with Allan," she said precipitately. "She dressed like a boy to work on the docks and be near him, win his friendship before revealing the truth."

"Huh," her father said.

Knowing that her excuse was far-fetched, and that it wouldn't resist much enquiry, she added as a last resort, "Pa, aside from kisses and caresses, what else could two girls do together?"

Her father remained silent but didn't hit Jason again. He seemed to be buying her argument that two women couldn't really do anything because the most important part was missing. Throwing a last glance at the body splayed out on the floor, he gave Kathryn an order. "Get dressed and take her home. I don't ever want to see her in my pub again. It's no place for a woman. And no point in her showing up at the docks for work tomorrow. I'm going straightaway to see Edgar the foreman."

McLeod left. Kathryn hurried over to Jason, slowly turning her onto her back. Grabbing a towel, she sponged the battered arch of her eyebrows. As she tenderly stroked Jason's hair and held her in her arms, she whispered sweet nothings to reassure Jason, who was barely conscious. "Forgive me, Jason. I'm so sorry. He would've killed you. I love you, but I couldn't…you're going to have to leave. I'll never see you again…"

A sob choked Kathryn. Tears freely ran down her cheeks while she quickly dressed. Without wasting another second, she took a water pitcher and wet a towel to delicately wipe Jason's face. Jason would have to walk; Kathryn wouldn't be able to carry her. "Get up, Jason. We have to get out of here. Please help me."

With great difficulty—cajoling, pulling, and tugging her along— Kathryn finally managed to get her to her feet and painfully negotiate the narrow stairway that led them outside. The walk to her room was an interminable nightmare, Kathryn's sweat dripping from her as she held Jason up and made her put one foot in front of the other.

Fortunately, once they reached the boarding house, Jason's landlady, though bitterly complaining, helped them go up the stairs to her room under the eaves.

"Who put 'im in this state?"

"My father," answered Kathryn, bitterly. "He caught us kissing."

The landlady pursed her lips. "If you young people weren't so impatient, this wouldn't happen. Especially with the pretty ones. Never trust them. They're the worst kind. Even my daughter was swooning over him!"

Once having settled Jason on her metal bed, Kathryn grabbed a piece of material, soaked it in water, and slowly wiped her battered face.

When Kathryn told the landlady, "I'm gonna stay with him a while to make sure he's all right," the unsympathetic woman sighed.

"It's against house rules, but I suppose that, in his state, nothing sinful can occur."

And with these words, the landlady exited the room, leaving Kathryn in despair.

❖

Two knocks on the door. The handle turned. Alarmed, Jason sat up in her bed, as best she could, reaching under the covers to grab the hammer she kept hidden there. Since she'd regained consciousness, fear never left her. She was expecting to see McLeod's huge shape appear in the doorframe demanding an explanation. The door opened slowly. Jason kept her eyes glued on the opening as it widened:

"Are you there, Jason? It's Allan."

Allan, Jason's best friend. Her sigh of relief didn't last long. Was he still her best friend? He must have learned the truth. He must have felt betrayed. Was he coming for revenge? Jason tightened her grip on the hammer as Allan entered the room.

His smooth face finally appeared in the darkness. With a few-days-grown beard and questioning eyes, Allan observed her. He couldn't miss the bandage and the enormous bruise on her face.

"Looks like McLeod had quite a go at you."

"What do you want?" Jason gripped the hammer she held under the covers.

"What are you hiding?"

Jason showed him the hammer without the slightest hesitation.

"Good God, Jason. I'm your friend!"

"Are you still my friend?"

Without directly answering this question, Allan asked another one. "Is it true what McLeod says? Are you a woman?"

Jason hesitated. How would Allan react if she answered honestly? He had always been a true friend, since the beginning. If he wanted to give her a beating in her state, hammer or not, it would be hard to defend herself.

"It's true."

Allan scowled. "Why?"

"Why what?"

"Why pass yourself off as a man, Jason? The guys on the docks are furious. They feel betrayed. They're talking about turning you over to the police, after they come here first to beat you up."

"And they sent you to scout ahead?"

"No! I didn't tell them where you live, but if they really want to find you…"

It wasn't necessary for Allan to finish his thought. If they really wanted to find her, it wouldn't take long. Helpless, Jason clenched her fists. She wouldn't be able to defend herself alone.

Despite the threat of the hammer she held, Allan approached the bed, taking the only stool in the tiny room to sit down facing her. "I want to help you."

Jason didn't know what to say. Without an answer from Jason, and obviously reading suspicion in her eyes, Allan sighed and took a white handkerchief from his pocket. "Kathryn asked me to bring this to you. She would've come herself, but her father won't let her out of his sight. She has asked for your forgiveness for having betrayed your secret, but she thought her father would have killed you."

Jason took the handkerchief, which was surprisingly heavy. Delicately, she opened the little package. There was money and… Jason swallowed. Tears came to her eyes when she brushed her fingers against a hidden lock of hair.

"You really love her, don't you?" Allan asked.

Unable to speak, Jason nodded. She would never see Kathryn again. Their love was doomed.

"You have to leave. Now that I know you're a woman, I looked into how to organize your departure for Australia. The reverend gave me the name of several organizations that take care of young women wanting to work over there as maidservants. The Salvation Army is one of 'em. That reminded me that I know someone who works there, a very good woman, my aunt's friend. I went there this morning before coming here, and she agreed to take you in for the time you need to get your papers sorted out and wait for the next boat for Sydney. The crossing is free, and a job will be waiting for you once you get there. Take your savings, dress yourself as a woman, and follow me. I'll take you there."

"I don't want to work as a housemaid, Allan."

"That's what I figured, but what's stopping you from disappearing as a woman after a month or two's work and reappearing in another place as a man? Australia is vast, and I don't think once you're over there that they'll be very particular."

Allan dug into his pocket. With his free hand, he grabbed Jason's and put money in it.

"You will need this to buy prospecting tools."

Jason opened her eyes wide when she saw the amount of money in her hand. She shook her head. "These are all your savings for Australia. I can't accept this."

"Consider it a loan. Once you've made your fortune in the gold mines, you can reimburse me with interest."

Allan hesitated and lowered his head as Jason stared at him. She couldn't believe such kindness existed.

"If you had told me you were a woman, we…"

"If I had told you I was a woman, you would've never let me work on the docks. Maybe you'd have wanted to marry me, and I would have refused. Or if I had accepted, my life would've been miserable. Yours too."

"I don't understand."

"Of course you don't. You're a man. My mother had fifteen children. Every day of her life I saw her working herself to sheer exhaustion in order to feed and clothe us while my father spent his evenings at the pub, and his Sundays with his friends. Men are free. They can do whatever they please, when they want. But what rights do we have, us women, apart from keeping house and having children? I want another life, Allan. I want to be free to walk down the street without someone accosting me. Free to travel, and free to love…"

"A woman."

Jason looked away. "Yes. Don't ask me why. I don't know myself. It's just the way it is."

Allan's callused hand gently closed hers over the money. "You're my friend, Jason, and nothing can change that."

Allan pointed to the bedroom door. "I will wait on the landing while you dress yourself as a woman. Do you at least have something to wear?"

Jason smiled slightly, for the first time since Allan arrived. "I have an old dress somewhere. Thank you, Allan."

Allan nodded before walking out the door. He too had felt betrayed when McLeod had told everyone that Jason was a woman. It had taken him two days to calm down enough to come over here. Truth be told, Kathryn had made him decide, had begged him to give Jason the handkerchief and its contents. Kathryn, and also the fact that he didn't like hearing his workmates bad-mouth Jason, wanting to make her pay for fooling them. When the foreman spoke about contacting the police, Allan decided to help his best friend, regardless of whether that friend was a man or a woman. They'd had so many dreams together. Allan, hidden by the door, wiped away his tears, cursing himself while vigorously rubbing his cheeks to rid any sign of this moment of weakness.

"I'm ready," murmured someone behind him.

Allan felt his jaw drop when he saw the woman watching him from the doorframe. Although her grey skirt and shirt appeared old and worn, they made the most of her small waist and pretty little bust. The bonnet on her head concealed her bandage, as well as the fact that her hair was too short.

"You're...beautiful," Allan said.

Jason didn't smile when she mechanically answered. "Thank you." She didn't want to be beautiful in the eyes of a man. Such a reaction made her feel degraded, appreciated only for her gender.

CHAPTER NINE

Sydney, Australia, 1914

When the steamship finally sailed into the Bay of Sydney after so many endless weeks at sea, Jason marvelled at the cliffs and hills that momentarily reminded her of home. Leaning on the ship's railing with the other young girls from her group, she silently took in the vegetation that grew increasingly lush as the boat progressed deeper into the bay.

"It's magnificent, isn't it, Laura? I hope the family I'm allotted to will be nice."

"Very beautiful" was Jason's succinct answer.

Since her arrival at the Salvation Army, Jason had only one desire: rid herself of the impractical dress that had been charitably given to her to replace her own, which was far too worn. When she dared suggest that some women in Australia must wear pants, the group's young girls had nervously giggled at the idea, and Mrs. Winter, their guardian, appointed to watch over them just before embarking on the ship, had once again put Jason in her place.

Jason and Mrs. Winter, a sour-tempered widow, had been at odds from the beginning of the voyage. Jason was too accustomed to acting and thinking like a man to subject herself to the widow's stiff, old-fashioned conventions without rebelling. She had had to hold her tongue and grit her teeth for so many weeks. But, glimpsing the buildings on the coastline, she knew she wouldn't have to wait much longer. Soon, she would find her bearings and get rid of this old dress to put on pants and once again become Jason McKellig, a free man.

Just a few more weeks of patience, Jason thought, to motivate herself. Go through immigration, collect the allowance given to new immigrants, settle in with the family they were placing her with, and, once everyone had grown accustomed to her presence, Laura McKellig would disappear forever. Oh, yes. Jason was in Australia, the country of her dreams, the country where everything was possible, the country where she would finally be free.

"This way, young ladies. Fetch your bags and get ready to disembark," Mrs. Winter ordered in her grating voice. "And no running. Well-mannered girls do not run."

With a determined step, Jason headed toward the cabin she shared with the other ten girls, but the look of disapproval on Mrs. Winter's face dampened her excitement at finally arriving in Australia. This old goat didn't appreciate her masculine demeanour and confidence, so she had threatened to place her in a strict family, and not as a lady's maid, even though Jason could read and write.

Lying on the minuscule bed stuffed into the storage cupboard that served, like an afterthought, as her bedroom, Jason bit the sheets so she wouldn't cry. Men didn't cry so she wouldn't shed a tear. For two long weeks she had been withstanding the cantankerous nature of the lady of the house, the mean-spirited cook, and the advances of the head of the household. She hated each and every one of them. She willed herself to be able to hold out long enough to receive the allowance granted to each new immigrant before leaving this wretched place, but she knew she wouldn't be able to refrain much longer from inflicting bodily harm upon one of them. She had to leave, get out of here, fast. What little savings she did have would have to be enough to pay her passage to go farther inland. Then she'd find work.

Once Jason had made her decision, she felt better. She jumped up out of bed, throwing aside her detestable, horrid grey dress, to grab her tattered and worn cloth satchel. She eagerly rummaged through her things to take out the shirt, pants, and cap she'd taken care to pack in London. Neither Mrs. Winter's reprimands nor the unpleasant remarks she received from the house owner's wife, who had searched through her personal belongings upon arrival, could dissuade her from parting with these treasured items. She had justified herself by saying they were all that was left of her poor, departed father.

After she bandaged down her bustline, she felt total delight as she slipped into her pants and shirt: a sense of power. The tears brimming in her eyes had evaporated, as if changing clothes allowed her to change personalities. She had resisted the urge to put on these garments night after night, only allowing herself to stroke them, hoping to draw enough strength to continue the next day. But tonight, it was over.

Jason hurriedly stuffed her old dress and other belongings into the bag in order to remove any trace of her presence in this house. Her bag and cap in one hand and her old worn-through shoes in the other, she slowly opened the door to her room and slipped into the dark hallway. Fortunately, her larder of a bedroom sat right next to the kitchen, where a back door led outside. Hopefully the cook had left the key in the door, as usual.

Jason tiptoed the few yards that separated her from the kitchen, then hurried to the back door. The key was there! Relief. Not wasting a second, she silently put her shoes and bag on the flagstone floor. Her blood was pumping through her veins, but she steadied her shaking hand enough to turn the key in the lock and slowly open the thick wooden door. The well-oiled hinges made no sound. Jason grabbed her things, carefully closed the door behind her, and started running frantically down the alleyway. The cobblestones hurt the soles of her feet, but she couldn't care less. Freedom was just around the corner. Without stopping, she ran through the streets until, out of breath, she had to stop.

Darting a quick look around to make sure she was alone, she put on her shoes, then grabbed the cap and placed it on her head. Her hair was too long. She'd have to find a barber. She could hear the noise of the sea and prudently headed for the shore. She took the dress out of her bag, and before she threw it into the wavelets, a fiery joy flared in her heart. She didn't know where her steps would take her, but at least she would be free. Hunger, exhaustion, the uncertainty of tomorrow—all this was better than submission. For the first time since she had left her room in London with Allan's help, she felt alive. Even the loss of Kathryn suddenly felt easier to bear.

CHAPTER TEN

Bourke, New South Wales, 1914

From the corner of his eye, all the while counting and recording the wool packs that were passing in front of him, Gary Lawson observed a distant figure with a bundle over his shoulder heading toward him. Judging by the stranger's gait alone, he knew he wasn't a swaggie or an Australian.

A bundle over his shoulder, the stranger approached Gary. "Good day, sir. I've been told you're the one to see about a job."

Gary took his time, focusing on the list he held. He checked a line on his inventory sheet while another wool load was taken from the wharf to the steamboat. It appeared from his accent that this lad was a Brit.

"Ted! Watch what you're doing!" Gary screamed at the man working the windlass, then turned toward the newcomer, who stood waiting patiently.

Ted raised his hand, but Gary was already shamelessly examining the stranger. Noting his muscular forearms revealed by the sleeves rolled up to his elbows, Gary instantly liked the candid, hopeful look in the young man's eyes.

"G'day, mate. You've come to the right place. I'm always needing extra hired hands this time of year, but you don't seem strong enough for this kind of work."

"I worked on the London docks. I can lift and carry my own weight," he instantly replied, "and I don't tire out as quickly as more muscled guys."

Gary smiled. Here was a serious young man. "Okay. We'll start with a trial period, and then we'll see. The wages are eight shillings a day. Be here at six thirty a.m. and ask for Billy, the guy over there with the big beard. You'll be on his team."

As Gary spoke, he kept checking his inventory sheet for each wool pack put on the loading platform.

"Name?"

"Jason. Jason McKellig."

"Irish? Scottish?"

"Scottish."

Gary turned his back to Jason after the conversation was over, but although Jason put her cap back on, she remained in place, her bundle at her feet.

Gary turned back toward him. "Something else?"

"A place to stay, sir. I just arrived in Bourke."

"Go see the Widow Dreyson. It's the last house along the river when you walk upstream. She rents rooms and has a good reputation."

The young man brought his hand to his cap as a sign of thanks, then grabbed his bundle by the strap and threw it over his right shoulder.

"Hey, young lad," Gary called out when Jason turned around to leave. "We're not in England so you can drop the 'sir.' Everyone calls me Gary."

Jason beamed and nodded at this tall, strapping man, whom she'd liked the moment she set eyes on him. He must be respected in these parts, and if she wanted to stay here for a while and make a place for herself, it would certainly be wise to be on good terms with him.

She took big strides to walk back up the wooden dock in the direction Gary had indicated. Having come by steamship, she had leisurely admired not only the town of Bourke, but also all the landscape along the Darling River. The contrast between the vegetation that bordered the length of the river and the red-earth lands that she could make out in the distance had struck a chord deep inside her. She had never seen anything so beautiful. And the birds! The seemingly endless variety of shimmering colours on the parrots constantly surprised her. Every day this country was carving out a place for itself in her heart that made her forget the cold and dampness of her native Scotland.

Most of the houses she strode by consisted of two stories. They didn't look anything like those in Scotland or England, even if the style was somewhat reminiscent of those places. Built of wood or brick and wood, they had wide balconies and verandas that denoted an architectural concession to the region's dry, hot climate. Even after six months, Jason couldn't help thinking about Allan. They had never, even with their overactive imaginations, dreamt of such landscapes. Whereas in Sydney, the houses were relatively close by one another, the farther Jason travelled from the coastal cities, the greater distance the houses stood from each other, even within a city. The last house on the Darling River was even farther apart from the others. She stopped in front of the two-story wooden dwelling. No fence. The front yard was very well kept, with rose bushes and golden chain trees framed by eucalyptus trees. It was hard to believe she was in a city. She took a deep breath. The fragrance from these large thick-trunked trees with their peeling bark was indeed unique.

As she was about to step onto the small path that led to the front door, a voice coming from the yard stopped her. "Over here, lad."

Noticing a woman kneeling behind a row of rose bushes, Jason walked over to her. The woman with the wrinkled face got up with difficulty, leaning on her rake. Jason immediately took off her cap and put her bundle down to help the woman stand.

"Thank you, young man. That's very kind of you. I'm no longer as well-oiled as I used to be."

"Ma'am," Jason answered, rocking from one leg to the other before the woman's watchful blue eyes.

"The body isn't working too well, but the head is still all there."

The Widow Dreyson gave a chuckle and grinned. A handsome lad. That would be a nice change from that drunkard Duran. She gave the new arrival another once-over. Although…was he really a young man? Not so sure. "I reckon you're looking to get a room."

"Yes, ma'am. My name is Jason McKellig. Gary told me that—"

"It's two shillings per night, with breakfast and tea, plus one bath per week. If you clean the stables and take care of carrying the straw and hay for the horse, I'll wash your clothes."

Jason quickly made the tally. It cost too much. She would have to search for something at a better price. As if the Widow Dreyson had read her thoughts, she added, "It's expensive, but the room is big and clean, and it has a balcony that looks out onto the street. Want to see it?"

Glancing at the balcony, Jason smiled at the old woman's determination. "Yes, ma'am."

Indeed, the simply furnished room was magnificent. Jason had never lived in such a lovely place. The view from the balcony was breathtaking with the eucalyptus trees, the river, and in the distance the red earth that went on forever.

"It was my daughter's room. She's married now and lives in Sydney. Since my husband died, I've been renting the room for company, but I don't let it out to just anybody."

Jason, overwhelmed by the landscape, barely heard what she was saying. Even if these great open spaces looked nothing like the Highlands of her childhood, the attraction she felt for them kept increasing.

"It's beautiful," she murmured to herself.

The Widow Dreyson watched Jason for a long time. What she could read in this young lad's face, she had seen on dozens of other faces—the call of the bush. Her own husband had never been able to resist it for long. After a month of sedentary life, the bush's lure was stronger than anything else, and Emma would never know when he would return...or *if* he would.

"So, does the room interest you?"

Still lost in contemplation, Jason barely heard her.

"Jason!"

"Huh? Yes, ma'am. I'll take the room."

"Emma. And I require a week's rent in advance."

Jason stopped smiling immediately. Fourteen shillings? She hadn't even had enough to buy something to eat since she had taken the steamboat. Lowering her eyes to hide her embarrassment at being broke, she stammered, "All things considered, ma'am, I'm not going to take it. It's pretty and everything but…"

When Jason took another glance at the landscape, Emma perceived a sadness mixed with pride on Jason's face. It didn't take her long to understand. "But you don't have any money."

Jason wanted to protest, but she couldn't help being honest. Her life was one big lie. She didn't have any money or any friends. All she had were her courage and pride.

"No. I start on the docks tomorrow. If you could keep the room for me, for just two days, I could come back and pay you and—"

"And what will you eat if you give me your two days' pay? Never mind. I'll be a decent soul. Give me just two shillings today, then four shillings per day for three days, and the room is yours."

Jason didn't even have time to lower her head before Emma put her hands on her hips, gave her a piercing look, and said, "You don't even have two shillings, do you?"

Jason shook her head. Then she reluctantly picked up her bundle she had left at the room's entrance and started to go.

"When was the last time you ate something?"

Jason turned around, but she couldn't look the widow in the eye. She was fighting against her tears when she admitted in a tiny voice, "A while ago."

"A while ago. It's not surprising you're so thin. And you think you're going to carry wool bundles tomorrow? On an empty stomach? Why didn't you say something earlier?"

Jason stared at the old woman without understanding.

The widow threw her hands to the sky and turned to the door. "Follow me...and leave your bundle. Ha! These new immigrants...you have to teach them everything!"

Not understanding, Jason did as she was told and followed Emma into the kitchen, which also served as the dining room.

"Sit down," Emma ordered her.

Jason complied and watched the widow place bread, a platter with cooked meat, a big knife, a plate, and a cup on the table.

"Eat while I make tea."

"I'm not asking for charity."

Emma crossed her arms over her chest. The schoolmarm glance she gave her made Jason immediately squirm in her seat.

"I'm not giving charity, but here, in the outback, we have a sacred rule. If somebody is thirsty, you give them something to drink, and if somebody's hungry, you give them something to eat. Life is too hard in this region not to help one another. If you ask nicely, not a single farm will refuse you a piece of meat or a day's work to pay for the supplies you'll need for your next journey. My poor husband took enough advantage of this custom for me to pay it back in kind."

Emma pushed the meat platter and the knife over to Jason, who, after hesitating a moment, dug in. While she cut into a big piece of meat, Jason watched Emma put the kettle on the fire, then sit down across from her. The mutton tasted exquisite, the fresh bread, delightful.

"How long have you been in Australia?"

"Six months, ma'am," Jason uttered between two mouthfuls.

"Call me Emma. I won't tell you again. You left with one of the last boats from England then?"

"Yes, ma...Emma. I was lucky the war was declared only after we had left."

Jason cursed herself. She realised she sounded like a coward, and she didn't want her landlady to think poorly of her. Emma slowly nodded before smiling. Then her expression grew serious again.

"I'm happy to see that not all young men have nothing but war on their minds. What nonsense it is for young Australians to go die so far from their homeland. And for whom? The English who exiled their fathers and mothers? You and I will get along just fine, Jason. Go on. Have some more meat, and then you'll go feed the horse. Are we agreed? I'll do your laundry, and you'll take care of the stables."

Jason, happy that everything was going so well, immediately nodded while chewing on the deliciously grilled meat. Emma got up to pour the boiling water in the tea before grabbing two big porcelain cups that she put on the table with the teapot.

"Sugar? Milk?"

"Sugar."

"I have never been able to drink my tea without milk. My poor husband always drank it black. He said that when travelling, it was difficult to find and then keep milk, so he'd rather not get used to it."

"Did he travel on horse?"

Emma's shoulders started shaking with laughter. "On foot. It's impossible to find anything to feed horses with once you head out west. Too much desert, not enough water. All swagmen travel on foot. But if you want to ride Margot, you can. She could do with a little exercising."

"I don't know how to ride. I never got to learn how."

"I can teach you if you like. It would be good for Margot. She's getting fat, and it'll remind me of my youth, when I taught my own daughter."

Jason couldn't believe how lucky she had been to be sent here.

As for Emma, despite her age, her heart fluttered. This young man had a charm that must be devastating for a young lass…and not so young!

"How'd you end up here in Bourke?" Emma asked, in order to regain her composure.

"I worked a few weeks in Sydney when I first got here, but I didn't like it. I came to Australia to find gold and become rich."

The end of Jason's sentence was practically inaudible, just a small murmur. Emma saw the disappointment on his smooth, handsome face.

"And?"

"I went to Broken Hill but got there too late. It was the end of the rush for individuals. There's just one big company there to exploit the ore, and apart from being employed by them, there aren't any other mining options. As I was broke, I worked for the BHP for a while, but I prefer big, open spaces. Holes in the ground aren't for me. So I hit the road again, working here and there. When I was farther downstream, I heard work was to be had up here in Bourke. So I took the first boat. I'll stay until the end of the season, and then I'll probably head out west. It seems there's still gold out there."

"You mean to go by boat?"

"No. I've had my fill of boats. I was sick as a dog the first two weeks between England and Australia. I'll go to Western Australia on foot if I have to, or by any cheap transportation I can find."

Emma sighed inside. She hadn't been mistaken when she had judged Jason as he'd looked into the distance. Once he discovered the grand open spaces, he would be just like her husband.

"Australia's a big place."

"I've got nothing but time."

After finishing his tea, Jason stood up. "With your permission, Emma, I'm going to introduce myself to Margot…and start cleanin' the stables."

Emma observed Jason from the kitchen window. His demeanour and gestures were typically masculine, but something about him gave an indefinable impression of femininity, and once again, Emma wondered at what she was seeing. Her instinct reminded her that appearances were deceiving. Hadn't her husband told her several stories about women dressed as men, who behaved so much like them that almost nobody could pick them out from the other swagmen? As much as these women were accepted in the bush, here, in town, you'd simply never see one.

When Emma walked out of her room, Jason couldn't help but give her an admiring glance. The new ash-rose dress they had purchased together the week before was extremely becoming. Jason and Emma's friendship had grown during the two months since Jason's arrival, and Jason often accompanied her when she ran her errands in order to help carry her packages or just spend a little time with her.

"You look ravishing, Emma. No man could resist you."

"Oh, you flatterer."

Emma stopped abruptly and frowned. "You're not expecting to escort me dressed like that. Are you?"

Jason heated with embarrassment. She lowered her eyes and

stared at the worn tips of her old shoes. She had given her everyday clothes a good brushing and polished her ankle boots, but she knew she looked more like an outdoor labourer going to work than a young man about to attend a party.

"I don't have anything else to wear. You know that. I had to buy work clothes, since mine were too old and ragged. I couldn't afford to buy Sunday clothes as well. Maybe in a few months, if I can save enough, but I need new shoes first."

Emma grew thoughtful. She listened to Jason's excuses for a few seconds. She shouldn't have embarrassed him with her comment, but she'd spoken without thinking. If they went to the party together and she kept her pretty dress on, everybody would notice Jason's poor-man's outfit. She didn't want to offend this helpful, thoughtful young man who had brought a gust of fresh air to the solitary days of the twilight of her life. She had an idea.

"Follow me. We'll be a little late, but it doesn't matter."

Emma took the stairs and headed for a tiny room where all sorts of objects were stored higgledy-piggledy. Jason had already been there once before, when Emma wanted a pedestal table that had been sitting up there for lord knows how many years.

"Open the trunk, and let me see what is still wearable. These are my dear, departed husband's things, and there must be something decent in there. You're about the same build, even if he weighed more. If you search carefully, you should find a pair of suspenders somewhere."

Jason opened the trunk but then hesitated. She didn't want any charity. The sidelong glance she gave Emma must have said so much that the latter started to chuckle.

"I know you won't accept charity, but I want an elegant escort on my arm. Otherwise, I'll be forced to wear one of my old dresses to be a suitable match for your outfit. You wouldn't deprive me of my yearly pleasure of impressing those horrid old gossips, would you?"

Jason swallowed. She was cornered. It would be inconsiderate to embarrass Emma, so she carefully removed the tissue paper that separated the layers of clothing.

Emma stopped her. "This one. This suit here should be perfect. He couldn't fit into it any longer, so the waist size should be right. Take this blue shirt too. It'll go well with your eyes. As for shoes, you'll have to make do with yours. You don't have the same shoe size. Here. Take this and go change."

When Jason came out of his room a few minutes later, Emma was speechless. Once again, her heart started fluttering, and she regretted not being twenty years younger. She slowly reached out and stroked Jason's cheek. It was the first time she had ever touched him. Such soft skin he had, not the slightest hint of whiskers.

"The lasses will be fighting over you," she murmured, feeling a bit jealous.

Jason, seeing the look in Emma's eyes, felt uncomfortable. She rocked from one foot to the other.

"If I were younger I would have kept you for myself," Emma admitted. "But I know when I'm beaten, and you are too handsome to stay by my side all night. I'll be happy enough arriving on your arm to make my friends pale with envy. Shall we go?"

Jason smiled and held out her arm to Emma, who took it.

The party was in full swing when Jason, accompanied by Emma, arrived in the main street. Many people had come from far away to attend Bourke's annual party. As they walked up the street, Emma would point out to Jason the different people she knew—a breeder, a farmer, the banker and his wife. The air was filled with the appetizing smell of grilled meat.

"Mrs. Emma Dreyson," someone called out behind them.

A man with a very thick beard came up to them and tipped his hat. His sun-weathered, craggy face contrasted strikingly with his snow-white hair and beard.

Emma smiled. "Pete. How are you? It's been such a long time."

"Yup. Since poor Joe kicked the bucket. And how're you? Sorry I haven't been by since Joe's death, but I was over near Melbourne."

"No harm done, Pete. I'm all right. I'm happy to see you again. This is Jason, my boarder."

Jason nodded, immediately intrigued by the man standing before her. She had seen several swaggies, as they were called, working on the docks, but had never dared speak with any of them.

Pete held out his hand, which Jason shook immediately.

"You a swaggie?" he asked.

"I work on the docks."

"We'll be seeing each other then. Gary hired me this morning."

Pete burst out in laughter when Jason scrutinized his fragile body.

"Hey. Not to carry wool. Though this old body of mine could give you a run for the money. I've been hired to clean the warehouses. I'm even going to sleep there. If stories about the bush tempt ya, come see old Pete whenever you like."

Pete gave her an appraising look. "You seem honest, sincere. Ya ever hunted kangaroo?"

Jason shook her head.

"You like the sound of it?"

Jason smiled broadly. "And how!"

"Then we'll be seeing each other again. Emma…"

And with a simple touch to the brim of his hat, Pete took his leave. Emma, who had silently observed the scene, was cursing herself for not intervening. Every Sunday since he had arrived, Jason had ventured out farther and farther into the bush with just a water flask and a long stick to chase away serpents or other creatures. Until now, the call of the bush hadn't been strong enough for him to leave several days at a time, but if Pete was taking him, Jason would follow, and she would find herself alone just as she did when her husband would leave for several weeks. Yet if Jason found a young lass for whom he would want to return…In her head, Emma started to make a list of the available girls she knew.

As they continued up the street, Jason heard a cheerful song with a catchy tune and lyrics that appealed to her.

"Emma, what song is that?" she asked as they approached the music stand.

"It's the swagmen's song, but every Australian knows it by heart."

All around them, men and women were singing together. Emma joined in while Jason tried to learn the words about waltzing Matilda.

On the last chorus, Jason began to sing, and after the song ended, she turned to Emma. "It's a nice tune, but I didn't understand all the lyrics, such as 'billabong' and 'coolibah' tree."

"You'll understand them once you've become a real Aussie."

Jason was about to answer when someone slapped her on the back so hard she almost made Emma, who was holding her arm, fall over.

"So, Jason, we'll make an Aussie out of you yet. Emma, you look simply ravishing in that dress."

"Gary. Still a flirt and a charmer. Your wife must be out of earshot."

A conspiratorial grin on his face, Gary leaned forward. "She's with her friends at the pie stand. If I were you, I would avoid hers."

"Pa!" came a voice from behind him. "If mum knew what you were saying about her pies…"

"And who's going to tell her, my dear Elizabeth? Not you? You avoid Mum's pies even more than I do. Emma, do you remember Elizabeth?"

"Of course I do. Do you think I've gone senile? How could I forget the person you talk about the most?"

"And this is Jason," Gary told his daughter. "I've spoken to you about him."

Jason, very proud that Gary had spoken well of her, pulled her shoulders back while beaming at Elizabeth, whose eyes were devouring her. Neither of them found the words to break the awkward silence.

Gary stood by with a mocking air when Emma frowned, then asked, "May I have this dance, Emma, while these two young people gather their wits?"

Although slightly worried about Jason's reaction to Elizabeth, Emma accepted the invitation and let herself be led to the dance floor. Hadn't she just been plotting, only a quarter of an hour before, to have Jason meet a young lady to make him forget the call of the bush?

Elizabeth could be this young lass. She had all the necessary qualities. She was pretty, with long, shiny, chestnut-coloured hair, doe eyes, and a very feminine figure. A fine young lady in every respect, but Emma had never really been fond of her. She found her too selfish, too much of a tease, with an over-indulgent father and a mother who so jealously watched her husband she never thought of anything else. Emma sighed. It was only a first encounter, nothing to get all worked up about—for the moment.

❖

"Gary, may I have a few minutes of your time?" Jason asked, planting herself right in front of him.

Jason nervously rocked from one foot to the other. It was the end of the workday, and the men were getting ready to leave for home or to go down a quick one.

"Man to man," Jason added when she saw the others waiting around to speak with the boss.

It was out of the question that anyone should hear her conversation with Gary. It was none of their business.

"Well, see you later at the bar," one of the men said, obviously realising he was in the way.

Gary, curious, frowned. What could Jason want? Not to leave, he hoped. "I'm listening, lad."

More nervous than ever, Jason wondered if she would find the courage to make her request. "Well. It's just that I…"

His curiosity piqued, Gary took out a pack of cigarettes and held out one to Jason, who eagerly grabbed it.

"I find Elizabeth mighty pretty, and I'd like to have your permission to court her," Jason spit out quickly before she lost her nerve.

Gary lit his cigarette, then held the match out to Jason, who leaned over to light hers before starting to cough and turn crimson red. Gary chuckled. He remembered how he had stuttered and sweated when making a similar request to his future wife's parents. Taking a slow drag from his cigarette, he took his time to inspect this lad from head to toe.

"How old are you, son?"

The young man cleared his throat and swallowed before finding his voice. "Twenty-one, sir."

"Twenty-one years old?"

Although surprised, because he wouldn't have guessed more than eighteen, Gary told himself that Elizabeth could do worse. Jason wasn't rich, but he was a hard-working and serious young man, something by no means insignificant; and he had never seen him drunk. Yep, his daughter could do worse, even more so since her reputation as a little pest had seemingly caused most local lads to stay at bay. He had often tried to speak to her about it, but to no avail. Would he be really giving Jason a gift? On the other hand, he didn't feel like having his daughter on his hands for much longer.

"Okay, son, but no funny business. I want your word of honour."

Jason's heart was racing. Gary had assented. She would be able to court Elizabeth openly. She beamed and joyfully held out her hand to seal their agreement with a handshake.

"You have my word. With your permission, I'm going straightaway to invite her to next Saturday's evening dance."

"Go right ahead, son, and if you have the time, come by the hotel bar for a drink."

Watching Jason quickly walk away, obviously eager to find Elizabeth and ask her the all-important question he had in mind. Gary realised he would most likely not return to join him at the bar now that he had the permission to make sheep's eyes at Elizabeth. Oh, to be young and single.

CHAPTER ELEVEN

"You reckon on comin' with me dressed like that?" Pete asked, seeming shocked.

Jason hesitated. She had put on her work clothes and had no idea what could be wrong.

"Uh, why?"

Pete burst out in laughter, revealing his teeth blackened by chewing tobacco and inexistent care. A moment later, a black gush spurted from Pete's mouth, landing not far from Jason's feet. Pete looked Jason up and down one more time before opening the flap on his satchel and handing over two rolled strips of fabric.

"Wrap the lower half of your legs in this, if you don't want the spinifex to rip your pants to shreds. It'll also stop insects and all kinds of critters from making a home in your family jewels. Believe me, tons of nasty things live in the bush, between ticks, spiders, ants, and other creatures whose name I don't know."

Jason grabbed the two rolls of fabric, crouched, and started wrapping them around her calves, careful to wind them tightly at the bottom. She was surprised at how soft the fabric was but didn't want to appear dumber than she was, so she refrained from asking what type of animal skin the wrapping was made of.

Pete smiled. "It's kangaroo. If the hunt goes well, I'll show you how to make a pair so they'll be supple but stay solid for a long time. Luckily the ground isn't that hard right now. Otherwise your shoes wouldn't make it," commented Pete, who turned and started walking away as soon as Jason stood back up.

She followed him, carefully observing how the old man moved, silently, with a minimum amount of effort—the gait of someone accustomed to walking for hours without stopping.

Minutes were followed by minutes, hours by hours, and Pete never stopped. He didn't walk fast, but with long regular strides, discreetly turning around from time to time, obviously to check on the newbie.

Although at first Jason had trouble keeping up the pace, after three hours, she forgot she'd been walking and started paying attention to the surrounding landscape. "Dry and flat" were the first words that came to mind. The trees were spaced so far apart, she didn't consider them a forest, let alone a wood. Sometimes, over long distances, she didn't see a single tree, and the ochre-red ground was covered with what the old man called "spinifex," a dreadful, thorny plant that pierced her pants above the protective puttee she was wearing and scratched her skin. When Pete stopped in the shade of an acacia tree, Jason raised her head and noticed that the sun was still far from its peak.

"We're going to rest a bit. Gather us a little wood for the fire so I can boil the billy."

Jason watched him from the corner of her eye as she followed orders. With an economy of effort, Pete took a pot and two small bags from his satchel. When Jason returned with an armful of wood, he had already started a fire with twigs and put the water, tea, and sugar in the pot.

"We didn't need that much, but it doesn't matter. Sit down."

Jason couldn't keep from asking the question she'd been wondering about since they'd seen the first kangaroos. "How come we didn't hunt the kangaroos we came across earlier?"

Pete chuckled. "Hey, lad. I thought you wanted to see what the bush was like?"

"Yes. That's right," Jason answered, a little surprised by Pete's comment.

"I hope you were paying attention during our walk. Did you see the galahs?"

"The whatsas?"

"The galahs. The pink and grey cockatoos."

Jason sighed and nodded. She had noticed them and admired their plumage.

"They're very playful. You'll see if you take the time to observe them. I imagine you also saw the black cockatoos."

"I heard them more than saw them. Although I've seen white ones in Sydney."

"They sure make a terrible racket. And not just them. As soon as you've finished your tea, we'll continue on, silently now, to get as close as possible to the group of roos that are just over there."

Jason opened her eyes wide, surprised. What kangaroos? Where? She watched in the direction Pete was pointing but saw nothing there.

"They're hidden by the eucalyptus grove, but don't worry. They're not going anywhere, and we'll have a nice piece of roo to grill up for our tea."

❖

The grilled kangaroo was so delicious Jason was still licking her fingers while Pete chipped off little shavings from his tobacco plug to roll a cigarette.

They had hunted and eaten in silence. Jason, somewhat disgusted, had watched Pete cut up the animal, carving the meat and skin he wished to save. When Pete had handed Jason the knife to take care of the other slaughtered kangaroo, Jason clenched her teeth and proceeded. Nothing in her life had prepared her for the Australian bush. Hearing Pete's stories was entirely different from the real experience. Somewhat unexpectedly she felt at home in this reality. In the bush, she could slowly forget England and Kathryn.

"Whole different world from what you know."

"Indeed." Jason smiled. "I was born and raised in Scotland. Over there, everything is green, and it rains all the time. There are mountains and old castles. The only thing that's the same are the sheep, so many sheep."

"Do ya miss it?"

"No. I'm happy here. And besides, war is raging in Europe…"

Realising what Pete might think, Jason hurried to say, "It's not that I didn't want to serve my country, but I had dreamt so much of Australia—"

Pete raised his hand. "All these young lads who've left to fight for England are fools. They'll never be thanked. The Poms think we're a colony whose only purpose is to serve them. Thanks, but no thanks. If there was a vote for independence, I'd be the first in line, but as long as this pack of galahs who govern us refuse to understand that the Poms see us as nothing but puppets, nothing's gonna change."

"You don't like the English very much. I imagine you were born here?"

"A pure Aussie, mate, and from parents all born here too."

Hoping not to upset Pete, Jason carefully asked the question she was itching to ask.

"Were your grandparents convicts?"

Pete burst out in laughter and threw his cigarette butt into the fire before answering in a cheerful voice. "One of my grandparents was a soldier stationed in Sydney. He deserted when his regiment was called back to England. Seems he had met a very pretty ex-thief, and they left together for the outback. I think, however, that he was struck by the call of the bush. My other grandfather came here when he was twelve, convicted for having stolen a loaf of bread while starving. That's English justice for you. It's best to steer clear of any authority. The only reality worth its while is the bush."

"Yet you came to work in Bourke," Jason remarked, adding a eucalyptus branch to the fire.

Pete stared at the flames that licked the dry wood. "Sometimes a man needs the warmth of a sheila and a few drinks with his mates. But Jason, there's no mistake. Marriage is the bushman's nightmare."

"But Emma…"

"Old Joe loved his wife, and he was torn each time he left for the bush. I could see the despair in Emma's eyes whenever I would come 'round. She must have hated me every time I showed up and took her husband from her. But old Joe, if you'd seen him, his eyes would shine anew, and he'd jump around like a joey filled at the prospect of the bush."

"Do any women follow their husbands into the bush?"

"Sometimes. In theory they cook and stay where the shearing takes place. You thinking 'bout Elizabeth?"

Jason nodded. She was thinking ever more often about her. She no longer remembered Kathryn's features clearly. Elizabeth's had replaced them.

"She won't follow you into the bush. She's not that kind of woman."

"Ah!"

"Come. I'll show you how to make strips for your legs, and if you like, next time I'll teach you to shoot. Knowing how to shoot and set traps is crucial if you wanna feed yourself in the bush."

The image of Elizabeth quickly vanished from Jason's mind. She burned with anticipation and jumped to her feet, which ached from having walked so much. She knew she'd collapse into her bed that evening from sheer exhaustion, but it would be with joy in her heart.

CHAPTER TWELVE

Elizabeth and Jason were sitting on a bench in the shade of a pepper tree watching the passengers get off the steamship in the distance. Jason brought Elizabeth's hand to her lips and softly kissed her palm.

"I'd like to go to Sydney one day," Elizabeth said. "Would you take me there?"

Jason winced. Sydney had left a bad taste in her mouth. She had no desire to go back, but she would do anything to please Elizabeth. Thinking it was the right moment, she dug into her pants pocket and took out a small box that she handed her.

"Jason?"

"Perhaps we could go to Sydney on our honeymoon? Elizabeth, would you do me the honour of becoming my wife?"

Elizabeth's mouth opened, then closed. For once she, who was never at a loss for words, was speechless. Without hesitating, she threw herself into Jason's arms and whispered "yes" in his ear.

Jason's heart burst with joy. She would have liked to jump up and dance, sing at the top of her lungs. "Open the box."

Elizabeth hastened to do as she was told. "Oh, Jason. It's magnificent," she said as she slipped the ring on her finger.

"Not as magnificent as you;"

"Oh, you…I love you so much."

Elizabeth's lips slowly approached Jason's. Their lips gently brushed together. Jason grazed hers against Elizabeth's cheek before returning to her lips and kissing her greedily. Jason immediately groaned with pleasure. Those lips had tortured her. Soon she told herself, but first she had to reveal her secret to Elizabeth. She would never try to conceal her true nature from the woman she loved.

"Elizabeth, I have a secret to confess. You'll see that it won't make a difference to the love we have for one another…"

❖

Emma was sitting on the back porch when she heard the front door slam shut so violently the whole house trembled. Jason? It certainly wasn't his habit to slam doors. He was always so careful that Emma often wondered if he had actually returned home. Intrigued, she shook the vegetable peels from her apron and got up. She didn't like to have to take the stairs more than once a day, but instinct told her this situation was important. The door to Jason's room stood ajar.

Emma softly called out, practically tiptoeing in. "Jason? Are you there?"

The sight of Jason lying curled up in the foetal position on his bed touched Emma's hardened heart for the first time in years. During the course of the last months, a true affection for this gentle, hardworking lad had grown in her, but since Jason had confided his wish to marry Elizabeth, she had been bracing herself, fearing things would go awry. Slowly, she sat down on the bed and placed her hand on Jason's shoulder.

"Come, come, dear. Tell me what happened. You'll feel better afterward."

Jason turned around and wrapped her arms around Emma to cry, and Emma affectionately hugged Jason back.

"Oh, Emma. If you knew. It's just horrible."

"Elizabeth?"

Jason nodded without answering.

"She refused your marriage proposal?"

Jason's sobbing increased twofold. What could the naive boy have said or done?

"Calm down, Jason. Please don't disgrace yourself. You're normally such a brave young lad."

Emma's harsh words felt like a cold shower to Jason, who tried to control her emotions. Emma…if she told her, would she reject her too? But then, she would find out from the others…Jason knew she would have to run away once again. Yet she had truly believed that Elizabeth would understand and accept her.

"I'm going to have to leave, Emma. I'm sorry."

"Explain, Jason!"

Jason shook her head. "There's nothing to explain. I asked Elizabeth to marry me. She first said yes, then no, and now I am the most miserable of all beings. I can't stay here. It's far too much for me to face every day. It's more than I can bear."

Jason took a deep breath, wiped her eyes, and then resolutely got up to start packing her satchel. She froze when she heard screams coming from the street and carefully walked over to the balcony and hid behind the curtain to peek outdoors. Seeing a dozen or so people heading straight for the house, the hair on her head stood on end. She hadn't expected this. All the horror of the situation appeared to her. "I have to leave quickly."

Jason turned around and found herself nose-to-nose with Emma, who had followed her to the window.

"They don't seem happy."

"No. Forgive me, Emma."

Jason then rushed to the door, but Emma's sharp voice stopped her immediately. "And how do you count on surviving, without anything?"

"I have no other choice, Emma."

Jason nervously glanced toward the balcony. The brouhaha was getting louder. Maybe it would be better to leave through the window.

Emma also looked out toward the balcony. "Go to my room, get under the bed, and don't make a move until I come get you myself. I'll take care of them."

Jason hesitated. What if one of them told Emma she was a woman? Would Emma then be bound to turn her in? She was risking everything to trust her.

"Go!" Emma ordered her. "Quickly. Without slamming the door."

Refusing to think that this woman whom she cared so dearly about could betray her, Jason hurried down the stairs and entered Emma's room for the first time. She slipped under the bed, and, out of breath, she stayed there, without moving, waiting to face her fate. Elizabeth had betrayed her, so why not Emma? Jason held back a heavy sob, feeling inexorably trapped.

Jason heard Emma walk down the stairs quickly, then stop and take a deep breath. Two powerful knocks sounded at the front door, and the sound of men talking loudly filled the house.

"What is this?" Emma asked in a harsh voice. planting herself in front of Gary, who was leading the posse of intruders. "How dare you enter my home without permission?"

Although Gary was a good foot taller than her, Emma didn't shrink back but held her ground. Folding her arms across her chest, her eyes on fire, she waited for an answer to her question. Gary, despite his own fury, hesitated. Emma was well-respected in the community. She knew he personally respected her. The men in the group behind him were speaking loudly, interrupting him.

"Quiet!" he roared. "Emma, we're looking for Jason."

"And what has he done that so many angry men are looking for him? Did he kill someone?"

Gary had a shocked expression. "No…"

An almost hysterical voice screamed from behind Gary. "That pervert had the audacity to ask for my hand in marriage and then announce that he's a woman."

It was Elizabeth.

Disgusted, Emma couldn't stop herself from showing her true feelings.

Obviously misinterpreting Emma's aversion, Gary added, "You see! That pervert fooled you too, Emma."

Gary took a step forward but had to stop immediately because Emma hadn't moved an inch. "Jason came home but immediately left out the back way," she said.

"You'll allow us to check all the same," Gary replied.

"I will not allow a posse of bloodthirsty men to turn my home upside down."

Emma saw the anger flashing in Gary's eyes. He thought Jason had fooled him, ridiculed him, so Gary was determined he would pay.

"Pa! This old hag is protecting him." Elizabeth was relentless.

"I will not tolerate that talk or behaviour in my home," Emma replied. "Gary, you can go check Jason's room…but you alone. The others have to stay here. Otherwise, you might as well go get the police."

Gary didn't want the police involved. What would the police do apart from putting Jason in jail, if that…No, Gary wanted to take Jason into the bush and there…the dingos would make sure that every trace of him was gone. Nobody made a fool of Gary Lawson.

"Okay. Wait for me here."

"Pa!"

"Shut your mouth!"

No one said a word for the next few minutes, which seemed like a lifetime to Jason as she lay tense under Emma's bed. The minutes went by without anyone saying a word. She heard nothing but Gary stomping from her room to the other bedroom and then the boxroom.

Emma was glowering at Elizabeth until the latter looked away. When Gary came back down the stairs with a heavy step, Emma said, shaking her head, "I didn't give you permission to search anywhere else in my home but Jason's room."

In response Gary pointed at a door at the end of the hallway. "What's inside there?"

"My room. I forbid you to enter. Apart from my deceased husband, not a single man has ever been allowed to cross that threshold."

Ignoring Emma's protests, Gary headed for the door.

Under the bed, Jason heard the handle turn and the door squeak open. She stiffened even more completely, and wished she were anywhere but there.

Gary turned the handle, opening it slightly. As he was about to walk in, a fragile hand grabbed his biceps.

"If you dare enter this room," Emma said, "I swear, Gary Lawson, that I will lodge a formal complaint and make you the laughingstock of Bourke."

They locked eyes for a moment. Gary glanced one last time around Emma's bedroom before stepping back.

"You, go search the stables," Gary ordered one of the men.

Through the windows, Emma saw several men walk around the outside of the house. "They better not upset my horse," she said.

"Good God, Emma. Whose side are you on?" Gary still sounded hysterical.

"That of God and justice, and not of those who want to take the law into their own hands. My poor husband warned me about men like you, Gary. And the rest of you? You should all be ashamed to want to partake in a lynching. Because this is what we're talking about. Isn't that right, Gary?"

The men stared at each other, hesitating. Finally one of them dared to speak. "We don't want to kill her, Mrs. Dreyson. Just teach her a good lesson. It's against nature for a lass to try and pass herself off as a lad and ask a young lady to marry her."

"And you want to kill Jason for that? Because if you didn't want to kill him, what else would you be doing at my place? You must realise that Jason won't be returning to Bourke any time soon?"

Jason heard the men murmur among themselves. No, they weren't planning on killing her. They weren't women killers. They obviously recognised the hate and the desire to kill on Gary's face and understood that they had been deceived. They didn't have a problem giving the pervert a lesson, but risking being hung for murder, that was something completely different. Slowly, the voices died down, one by one, and, finally, the men filed out of the house and headed back to town, leaving Gary and his daughter in Emma's living room.

"Leave my home," she said. "And if you want some advice, Gary, if I were you, I'd get a firm hold on my daughter before she makes you the laughingstock of the whole county."

Before leaving, Elizabeth, dragged out by her father, threw a dagger-filled glance at Emma, who replied with a mischievous smile. Without hurrying, Emma closed the heavy front door, then headed for her room, whose door had remained open.

"I'm going to keep peeling my vegetables, Jason. You stay put until I come back for you."

Emma then closed the door and calmly returned to tending to dinner.

At nightfall, Emma came to get Jason, who crawled out from underneath the bed with difficulty. As she wiped the dust off her shirt and pants, Emma apologized. "At my age I can't clean under the bed any longer."

Despite the darkness, the sad expression in Jason's eyes melted her heart. She saw such disappointment in those beautiful blue eyes.

"Come on," she said. "Let's have something to eat. Dinner's ready. I don't think anyone will come to bother us this evening."

"Thank you, Emma. You—"

"We'll have a talk, but let's eat first."

The meal was silent, contrary to their usual chatter. Jason picked at her plate without daring to look Emma in the eye.

After a few minutes, Emma sighed. "I know you're not hungry after everything that has happened, but you have to force yourself. You'll be leaving tomorrow morning just before dawn. I prepared a bag with bread, meat, tea, and sugar that will last you a few days. You must leave this county if you don't want anyone to learn the truth, especially if you intend to keep on living as a man."

At those words, Jason's face brightened. "You're not blaming me?"

"Why would I? My dear departed husband told me stories about women who lived like men. He had the greatest respect for them and how brave they were."

Jason opened her eyes wide. "There are other women? Like me?"

"Just like you, I don't know. Perhaps they aren't silly enough to make marriage proposals," Emma said with a grin. She took a sip of tea. "Did you think there was nobody else like you?"

Disconcerted by Emma's words, Jason didn't answer. She'd always believed she was the only person who was different, but if there really were others…What she wanted more than anything was to be in a calm, quiet place where she could think things over. She glanced out the kitchen window and saw violet-pink coloured filaments in the sky.

"You'll leave for the bush and stay there, right? I've seen the fascination you've had with the bush since the day you came here. Some are afraid. Others can't live without it. Life as a swagman is difficult, but you are a courageous woman. Follow me."

Emma got up and led Jason into a corner of her tiny living room, where she pointed to a pile of things on the floor. "My husband's bush gear. It's yours now. Let's just make sure it's in good enough state to use."

"I can't accept this."

"You don't have a choice. Your belongings won't last more than a couple of weeks out there, and if you won't take this, nobody will. It was out in the stables."

Jason nodded. She had seen the swag in the stables before, had touched it dreamily without daring to undo it.

"Go on. Open everything up, and I'll bring you the clothes that go with it. They might be a tad big for you, but where you're going, nobody will care."

Jason kneeled before the washed-out blue swag. She removed the pouch that was tied to one of the straps before attacking the straps themselves and unfolding the bedroll. She opened the flaps to touch the nice, thick fabric of the bluey that lined the inside of the bedroll. It offered perfect protection from the thorns and pebbles, and the upper flap would protect her from the wind and desert cold.

"Just slip the two blankets between the tarpaulin, and you have a nice, comfy bed," Emma said, coming back with her arms full of things. "It's really just a big bag sewn up on two sides with a flap to cover the head in case of wind or a sandstorm. If you can get yourself a solid walking stick, you can use it as a stake to make a sort of tent with the swag. I found two shirts and two pairs of pants in pretty good condition. Go get your belongings, only those you can't part with, and I'll show you how to roll everything up to make your swag. I watched my husband do it so many times I could do it with my eyes closed."

Jason stood up without a word and went to get her things. She didn't have much, but she knew it was already too much for the life she was about to begin.

Forcing herself to forget what had happened that afternoon, her heart full of sorrow, she emptied the drawers and spread her few possessions out on the bed. What should she take? Certainly not the suit Emma had given her for the party, nor her dress shoes that she was still wearing.

Jason quickly undressed and threw on a pair of work pants and a shirt. When her eyes rested on the bush boots she had just bought last month, she smiled for the first time in hours. All the real Australians wore them, and she couldn't resist having a pair. That and a knife.

Jason put on her still-new-looking boots with the help of the loop at the back of the shoe and slid the knife into her pocket, along with her small savings that remained after having bought the ring. Chasing away her grim thoughts about her unhappy love affair, she stuffed into a small pouch a sewing kit, two bandages to hide her breasts, and the envelope with her falsified birth certificate. The rest would belong to the past. Jason picked up the bush hat that Emma had offered her, placed it on her head, and resolutely turned her back on what had been her life until that moment.

When she returned to the living room, Emma looked her over from head to toe. Then she nodded approvingly. Jason felt a pinch in her heart for this wonderful woman whom she was going to abandon.

"You're a handsome young man. It isn't surprising that all the girls run after you."

"For all the good it does me," Jason answered bitterly.

"You'll find your perfect match one day. Trust me." Emma gently stroked Jason's cheek. "How old are you?"

Although the question surprised Jason, she didn't let it show. "I'm twenty-one. I'll be twenty-two next May. Why?"

"You have time to find true love. You have your whole life to live."

Jason shrugged, sceptical. Deep down, she was convinced that love just wasn't for her. Never again would she reveal who she really was. Never again would she let herself be vulnerable enough to fall in love with someone. She swore to it.

"How do you roll a swag?" she asked.

Emma chuckled at this obvious change of conversation. The subject was too painful now, but maybe in the future, Jason would be able to talk about it, even if it wouldn't be with her. Emma leaned over the bedroll with a heavy heart. She would never again see this young woman who was so very different from any other woman she had ever known.

"Open the bedroll and put your change of clothes in the part that will be level with your back when you're sleeping. The clothing will also serve as your mattress. Then, slip the blankets inside over the clothes, as flat as possible. Fold the flap over it all."

Jason followed her orders as well as she could while Emma watched.

"Roll the heavy or pointy objects in the middle of the swag so they are well cushioned. Here. Put in this billy can and the frying pan. Stick your little pouch inside the billy. Yes, just like that. Time may start creeping by out there. Since you know how to read, I thought you'd like to have a book."

Emma gave her a collection of short stories by Kipling. The cracked-leather cover showed it had seen better days.

"It's one of the books my husband would take with him. Enjoy it. He'd be happy to know it's going back out on the road."

"I don't know how I will ever be able to thank you."

"You can thank me by staying safe and sound. Go on, now. Roll up that swag for me, nice and tight."

Keeping back the tears that were welling up in her eyes, Jason got to work.

"Now wrap one of the straps around the centre of it, tighter. Good. Place the other two straps, one at each end. Not bad for a beginner. Make sure everything is as tight as possible so the swag doesn't come apart while you're walking. Here. Take this."

Surprised, Jason grabbed the big grey towel Emma was holding out to her. Not knowing what to do with it, she turned it around several times in her hands. "I should have packed it inside."

"No. It will serve as your shoulder straps. Attach it to the other end strap, and it will be comfortable. You can use it to wipe off your sweat. I finished filling the pouch while you were upstairs—tea, sugar, meat, bread, flour, salt, and yeast to make bread. Hook on the tin cup, and you're all set."

Jason did as she was told. One question, however, was bothering her. "Why didn't you put the cup with the billy?"

Emma grinned. "You're not going to want to have to undo everything just to make tea."

Jason nodded. She had so much to learn. Suddenly, the bush didn't seem as attractive as it once had. Thankfully she'd spent a bit of time there with Pete before he left last month.

"Do you know where you want to go?"

"I haven't thought about it. Everything has happened so quickly. Maybe back to Broken Hill."

"If you want some advice from an old bushman's wife, avoid Broken Hill. It has too many people, too many disappointed miners. Go west instead, all the way to the Dingo Fence. Afterward, you can follow it either north or south. It's your choice. You'll find work at the fence and in all the neighbouring farms. But never forget that water is precious, and the position of the wells and water holes will determine your path. Also, keep in mind that you can always get something to eat at the farms, whether or not there is work. The other swaggies that you're bound to meet on the way will teach you the rest. Sleep in the stables tonight. When I get up tomorrow morning, you should have been gone for hours. Good luck, Jason."

Without hesitating, Jason threw herself into Emma's arms and hugged her as tightly as she could. She would never see her again. Then Jason gave Emma a last kiss on the cheek and let go. She heaved her swag and satchel onto her shoulder before quitting the house for the last time. Tomorrow, the bush would be waiting for her…at last.

❖

"And she left, just like that?" Jeremy asked, surprised at his great-grandfather's, or rather great-grandmother's courage.

Would he have had the same courage, the strength to leave for the unknown? He, who had never really left Willowra. He loved this land too much to go live elsewhere, like Gab. Jeremy glanced at his sister. He knew that she also loved this land. But she'd chosen to live her life, her "difference," without having to face her family. Her return with Tess, even if Victoria had forced it, demonstrated the strength of his sister's character. He wasn't sure he would have been able to face his fears if he were in her shoes. The respect he had always felt for Gabrielle, even if he kept it well-hidden, increased a notch.

"Yes, she travelled all alone," Victoria said. "She met other swaggies who taught her the ropes—good places to find work, how to shear sheep. Jason followed Emma's advice and travelled along the dingo fence southward, then continued along the southern coast until she reached Western Australia and finally Willowra. The year was 1922."

"All of that, on foot?" Gab couldn't get over it. Could anyone be brave enough, or crazy enough to want to walk across almost all of Australia from east to west?

"Mostly. Maggie wrote that Jason even crossed the Nullarbor Plain on foot and worked on the construction of the railroad. When I was a child, Jason often spoke about his life as a swaggie. Some of those who came to Willowra for the shearing season were friends from that period. I remember them well. They were all rather colourful characters."

"And no one ever suspected anything about her sex?" Gabrielle asked.

Victoria shook her head with a smile. "You've seen Jason's photo?"

Gabrielle nodded. Yes, she had seen the picture of this handsome man. She could easily imagine how all the young girls would swoon over him, while Jason must have been suffering because she felt so different. Gabrielle understood. She had felt like that as a teenager, and even later…until she met Tess. How had Jason experienced her difference the first time she realised she was attracted to women? "In her day, and here, of all places, it couldn't have been easy to deal with her sexuality," she said.

She addressed her grandmother. "What was Jason: a lesbian? Transexual, trans…?"

Victoria burst out in laughter and looked affectionately at her. "All these modern words to classify and put people in different boxes, Gabrielle. It certainly never crossed my father's mind to try to define himself. He just wanted to exist and be happy. Personally, I think Jason was a lesbian. According to Maggie's diary, Jason never rejected his body, or his sex, only the constraints linked with being a woman and loving other women at the beginning of the twentieth century."

Victoria continued to speak. "Only recently have these constraints relented. People's ideas do evolve, but it's a very slow process. When I see a gay pride parade on TV, I think times have really changed. All these protests and demands should lead to new laws, and maybe even marriage soon, like in some other countries."

She paused and sighed. "I would have very much liked to marry Ginger. I might have been able to continue my existence as Victor McKellig after the war, but I wanted to be me, unlike Jason, who was forced to control his emotions to appear more masculine. She suffered a great deal, according to what Maggie wrote."

A wave of sadness settled over Victoria's face while, with the tip of her finger, she retraced the cover of the notebooks lying before her.

Simone grumbled in the silence that had settled in the room. "All this doesn't bring me any closer to knowing what happened to my father. And don't think I didn't realise what you and my mother were doing in your bedroom at night."

Victoria gave an exasperated huff. Simone, stiff-backed, had an aggressive expression, which wasn't a good sign. Years and life experience had changed nothing about her. She'd left Willowra angry, and her anger had never faded. What had become of the little girl who would come running into her arms to hear stories about the bush? She'd disappeared at adolescence. Why? Victoria didn't know. She plunged her steely blue gaze into Simone's, cutting through the silence like a whip. "You're in too much of a hurry, Simone. This day is mine, and I will do with it as I please."

Simone gasped and then held Victoria's gaze for a moment more before lowering her eyes and clenching her fists under the table.

Gabrielle wondered why Simone was so angry with Victoria, and with her as well? Simone glared at her and Tess like she would like to spit on them.

"Anyone feel like making tea?" Victoria asked.

"I'll go," Aurore said.

"Let me do it, dear," Thomas said. "You've already slaved away for our meal, and if I know you well, the water must already be hot."

"What a story!" Jeremy murmured. "One helluva character!"

Gab raised a brow and wondered if her brother was referring to Jason or Victoria. Indeed, this family was much more unusual than she had realised. She wanted to know more about its members.

PART III: MAGGIE

CHAPTER THIRTEEN

Willowra, Western Australia, 1922

A distant figure slowly made its way through the mid-morning's already oppressive heat. Step by step, the figure drew closer to its destination: a eucalyptus grove glimpsed an hour earlier from atop a low barren hill. Details had come into focus for the foot-traveller as he progressed across the scorched terrain: trees, a windmill. A satisfied smile then broke across his sun-tanned face, which was partially hidden by the wide brim of a kangaroo leather hat: *looks like the shepherd encountered two days earlier hadn't been lying.* Prompted by years of habit, callused hands repositioned the swag belt that had slightly shifted on the figure's back. Perspiration beaded on the swagman's face and neck, soaking his ochre, dust-covered shirt with sweat. The rough canvas pants that had once been brown weren't in a much better state. It didn't matter; there was no such thing as a rich swaggie. A swaggie's wealth was his freedom, which at times came at a steep price.

The rugged brown leather boots crunched against the ochre-coloured earth at a steady pace. The swaggie's pale-blue eyes checked the direction once again while making note of a group of incongruous angles jutting underneath the windmill. Buildings! Not just a cabin or a shelter, but an entire group of buildings. His instinct hadn't failed him when he had spotted that group of trees from afar.

Naturally, even before meeting the shepherd and his herd, the swaggie knew he was on a sheep station because of the pens he had spotted on his journey there. Unlike other swagmen, he didn't really care for sheep-shearing, even if it paid well, but he didn't always have the choice. He much preferred the work that went with running a station. That year, he had decided to try his luck in this remote corner of

Western Australia well before shearing season. Less work might have been available out here, but he would find less competition also.

After years of wandering on the beaten, but much more often off-the-beaten track, he wanted to rest, settle down a bit. His age, undoubtedly. The swaggie laughed at himself. Twenty-nine years wasn't old, but seven years of wandering would age anyone quickly. When he'd arrived in Australia, he hadn't imagined his life would be this way. No, frankly, not this way at all. The sound of two barking dogs nearby brought him back to the present. He had never been the kind to feel sorry for himself, even if once, a very long time ago, and only for a short period, he had taken refuge in drink. Ignoring the growling of the herding dogs, he walked with a firm step to the main house.

The swagman was surprised to find no sign of life once he had climbed the porch's three wooden steps. He took off his hat and slipped his swag strap over his head before letting it fall to the floor. The dogs had stopped growling, although they still kept a watchful eye on the intruder; their job was to herd sheep, not mind humans. He wiped the sweat from his forehead with his sleeve, thus smearing the dust on his face.

A water bucket and a ladle hanging on a hook next to the front door tempted him more than he could bear. He delighted in gulping down the fresh water that ran down his chin, soaking the front of his shirt. After pouring water from the ladle onto the nape of his neck, he straightened back up and contemplated the courtyard.

"Seems your master isn't home. That right, doggies? Do ya think there's work for me here?" The two dogs wagged their tails in unison to the sound of his voice. The darker-haired dog sat down, then tilted his head to the side as if to better hear what he was saying. "Maybe. Maybe not…"

The swaggie gave a sweeping glance, taking in the different structures dotting the homestead. Horses in a paddock near the stables; a barn; a long, rectangular structure that probably was the shearers' dormitory; a storage shed that had to be for tools and materials; and, farther to the side, a woolshed with its pens and the wool storehouse. All the vegetation around the two structures had been removed to prevent brushfires, so prevalent in the area, from reaching them. Sheets drying on a clothesline not far from the house attracted his attention. He put his hat back on and walked down the steps to get a closer look: sheets, shirts, pants, dresses—a couple, with no children.

A young couple perhaps. Then again, a station as big as this one cost a lot, so maybe an elderly couple with grown children. But if that was right, at least one of them would have stayed behind.

While examining the surroundings, the swagman spotted a heap of wood piled higgledy-piggledy next to carefully arranged logs stored under a shelter. The swaggie's stomach growled at the prospect of a hot meal cooked by the missus in return for some honest work. He rolled his sleeves above his elbows while walking over to retrieve the ax stuck in a block of wood. He took off his hat and hung it on a wooden peg that stuck out from the roof. It was neither the first time, nor the last, undoubtedly, that he would earn a hot meal in return for chopping wood. The muscles on his forearms grew taut as he grabbed the ax and removed it from its stand.

Two hours later, when the swagman, drenched in sweat, stuck the ax back into the piece of wood with a weary gesture, the heap was gone. Neat logs were piled under the shelter with the others. No doubt he would have a good meal for his reward when the boss returned. His damp shirt sticking to his back, he put his hat back on his head before picking up his bluey.

The two dogs, having decided this stranger represented no threat, were now sleeping peacefully under the house in the shadow of the wooden porch. Still observing everything around him, the stranger slowly walked toward the building he figured to be the shearers' quarters. Ten beds, each with a rolled-up mattress and a few pieces of furniture in a sorry state confirmed his assumption. The side door must lead to the shearers' canteen. *Empty, this time of year.*

He flicked away layers of dust from the bed with his hat before putting down his gear and unfastening the buckles that kept the rolled bluey and material in place. Inside, the sparse belongings acquired over many years of wandering: an almost-clean spare shirt, a thick kangaroo-leather jacket for the cold nights, and a rifle.

This rifle told the story of a friendship between two swaggies: an old-timer who knew all the ropes but was a little too fond of the bottle. Yet he was soft-hearted enough to take a young man, who knew nothing about life in the Australian great outback, under his wing. Upon his death, in a place that had no name, the old bloke had left his protégé his only possession: a rifle. The latter owed his life to that old man.

The idea of finally being able to wash up chased away the swagman's sad memories. He grabbed the almost-clean extra shirt from his swag and tried to shake out the wrinkles. Then he grabbed a piece of frayed material and a rolled-up strip of cotton and went over to the well. The basin filled to the brim with water pumped by the windmill appeared like a miracle after the long journey across the desert. How many times, having come 'round a canyon bend, had his heart swelled with enthusiasm at the sight of a river bordered by white-trunked eucalyptus trees? What a delight to be able to swim!

Making sure that he was still really alone, the swaggie removed his hat, placing it on the edge of the basin, followed by his sweat-drenched shirt. He then carefully unrolled his torso bandage and removed his pants and belt, to which a hunting knife was attached. The naked body thus revealed no longer had anything in common with a regular swaggie. Except for the deeply sun-tanned arms and face, the rest of the swaggie's body was pale white: a woman. She cleaned herself, vigorously scrubbing every square inch of her with the frayed cloth as soapy water ran slowly down her features which, in spite of being chiselled and toned, remained unmistakably feminine. She grabbed the bucket of water, pouring it slowly over her head, and torso, before shaking it off like a young dog. She rapidly wiped off the excess water, the crisp air of the arid land drying her before she'd even buckled her pants.

In an expert, oft-repeated gesture, she wrapped the long cotton strip over her breasts, thus concealing the curves which, unaltered, would have triggered many an embarrassing question. Not that there weren't men who actually had more imposing chests than she, but they also had the physique that came with them. The clean shirt on her back, she once again hid her sinewy body.

❖

A wagon stopped in front of the house. The swaggie got up from the shaded corner where she had been napping. The two people in the wagon gave no sign of being surprised to see a man suddenly come out of the shadows.

"Sir, ma'am…" she said, touching the edge of her wide-brimmed kangaroo hat. "Jason McKellig at your service."

"I'm Aaron Sterling. This is my wife Margaret. Looking for odd jobs in the area?"

Jason nodded, uncertain, before adding, "I chopped the wood to make myself useful while waiting for you, boss, and I folded the laundry when it was dry, ma'am." When the swaggie heard Margaret (or Maggie, as her kin probably called her) clearing her throat and with a look of dread in her eye, she hurried to add, "After I washed up and changed, of course. I put the laundry on the kitchen table so it wouldn't get dirty. I hope that's okay with you, ma'am?"

Maggie seemed to relax a bit. "Yes. If you want tea, it's time I get it on. Mr. McKellig?"

"Ma'am?"

"Could you help my husband unload the wagon? That'll save time, and we can eat sooner."

Although the swaggie was surprised the order came from the woman, she quickly agreed. When she moved closer to the man to unload the wagon, she noticed that the boss's eyes were glassed over. Whiskey must have been flowing earlier that afternoon.

"Boss?"

"Help me with the crates, Jason. They go in the shed."

The "boss" pointed to a building next to the dormitory with his chin, before grabbing the first crate. Jason wordlessly picked up the next one and followed the same path. Less than an hour later, as Jason unharnessed the horses, after having put the wagon away in the barn, Margaret came over to her.

"Tea will be ready in a half hour, Mr. McKellig."

Maggie hesitated. Many swaggies had passed through their sheep station over the years. Some were good workers, others good for nothing, but not a single one had ever folded her dry laundry. That had surprised her, to begin with, but she astounded to discover that the laundry had been folded just the right way. This swaggie is different, she thought.

"Would you like to eat with us in the house, or alone, outside?"

The pair of intelligent blue eyes seemed to sparkle, even if the swaggie's features remained inscrutable. The man facing her had to know that, in theory, helpers ate separately from the bosses, and she discerned that the question visibly surprised him.

"The dining hall for seasonal workers hasn't been cleaned since the last shearing season," she said, to justify herself.

"I cleaned up a bit to put my belongings in it, ma'am. I can eat there if you give me a broom to sweep up...if it's not too much bother, of course."

"Come find me when you're done. I'll give you what you need."

Without another word, Margaret turned around abruptly and

went back to the house. This swagman was *definitely* unlike any other. Swaggies generally weren't big on cleanliness. She glanced at the clothesline where a shirt, faded from bad weather, but clean, was hanging. Keeping him on for a few days to do the odd jobs that Aaron never got 'round to might be a good idea…if Jason McKellig agreed, of course. These swagmen were anything but reliable. The shearers at least stayed for shearing season, but swaggies came mostly off season, and as soon as the open spaces called them, nothing could hold them back.

Through the kitchen window, Maggie watched the man put the horses in the corral. From the very first glance, she had noticed his youth and fine features. The square and determined chin was that of a grown man; however, the pitch of his voice and his smooth, beardless skin reminded her of a teenager. The swagman walked toward the house with the ease of someone who was used to covering well over twenty miles a day. In a certain way, Maggie admired these free spirits, who could come and go as they liked, even if she didn't envy the uncertainty of their every morrow.

After a light knock at the door, Jason immediately removed his hat and came into the kitchen.

"Ma'am."

"There's a cup of tea ready, Mr. McKellig. Help yourself," Maggie said, pointing to the tea kettle resting on the wood stove. "Treat yourself to a few biscuits while I finish up the meal. Once you're done, you'll find the broom in the cupboard. You'll also find rags and a pail to wash the floor if you feel up to it."

Without hesitation, Jason poured the dark tea into a cup set on the table. He added two sugars, then took a sweet biscuit from a large porcelain china jar that Maggie kept filled. He chewed his biscuit slowly, looking around. Maggie knew that most people around here didn't usually treat swaggies any better than aborigines, but she felt sorry for them in general. And this one seemed somehow special. She opened the oven door to check if the bread was done, the contents of the pot simmering on the stove.

"Is the boss here, ma'am?" Jason asked.

"He's resting," she said, embarrassed. "You can ask me if you have any questions."

"Not really a question," he replied, taking another biscuit. "I just wanted to know if you'd like me to feed the horses after I've eaten tea, or if the boss is going to take care of it."

"I'll take care of it. You have enough to do trying to make the dormitory fit to live in."

Maggie hadn't dared explain to the man, Jason, that her husband was sleeping off his drinking binge and probably wouldn't emerge until morning: a state of affairs that had only gotten worse over time. The moment Aaron went into town, he came back drunk…if he came back at all. Maggie had helplessly watched the situation deteriorate since the doctor had confirmed that she would never be with child.

When the doctor had given them that news, the anger in Aaron's eyes had shaken her to the bone. She'd been afraid of him for the first time. They had both imagined their home filled with children who would help their father with the property as they grew older. As for Maggie, although no longer afraid of Aaron, she'd become increasingly withdrawn. And Aaron had started drinking. Could she really be upset with him since, according to the doctor, it was her fault? Jason's gentle voice interrupted her private thoughts.

"With your permission, ma'am, I'll go now to clean a part of the dormitory."

Maggie watched the man rock from one foot to the other. She nodded and then sighed as he left the kitchen with a broom in his hand. Was having to ask a woman's permission that difficult for him? If that was the case, he wouldn't stay for long at Willowra once he realised that Aaron had lost interest in everything—except the bottle.

Thankfully she'd been able to convince him to hire dependable farmhands that year to mind the sheep. But what would happen next year? And who will manage the shear and negotiate the price of wool? Would the men obey her? Chasing these depressing thoughts away, she lifted the lid to the cast-iron pot and stirred the stew.

❖

Maggie rang the cowbell twice and heaped a mess tin with beef stew as she waited for the swaggie to arrive from the house. Through the window she saw Jason wipe the sweat from his face and run his fingers through his short hair before he knocked on the door. As she handed him the tin, she noticed his gleaming eyes, twitching nose, and rapid gulps. The poor thing was practically starved, she thought.

"Ma'am," she said, as Maggie cut a piece of pound cake. She gave him a generous slice of it, as well a large hunk of the hot bread she'd just pulled from the oven.

"I put tea, sugar, and bread in a bag. You'll find a kettle and dishes in the cupboards, as well as candles. Breakfast is at five thirty. My husband will give you the list of chores then."

Realising that was all, Jason took the mess-tin of stew and the small canvas bag sitting next to it. "Good night, then, ma'am. I'll see you in the morning."

"Good night, Mr. McKellig."

Arriving in the canteen, Jason immediately put the mess-tin and bag on the table before grabbing the cutlery she had washed and prepared earlier. The beef stew was delicious, tender, and the potatoes were cooked just right. After wolfing down several big spoonfuls to tame her hunger, she took time to remove the items stored in the bag. The freshly baked, hot bread crunched when she broke off a piece. The cake was a sort of pound cake that she would save for later with her cup of tea. She would have to search for the kettle, but she couldn't resist finishing the wonderful stew first. After a last piece of bread to soak up the sauce at the bottom of the tin dish, Jason leaned back in her chair, sighing contentedly. She could easily get used to meals like this every day, living on a sheep station with a woman by her side; a woman who would love her despite her difference.

Jason abruptly stood up, knocking the chair over. No point in dreaming about something that could never be. Hadn't the old man she had wandered with said that a swaggie couldn't allow himself to have dreams, that broken dreams broke the men who dreamt them? The old man was right. That was why, over the past seven years, Jason had never stayed more than a few weeks in one place. Too many broken dreams, too many romantic disappointments, too many betrayals had thrown her into the swagman's harsh life. But she had no regrets.

She opened the cupboards, searching for the tea kettle. It would take too long for the water to boil if she waited for the small wood-burning stove she'd just lit to be hot enough, so she took a pair of tongs and removed the top from the burner to put the kettle directly on the flame. Tomorrow, she would start the fire before dinner; she hadn't had enough time this evening.

Her third cup of dark tea in hand, Jason lit a candle. She went over to the beds with their rolled mattresses to choose one. After kicking a couple of bedposts to test for sturdiness, she chose the bed farthest from the still-open door, as it appeared to be the most solid. Carefully grabbing hold of the mattress, she took it outside to shake it and check in passing that no insects or animals had nested in there. Tomorrow she'd shake out and check all the others. For this evening, after that good hearty meal, she started to feel tired.

She put the mattress on the bed, undid her swag, setting it up on top of the mattress, then after having closed the door and snuffed out the candle, she went to bed and fell immediately asleep.

Later that night, after Maggie had washed up after tea and completed the chores she'd neglected that day because of their all-day trip in the wagon to buy supplies, she readied herself for bed. When she entered their bedroom, Aaron, who had fallen asleep sprawled diagonally across the bed, was snoring so loudly she decided to once again sleep in her parents' bedroom. It was strange that, after all these years, neither Aaron nor she had thought about taking that room, which was the most spacious of the three bedrooms. As a young couple they had come to live with her parents and had taken over her childhood bedroom. They hadn't moved out of it since, even when her mother passed away six months after her father.

Maggie sighed when she thought of her parents, who would be devastated to see their beloved sheep station falling apart. It was a good property. Not the richest in the county, but with enough revenue to never be wanting for anything. Her parents had even put running water in the house in the months before their passing. That had caused a lot of talk in town, where few people could afford such a luxury. They'd had to install a new windmill, but her father, despite the cost and Aaron's objections, didn't budge. Maggie was happy for it now. It had made her life simpler and, in particular, given her the extra time she needed to take care of the chores that Aaron neglected.

She hoped that Jason McKellig would be just as good a worker as he had showed himself to be that very day, and especially that his pride was somewhere else than in his pants. He would have to be willing to take orders from her if she wanted anything to get done. She could easily lose a day's work waiting for Aaron to rise to the task.

As she slipped her nightgown over her slender shoulders, Maggie couldn't help but think about this strange man. *Handsome, polite, industrious...but probably just as much as a boozer as Aaron. Only time will tell.*

CHAPTER FOURTEEN

"Ma'am."

"Mr. McKellig, come in and help yourself to some tea while I get a plate ready for you," Maggie said. "My husband will be here soon. Eggs and bacon?"

"Perfect, ma'am." Jason poured himself a large cup of tea and smiled broadly. Maggie filled his plate with two fried eggs, three strips of bacon, and a hunk of bread that she had baked this morning.

The poor man beamed as he began to eat. When was the last time he had eaten home-cooked food? It was a pleasure to prepare meals for someone who obviously enjoyed them so much.

The newcomer was already sipping his second cup of tea when Aaron walked into the kitchen.

"Mornin', boss," Jason said, sounding as if he'd had a good night's sleep and was ready to do whatever chores were necessary around the place.

"Mornin', Jason, Maggie." Aaron planted a light kiss on her cheek. "You should have woken me earlier."

She stiffened. "Eggs and bacon this morning. I've got a bag ready with lunch."

The atmosphere at breakfast was as chilly as usual. Maggie wondered if the swaggie noticed it, as well as Aaron's surprise at her comment about his lunch bag.

"I thought I'd go back into town to negotiate the price of the ram with O'Connor," Aaron said. "He didn't strike a deal yesterday. Jason can take care of the farm work today. I'll show him the property tomorrow. In any case, I have to check all the paddocks."

Both Maggie and, obviously, Jason, who prudently kept her mouth shut, noticed the aggression in Aaron's voice. As Maggie sat there sipping her tea and looking from Aaron to Jason, she again wondered if Jason noticed anything amiss. Aaron's aggressive tone was so obvious, a person would have to be very calloused not to detect it.

Maggie spoke up. "If the paddocks aren't ready for shearing, Aaron, the sheep can't be herded, and the whole year's work will come to nothing. There's only two months left before shearing season. Negotiating with O'Connor isn't a priority."

She figured Jason would be surprised that she dared stand up to her husband in front of a swaggie. It was unusual for a wife to contradict her husband in the presence of a witness, even when she didn't agree. But Maggie had to take a stand if she wanted the sheep station to survive Aaron's negligence. As usual, Aaron didn't react overtly, mainly because he didn't exactly have a clear conscience.

"All right. We'll go inspect the damn paddocks today! Jason, go get the wagon ready. You'll find all the material we need in the shed."

Jason immediately pushed his chair back, stood up, and took his leave. Then he left the kitchen and disappeared into the morning's first light.

"You had to contradict me in front of the farmhand!" Aaron growled. "How do you expect me to get him to work if he doesn't respect me?"

Maggie shrugged. Her frustration had been growing for weeks now, and today was the last straw. "If you thought less about going drinking at the hotel pub and more about working on the property, I wouldn't have contradicted you. You've been neglecting your work for weeks now just to go get drunk. Coming home at all hours…when you do decide to come home! What's the matter with you, Aaron? The sheep station meant everything to us."

"The sheep station meant everything to *you*!" Aaron spat out. "My work here was for the future. I'd been building something we'd pass on to our children, but that was before we…"

The sadness in Aaron's voice stopped Maggie from spewing out the acrid comment on the tip of her tongue. Overwhelmed with guilt, before she could find the words to calm their pain, Aaron had already stormed out of the house, slamming the door behind him. What could she do to restore the harmony they once had? They'd fought in the past, but they'd always been able to reconcile during the following hour or day. Since the doctor's pronouncement, a wedge had been driven between them, creating a rift that grew bigger each day. What had happened to the man she married? The one who was reasonable about his drinking, who went to the pub only on Sundays after church when Maggie went to visit her friends?

❖

Jason kept quiet while Aaron drove the horses down the neglected path. Stones needed to be found to fill the dried-out holes in the road. Since they had left the homestead with the wagon loaded with material, they hadn't exchanged a single word. Seeing that Aaron was heading North, Jason decided to speak up.

"There's a gaping hole in the paddock west from here, boss. I walked right by it on my way here."

Aaron left the path and headed in the direction indicated by Jason without taking his eyes off the horse team.

"A dead eucalyptus fell on the fence and tore the barbed wire." Aaron whistled between his teeth. That wasn't going to be easy to repair. It probably meant spending the day, and they would need saws and axes. "Dang! We don't have the right tools to get rid of that tree."

"I put an axe and saw in the wagon, boss, figuring we were going to check the paddocks and that you'd wanna fix it."

Aaron turned his head to stare at his temporary hired hand. "You could have mentioned it earlier," he grumbled.

"I was going to tell you at breakfast." Jason didn't need to add anything else.

Aaron spat. "Women! Always putting their noses where they shouldn't! You got a woman somewhere, Jason?"

"No, boss. Never managed to keep one…not enough money, too much time on the road." Jason didn't like to lie, but how could she explain to a man that she hadn't touched a woman in seven years, not since Elizabeth…Elizabeth and her betrayal. Aaron would never be able to understand her abstinence and would suspect something was amiss. Trouble was the last thing Jason was looking for.

"Talkin' 'bout money, did the missus tell you how much I pay?"

"No, boss."

"Room and board, plus four shillings every Saturday evening," Aaron replied, relieved that at least Margaret hadn't overstepped her bounds in that area. "You can come to church with us on Sundays, and afterward I'll take you to the pub, or rather the bar, which is in Norseman's only hotel."

Jason held back a smirk. "I won't say no to a visit to the pub, boss, but if I can be frank, the less church for me the better."

"Couldn't agree with you more, son, but don't ever say that to the missus. If you want to stay in her good graces, you can't get out of goin' to church."

Jason groaned inside. She believed in God, but go to church? It had been at least five years since she'd set foot inside one, and the last time was only because the boss's wife was the worst kind of holier-than-thou person who forced all the workers and staff to go. A cheapskate of a woman, without an ounce of charity in her entire being. Jason hadn't stayed long working for them.

Three hours later, when Aaron decided it was time to stop for lunch, the tree that had destroyed part of the fence had been cut and removed, and the stakes had been replanted. It would be easy to install the new barbed wire now. Jason took off her leather gloves before sitting down on one of the thick branches from the eucalyptus tree that had been cut down, while Aaron took the bread and cooked mutton from the bag. A kettle was already on the fire.

Ignoring the hot summer sun, Aaron and Jason ate in silence, sipping their boiling hot tea. Aaron turned to look at the swagman who, this morning, had worked like a dog. This swaggie sure knew how to handle an ax. "You lookin' for work for a few months or just a few days?" Aaron asked, handing a wad of tobacco to Jason once they were done with their meal.

Jason shook her head at the offer. After having started to chew tobacco like the other swaggies, she'd stopped once she'd realised it was yellowing her teeth. She had always been proud of her straight, white teeth, and the women liked them as well.

"I could do with a few months' work. I wouldn't mind settling down for a while."

"I have work until at least after the shearing, if you're not lazy. The only thing is that, if I'm not around, you'll have to take orders from the missus."

Jason nodded yes. Most of the swaggies she knew would never have done that, but women were generally better organised than men and, furthermore, better workers. Most women took care of the house, the cooking, the children, and on top of all that handled many of the chores on the farm.

"So, we have a deal? How about a little pick-me-up then?" Aaron handed Jason the flask he'd just taken out of his pocket. Although she took only a small sip, the amber-coloured liquid burnt Jason's throat, almost choking her. "That's one stiff drink," she murmured with a hoarse voice.

Aaron laughed heartily before taking a few good swigs himself. "Homemade. I'll show you. Let's finish up. I wanna make sure this part of the fence doesn't have any more holes so the sheep can't get out once we put them there."

When Maggie heard the wagon, she wiped her hands on her apron before stepping out to greet the men. She was happy that Aaron had spent the entire day working. That hadn't happened for at least three months. Was Jason McKellig's arrival a good omen? Having a farmhand at the house might be just the thing that could push Aaron to reinvest himself in the land. As soon as the wagon stopped in front of the house, Aaron jumped out. The dogs made a great fuss over his arrival, while Jason took the reins to head for the barn.

"Productive day?" Maggie asked, from the porch.

"Two large holes in the Dead Tree paddock. Took us the whole day to mend."

Maggie opened her eyes wide in surprise. Two big holes?

"How did that happen? Thieves?"

Aaron shook his head, avoiding her eyes when he replied. "Nope. Fallen tree. And the water tore out the stakes at Dingo Creek."

Maggie bit her lips to keep from speaking. She knew the cause of the two holes as well as Aaron did—the big storm two months earlier. He should have checked the property back then.

Anger swelled in her chest. He could neglect her if he wanted to, since she was infertile, but she wouldn't allow him to neglect the sheep station. She swallowed the caustic comment in her throat because of Jason, who had just returned from the barn. Obviously seeing the anger flash in Maggie's eyes, Jason started swaying from one foot to the other.

"Should I feed the horses, boss?"

"No. Just unhitch them and put them in the corral. I'll take care of it later. You put in a good day's work, Jason. Go get yourself a cup of tea in the kitchen with a few biscuits while waiting on dinner."

"Okay, boss. Ma'am…"

Jason quickly left, not wanting to be included on the receiving end of Margaret's anger. However, as she served herself a cup of tea, she couldn't help but overhear Aaron and Margaret's stormy discussion. The open window and walls partially made of wood did nothing to mask their conversation. "You mean to say that you haven't been to check the paddocks in over two months? After the storm we had? Aaron…"

"Stop it, Maggie. I had other things I needed to tend to."

"What, exactly? Drinks at the pub?"

Jason now understood Margaret's anger. She had a legitimate reason for being upset. She also knew that a man didn't like it when a woman called him on his faults. Especially since Aaron had to be aware that Jason could hear their conversation. More accustomed to big, open spaces, Jason suddenly felt trapped in this kitchen, even though it was of respectable size. Ignoring the consequences, she left the kitchen, walking right past Margaret and Aaron to head for the dormitory. After all, she hadn't finished cleaning, and she intended to live in a clean space if she meant to stay the next few weeks. Margaret and Aaron's problems were none of her concern. Work, something to eat, and a little money were enough to make her happy.

Later, when Maggie walked into the workers' quarters with Jason's dinner in hand, she was astonished to see him at the table reading. Decidedly this man was full of surprises. She didn't have the time to recover herself before realizing that his blue eyes were set on her. Jason's smile went straight to her heart.

"Tea," she said as she placed the mess-tin and the canvas bag on the table. "Irish stew. My grandmother's speciality."

Jason's eyebrows popped up.

"My grandfather's family always considered that he had married beneath his station. An Irish girl, how horrid. They came to Australia with their children to escape such prejudice. Contrary to popular belief in England, not every Australian is a convict. Only my father's parents," Maggie added with sparkling eyes. She stood there waiting for Jason to confide in her in return.

Jason was struck by Margaret's beauty when she smiled so unreservedly. It took her a while to understand that she was waiting for her to tell something about herself. Finally, Jason took the hint and said, "Oh, um…I was born in Inverness, but I lived in London for two years before coming to Australia."

"You're an Englishman?" A bit of sarcastic surprise came through Maggie's voice.

"No, ma'am," Jason said. "A Scotsman…and now an Australian."

Maggie wanted to laugh at the indignation in Jason's voice.

However, things had been so bad that evening with Aaron, she didn't feel like poking fun. Plus, joking around with a farmhand wasn't correct behaviour. What was she thinking? Aaron would be annoyed with her.

"My apologies, Mr. McKellig. You speak like a native."

"No harm done, ma'am."

"I'll leave you to your tea then. Good evening, Mr. McKellig."

"Ma'am."

Watching her leave, Jason turned red when thinking of the way she had reacted to Margaret's teasing. Did she realise how breathtaking she looked when her smile brightened her perfectly oval-shaped face? And the flash of humour in her golden eyes? *She's the boss's wife—you don't have the right to think of her that way, Jason. And at any rate, if she knew you were a woman, she would undoubtedly throw you out.*

The next morning, even though Jason felt nervous about finding herself alone with Margaret in the kitchen, she didn't let anything show. Margaret, like the day before, greeted her with a smile while serving breakfast. "Steak and buckwheat pancakes. I hope it's to your liking, Mr. McKellig."

Jason nodded promptly before sitting down and cutting a piece of steak that she immediately stuffed in her mouth. She moaned with pleasure; again, the steak was so tender.

"It's the best breakfast I've had in months. I've eaten better in the last two days than the last year put together."

"Thank you, Mr. McKellig. I appreciate heartfelt, or should I say *belly*-felt, compliments."

A flash of mockery in Maggie's eyes made Jason immediately blush before stuffing another piece of meat into her mouth to hide her reaction. "Do you know if the boss wants to continue with the paddocks today?"

Maggie's good mood vanished, and she clenched her teeth to keep down the bile that was burning her stomach. "Aaron went into town, but you can fix the roofs."

"The fences are more important. With your permission, ma'am, I'll take the wagon and continue checking them and repair them where needed."

Maggie had never expected to hear such a suggestion. She'd hoped that Jason wouldn't be too reluctant to take orders from her but had never imagined he would go so far as to volunteer to accomplish a task that was already difficult for two. She slowly nodded.

She was a bit perplexed as she watched Jason finish his plate, but little by little, an idea started coming together.

Jason said, "I didn't unload the wagon yesterday, so I'm going to leave as soon as I hitch up the horses, unless you need help in the stables or—"

"In truth, I was just thinking that if you could help me feed the animals, I could come with you to help fix the fence." Maggie took off her apron.

Jason opened and closed her mouth several times without uttering a sound.

"Close your mouth, Mr. McKellig, and come help me."

"Ma'am..." was the only word that came out of Jason's mouth as she stood up to follow Margaret.

Women in the outback often rolled up their sleeves, even for the most difficult tasks, but never would Jason have imagined Margaret to be one of those women. Too slender for heavy work, a small voice murmured in her head. Understanding how deceiving someone's physical appearance could be, she tried in vain to hide her smile. When Margaret turned around and gave her a strange look, Jason realised that her demeanour might appear strange. She tried to squelch the flash of humour that threatened to shine in her eyes before she found her voice again.

"Appearances can be deceiving, ma'am. I can't imagine you fixing a fence."

With an exasperated wince, Maggie put her hands on her hips. "Who do you think helped my father before I was married, Mr. McKellig? My older brother died of an infection when he was thirteen, and my younger brother hadn't yet learned to walk. My mother never regained her strength after her last pregnancy, yet the work had to get done. Now, go feed the cattle while I take care of the fowl. I want us to set out as soon as possible."

❖

When Maggie called Jason for their lunch break, she didn't have to be asked twice, letting the roll of barbed wire she held in her arms fall to her feet. All morning long she couldn't help but admire Margaret's determination and dexterity with tools. Jason had blushed a few times when Margaret had caught her admiring glances.

Now Jason wordlessly squatted down to face Margaret sitting on a log on the other side of the fire. She poured a cup of tea and started sipping it, keeping to herself. When she gazed again at Margaret, their eyes met. Jason looked away.

"Does it embarrass you to work with a woman, Mr. McKellig?"

Jason looked up yet again, surprised. She could read the provocation in Margaret's eyes. "Not at all, ma'am."

"Then why do you keep glancing at me from the corner of your eye? I like frank and candid men, Mr. McKellig. Those who say what's on their mind."

While chewing her bread, Jason tried to think of an appropriate answer. She sighed. "I was just admiring your dexterity."

The compliment made Margaret blush this time.

"And...I don't know how your husband will react to the fact that we worked together on the fence. Some men are..."

"Jealous?"

Margaret gave a big, beaming smile, and Jason blushed now.

"Possessive."

"I see. Please be reassured. Aaron has never been possessive, and he's even less so now."

Jason nodded. She understood the bitter words hidden behind this answer. Why did men start drinking and neglecting their wives? Especially such an attractive lady as Margaret, who had enough courage for both of them. If she were in Aaron's place, she would cherish this woman. Men were so stupid.

CHAPTER FIFTEEN

After the minister pronounced the closing prayer, Jason couldn't quite hold back a discreet sigh of relief. Seeing how quickly some people left the small church, she realised she wasn't the only one who hadn't particularly enjoyed the sermon, but in her case, it had little to do with today's subject, which was fidelity. In the eyes of the church, the law, and everyone, she was guilty: guilty of dressing like a man, guilty of being attracted to her own sex. Yet wasn't she also a child of God?

Forcing herself to stay in Margaret and Aaron's wake, Jason followed them out of the church and faced the late-morning's burning-hot sun. Just a few yards ahead of her was the main street, with its rows of small buildings and warehouses on either side. She didn't find it surprising that some of the structures were permanent, while the majority were temporary wooden ones. The rich needed a showcase for their money in this town lost deep in the Australian bush.

"Well, Maggie, I'll leave you with your friends. I'll do the rounds with Jason, introduce him to everyone. If he's staying for a few months, he needs to know who's who."

Margaret's face immediately tensed. She apparently knew where Aaron was going to introduce Jason, which meant she might end up having to take two drunkards home instead of one. Probably only the presence of other people stopped her from spitting out the unpleasant remark on the tip of her tongue. *Men.*

"You know where to find me when you're ready to leave," she said.

Aaron nodded at her, then quickly went on his way. Jason made sure to salute Margaret with a tip of her hat and a slight apologetic smile before hurrying to follow Aaron. If she turned around to look at Margaret, she would see her standing there as straight as could be, observing them with a disapproving expression. Deep down, Jason felt sorry for her. In reality—and she would never have revealed this to anyone—working with Margaret was much more rewarding than working with Aaron. She loved hearing Margaret tell her about the books she'd read, and Margaret seemed to very much enjoy hearing about Jason's adventures in the bush. Did Aaron have any idea what a treasure he'd married?

"G'day, Ben," Aaron said as they entered the hotel bar.

"Aaron. So whaddya think of Reverend Andrew's sermon today?"

As Jason watched, the two men exchanged a knowing smirk. Visibly not everyone agreed with the reverend's sermons.

"What can I say that I've not already said? Instead, let me introduce you to my new station hand, Jason McKellig. Jason, this is Ben Smith, the owner of the only hotel and bar in Norseman. You won't find a better beer for at least two hundred miles around."

Ben, a smile on his lips, nodded at Jason. "A swaggie, eh? Come from far?"

"I've covered some ground in my day."

"Whaddya have?"

Jason licked his lips. "A beer is vital after a sermon."

Ben guffawed. "Seems he's one of ours, Aaron. You did right to bring him here. You'll have the usual?"

"I knew you'd get on fine with Jason, Ben. He's a good worker with a sense of humour."

As Ben placed two beers and a shot of whiskey on the counter, a deep voice called out to him. "Ben, two beers over here. Aaron, join us."

Without waiting for an answer, the two men who had just entered sat down at a table. Aaron grabbed his beer and whiskey and went over to sit with them, followed by Jason. As everyone was settling in around the table, Aaron introduced them to his new worker. After a few polite questions, the conversation turned to the price of wool and politics.

Jason listened to the discussion without taking part in it. She didn't feel comfortable in this dim, confining bar now that she was accustomed to wide, open spaces, but what made her feel even more uncomfortable was Tom O'Connor, Aaron's so-called friend, who kept ordering beer after beer for him. He would have done the same for Jason, but she made sure to drink hers very measuredly. Aaron was right; the beer here was good, but vicious because it was strong.

A question came to mind each time someone ordered another beer for Aaron. Why did Tom O'Connor and Edward Carrington make him drink? Even if the latter had the habit of drowning his worries in alcohol, it didn't seem that, left to his own devices, he would have consumed so much.

❖

The tea hadn't yet been served when Mary made a comment about Reverend Andrew's sermon. "Who do you think his sermon was meant for? Jonah, Ted?"

"I have no idea. Perhaps it wasn't for anybody in particular…"

"Really, Ann? As if you didn't know that Pastor Andrew draws inspiration for his sermons from people who come to the parish seeking guidance."

"Even if it wasn't for anybody in particular, the subject of the sermon must have struck close to home for quite a few."

"What are you getting at, Nelly?" Ann asked.

"That men, by nature, are unfaithful."

"You're too cynical. Your mind's playing tricks on you."

"By the way, Maggie. Who was the adorable-looking young fellow sitting next to you? I've never seen him in town. Are you hiding something from us?"

Without really knowing why, Maggie blushed slightly. "Jason McKellig. A swagman who arrived last Sunday. He was there when we came back from town, and you'll never believe it. Not only had he cut all the wood, but after showering himself, he folded my laundry."

"Incredible."

"Well, knock me over with a feather," one of the women exclaimed.

"In any case, I wouldn't mind having him over for a cup of tea. Not one bit. He's as cute as a button. If you can't find enough work for him, send him to me."

"Mary!"

"To repair my shed," Mary quickly added, a naughty grin on her face.

"Hmm. Maybe Pastor Andrew's sermon wasn't meant just for men."

"Oh, Nelly. What harm can just looking do? In any case, judging by the way Charlotte and her girlfriends were eyeing him, he won't be alone for long if he spends any time in this town."

"Don't forget he's just a swaggie. I don't believe Edward Carrington would appreciate his daughter associating with a vagrant."

A wave of anger overcame Maggie on hearing Ann's words. But just as she was about to open her mouth to defend Jason, her instinct stopped her. What would her friends think if she praised him? In one short week this man had been able to earn her respect and friendship. And she had to ask herself why she suddenly felt so sad at the prospect of Jason having a young girl on his arm.

"Because you think your Rebecca did ignore him?" Nelly added, teasingly.

"My daughter? I haven't noticed a thing."

"Maybe you were too busy ogling him yourself, Mary," Ann quipped.

Mary's indignant look upon hearing the comment made the other three of them break out laughing. She couldn't stay mad for long, however, and finally burst out in laughter herself.

"Found out. If our men had the slightest inkling of what we spoke about on Sundays, they wouldn't let us get together. But it feels so good to talk about something other than wheat sacks, canned goods, or the price of lard."

"Consider yourself lucky. Try being married to a stationmaster. The only subject is trains."

"Oh, and you think it's better, Ann, to be married to a man of the law and have to cook for the drunkards your husband picks up on a…?"

Nelly interrupted herself. Turning red, she felt ashamed. None of them had forgotten that her husband had picked up Aaron several times these last months for disturbing the public peace when he was plastered.

Tears formed in Maggie's eyes, but she held them back. She, whose parents had practically founded this town, who was so well-respected, had been repeatedly humiliated by her disillusioned husband.

"Would anyone like another cup of tea? A scone, Ann?"

"With pleasure," Nelly answered in a gentle voice.

"Maggie?"

"A bit of tea for me too, Mary…and well, yes, why not a scone?"

An hour later, the four of them were still chatting when the living-room door opened. Rebecca came in, her eyes gleaming. "Mother. A man's here for Margaret."

Rebecca stood to the side to let the new arrival come in. Hat in hand, Jason greeted the women. "Ladies, ma'am…"

Maggie saw the hesitation in Jason's eyes. She glanced at him with a questioning look.

"I've just come to tell you, ma'am, that we can go back to Willowra whenever you like. We're waiting for you in the wagon. I've parked it on the side."

Jason gestured in the direction of the wagon, and Maggie immediately understood. Aaron must have been drunk, and Jason didn't want to embarrass her in front of her friends. She was greatly touched that this man was showing his concern for her reputation. Once again she asked herself who Jason McKellig could really be.

"Won't you have a cup of tea and a scone before leaving, Mr. McKellig," Mary offered. For once her daughter hadn't run out of the room, but Maggie suspected Mary had invited Jason to satisfy her own curiosity.

Jason, after a brief hesitation, sat down in the chair pointed out to him. Rebecca, forgetting all her manners, pulled up another chair and inspected Jason.

Maggie watched Mary and Nelly chat with him. He slowly drank his tea served in a porcelain cup, taking small bites of his jelly-covered scone. What a strange swaggie. He seemed as much at ease at a tea party as when repairing a fence. Obviously this man had a certain education. What could have put him out on the road? Alcohol? He didn't seem like a drunkard. Gambling? He would have been at the pub playing cards if that had been the case. Love? Maggie's heart pinched. Oh, yes. A broken heart. That seemed so much like him, and at the same time a man as handsome as he could easily find consolation.

Despite being lost in her thoughts, Maggie couldn't help notice what Rebecca was up to. She was pretty and young. Her parents had money, thanks to their general store. She was a good catch for whomever would be interested in her. A pang of jealousy struck Maggie's heart. She didn't want Jason to become interested in Rebecca. Without warning, she surprised herself and probably everyone by standing up suddenly. "I think it's time for us to go, Mr. McKellig."

Although Jason and the others noticed Maggie's sharp tone of voice, no one said anything, apart from Rebecca who, clearly disappointed that the object of her attention was about to be taken away from her, blurted that Jason hadn't yet finished his tea.

Jason stood up. "Thanks again for the tea, Mrs. Johnson. The scones were delicious. Ladies. Miss."

As Maggie prepared to leave, saying good-bye to her friends, Jason hurried to the door to open it for her. It had barely closed behind them, when Mary fell heavily back into her armchair. She sighed before adding, conscious that her daughter was still present, "What a charming man this Mr. McKellig is."

"He's got all the right manners," Ann confirmed.

"And he's so cute," Rebecca added dreamily. "Oh, Mother. We have to invite him to dinner. Don't you agree?"

Mary sighed without answering. Just what she needed, her daughter in love with a swaggie. Even if he was handsome and polite, marrying a swagman wasn't what she and her husband had in mind for her.

As they approached the wagon, Maggie glanced at the shape slumped in the back. She shook her head while motioning toward the reins. Jason climbed up on the bench in front of the wagon and sat down. Maggie took Jason's extended hand and sat down next to him.

Riding in silence, Maggie could hear Aaron's loud snoring despite the noise of the horses' shoes clip-clopping on the hard ground and the squeaking wheels. Lips pinched, she stared straight ahead.

Even Jason, who hadn't known her very long, apparently recognised the anger she was holding back. "Thank you, Mr. McKellig."

Jason turned to her with a questioning expression.

Maggie pointed to Aaron. "For not saying in front of my friends that my husband was sloshed, even if they must have guessed it. Thank you also for having taken care of Aaron. You've been with us for only a week, and I already don't know how I will manage without you."

Margaret's voice broke after having so clearly expressed her powerlessness. She tried to make out what Jason was thinking, but he just nodded before turning to watch the road.

Secretly, Jason was thankful the horses didn't need her to guide the wagon. Margaret's thanks and admission had touched her deeply, but a swagman couldn't go soft or tenderhearted. Today, Margaret had thanked her, but tomorrow, she very well might ask her to leave. Getting attached could only do her harm. All the more so because Aaron could end up becoming jealous if he realized his wife had become rather friendly with their station hand.

"Why aren't you married, Mr. McKellig? A handsome man like you must attract a lot of women's attention. I saw the reaction of all the young ladies today."

Jason, apparently lost in his thoughts, seemed startled by Margaret's frank question. His eyes big and round, his cheeks red, she turned to Margaret, but no sound came out of his mouth.

"Was I too frank?" Maggie gently asked, surprised at her own curiosity about this silent man.

"Yes...no...it's just that I'm not accustomed..."

Jason turned scarlet. Margaret, seeing his embarrassment, let out a small laugh to hide her own. How could she tell this man she hardly knew that he was even more charming when he blushed? Silence set in, only disturbed by the noise of the travelling wagon. Even Aaron had stopped snoring.

"Should I conclude that you are not going to answer my questions?" Margaret insisted.

"I...I wanted to get married, a long time ago...but she wouldn't have me," Jason murmured under his breath, the pain still alive in his voice.

"She was a stupid young woman then. How long ago?"

Jason hesitated. "About seven years. I was young and stupid. I hid some things from her, and I hadn't been able to predict that she wouldn't know how to face certain truths. I thought she loved me, but in the end, the opinion of others was more important to her. You can reassure your friends that I have no interest in their daughters. I prefer the company of women my age. Their conversations are more enlightening."

Just when Margaret was about to ask more questions, Jason quickly added, "Your husband's friends are peculiar."

The abrupt change of subject made Maggie immediately understand that Jason wouldn't say anything else about his past. "What do you mean by that?"

"They push him to drink, and I don't understand to what end. I observed them. As soon as the boss's glass was empty, they ordered another one. They tried to do the same with me, but I know how to pace myself. They couldn't reasonably offer me another beer when I hadn't finished the one I was drinking...very slowly."

"You mean to say that Tom O'Connor encourages Aaron to drink?"

"Him and Edward Carrington."

Maggie tried to hide the rage that surged through her. "I never trusted them. But I don't understand why they would do such a thing. Aaron's been meeting them every Sunday for years. It's true that, before, he didn't come back rotten drunk."

Maggie reflected for several minutes. The question "why" turned in her head constantly. She had to know. She had never recoiled when faced with an obstacle, and she refused to start at thirty-seven years old. An idea came to her. What she was thinking could work, but she couldn't pull it off alone.

"Do you think you could help me, Mr. McKellig?"

"Ma'am?"

"It would be a great favour to me if you could accompany Aaron every Sunday. And you could do me even a bigger favour if you kept your eyes and ears wide open."

"You want to know what's brewing?" Jason smirked, feeling mischievous.

"I'll pay you, of course."

"Not to worry, ma'am. It will be a pleasure for me to help. And also, you should never betray a friend. That's a swaggie law."

A small smile brightened Margaret's face, the first since they had left town. Jason's heart almost stopped beating. This woman was so beautiful.

"You're a good person, Mr. McKellig. I hope you will stay with us for as long as possible."

After that compliment, Jason had trouble finding her voice. "Thank you, ma'am. With a boss who cooks so well, I'm in no hurry to go anywhere. And soon I'll be so fat I won't be able to walk."

Margaret chuckled, which filled Jason's heart with joy. For once, the three hours between Norseman and Willowra went by quite pleasantly.

CHAPTER SIXTEEN

Jason checked herself one more time in the small mirror fragment to make sure she was presentable. With the wages she had earned in the last three weeks, she had been able to buy a shirt and a pair of pants. Although the fabric was just canvas, the clothes were new, and she felt proud to go to church this Sunday with Maggie and Aaron without looking like a pauper. She had gotten up early to wash all her work clothes and get ready. She stuck her comb in a bowl of water one last time to smooth down her short blond hair.

Even if she refused to admit it, deep down Jason knew that all her sartorial efforts were aimed toward pleasing Maggie. In her heart, she no longer called her Margaret, but Maggie...as Aaron did. Jason sighed. This infatuation would lead her nowhere, but she couldn't help admire Maggie's courage and dignity while faced with her husband's neglect.

Increasingly, he had eyes only for the bottle. Aaron wasn't a bad bloke, but alcohol could destroy the best of men. And then there were his so-called mates. Jason had silently gnashed her teeth last Sunday when she had inadvertently overheard a conversation between O'Connor and Carrington. What truly interested them was Maggie and Aaron's property. Unfortunately, she had overheard only that one sentence. Today she hoped to find out more about their schemes.

Jason hurried out of the workers' quarters to get the wagon she had hitched before changing. It was out of the question to dirty her new clothing before Maggie could admire her. A sad inner voice reminded her that Maggie was married and that, even if she hadn't been, she wouldn't be interested in a swaggie, and a woman to top it off. Her face felt frozen.

She brought the wagon round to the front of the main house and stepped down from it. A few minutes later, Margaret and Aaron came out. While Aaron didn't even glance at her as he climbed up onto the wagon, Margaret stopped in place when she saw her. She took her time, looking her up and down. Slowly, a knowing smile brightened her face.

"Mr. McKellig! Dressed that way, you're going to make more than one damsel swoon."

Jason couldn't resist her. She smiled back at her, blushing all the way to her ears. Embarrassed, she quickly climbed into the back, letting Maggie sit down next to Aaron. Even Aaron grinned at Jason. That was a first.

"Well, well, lad. Who're you aiming to please? I noticed quite a few sheilas were running after ya, but you never seemed that interested. You're a clever little sneak. But quite right. The more you ignore them, the more they come running."

Jason didn't dare look up, afraid of meeting Maggie's eyes. She was afraid of seeing in them...she didn't know, but she was certain she wouldn't like whatever it was. How could Aaron be so insensitive to say such things in front of her? If Maggie had been her wife, she would have cherished her; she would have promised her the moon. The wagon brusquely jolted ahead, reminding Jason that she was just a seasonal worker.

❖

"Comin' to have a drink, Jason, or do you have something better to do?" Aaron smirked knowingly at her.

Jason knitted her eyebrows. How could the man be such a lout?

Aaron then burst out in laughter and headed for the hotel. "Dressed like you are, I would've thought you had a secret tryst with a sheila. The lassies couldn't keep their eyes off you in church. And don't tell me you didn't notice. Carrington won't necessarily be overjoyed that his daughter was making sheep eyes at ya. But in your shoes, I wouldn't deprive myself of a lil' flirt."

Once again, Jason grew hot all the way to her ears. She stammered in a hushed voice, "I've got no interest in these girls."

Aaron stopped and looked at Jason suspiciously. "Say. You're not one of those pervs who prefers...you know, messing about with... boys."

Jason opened her eyes wide in surprise. "No!"

The denial was so sincere Aaron seemed immediately relieved. "So then why don't you go have some fun? I'm sure several would be far from baulking, if you gave 'em the chance. As long as you don't knock 'em up"

Jason sighed. "It's a long story, boss. Sheilas and me—we never quite see eye to eye. And then, if I plan on sticking around, I don't want folks thinking I'm a petticoat-chaser."

Aaron teased her. "So you're thinking 'bout staying in these parts?"

"Could be, boss."

Aaron smiled widely as he slapped Jason good-humouredly on the back on their way to the pub. "And you swear there's no sheila behind this?"

Jason followed Aaron without answering. What could she possibly say? That she only had eyes for Maggie, Aaron's own wife? The bloke certainly wouldn't be happy with that.

Like every Sunday since Jason had come to the sheep station, she ended up driving the horses home, with Maggie sitting next to her on the bench and Aaron blind drunk in the wagon. Like every Sunday, she had gone to fetch Maggie at Mary's place, without mentioning Aaron. And like every Sunday, Mary had offered her a cup of tea and cookies, which Jason had politely eaten as Rebecca watched her with great interest.

Maggie sighed, and Jason looked at her questioningly.

"I don't know how long I can stand to watch him destroy himself this way. I feel so helpless, so much at fault."

"It's not your fault if he drinks, ma'am," Jason dared to say.

"He drinks because I'm barren."

Maggie's voice broke. She seemed to try to hold back her tears, but there was no stopping them.

Jason, feeling a pang of anguish for her, gently placed her hand on Maggie's shoulder.

"Pardon me, Mr. McKellig. It's not my way to feel sorry for myself."

Jason removed her hand. "Crying can help, ma'am, but whiskey never can do any good. You could adopt perhaps. There are so many children without parents just asking to be loved."

Jason's directness might have surprised Maggie a little, but she took advantage of Jason's attentive ear. "I would have loved to adopt, but Aaron won't hear of it. He wants blood heirs. Why are men so proud? As if adopting a child made them less virile."

She spit her words out angrily. All Maggie's accumulated frustration with Aaron over these past months came out in her tone of voice. Jason remained quiet. What could she possibly say about a man's wounded virility and pride?

"Forgive me, Mr. McKellig. I'm mad at myself, and at Aaron. The whole thing makes me feel pathetic."

"I understand, ma'am. Boss doesn't know how lucky he is to have a woman like you." The words had hardly come out before Jason already regretted them. What would Maggie think? The eternal silence before her answer was torture to Jason. Why had she said that? She had no right. She...

"Thank you, Jason," Maggie whispered under her breath.

Jason nodded while keeping her eyes straight on the road ahead. If she even glanced at Maggie just then, her eyes would betray her. It was the very first time Maggie had uttered her Christian name.

❖

When Jason came into the kitchen to pick up her evening meal, she found Maggie sitting at the table, her head in her hands. Jason hesitated. Should she turn around and leave? Standing in the doorway, she was at a loss as to what to do or say.

Feeling a presence, Maggie looked up. Jason's eyes were filled with such wonder and compassion, Maggie's heart skipped a beat. Jeez, this man was handsome. And he had so many qualities—everything to make him a good husband, father, and lover. She sighed.

The tears she had cried when she was alone were not just tears of regret over her failed marriage, but also sobs over the love she felt for this man who had just recently entered her life. Today she had realised, that for the very first time ever, she had fallen in love. Jason was constantly in her thoughts, night and day. Worse, she intuited that the feeling was mutual, which was unbearable. If Aaron hadn't been so physically and emotionally absent, he would have long ago noticed the glow of desire in Jason's eyes when he glanced at her.

"I just came to fetch my mess-tin, ma'am...I..."

"Stay, Mr. McKellig. I don't feel like eating alone tonight."

The imploring look in Maggie's eyes won over all reason and

drowned out the little voice in Jason's head that screamed this wasn't a good idea. Jason put her hat on the buffet before sitting on the nearest chair, while Maggie got up to serve tea for both of them.

As soon as Maggie put Jason's plate down in front of her, she saw a bright smile light up Jason's weather-beaten face, and her own eyebrows popped up questioningly.

"I have never eaten so well as since I arrived here, but your beef stew is really my favourite."

Maggie would have liked to tell Jason that she knew, and that was why she had fixed it for him today, to please him and see the smile of delight on his face, the perfect white teeth in his mouth, and his shining blue eyes. But admitting all that certainly wouldn't have been reasonable.

"It was my father's favourite as well, and my mother made it every Sunday. Every time we went into town, she would buy a large cut of beef to make my father happy."

"You miss your parents."

It was less a question than an assertion. Maggie nodded. "And yours?"

"No, not really. I never knew who my father was. The man who raised me was always out and about. My mother died when I was ten, so those days seem very distant to me, and my memories are vague and few."

Maggie would have liked to know everything about this man facing her, but she could tell that talking about his past made him uncomfortable, so she changed the subject. "Were you able to find out what O'Connor and Carrington are up to?"

Staring her in the eye, Jason slowly chewed a piece of meat before swallowing.

"The only thing I learned is that your land interests them. How? Why? I can't tell you. I'm sorry…" Jason sighed.

Maggie put down her fork and knife on her plate. "Our land? They want to buy it? And they think Aaron will sell it to them under the influence of spirits?"

"I really don't know. Perhaps something of the sort."

Maggie uttered a dry, mirthless chuckle. "Aaron doesn't own the land. It's mine. It's the one thing my parents insisted upon when I married Aaron. They wouldn't hear of anything else. My father's will was even more specific. He earned this land with his own blood, sweat, and tears in the Coolgardie mines. The gold allowed him to buy Willowra, and he wanted the property to belong only to his direct descendants."

Jason smiled with apparent relief. "I was afraid Aaron would do something stupid, and you would find yourself out on the street. He certainly didn't brag about that to his friends."

"No. I suppose that must have hurt his pride. Men...You have to forgive me, Mr. McKellig. I seem to forget that you're one too..."

Jason moved uneasily in his seat, and Maggie burst out laughing. She was teasing him.

"My friends are a bad influence. Spending several hours complaining about our respective husbands every Sunday has coloured my thinking."

Maggie grew serious again, too serious. "I feel very comfortable with you, Jason, probably too much so, but I don't know how to stop it. It's something I can't resist."

"You're a married woman, ma'am," replied Jason as he hurriedly leapt to his feet. "Eating together wasn't a good idea."

Maggie was still sitting when the kitchen door closed. She could hear Jason walking away toward the dormitory. "My God. Whatever possessed me to say such a thing?"

Maggie went to her parents' bedroom without cleaning the kitchen and collapsed onto the bed, relieved, letting the tears come and soak her pillow. Aaron was in a deep drunkard's sleep, like he was most nights.

CHAPTER SEVENTEEN

Before the shepherd arrived with the sheep, Aaron and Jason checked that everything was ready for gathering them on this far side of the station. The logistics and timing were very specific, like clockwork. All the sheep couldn't arrive at the same time in the paddocks, which were adjacent to the shearing shed.

"You've taken a liking to Maggie, haven't you?"

"Boss?"

"Don't think I haven't noticed the way you look at her. Worst, she seems to be interested in you too."

"Boss, I never...the missus is a handsome woman, but I would never..."

"Don't you worry, Jason. If you want her...if you want a barren woman, she's all yours!"

Aaron spat out the last words with such venom, Jason recoiled. She should have realised he would notice her interest in Maggie. In the month since their conversation in the kitchen, she had forced herself to never stay alone with her too long, and to not speak of personal things when they had to converse in the interest of Willowra station, or when Aaron had gone into town and they had no other choice but to work together. Jason was conscious, however that, despite their efforts, their attraction to one another kept growing with each passing day.

The arrival of the seasonal workers for shearing season had been a welcome distraction. Jason had been too busy to think of Maggie while working as the foreman, allocating jobs in Aaron's absence. Jason knew she should have left, that this attraction would lead to no good, but every day she found another excuse to put off her departure. She couldn't very well leave Maggie alone in the middle of shearing season. It wouldn't be decent of her. And not alone with Aaron sinking deeper and deeper into the bottle. Afterward, when everything was squared up, at the end of shearing season, she would go.

Aaron suddenly climbed up onto the wagon and gave the reins a snap. Without reacting, Jason watched him drive off in the direction of town. She never would have imagined that Aaron would abandon her there, without any water and farther than a two-hour walk back to the house. Especially since this wasn't the first time they'd travelled far out to work together. They had already checked up on most of the different sections of the station.

After taking one last glance at the cloud of dust that rose in the wake of the wagon's passing, Jason started to walk, with her long swagman's gait, back in the direction of the house. What did it matter that it was almost noon?! What did it matter that she didn't have any water? She'd been through worse.

When Jason finally reached the homestead buildings, she hurried over to the water bucket on the main house's porch and gulped down as much as she could from the ladle before pouring the rest on the nape of her neck. Then she started to drink again.

"Where's Aaron? I thought you left together."

"He decided to go to town," Jason calmly replied.

"But look at the state you're in! Where did he leave you?"

Anger shone in Maggie's dark eyes. She obviously saw the sweat running down Jason's dusty face, leaving streaks on her cheeks, the sweat-soaked shirt bottom. Maggie knew the country well enough to understand that it would take a long, sustained effort to put someone in that state.

"At the paddock that borders the Andersons' property?"

Maggie's gasp of surprise made Jason react immediately. "A little walk to get me back in shape. I've become lazy using horses all the time."

Before Maggie lost control of her anger, Jason took a few steps toward her. "Aaron was furious. He thinks something's going on between us. I'm planning to leave, Maggie. It's for the best."

"No. I need you. With Aaron constantly drunk, you can't go before the end of shearing season. You can't abandon me now."

Jason nodded at her, then turned to walk to the shearing shed. Maggie watched him walk away. He had called her by her Christian name again. She had dreamt of this moment for a long time. She would never tire of hearing him say her name. He couldn't leave. She had to make sure of it. She wouldn't let him go.

❖

Maggie mechanically kneaded the bread dough. As she firmly worked on the flour mixture, her thoughts drifted as she mulled over Jason's last words. He couldn't leave; she couldn't let him. But how could she make sure he stayed? If only Aaron was…No, she thought to herself. Don't go down that road.

Maggie wasn't even angry at Aaron anymore. She saw no point in losing her time and energy over a drunkard intent on ruining his own life and that of those around him, especially her. When she'd learned that Aaron had abandoned Jason at the paddock, she had immediately become furious…until Jason had pronounced those fateful words. Tears formed in her eyes without her even noticing; they ran down her cheeks, mixing with the dough she was kneading. She couldn't stop, didn't want to stop. If she did, her world would collapse, and the man she loved would disappear forever. She had a strange feeling of loss and pain deep inside. She held back a sob and finally, with the back of her hand, wiped away the tears running down her face.

The sound of a wagon and horses approaching didn't even attract her attention. She was lost in her world, a daydream where Jason took her in his arms and whispered sweet endearments in her ear. Only after a carriage stopped in front of the kitchen window was she called back to reality.

Maggie's eyes popped wide open when she saw Mary and the pastor, sitting next to her. She quickly wiped her hands on her apron to go outside and greet them. Although she had noticed, when she came out onto the porch, their sombre expression, seeing a wagon with a horse attached to the back and led by the police sergeant, struck her dumb. It was her wagon.

Maggie swallowed several times before turning to Mary, silently asking for an explanation. What she read on their faces caused her to stop breathing: Aaron?

"Aaron!" she screamed, hurrying over to her wagon. "Aaron!"

Although she immediately recognised her husband's worn boots, she climbed into the wagon and tore away the blanket covering the top of the body before anybody could stop her. What she saw nearly made her faint.

"Oh my God. I didn't want this. I was angry, but I didn't wish this. Not this."

She started sobbing loudly as she stared at her husband's ravaged face. Hands came to force hers to let go of the blanket and covered Aaron's body again. The same hands hugged her tightly, helping her walk back to the house.

"Mary?"

"I'm here."

"Mary, I didn't want this. Not this."

Mary sighed. How many times had Maggie complained about Aaron's behaviour these past months during their weekly tea party? She had intimated several times that if Aaron didn't come back to Willowra, it wouldn't be a great loss. Many of them had already spoken words such as these in reference to their husbands when they acted like children—only words—but now they were engulfing Margaret with guilt and pain.

Jason hurried as quickly as she could to the house after one of the teenagers who had been hired to transport fleece between the shearing shed and the press alerted her. She hadn't heard the arrival of the horse and wagons. She had too much to work out in her mind. Torn by her love for Maggie, Aaron's anger, and her own fear of being rejected, engrossed in her work along with the hangar's deafening noise, she had been entirely preoccupied. Yet, as soon as she saw the wagons and who was present, she knew a tragedy had occurred. She saw Mary take Maggie in her arms and accompany her into the house, followed by Reverend Andrew. Jason would have liked to be in Mary's place, but that would have been inappropriate.

"The next days aren't going to be easy," a voice said from behind, surprising her. It was Sergeant Wilson.

After a beat, Jason found her voice. "What happened?" She pointed to the wagon and the long mass laid down at the back.

"A heavily loaded wagon ran over him. He was drunk and crossed the street without looking. Everything happened so quickly. The witnesses said the wagon's driver couldn't have avoided him. When the doctor arrived, Aaron had already stopped breathing. Seeing how much he's been drinking these past months, an accident was bound to happen."

"Anyway, now it's too late."

Wilson nodded. He had seen many a life ruined by alcohol since he'd become a policeman. Aaron had always been one who enjoyed a drink, but these past months a drink had become a bottle, and certain people had been encouraging Aaron, taking advantage of his weakness. But to what end?

"With this heat, you should bury him quickly."

"Tomorrow." Jason nodded. "Can you spread the news and ask Reverend Andrew what time he wants to have the ceremony? I'll take care of the coffin and the grave."

"That works for me."

"So I'll tend to him then." Jason motioned with her chin toward Aaron's remains. While the sergeant went inside the house, Jason called over the cook, hired for the season, who had been watching what was going on from afar. An old but still strong man, the former shearer had a limp due to a poorly treated broken leg.

"What an ugly sight. He's all messed up. The missus boss is going to have nightmares. She—"

"Shut your mouth, Peg-leg, and help me carry him to the room at the back."

The man with the limp would have liked to insult Jason in return, but he had enough experience to know when to hold his tongue. Aaron was the boss, but Jason had hired him. He'd hired all the seasonal labourers and been giving orders from the beginning. On top of it, he'd noticed the way the missus boss looked at Jason, as well as the way Jason looked at her. The boss's death should make things a lot easier for those two.

"I'm going to take care of the body. As soon as the men finish the day's shearing, find two volunteers to dig the grave next to the other ones."

"Yes...*boss*."

Jason snapped her head up. The ironic wince and cocky smile on the cook's face were a clear warning. If she wanted the shearing season to end well, she would have to establish her authority immediately. Until now, the men probably thought she was merely conveying Aaron's orders, when most of the instructions came from Maggie, or from herself. But with Aaron's death, it would be more difficult to rein in these tough guys, who were likely to refuse to obey a woman. Jason kept her eyes on the cook's without moving until the cook looked away, clearly embarrassed.

"Well, if there's nothing else, I'll go back to me kitchen."

"Let me know when you've found two volunteers."

Without paying the cook any more attention, Jason turned toward

Aaron's body. She sighed. She didn't like the prospect of preparing a corpse for burial, but she'd had experience doing it. Most of the time it was enough to dig a hole, then fill it up with earth and cover it with rocks because of the dingos. But here she'd have to clean him and dress him in his Sunday best to make Aaron presentable until morning. She started to methodically undress him.

❖

Everyone ate their well-deserved mutton curry in silence, their heads down. The news of the boss's death had thrown a heavy veil of silence over these workers who were accustomed to hard knocks. The question of their wages was on everyone's mind, but nobody dared bring it up.

Jason, although she had no doubt that Maggie would pay them, hadn't tried to reassure the workers. After all, she wasn't anything more than an employee, just like them. She would have given all her meagre possessions to be with Maggie right then and there, to comfort her…

The sound of the canteen door opening made everyone look up. Reverend Andrew stood in the doorway, his imposing figure outlined against the blue sky. Hesitant as to how to address these hardened men, he squared his shoulders and finally stepped inside. Jason, like the others, watched him silently. Reverend Andrew cleared his throat. He was both accustomed to and enjoyed giving sermons, but today these men didn't need a sermon.

"You have all been told of the sorrowful events that have just struck this station. Mrs. Sterling will need your unwavering support in the days to come. I know many of you must be wondering what is going to happen in the next few days, and I intend to tell you. Tomorrow morning at eight a.m., every one of you will attend the boss's funeral. After, you will return to the shearing shed, because the shearing cannot wait. I want each of you to swear on the Holy Bible that you will finish the job you have started."

Reverend Andrew took a Bible from his pocket and held it out. "Gentlemen, swear before God!"

Jason was the first to stand. Little by little, one by one, the men followed her example until everyone was on his feet.

"Mr. McKellig, Margaret Sterling asked if you would be so kind as to continue on as foreman."

"Of course, Father. Tell her not to worry. The men and I will shear the sheep and bale the wool. Isn't that right, mates?"

"Yeah!"

"Of course!"

The chorus of support that burst forth reassured Andrew. You could never quite tell what seasonal workers were thinking. He nodded, satisfied with their response. "Thank you, gentlemen. Mr. McKellig? May I have a word with you, please?"

The minister pointed outside. Jason hastened to the door. Once outside and sitting in the shade of a big eucalyptus tree near the stables, Reverend Andrew took off his hat and wiped his hand across his bare head. "It's so warm these days. Winter is a long time coming this year."

"Yes."

The reverend was visibly embarrassed. Jason wondered why. What had Aaron said before dying? Had he spoken of his suspicions?

"The shearing will be over in one or two weeks' time."

"Yes. That's about right."

"What do you plan to do afterward?"

"I haven't decided yet."

Giving Jason a piercing look, Reverend Andrew tried to make his words as convincing as possible. "In the name of Christian charity, if you would agree to stay on for some time longer, at least until Mrs. Sterling sells."

Christian charity? Had the situation not been so tragic, Jason would have burst out in laughter. Sell? Maggie sell? Never! She'd never sell. These lands were hers; they were her entire life. The reverend was dreaming if he thought she could part with the station. Of course, she, Jason, would stay, but surely not for the reasons the minister suggested.

"I'll stay until the missus boss tells me it's time to go."

The reverend was relieved. Swagmen didn't like to take orders from women. But this swaggie was a good man. The regulars at the pub had told him Jason barely drank and took care of Aaron when he was intoxicated. But nothing could replace having a good talk, man to man, to get to know someone.

"God bless you, Mr. McKellig. You are a good man."

Andrew squeezed Jason's shoulder as they both stood up. "I'll see you tomorrow at the the funeral."

"The missus?"

"Mary Taylor will spend the night."

Jason nodded, then put her hat back on and returned to the dormitory under the pastor's watchful eye. She would need a volunteer to help make a coffin from the planks of wood stored in the shed.

❖

Maggie sat down on the edge of her bed. She took a deep breath before getting up again. Standing in front of the enamel wash basin, she poured some water into it and washed her face. The initial shock of Aaron's death was over. The first wave of guilt as well.

His death wasn't her fault. How could she be responsible for the amount of alcohol he'd swilled down? If they didn't have any children, it was God's wish. But why? Since they had been married, she had prayed to God every Sunday to give her children. In vain! And now Aaron had died just when she realised she had feelings for Jason. Did the events of her life hold a divine message?

Alone, facing her mirror, Margaret smiled, then grimaced. *Poor lass. If you start thinking that way, it's the beginning of the end!* For someone as practical-minded as she, seeing a divine message in Aaron's death signalled that she was cracking up. Maggie shook her head. NO. Aaron was dead because he'd chosen alcohol over her. With these comforting thoughts, Maggie then left the room. She hadn't taken three steps when she found herself nose-to-nose with Mary. They bumped into each other, making the teacups on the tray she was holding clatter.

"Phew, Maggie. That was close. I didn't expect to see you pop up like that."

"Sorry. You made tea. I'd love to have a cup. Let's go back to the kitchen. It's not late enough for me to stay in bed."

"Are you all right?" Mary asked as they sat at the table drinking their tea.

"I'm starting to get over the shock…"

Mary kept quiet, sensing that Maggie had something else to say. She watched her friend slowly stir the tea in her cup.

"I was so angry with him this afternoon. He abandoned Jason a good two hours away from the house—on foot, without any water—so he could go into town and drink. Why, Mary?"

Mary sensed the real question wasn't why Aaron had abandoned Jason. She wasn't sure what to say. "Some men are weak. They need something to make them feel strong. For many, it's spirits." She hoped she was saying the right thing. "I'm sorry, Maggie. We were all fond of Aaron. He was a good man."

Maggie nodded. *A good man and a drunkard.* Was that all that would remain of Aaron in people's hearts?

"Where is he?"

"In the room at the back. I think Jason tended to the body."

Upon hearing Jason's name, Maggie looked up. She should have been the one to prepare Aaron's body, not Jason. Keeping her thoughts to herself, she began to stare into her teacup again. "I suppose we'll bury him tomorrow."

"Eight tomorrow morning. Wilson is spreading the word around town. Father Andrew is speaking with the seasonal workers right now. He decided to make them promise to stay till the end of the shearing."

"Oh my. Of course. The shearing! I have to speak to Jason McKellig about this." Maggie began to get up.

Reverend Andrew walked into the kitchen as she was finishing her sentence.

"No need to trouble yourself, Mrs. Sterling. I spoke directly to Jason. He's taking care of everything. I hope you won't mind, but I took the liberty of naming him foreman on your behalf."

"You did the right thing, Father. He's a man who can be trusted. For the three months he's been here, we've always been very satisfied with his work."

Maggie sighed. Weariness shone in her eyes, thought Reverend Andrew, but she had a determined expression.

"If the funeral is tomorrow, I have to get the food ready for after the service."

"It won't be necessary, Maggie," Mary said. "Wilson plans to ask everyone who is coming to bring something. You know it's the tradition when there's a sudden death."

"Yes, but I can't sit around and mope until tomorrow morning. Father, you'll stay for tea, won't you? I have cutlets, and I can fry some potatoes."

Andrew understood that Maggie needed to keep herself busy in order to deal with Aaron's death. Furthermore, he was hungry, and the return trip to town would be long. He readily accepted Maggie's offer.

CHAPTER EIGHTEEN

"Mr. McKellig," Maggie called out to Jason as he headed for the canteen.

Ignoring the fatigue of this endless day that had started with Aaron's funeral and finished with the shearing, Jason approached the house. She couldn't keep from studying Maggie's face, trying to read the emotions expressed on it.

"Ma'am?"

"How did the day go?"

"We finished the Walonga-pasture sheep. The shepherd has already set out to take them back. If we can keep up this pace, we'll be done with everything in a week's time."

Maggie forced a smile. In fact, she had forced herself the entire day to keep up a brave face, but she was overcome with depression. She should have been more careful before she spoke, but the words came faster than she could think. "Share a meal with me this evening."

Jason blushed, then nervously glanced at the dormitory, where the seasonal workers had just returned, as their work was done. Maggie understood Jason's hesitation, but she couldn't care less. "It doesn't matter to me what they say, and I don't feel like eating alone this evening. Are you afraid of gossip, Mr. McKellig?"

The distress in Maggie's voice went straight to Jason's heart. "Not if you aren't, ma'am."

"Good. Tea will be ready in an hour."

With a grin, Jason touched her hat to take leave of Maggie. As she headed for the dormitory, she found it difficult to control her erratic heartbeat. She had already shared a meal or two with Maggie, but Aaron had been snoring in the next room. He had been the invisible obstacle between them, the insurmountable barrier.

Today, this barrier was no longer there, and Jason felt the overwhelming weight of the feelings she had for Maggie and her fear of being rejected. Although she knew that nothing would happen so soon after Aaron's passing, since his grave was still fresh, and as long as the seasonal workers were still there, the possibility didn't exist…But now a glimmer of a possibility did.

Yet Maggie thought Jason was a man, and as soon as she learned the truth…The painful memory of Elizabeth suddenly surfaced to haunt her. Jason shook her head as if she could rid herself of her deepest fears. This evening she was having a meal with Maggie and needed to be clean and presentable.

"Hey, Peg-leg. Don't bother with a plate for me. I'm eating with the missus boss tonight," Jason nonchalantly called out upon entering the canteen. "I'm gonna speak to her about our pay. If someone has a question, let me know, and I'll bring it up with her."

Avoiding the cynical sparkle in the lame man's eyes, Jason headed for the dormitory to pick up some clean clothing.

"You're sure quick on the draw."

The room instantly fell silent, everyone waiting to see Jason's reaction. Her back to the lame man, she sighed. She had expected this type of remark. All day long she'd wondered how she'd react when it came. Now she had to face it. Her clean clothing in her hand, she slowly turned around. "And what do you mean by that, Peg-leg?"

"I don't mean a thing. I have eyes to see," the man added, with a sarcastic scowl.

"So you're not just lame, but blind, with perv ideas I wouldn't dare mention to Father Andrew. Missus boss is an admirable woman. Who do you think was running the station while her husband drank himself to death? I've seen her be crying in a silent rage and then pick herself up each day to go on. You're afraid for your wages? I know she'll pay each and every last one of you, even if she has to go without food. Now, what are you? Men—or gossiping ninnies?"

Without bothering any longer about the lame man—who had better forget about seeking employment here next year—Jason left the dormitory for the storage area she had converted into a shower a few weeks after arriving on the station. Protected from prying eyes, she let the deliciously cool water flow down her. And although many of the men ignored its existence, several of them had seemed rather glad to find this private area that allowed them to clean themselves out of sight of the missus.

❖

Maggie scrutinized the man who entered her kitchen with a confident step, immediately removing his hat, as was his custom. Maggie also saw his uncertain smile. Jason knew just as well as she that, with Aaron gone, their relationship was bound to change.

"Have a seat, and I'll get you the stew."

The dinner began in silence. Halfway through her meal, Maggie put her fork down and looked Jason directly in the eye. "You're not very talkative this evening."

Jason put down her fork, lowering her eyes before plunging them into Maggie's golden gaze. "I just don't know what to say. The boss's death...I'm so sorry. If I had gone into town with him..."

"He didn't want your company. Otherwise, he wouldn't have left you out in the middle of nowhere."

Maggie's formal tone felt like sharp stabs to Jason's heart. She would so much have liked to take Maggie in her arms, whisper sweet words of comfort in her ear, and call her by her Christian name. Instead, she simply said, "He was angry."

Maggie recalled the conversation she'd had that day with Jason, how she'd made him promise to stay until the end of shearing season. "You won't leave, will you? Not until after we finish?"

"I promised Father Andrew to be here as long as you need me. He seems to think you're going to sell."

And if I wanted to keep you forever, Jason, would you stay? Conscious of the silence that had settled between them, Maggie forced herself to hear Jason's words. *Sell?*

"I have no intention of selling."

Maggie's firm, determined voice reassured Jason. "That's what I thought. But the reverend is convinced that a woman alone can't manage Willowra. He doesn't know you."

Maggie beamed at the compliment. "This morning, O'Connor more or less offered to buy me out, but I made him understand that this wasn't the time. I don't reckon he's going to be asking again soon. They're all mistaken."

Jason, chewing her food, gave Maggie a surprised look.

"And I'm not alone as long as you're here."

Suddenly, the food in Jason's mouth became hard to chew. Despite the lump in her throat, she forced herself to swallow. What was she committing to? And, especially, would she be able to resist Maggie's charm? She continued to eat and completely changed the subject.

"We have some good shearers this year. Rick does it with a gun. I've seen a few like him at work before. They tally more than 200 sheep a day. It's quite a thing to behold. The guys are placing bets for him to beat his personal record of 235 in one day. I've never gone over 132 myself, and when I did, I thought I'd collapse, between the heat in the shed, the thirst, and the flies…"

Maggie listened to Jason distractedly. The change of conversation signalled a number of things. Reminding herself that her husband had been buried only that morning, she wanted to chase away her feelings for this man sitting across from her, but she was powerless to do so. This lack of willpower should have scared her, but she was happy enough to listen and smile at Jason as he went on about wool.

When, like every Sunday, Rebecca announced Jason's arrival, Margaret and her friends turned toward him.

"G'day, ladies. Just to say that the wagon is ready when you are, missus boss."

Jason started to go. And like every Sunday, Mary extended an invitation. "Mr. McKellig. Don't leave so quickly. Come join us for a cup of tea. Our husbands avoid us like the plague every Sunday…I wonder why?"

With her hand, Maggie covered the smile that immediately came to her mouth. The word avoid wasn't strong enough. They hightailed it away from them. She looked at Jason, once again surprised at how easy and collected he seemed here among all these women. Did he really enjoy having a cup of tea with the four older ladies that they were— well, five, counting Rebecca, though she certainly wasn't old.

"With pleasure, ma'am," Jason said while putting his hat on the side table. "It's not every day that I have the opportunity to drink my tea among such delightful company."

"And a flatterer on top of it," Ann murmured between her teeth. "I'm not the lucky kind. Such a dear, charming man has never knocked at my door."

Nelly burst out laughing, surprising the others who hadn't heard

Ann. Everyone's eyes were now on her, and she wasn't going to get away with it. Blushing, she cleared her throat and avoided looking at Jason.

"Ann said she would like to find an odd-job man who had such refined manners."

Jason was about to thank Ann when all the women burst out in laughter.

Maggie, pulling herself together between guffaws, tried to explain to Jason why they were acting that way. "The swaggie they hired last season was toothless, chewed tobacco and cursed at the end of each sentence."

"I never dared get close to him for fear of getting hit with tobacco spittle," Ann added, wincing in disgust. "It would run down his beard. Yuck."

Jason grinned. "I know the type. I've met plenty. Elder folk who spent most of their life humping their blueys from station to station. They're not a pretty sight, but they're generally honest fellows."

Like the old bloke who'd helped her at the beginning, Jason thought. You can get used to anything, especially if your survival depends upon it.

"Tell us a story about one of your adventures, Mr. McKellig," Rebecca begged, not without charm. "Everything you've experienced is so fascinating."

Jason discreetly rolled her eyes, which didn't escape Maggie's or the other women's attention. Mary seemed just about to come to Jason's rescue when Maggie asked, "Could you tell us about London instead, Mr. McKellig? You've been there, haven't you?"

"Yes, missus. I worked there for two years."

"You know London? I'd so much like to go there, this—"

"Rebecca! Let Mr. McKellig speak."

Rebecca threw herself back in her armchair, pouting. If only she could have Jason all to herself. Why did he come to town only on Sundays, and always with Margaret?

"London is a huge city, where the finest neighbourhoods rub shoulders with the slums. The fog can grab you by the throat for days on end, and the only thing you want to do is escape or die. The filth in some areas is revolting. Yet you can visit magnificent monuments that show all the wonderful things man is capable of."

"But you don't like it."

"No, ma'am. To be happy in London, you need a lot of money.

Otherwise, it's all hunger and misery. Here, we have dust everywhere and in everything, but even without money, a determined and courageous man can live decently."

"A little more tea perhaps, Mr. McKellig?" Mary offered, to chase away the heavy atmosphere...

A smile immediately returned to Jason's lips. "I would never turn down such an excellent tea, ma'am."

Chapter Nineteen

Maggie wiped her damp hands on her apron as soon as Jason joined her in the kitchen. The smile on Jason's lips made her heart jump.

"Gone?"

"Yep. All of them. I have to admit I won't mind having a bit of peace, missus boss. Not to mention that it made me nervous having to handle all that money."

Maggie laughed. She'd had to really push Jason to be in charge of paying the seasonal workers. She had convinced him by explaining how uncomfortable she felt handing money over to these men she hardly knew.

"What about handling your own money, then?"

Jason nervously glanced in the direction Maggie had pointed to on the table. Her heart raced when she saw the number of banknotes waiting there. She was so surprised by the generous amount that she stared at Maggie. "It's…too much."

"You earned it, Jason. As foreman you were responsible for everything, and that was already the case well before Aaron's death."

Jason shifted her weight from one leg to the other. She didn't know if this uncomfortable feeling was due to the money on the table or the familiar way Maggie was speaking to her. How many times had she dreamt of Maggie calling her by her first name? How many times had she wanted to call her Maggie and not "missus"? Also, the presence of the seasonal workers and the dread of their gossip had prevented her from spending more time than had been strictly necessary with her.

"Take it," Maggie insisted.

"Thank you, missus."

A tiny smile appeared on Maggie's lips, a mischievous look in her eyes. Jason gulped.

"As of today, I want us to take all our meals together. Eating alone is too depressing."

Jason nodded, nervous.

"And if I could call you Jason, and you call me Maggie…"

"What will people think?"

"In public, if you're more comfortable, you can call me missus. But not when we're alone. And one last thing. I want you to have Aaron's clothing. It's probably a little big, but I'll fix it to fit you."

"Missuh…I can't, Maggie. It's too much. I…"

"What do you want me to do with it all, Jason? Give it to strangers? Some of those shirts were my father's. I don't want people that I don't know wearing them. And as you are staying on to work here, I want you to be dressed correctly, even for your everyday clothing. What will the neighbours think of me if they see you in your old patched-up rags? They're going to think I'm cheap, which isn't the case."

Convinced, Jason raised her hands in surrender.

"You can also have Aaron's room."

At these words, Jason's heart started to beat wildly. It was out of the question to sleep under the same roof as Maggie. It would be pure torture.

"No, thank you, ma'am. I prefer the dormitory."

Maggie sighed. She knew how to pick her battles. The vehement look in Jason's eyes and his flat refusal told her that even if she insisted, she wouldn't get her way. She couldn't win them all. But losing a battle wasn't losing the war, and she wasn't a woman to give up easily. An opportunity would come up one day to justify having Jason near her.

"Okay. The next few weeks will be busy with getting the ranch back in order and repairing the tools, but afterward I'd like you to go to the neighbouring towns to see if you can find a buyer for next year's wool."

Jason screwed up her eyes. She didn't understand. O'Connor paid a good price for the wool. Why would they go elsewhere?

"O'Connor is pressuring me to sell my land," Maggie said. "When I refused, he implied that my wool may not interest him so much next year and…"

She stopped herself. She didn't want Jason to know what else O'Connor had implied.

"And?"

"It's not important. I have to get on with my cooking." She turned away to finish washing the carrots.

"Maggie! I have to know what O'Connor's up to if I want to be ready to confront him."

Continuing to clean her vegetables, Maggie, trembling, voiced her deepest fear. "He suggested that he could hire you away from here at a salary I couldn't compete with."

Jason's anger immediately raced through her. She was angry at O'Connor, but also at Maggie, for believing she could be bought off so easily. She impulsively approached Maggie, grabbed her arm, and turned her around to face her. The tears gathering in those golden eyes immediately checked Jason's anger, stirring up her desire to protect this woman who was standing in front of her. She would have liked to take her in her arms, but a last bit of self-control stopped her.

"Oh, Maggie! Never. You hear me. I would never, ever let myself be bought off by O'Connor or anyone of his kind. I'm here for you— not for the land, or the money, but simply, and entirely, for you."

Realising what she'd just admitted, Jason let go of Maggie's arm and took a step back. "I'm sorry…I shouldn't have said that…I…"

"Jason…"

Maggie reached out to stroke Jason's cheek, but he took one, then two steps back, turning around to leave.

Immobile, incapable of pronouncing another word, Maggie watched him go. Her legs like cotton, she collapsed onto the nearest chair, her wet hands dampening her dress. As she repeated Jason's words in her head, joy slowly started creeping into her heart. Jason reciprocated her feelings. She'd suspected it, but having it confirmed was the greatest gift she could ever receive. Now, there was just this minor detail: Jason had run off after making his confession.

She understood that she would have to go slowly to overcome Jason's fears. She needed to prove to him that she wasn't like that other woman who had broken his heart. Whatever happened, she would love him for who he was. Proud of her resolve, she returned to her vegetables. Tonight's meal would be interesting, to say the least.

❖

Jason slowly sipped her beer, her sole resting on the bar's copper foot rail. She imagined Maggie and her friends commenting on the pastor's sermon about stingy people. This time of the year, when, after all the wool had been sold and whatever profit remained was deposited at the bank, Andrew clearly had hoped some of that money would find its way to the church in donations. He must have received less than expected, thus the inspiration for his sermon about stinginess.

"Hey, mate. How are ya?" Ben the bartender asked.

"Happy the shear is over and the shepherds have returned to the pastures."

"Not surprising, knowing how difficult the month must have been at Willowra."

Jason took another sip of the fresh, cool beer. She hadn't been asked a question, and she wasn't the type to gossip.

"You gonna stay on?" Ben asked directly.

"A while longer. I promised the reverend after Aaron's death."

Ben wiped a beer glass dry with his old grey rag before putting it away with the others. He had observed Jason these last months. He wasn't the type to talk too much or drink too much. Was the gossip about Jason and Maggie true? Ben doubted it. He knew Maggie pretty well; they had been schoolmates. He'd even considered courting her for a while, but Aaron had come and stolen her away from him. Maggie certainly wasn't the kind to flirt when she was married, or as a young widow. And the fellow sitting in front of him was much too serious and honest to engage in any dallying. No. People were wrong or too gullible. They'd believe anything.

"It's good Margaret won't be all alone out in Willowra."

Jason nodded. She did wonder how she was going to survive eating every evening with the woman who occupied her thoughts every second of the day. While working at her chores and duties, she could stay away from Maggie, but once evening came…

A loud voice rang out behind her. "G'day, mate."

Jason turned her head to greet O'Connor.

"Won't you come join us?"

Jason glanced in the direction O'Connor was pointing. Carrington, Keller, and Hicks were already sitting at a corner table. The banker, judge, and general-store owner. All the town notables and not a single sheep farmer among them.

"No, thanks. I've gotta pick up the missus boss as soon as I finish my beer."

O'Connor squinted in anger. It was very rare for someone to reject his invitations, and he didn't like it one bit. Especially when that person was a good-for-nothing.

"Come finish your beer with us."

Despite the friendly look on O'Connor's face, Jason understood this was an order. Not obeying would make Maggie's life that much more difficult, so Jason wordlessly picked up her beer and followed O'Connor to the table, where introductions were made.

"Everything going all right at Willowra?" Carrington asked, nonchalantly.

"You're the banker. You should know better than me."

Jason's sarcastic answer surprised everyone. Carrington nearly blushed, seeming a little embarrassed.

"We're merely thinking about Maggie's well-being, McKellig," Keller said, coming to Carrington's defence.

Jason looked the judge right in the eye and calmly took another sip of beer before answering, keeping her gaze planted firmly on O'Connor: "By pressing her to sell?"

"A woman can't run a sheep farm all alone," O'Connor said.

"Who do you think was running Willowra while Aaron drank the days away with his *mates*?"

The way Jason pronounced the word mates made everyone realise she meant just the opposite. Hicks and Keller exchanged a hesitant look. Had they been misled? O'Connor had told them Aaron and Maggie wanted to sell even before Aaron's death. O'Connor wanted to buy Willowra, but he needed partners.

Jason swallowed her last sip of beer, then stood up. "Sorry, but the missus boss is waiting for me. Good day, gentlemen."

Boiling over with rage, O'Connor realised this swaggie had manipulated him like a joey. The words exchanged by the others, who he'd thought would be his future partners, now made his dream of becoming a sheep-station owner disappear before his eyes. He cursed this blasted McKellig and Margaret along with him!

CHAPTER TWENTY

"How could such a large hole be made in so short a time?"

Perceiving a barely veiled reproach in Maggie's voice, Jason replied defensively. "The termites probably ate one of the main stakes, and last week's wind pushed the bushes right through the barbed wire, ripping out the stake along with several others after it. I should have taken notice of the lil' heap of earth at the foot of the main stake. It's a sign of termites. Now instead of replacing one, we have to replace four!"

Maggie realised Jason was trying to justify something that wasn't his fault or responsibility. She would have confided that her remark wasn't particularly aimed at him, but for the past two months, since the incident in the kitchen, she'd felt as though she had to walk on eggs with Jason and avoided alluding to anything personal. Even if Maggie had always perceived Jason as a man of few words from the first day they met, the little he did speak helped keep a connection between them. But now Maggie desperately felt a rift growing between them a little more each day. She was fed up that their only topic of conversation was Willowra and sheep, when all she wanted to hear were sweet nothings.

"You are not responsible for the termites, Jason," she said, jumping down from the wagon. "Let's get started if we want to mend this before sundown."

They wordlessly put on their thick leather work gloves to handle the barbed wire and bushes still stuck to it. Thus they started the long, slow process of removing the old collapsed enclosure to replace the stakes. Jason tried not to think about the hardest part, when the old wire had to be pulled taut again around the new posts. But for the sake of economy, they didn't have a choice.

Under the still-hot winter sun, they worked together in perfect harmony without having to exchange a word, only stopping briefly for a mid-morning snack. When it was time to break for lunch, Jason was proud of the work they'd accomplished. All the new stakes had been driven into the ground, waiting for their wire. She glanced at Maggie, who was busy working around the fire. Heading over to her, Jason picked up a few brittle eucalyptus branches.

"I think it's time to build up our strength. Tying the barbed wire on the stakes isn't going to be a picnic."

Maggie grinned at Jason as she handed him a cup of tea and a sandwich. As usual, Jason's heart skipped a beat upon seeing that marvellous smile. Since her confession, she hadn't been able to speak to Maggie. That upset her, but her feelings were just too strong. She dreamt of Maggie at night, and during the day too, while she was on her horse, surveying the huge property in order to check on the herds. Yet, when in her presence, she lowered her eyes for fear Maggie could all too well read her thoughts. Jason was so afraid of being rejected by the woman she loved she felt completely paralysed, even when it came to her daily tasks.

"It's going to be tough. Even if we pull with the strength of bulls, I'm sure we'll end up a half-inch short."

"Three-quarters," Maggie countered.

Jason glanced over at Maggie. Her sparkling eyes were an open provocation. She played along.

"An apple pie tomorrow if it's a half inch."

"Deal! And if I win, you're the one who'll make the pie."

Jason almost choked on her tea. "You're not afraid of dying before your time?"

"The fact is, I don't know any swaggie who doesn't know his way around a kitchen."

"Making stew has nothing to do with baking a pie," Jason exclaimed, laughing.

Maggie clucked her tongue. "Don't back out now just 'cause you're afraid of losing—"

"It's your funeral. The bet is on."

Jason grinned at Maggie, to the latter's great delight. Oh, how she'd longed these last months for this type of familiar, easy talk between them.

"Okay. Let's see who ends up making the pie. Or have you changed your mind?" Maggie gathered their teacups and threw the rest in the fire to quench the flames.

Cut to the quick, Jason got up, picked up the box of nails and the hammer from the back of the wagon, and headed for the farthest stake. There, without even bothering to put her gloves back on, she nailed the end of the wire to the highest part of the post, making sure to waste as little as possible.

Meanwhile, Maggie, who has already slipped her gloves on again, took the end of the barbed wire Jason had nailed and started to pull it toward the main post. Once she finished hammering in the second and then the third staple, Jason came over to help her.

"I'll pull, and you attach it to the middle post."

"I think it'd be better if you pulled on it with all your might, while I first attach the wire to the main stake. Otherwise we'll never make it."

Maggie followed Jason's orders without protest. With just a few confident hammer strokes, Jason nailed the wire to the post.

"I didn't overtighten it on purpose, so it'll have a little give. We'll need it. Ready?"

Maggie nodded before grabbing the other end of the wire and walking to the last stake.

"Too short, by at least an inch. Looks like *you*'re going to be baking the pie," Maggie gaily announced.

Jason couldn't believe her ears. A whole inch! She came over to see for herself. "It's because you haven't pulled on the wire nearly hard enough."

"And what do you think I've been doing? Taking a nap?' Maggie said, red-faced from the exertion.

Slipping the hammer into her belt, Jason, determined to win, positioned her hands on either side of Maggie's and started heaving. United by their effort, their arms and shoulders touched.

"A half inch! You're the one who's going to bake the pie for me." Jason, smiling widely, turned her head to Maggie. They were so close Jason could feel Maggie's panting breath on her face.

When Maggie looked up, her gaze fell on Jason's lips. Barely able to think, she murmured, "one...," then placed a kiss on those lips.

Although surprised, Jason, forgetting her fears as well as any conscious thoughts, hungrily tasted Maggie's lips. She felt Maggie's tongue coming to meet hers, setting the passion ablaze within her. Without completely realising it, she had let go of the wire, and now her hands were sliding over the length of Maggie's body to settle on her hips, pulling her close.

When, out of breath, they stopped their passionate kiss, Jason returned to her senses. Maggie could read the panic in his eyes. She anticipated the fact that Jason might try to run off, so she advanced toward him as he backed up right into the wagon. Maggie then plastered herself against him so he couldn't move.

"Maggie…"

"Jason. I've wanted this for so long…"

All of Jason's senses were screaming for Maggie as her entire body was pinned against her. Her heart pounding wildly, Jason desperately tried to stop her. "You mustn't. You're going to regret it, you—"

"Shh…"

Maggie's fingers, free of her gloves, softly traced the outline of Jason's lips.

"Kiss me…"

The fire in Maggie's desire-filled eyes overcame any hesitation Jason might have had. Once their lips had met again, their tongues intertwined for long moments until their kiss was interrupted—to take a breath.

"Take me," Maggie whispered into Jason's ears.

Without waiting for an answer, Maggie pulled the glove off Jason's hand and placed it on her breast. While Jason's caresses made her shiver and close her eyes with pleasure, she quickly undid her own work shirt and work pants buttons. What a good idea it had been not to wear a skirt this morning.

When Jason felt Maggie's bare skin under her fingers, her senses went wild. The rush of blood to her clit made her feel like she would explode. Blinded by this pent-up desire, Jason stuck her hand into the wagon to grab the tarp, which she quickly spread onto the ground and then laid Maggie down on it. Once again her lips were on Maggie's while her fingers caressed her breasts, her stomach, and strayed down to explore her most intimate parts. Every moan that came from this gorgeous woman's mouth increased Jason's desire. While she sank into the depths of Maggie's trembling body, Jason herself was overwhelmed and climaxed.

Panting, incapable of speech as their orgasms had been so powerful and quick, they hugged each other, closely.

"I love you, Jason," Maggie dared to say while stroking the cheek of the person resting against her. "You are the man I have been waiting for my entire life. I know that now."

These words forced Jason to return to the harsh reality of her situation. She had remained entirely dressed, and Maggie still didn't know the truth. Jason wasn't just afraid. She was terrified. She rolled over to her side, sitting up and turning her back to Maggie.

"We have to finish repairing the fence," Jason said in a hushed voice. She then stood and, with a heavy step, went to pick up the barbed wire again.

A stab in the stomach couldn't have made Maggie hurt more. How could Jason treat her this way? Her anger, though, immediately faded when she saw Jason's shoulders slumped with sadness, his mechanical gestures and overall air of misery. She didn't doubt the desire and love she saw in Jason's eyes, but she'd also seen fear there. Why? Why hadn't Jason penetrated her? Why did he use only his fingers to make her come? As she dressed, these questions swirled in Maggie's head. He did know she was barren, didn't he?

Maggie walked over to Jason.

"Jason…"

"We're going to have to add wire. We'll never be able to reach the stake otherwise." Without waiting for Maggie's answer, Jason walked to the back of the wagon. She tried to stay calm after this absolute lapse of control. Terror raced through her—fear of what would come next. It was childish to refuse to have this conversation now. But having to face the disgust she suspected she would find in Maggie's eyes once she knew the truth was unbearable, especially after the harmony of love their two bodies had just sung.

"Jason! We have to talk," Maggie said with great resolve, her hands on her hips. Maggie hadn't moved from her position next to the post. She was surprised a man like Jason, responsible and calm, couldn't take responsibility for his acts.

"Later, Maggie…this evening."

This evening…sounded like a death sentence to Jason. She couldn't think about it. Otherwise she would end up immediately heading for the bush and its salutary, heart-healing ways.

Maggie knew enough about men to realise she shouldn't insist. This evening then. Oh, how terribly long the afternoon was going to be!

❖

Once back in the dormitory after having unhitched the horses, Jason panicked. Without considering the consequences, she took her belongings out of the closet and set them on the central table. Of her belongings from when she first arrived, only the old man's rifle and her swag remained. The rest she had purchased, except for the pile of Aaron's clothes. She had too many things and couldn't take them all, especially because she would need to pack flour and dried meat. How could she gather provisions from the pantry without making Maggie suspicious?

At the thought of Maggie, Jason brought her fingers to her nose. Even though she had been wearing thick leather gloves, she could still smell Maggie on her. Memories of their afternoon came flowing back to her: their kisses, her skin, her gentle touch. She couldn't run off as long as Maggie hadn't chased her away. Her heart would be broken, but it was better than leaving without ever knowing whether by some remote chance Maggie might have accepted her just as she was. If only she weren't so afraid. Tears came to her eyes. Her legs weak with emotion, she collapsed onto the bench and put her face in her hands.

"Jason? We have to…"

Maggie stopped short when she saw all Jason's belongings on the table. She had to hold on to the doorframe so she wouldn't lose her bearings.

"You can't leave! Jason, not after this afternoon…"

As soon as she saw Jason's shoulder's shaking with great sobs, she couldn't speak. Immediately, all her emotions faded except one: the love she felt for this man. She sat down on the bench next to Jason and took him in her arms, held him tight.

Jason didn't resist. She was finally where she wanted to be, even if it hurt her to think this might be the last time. She sobbed harder.

Maggie rested her cheek on Jason's head and stroked his blond, silky hair with one hand while she gently caressed his back with the other. The bandage that ran across his back stopped her fingers. He had never mentioned an injury, but her emotions were too strong for her to pay much attention. She couldn't keep herself from touching Jason, from kissing his head, rubbing her cheek against his hair. She could have spent hours bringing solace to this vulnerable man who was so docile in her arms.

Jason was no longer sobbing. Her arms wrapped around Maggie's waist, her head against her neck, she savoured these wondrous moments. She weakly resisted Maggie, who was forcing her to look up. The love she saw in Maggie's sun-filled eyes once again brought tears to her own.

Maggie slowly wiped away the new river of tears flowing down

Jason's cheeks. Then she couldn't hold back her own tears when she saw the distress in Jason's blue eyes.

"Don't cry, Maggie," Jason whispered. "Don't cry. I'm sorry... I'm so sorry."

"You were going to leave without saying anything. Why?"

Jason shook her head. "I wanted to go, but I couldn't. I love you, Maggie, but I'm so afraid you're going to hate me after I tell you my secret..."

"Whatever your secret may be, it won't change my feelings for you."

Jason doubted that. She wanted to pronounce the fateful words, but they were stuck in her throat.

Sensing his inner conflict, Maggie placed her fingers over Jason's mouth. "If you promise not to run off, I think we should each clean up, change into fresh clothing, and meet in the kitchen for a cup of tea and a snack so we can talk. That will give us a chance to calm our nerves a bit. Okay?"

Jason nodded. She could never leave without having spoken to Maggie. And she'd feel better after a shower. "So I'll see you up at the house in a little while."

After having planted a light kiss on Jason's lips, Maggie got up and headed for the main house. She too needed to clean herself up and think. She wanted Jason to make love to her again, and not tomorrow, but she needed to heat the water for the bath and make something to eat. If everything worked out as she hoped, she wouldn't have time to cook a hot meal. A cold plate would do.

What could this secret that terrified Jason be? How could he imagine that she could reject him, whatever it might be? Was he impotent? That would explain the way he'd touched her this afternoon. Yet Maggie was sure he'd had an orgasm. *Someone who is impotent can't.* Now that she thought about it, maybe he hadn't had one. His pants were dry. When that had happened to Aaron before their wedding, it had left a large spot on the front of his trousers.

When Maggie sank into the delicious water, even if it was lukewarm, she sighed with happiness. Tilting her head back to rest on the edge of the hip bath, she closed her eyes. Jason's smell, his silky hair and soft skin...she smiled. With Aaron, she'd always had to be careful of his thick beard. She suddenly opened her eyes. She knew some men had almost no hair on their faces, but the memory of her fingers on Jason's cheeks reminded her that he was entirely hairless.

Slowly, she traced her fingers across her own cheek. Like a woman's cheek...A woman? Jason? No. He couldn't be.

Maggie got out of the water with these silly thoughts and dried herself. She dried her small breasts, which she didn't like. Men preferred big-breasted women. Jason's bandage. If he was a woman, what better way to hide his breasts? She had never seen him bare-chested, and he had made himself a private, safe corner to wash...where no one could surprise him. Now, everything took on another meaning: his way of walking, height, the folded sheets, the tea with her friends, the woman who had rejected him, his fear that she, Maggie, would reject him also. Could she love a woman? Would that change her feelings for Jason? Making love would certainly not be a problem. Never had she had such a strong orgasm. She quickly dressed.

Maggie put the kettle on the fire with mechanical gestures, thoughts spinning in her head. Everything was ready. All she needed was the hot water. When Jason came into the kitchen with an uncertain step, Maggie was finally able to see the woman under the man's clothing.

"A bit of tea?"

Jason responded with a shadow of a smile. How was she going to tell Maggie? Even if she felt clean and more in control than before, the words wouldn't come easily.

"I took out some cold meat. I thought you might be hungry."

As she spoke, Maggie drew closer to Jason. The desire Jason could see in her eyes was like being punched in the gut.

Maggie brought her hand up to Jason's face and caressed the velvety skin on her cheek.

"Kiss me."

The lips that took Maggie's were cool and hungry. Immediately all her senses were floating—it was like flying! She had wondered if she could love a woman, and here was her answer.

Without stopping their kiss, Jason slowly backed Maggie toward the kitchen table. Even if Maggie rejected her, she wanted to possess her one last time. She would have to get ahold of herself if she didn't want to come before she touched Maggie, but her starved body wouldn't listen. Slow down, a voice murmured inside her, but Jason desired this woman too much to control herself much longer. She grabbed Maggie by the thighs to sit her down on the table, then pulled her skirt up over her stomach and knelt between her legs.

Maggie would have liked to keep Jason's lips on hers. Despite feeling Jason's hands on her hips, the solitude that seized her was unbearable. She cupped her hands around Jason's face to pull him back, but then Jason's lips touched her most intimate parts. Closing her eyes with the intense pleasure, Maggie kept Jason's head between her thighs. She moaned more strongly when two fingers penetrated her just before the delightful spasms started, and she felt as though she were falling into an endless well of pleasure.

Panting, Jason stood, pulling Maggie into her arms. Her brunette hair against her shoulder appeased her overwrought senses. Jason had come as soon as her lips touched Maggie's most intimate parts, but she still didn't feel sated. She could have spent the night making love to Maggie. No, not just the night—her entire life. She cradled Maggie against her, stroking her hair until Maggie, regaining her breath, looked up and smiled at her. That smile! Jason's heart melted. She lowered her head to give Maggie a tiny kiss on the lips, but the passion-filled lips that met hers drew them into a streamy, sensual embrace, lips against lips, tongue against tongue…

Maggie freed herself from the table and grabbed Jason's hand. "Come."

It was only when they arrived in Maggie's bedroom that Jason understood the moment of truth had arrived. Maggie had already started undoing the buttons of Jason's shirt. Jason's hands closed over Maggie's, stopping them briefly.

"Undress me while I undress you," Maggie whispered. "I want you naked and in my bed tonight."

"Maggie…"

"No. No more words, no more fear, Jason. Just show me how much you love me, just as I want to show you how much I love you."

Maggie freed her hands from Jason's, who resigned herself to having her secret revealed and her heart broken.

With a steady gesture, Maggie pushed aside the flaps of Jason's shirt, sliding it down her shoulders. The bandage she'd expected was there, held in place with a safety pin, which she hurried to undo.

As Maggie undid the bandage, Jason couldn't breathe.

Without taking her eyes off the lovely little breasts that had just been revealed to her, Maggie placed her hands gently on Jason's shoulders, slowly sliding them down over her torso. Jason's nipples hardened at the touch of her warm hands and the cold air. Maggie would have liked to pause, but she had to get on with undressing Jason entirely to end his fear once and for all. She had been right; nothing could stop her from loving this person…and Jason's skin was so soft! She skilfully unbuckled Jason's belt and pants buttons. She let the pants drop to the floor. Then she took a step back. She glanced directly into Jason's petrified eyes before taking a sweeping look at the superb, muscular body standing before her. She then made sure to gaze right into Jason's face. "You're beautiful, Jason. Very beautiful. Undress me."

Jason had expected a wince of disgust, but all she saw was wonderment. She couldn't believe her eyes, or her ears. She forced herself to move. Slowly, she raised her arms and started undressing Maggie until they both were naked, facing each other. When they touched, skin against skin, Jason moaned. It had been such a long time.

CHAPTER TWENTY-ONE

Maggie stretched languorously in bed, like a cat. What a night! She felt the other side of the bed where Jason should have been. But the sheets were cold, and an icy feeling immediately ran through her veins. She sprang up, her eyes wide open, her heart racing.

"Jason, no!" Maggie murmured at this sad reality that broke her heart.

Feeling nauseous, she sat, all alone, unable to move. Why had Jason left? The night they had just spent together had been fantastic. She had never imagined anyone could experience such pleasure, but the most incredible thing had been when she made Jason come. What power…but why was she alone this morning?

It took a moment for Maggie, paralysed with fear, to understand the noise she was hearing. At the sound of pots and pans banging together, she sat up straight, hope filling her. Jason was here. She hadn't left her. She fell back on her pillow like a rag doll. She swallowed mouthfuls of air and massaged the skin over her heart until she felt calm. And just when she was about to get up, the bedroom door opened with Jason holding a tray in her hands.

The bright smile that welcomed Jason made all her final apprehensions fly away. Maggie clearly didn't have any regrets. Jason cursed herself for having waited so long to tell Maggie the truth. When Jason had waked before dawn, she had been afraid Maggie would regret their wild night together. The liberty of their lovemaking had reminded her of long-ago afternoons spent with Kathryn, her first lover.

But the years that had passed, filled with bad experiences, had demoralized Jason. She had feared Maggie's reaction this morning. So she took her time—got up, fed the animals, cleaned the stable, and prepared breakfast. When the sun was already fairly high, she started to wonder if Maggie might be hiding in her bedroom. So Jason had forced herself to make tea and take Maggie her breakfast in bed.

She silently placed the tray next to Maggie.

"Breakfast in bed? It's shocking."

Now that she was reassured, Maggie felt in a playful mood. She hungrily eyed the pancakes and jam. Seeing only one cup of tea, she frowned. "Aren't you going to have breakfast with me?"

"I left my cup in the kitchen. Be right back."

Maggie could sense the nervousness in Jason's voice and her jerky movements. She sighed. They would have to have a true discussion this morning. She didn't want to, but she couldn't let Jason shut down, wrapped in fear and silence.

Jason came back with her cup but just stood there, apparently not knowing what to do with herself.

"Either you get undressed and come to bed with me, or I'll dress, and we'll eat in the kitchen," Maggie said in a mocking tone. "I feel vulnerable because you have clothes on and I don't."

Seeing that Jason was too scared to move, she ordered in a husky voice, "Undress."

Jason licked her lip and drank a sip of tea before placing her cup on the night table before taking off her clothes. Pushing the tray aside, she joined Maggie in bed but didn't touch her.

Maggie turned onto her side to better admire Jason. With the tips of her fingers, she traced the outlines of her upper arm. "When I woke up alone, I was afraid you'd gone. Never do that to me again!"

"Maggie…" Jason grabbed the hand that was making her crazy with desire with its light touch. Staying focused on Maggie, she very softly kissed each of her fingers. Desire immediately lit up Maggie's eyes.

"No!" Maggie said, taking her hand back. "Before anything else, we need to talk."

"Talking isn't my strong suit. You know that."

Maggie couldn't resist the uncertainty in Jason's eyes. She caressed her cheek.

"What do you want, Jason?"

Jason frowned.

Maggie smiled. "I think you understood me. Now that we've made love, are you going to leave? Or do you want something else?"

Maggie's cold tone upset Jason. She opened her mouth, but

nothing came out. And then, finally, she said, "I love you, Maggie. If you'll have me, I'll stay until you grow weary of me."

Tears formed in Jason's eyes. Maggie immediately took her in her arms, giving her a suffocatingly tight embrace.

"And what if I never grow weary of you?" Maggie asked her in a breathy voice.

"Then I'll stay until death do us part."

"Oh, Jason…stay, my love. You are the light of my life."

Tears rolled down Maggie's cheeks. She had felt so old and useless with her barren womb. Now, with this crazy love, came a newfound youth. She had never felt a love so strong for Aaron, never with a force that gave her the strength to face any obstacle. A wave of guilt overcame her, quickly chased away by Jason's feather-light kisses on her neck. The joy of feeling alive and desired ran through her.

❖

"We're indecent." Cooking at the stove, Maggie softly chuckled.

"Why?" Jason, without taking her eyes off Maggie, was sipping her tea.

"It's well past noon, and we've just gotten out of bed."

"So? The animals have been fed, and the world won't stop turning because we spent the night and morning making love."

"The world won't stop turning, but imagine the gossip in town if somebody learned…" Maggie joked. "The widow and the swag-woman."

Jason grimaced. The outside world posed their greatest danger. If the truth ever came out, Maggie couldn't handle it. "Nobody can know."

Maggie stirred the sautéing onions in the pan and then looked at Jason with a serious expression. "What do you mean, nobody can know? Do you think I'm going to be able to hide for very long that I've fallen in love? Mary will see it immediately, and then…"

"That's not what I mean, Maggie."

"Oh. You mean the fact that you're a woman."

Jason nodded.

Maggie kept silent. The sound of the onions cooking distracted her. She grabbed the wooden spoon and stirred them again.

"There will be gossip and talk about us, especially since you've been a widow for only two months, and because I'm a swaggie. But we can face it, and then people will quickly move on to other subjects and ignore us. However, if they learn I'm a woman…"

"They'll feed us to the lions."

Jason stood and went over to stand right in front of Maggie. Her eyes were full of a great sadness.

"I'm sorry. I don't want to force you to lie. Perhaps it would be better for me to go…"

Maggie put her hand over Jason's lips. "Stop that! If you want to go, don't use that excuse."

"I don't want to leave you. It's just that…"

"You want to protect me. But I can fight my own battles. I agree with you, though. They can never learn that you're a woman. The rest we'll handle as it comes. For the moment, my dear, beautiful girl, let's be happy. Let's keep things to ourselves."

"Man."

"What?"

"You have to keep of thinking of me as a man. If not, you'll end up accidentally betraying yourself. I'm a man. My name is Jason McKellig, and I'm a swaggie. The only moment when you can think of me as a woman will be when we make love in the privacy of our bedroom."

Maggie nodded. Her face lightened up.

"What's your real name?"

"Maggie! That's not going to help you forget I'm a woman."

"I want to learn everything about you, Jason, about your life. But first, what is your real name?"

Jason sighed. "Laura. Laura McKellig."

A shadow of a smile appeared on Maggie's lips. "I much prefer Jason. It suits you better. Now, if you could find something to do so I can get on with my cooking."

Maggie gave Jason a quick kiss on the lips, then turned back to the stove. The onions were starting to stick to the bottom of the pan.

❖

Maggie squirmed in her chair under her girlfriends' scrutiny. These last few days she had been walking around wearing a blissful smile, and even at church this morning, she hadn't been able to stop thinking about making love with Jason.

"And would you like to tell us what's making you so happy, Maggie?" Mary asked.

"I don't know what you mean."

"Bah!"

"Hmff! She thinks we were born yesterday," Nelly added.

"You know very well we won't let you out of here until you spill the beans," Mary said with a big grin. "It wouldn't have anything to do with a handsome man named Jason?"

"Mary!"

Maggie's cheeks went fiery hot. She lowered her eyes and stared intently into her teacup. It was difficult to hide that she was shaken.

"Maggie?" Ann questioned her. "How could you say such a thing, Mary? Maggie just lost her husband."

Mary motioned with her chin to Maggie, who was still blushing furiously but had finally decided to face her friends. She could tell just by looking into Mary's eyes that they would be understanding. All she had left to do was admit the truth:

"You're right, Mary. I'm more in love than I've ever been in my entire life."

"But you just became a widow, Maggie. How could you…?"

Ann was indignant at the idea, but Maggie had expected her reaction. And how would she react if she knew Jason was a woman?

"I know, Ann, but Jason's…special. Truth be told, I've been attracted to him since his arrival. He's different from any other man I've ever met. And he loves me too."

Ann's mouth dropped open as she stared at Maggie.

"They're all charming at the beginning, but then things change." Bitterness filled Nelly's voice. She didn't hide from her friends that her husband had a quick temper and a heavy hand. However, Maggie remembered the love in Nelly's eyes as she'd looked at him when they were first married.

"Not Jason. He's lived long enough to stop changing. He's too attentive. He's been that way since the beginning."

Mary sighed. She wanted to be happy for her friend. Suppressing her questions, she simply smiled. Jason had indeed seemed like a good soul, but was he really in love with her, or was he taking advantage of a well-off widow?

Ann didn't have any of Mary's scruples. "What makes you think he isn't jumping on the occasion to settle down? After all, you're rich, with all the land you own. Maybe he's tired of being stone broke."

"Excuse me?"

"Ann!"

Nelly's intervention cut off Maggie's reply. She closed her eyes to collect herself. She would never allow anyone to speak poorly of Jason.

"You don't know him, Ann. If you really did, all your doubts would disappear. You—"

The door opened.

"Look who I found in front of the house," Rebecca proudly announced. "He was sitting on the bench outside."

"I didn't want to shorten your visit, missus." Jason made an excuse for Maggie's frown. "I'd finished my beer, so I was waiting…"

Maggie beamed at Jason's attempt to save appearances.

"Can you leave us, Rebecca?" Mary asked.

"But Mother…all right, Mother."

Rebecca regretfully left the room without taking her eyes off Jason. How could her mother dare humiliate her that way? She, who impatiently waited all week long to see Jason on Sundays. She was sure Jason had noticed her. Who didn't? After all, she was young and pretty, with wealthy parents.

While Rebecca closed the door behind her, Mary's smile grew brighter. Jason swallowed. Why did she have the impression that she was a mouse in front of a hungry cat?

"If you haven't finished, missus boss, I'll wait outside."

"You wouldn't deprive us of your charming presence, Mr. McKellig. Especially after what Maggie has just told us."

Maggie's face was bright red. Ann was wearing a sulky scowl, Nelly was smiling ironically, and everything was clear as day to Jason. Maggie had told them. Jason's heart soared.

An enormous smile enveloped her face when she turned to look at Maggie.

If Mary had any doubts about Jason's feelings for her best friend, they faded when she saw the sparkle in his eyes when he gazed at Maggie. The kind of love Mary saw there made her once again regret the reasonable match she'd made and think back to the love of her life that she had let get away because he was penniless. She envied her friend.

❖

Powerful arms encircled Maggie's waist. She smiled. Jason lying close against her back, the feeling of her chin resting on her shoulder… Maggie closed her eyes and sighed happily.

"If you want to eat, you better let go…"

Jason was dying of hunger but couldn't yet let go of this silky body she was holding in her arms. Every morning she woke up, amazed that she had Maggie by her side. She liked to watch her sleep peacefully, snuggled up against her…yet she couldn't shake off a surge of anguish reminding her that all good things usually came to an end.

"The delicious smell of apple pie wafting in here makes me think I won't die of hunger any time soon…"

A kiss placed on Maggie's neck made her shiver with pleasure. Aaron had never been so tender or attentive, even in the early days of their marriage.

"You spoil me too much," Jason said. "I'm going to become so fat the horses won't let me ride them."

Maggie laughed freely as she turned around in Jason's arms to face her. She caressed Jason's soft cheek and stared deeply into her clear, blue eyes.

"We have time until that day comes, my love. After months of eating my cooking, you haven't gained an ounce. Come on. Let's have something to eat, and we'll talk of these trivialities after you've recovered your strength."

Jason yielded to Maggie's wisdom. She had left very early that morning to visit the shepherd of the western pastures and take him supplies. Unravelling herself from Maggie's warmth, she sat down on a chair at the table while Maggie started filling two plates with grilled mutton and potatoes.

"Any problems with Henry?"

"No. But I don't think he'll stay next year. Manual labour is hard to find, and I'm wondering if we shouldn't hire mulattos instead of whites."

Maggie swallowed her food before commenting. "I'm not sure they're trustworthy."

"Willowra is yours, so it's your choice, Maggie. It was just a suggestion."

She scrutinized Jason for a long moment. No bitterness or insulted pride. It truly was just an idea, not a desire to force her decision or run things. Despite what her friends thought, Jason had never tried to take over Willowra.

"People in town are starting to gossip."

Jason, surprised that Maggie had changed the subject, took a moment before understanding what she was referring to. She frowned and tried to hide the anxiety pumping through her. How would Maggie deal with the gossip?

Maggie stared at Jason, who looked back at her silently. She saw how tense she was. Her jawbone was jutting out, her fists clenched so hard her knuckles were white, her blue eyes afraid. Maggie shook her head and put her hand on Jason's, forcing her to relax.

"Haven't you understood by now that I don't give a fig about gossip, Jason? Having you here by my side is the most beautiful thing that has ever happened to me. Look at me. Do you have the impression that I'm miserable and upset?"

Jason, unable to say a word, shook her head. She wanted to believe Maggie, to be reassured, but old fears rose in her.

Maggie caressed Jason's cheek. "Jason," she asked in a husky voice. "Will you marry me?"

Jason's mouth fell open and closed again without making a sound. Her blue eyes opened as wide as possible, as if to hear better. Maggie's proposal had shocked her.

"I am aware that you're not one for words, Jason, but I'd like to have an answer. A simple yes or no will do," Maggie teased.

Jason cleared her throat, took a deep breath, and cleared her throat again, as tears rolled down her face. She jumped into Maggie's arms. "Yes. If you'll have me."

Maggie stroked Jason's soft hair as she gently squeezed this crying woman in her arms. She had hoped for a "yes," but not to make her cry. At that moment, Maggie understood what this all meant to Jason: her unequivocal acceptance of her for who she was. Entirely. She silently rocked the love of her life, whispering sweet words in her ear, words she had never before uttered.

❖

"If you won't marry us, Father, we'll find another pastor!"

Reverend Andrew stared at the couple standing before him. He certainly knew enough about Maggie to believe she would make good on her threat. She had inherited her father's strong character; he remembered the countless times over the years he had argued with

Ralph on various subjects. He studied the man standing next to Maggie, who hadn't said a word since their arrival.

Reverend Andrew had heard the rumours without paying them much mind. Wasn't he the one who had personally asked Jason to stay on and help Maggie? He'd helped her all right, right into her bed! For the pastor had no doubt that they had already sinned—the marriage would be nothing but a formality. He was incensed, but he wasn't stupid. If they married elsewhere, he could say good-bye to the donations Maggie made to his church. Why couldn't she see that this enterprising pauper was manipulating her? "Love is blind," a little voice in his head reminded him.

The father observed the couple more closely, especially the way Jason looked at Maggie. Was he really in love then?

Defeated, Reverend Andrew gave in with a sigh. "Okay. I'll marry you, but not until next month."

Andrew raised his hand to stop the argument forming on Maggie's lips.

She closed her mouth.

"I want a proper grieving period of at least six months between Aaron's burial and your marriage."

"So be it," Maggie murmured before turning away.

Jason simply nodded before following her future wife out of the church. They would be married next month. She forgot the pastor's dissatisfaction and the gossip that the announcement of their marriage was bound to spark, and a huge smile came to her lips. She was going to marry the woman she loved, and this would be the happiest day of her life.

"Father Andrew's attitude didn't seem to upset you," Maggie, surprised, said once they stepped outside.

"He's going to marry us, whether he's happy about it or not. It's the only thing that counts. The rest doesn't matter."

CHAPTER TWENTY-TWO

Norseman, Western Australia, 1924

On this Sunday morning, after having shaken hands with their acquaintances, Jason led Maggie into the church. Maggie insisted on following this ritual, even if Jason had made it very clear that God and she didn't get along particularly well. And her feelings of doubt had only grown stronger because of Father Andrew's attitude toward their marriage several months earlier. Jason was still angry that they'd had to threaten to go elsewhere to convince him to marry them. Every time they set foot in the church, she thought of that scene. So when Father Andrew approached her before they entered the church saying he wanted to have a word, she was extremely surprised.

"Maggie, I'll catch up with you."

Although curious, Maggie went inside the church alone and took their usual spot. From where she was sitting, she could see Jason and the reverend exchange a few words before Jason came in and Father Andrew strolled to the pulpit to conduct the service. Maggie gave Jason a questioning look.

"He wants to see me after church. Don't ask. I don't know why."

Maggie nodded, enjoying the fact that they understood each other without having to exchange a word. This connection had existed since they first met but had strengthened with time. They had been married six months now, and she had never felt so happy and complete. Even the people who had most opposed their marriage, those who had accused Jason of being an opportunist, had changed their minds. Their mutual happiness was so obvious people couldn't help but smile at it. Yes, Jason was indeed her Mr. Right, as Mary had said.

After services, while everybody started to file out of the church, Jason and Maggie stayed behind.

People in the congregation made the usual comments.

"What a sermon!"

"To imply that we neglect our children?"

"Does he think we don't love them?"

Maggie looked tenderly at Jason, smiling.

"I'll wait for you at Mary's. Don't hurry. Given Father Andrew's sermon, we'll probably have a lot to talk about. But if you want to join in, I'm sure my girlfriends would love to hear a man's point of view."

Maggie's eyes were sparkling with humour. Jason couldn't stop from giving her a quick peck on her cheek and whispering in her ear, "You're the one I want to have a conversation with…but one without words."

Maggie went scarlet red. She gave Jason a look of outrage and seemed about to answer back when someone behind her cleared his throat. Father Andrew, standing at the end of the pew, glanced at Maggie, then at Jason. He couldn't have any idea what they were up to but seemed too preoccupied, probably with what he wanted to discuss with Jason, to care about Maggie's blushing face.

Maggie skedaddled out of there before he could ask any embarrassing questions.

"You wanted to speak with me, Pastor."

"Let's have a seat."

Andrew pointed to the nearest bench. "What did you think of my sermon, Jason?"

Not understanding what the pastor was getting at, Jason took her time answering.

"I thought it was good."

"But…"

Jason sighed. "But I don't have any children, and according to what I know about this community, not many people must feel concerned about what you said. I haven't noticed any neglected or abused children since I've come here. A few farmhand families let their kids run around unsupervised, but nothing worse than I've seen other places. As for children born out of wedlock, I'm too new here to know if there are any."

"And you don't listen to gossip."

"Nope. And Willowra's too isolated."

The reverend passed his hand through his thinning hair. "Listen, Jason. I think I misjudged you from the beginning. I'm not blind, and I can see the joy on Margaret's face. My hurt pride prevented me from accepting what was obvious. I've spent a good amount of time reflecting these last months. You would have stayed even if I hadn't asked you. Isn't that so?"

Jason nodded, wondering what the pastor was getting at.

Andrew took a deep breath. "I suppose you know Margaret is barren. Aaron wasn't very discreet…"

Jason nodded again, keeping her eyes riveted on the pastor.

"Have you considered adoption? I know Aaron was against it but—"

"We have thought about it."

Growing visibly more uncomfortable, Reverend Andrew took his courage in his hands.

"I know you've been married for only six months, but the parish has taken in a little three-year-old boy, whose mother died last Thursday. The Widow Johanson is taking care of him for the moment, but we're going to have to place him in an orphanage if nobody wants him."

"His father?"

"Is dead as well. He never acknowledged the child but spoke of him in private to me after he was born. It would show true Christian charity if you agreed to take care of the little one."

Jason screwed up her eyes. Something told her the pastor wasn't being entirely honest. "I'm not against the idea, Father, and I think I can convince Maggie…"

The reverend gave a sigh of relief.

"But I want the whole truth."

The pastor hesitated. In the past year that he had observed this man, he had seen him act with nothing but honesty, courage, and goodness. If he believed what the members of the parish said about him, Jason McKellig was never drunk, rude, or aggressive. And he never cheated on his wife. There was no doubt about this man's integrity. A child adopted by Maggie and Jason would be cherished and well-treated.

"John Aaron Berkel is the son of Mathilda Berkel and Aaron Sterling."

Jason opened his eyes wide in surprise. Maggie's husband had fathered a child out of wedlock.

"Both parties have confirmed it. Mathilda grew depressed after Aaron's death. She'd lost her son's father, but also an important financial support. As her illness had prevented her from working these last months, Christian charity looked out for the welfare of her and the child. I know Aaron never told Maggie about it, but I thought it would be a good thing if…"

Father Andrew stopped, overcome by his doubts again. Could a woman agree to raise her dead husband's illegitimate child? Faced with Jason's silence, he added, "Perhaps it would be better not to tell Maggie who the little guy's father was."

"Can I see the boy?"

Pastor Andrew couldn't repress his smile. That Jason wanted to see the child was a good sign. "Of course! Mrs. Johanson, please bring little John in here."

Jason gave the pastor, who was smiling, a quizzical stare.

"I'm an optimist. You're going to love the wee lad. You'll see."

Jason recognised the grey-haired woman who came in as the Sunday-morning organist but hadn't known her name until today. The Widow Johanson was holding the hand of a little boy, dressed in clothes far too big for him and staring with great interest at Jason. What could the pastor have told him? Only when the widow brought the boy all the way over to Jason did she realize little John had tears in his eyes. She automatically crouched down so as not to intimidate the child.

"Hello, John. My name is Jason," she said in a gentle voice, offering her hand to the little boy.

John hesitated in front of this stranger, but the man's kind smile overcame his reluctance. He put his hand in the stranger's big, callused one and shook it like his mother had taught him.

"Hello, sir," he politely said when the widow tapped him on the shoulder.

The tiny boy's barely veiled distress broke Jason's heart. Could this be the chance for Maggie and her to finally have a family? What did it matter that the child wasn't a baby? A child was a child, and Maggie would make a wonderful mother. But would she make a good enough father? *I can always try. Anything would certainly be better than an orphanage.*

"My wife and I have a sheep station outside of town. Would you like to come live with us?" she heard herself say to this little boy who hadn't taken his eyes off her.

Before the child had time to understand what Jason had just said, the Widow Johanson answered for him. "But of course he would be happy to live in a place with lots of sheep and horses. Isn't that right, John? He loves animals."

Jason stood up and watched the child, who had lowered his head as if to hide his silent tears. She had trouble suppressing an urge to grab the Widow Johanson and shake her until she understood that this child was terrified. Jason was surprised to see how strong her instinct to protect John was.

"Does he have any belongings?"

"A bag. I'll go fetch it," the Widow Johanson replied quickly.

As soon as she walked away, Father Andrew said, "You have to forgive her. Young children at her age...But for Maggie and you—"

"I still haven't made a decision, Pastor," Jason said. "But don't worry. We will take good care of John."

"I don't doubt it at all."

Wasting no time, Jason grabbed the bundle of belongings the widow had brought him and took the silently crying little boy by the hand. After a last good-bye, they walked down the church's centre aisle to the door.

Jason didn't know how she would announce to Maggie that John was her late husband's son, but she would tell her the truth as soon as she could. From the beginning, their relationship had been based on trust, and it would stay that way. As soon as she reached the wagon, she threw the boy's bundle into the back and hoisted John up onto the driver's seat before climbing up next to him.

The child was terribly scared. He couldn't begin to understand all the drastic changes that had occurred in his life over the last few days. This wasn't the first time he'd ridden in a wagon, but he'd always been placed in the back.

"You want to drive?" Jason asked, pointing to the reins.

John opened his eyes wide, surprised. The man named Jason was going to let him drive the wagon? He wiped away his tears with the back of his sleeve and grinned a little.

"Go on. I'm going to show you how to do it."

Jason pointed to the space between his legs. John quickly went there, and Jason put the reins in his hands, and then her hands over them. "You shake the rein with a sharp snap, and you call out, 'Giddyup.'"

The two horses immediately responded and started moving forward. John, all smiles, kept repeating "giddyup" and shaking his hands. Luckily the harnessed team, used to Jason, didn't respond to John's promptings to go faster.

"Pull to the left, John. Like that. That's right. Now jerk both reins back to stop them. Very good! You're a born driver, I'd say."

The proud look on the child's face warmed Jason's heart. Placing a hand on his shoulder, she spoke to him kindly. "I'm going to get Maggie, my wife, and then we will all go together to your new house. Okay?"

John nodded.

"I won't be long. Wait for me and don't touch anything."

Jason jumped down from the wagon. Without losing any time, she walked into the house and was greeted, like every Sunday, by Rebecca. "Mr. McKellig. What a nice surprise! I'm so happy to see you again."

Jason held back an annoyed sigh, remembering the girl's adolescence. Despite the fact that Jason was now married, Rebecca still hadn't given up and continued to flirt with her every Sunday.

"G'day, Rebecca. Could you please go tell Maggie that I'm waiting for her by the wagon?" Jason immediately turned around to leave again.

Rebecca quit smiling. Jason wouldn't be visiting her mother and her friends today. "Mr. McKellig, my mother and her friends expected you to join them for a cup of tea."

Although she was a nonviolent person, Jason would have liked to strangle the girl. When was this stuck-up child going to accept her marriage with Maggie?

"I can't, Rebecca. Please let my wife know," Jason answered, emphasizing the word "wife."

Jason turned around. A teenage girl's obsessions weren't her problem. What interested her was the little boy watching her with huge eyes as she returned to the wagon.

"How are you doing, son? You see. I was quick. Now, will Maggie hurry too? I don't know. When a woman is chatting with her girlfriends, they often forget the time."

If Maggie heard her playing at being "the man of the house," she would really give it to Jason. In a softer tone, she added, whispering in John's ear, "Of course you should never point it out to her, little buddy. Otherwise, no dessert for us."

John stared at this adult, wondering if he had correctly understood. Could adults also be made to go without dessert? The man with the soft and gentle voice was very kind.

"Do you want to get a closer look at the horses? Come here, and I'll help you get down," Jason offered when John nodded yes.

Jason took John in her arms but, contrary to what John probably expected, didn't put him on the ground. He locked his arm around Jason's neck and settled himself in comfortably against her.

Ten minutes later, Maggie found them petting the horses. She stopped immediately at the sight of this scene, staring and letting her mouth hang open. Who was this little boy in her husband's arms? Jason, catching sight of her, broke into a beaming smile. While she continued to softly speak to John, she headed over to Maggie.

"John, this is Maggie—my wife and your new mum."

"Maggie, this is John, our son. He is three years old and is a very good boy. Isn't that right, John?"

John immediately understood what Jason expected of him and held out his hand. "G'day, ma'am."

Although shocked by what was taking place, Maggie was clear-headed enough to shake the little hand held out to her. "G'day, John. Welcome."

Maggie didn't understand what was going on, but she supposed Jason would explain it all later, when they were alone. She threw a questioning look at her.

"Later," Jason said, kissing her on the cheek.

❖

Night had just fallen, chasing away the day's stifling heat, when Maggie walked into the kitchen.

"Is he asleep?"

"Yes, but it wasn't easy. He was exhausted yet overexcited after discovering Willowra. I thought he'd never slow down."

Maggie gratefully took the cup of tea Jason held out for her. She took a long drink before sitting down at the table, tired from the day's events. She had many questions, and it was time for Jason to do the talking.

"So?"

Jason softly sighed. She had spent the whole trip back and all afternoon wondering how to break things to Maggie. Nothing had come to her. She had no solutions.

"Reverend Andrew asked me if we were considering adoption, and when I said yes, he had John come see us. His mother died last Thursday, and if we hadn't accepted him, he would have been sent to the orphanage. So I took him by the hand and put him in the wagon."

Jason stopped herself. She could practically see the wheels and gears turning in Maggie's head. If she thought she could get away without saying anything, she was wrong.

A small smile spread on Maggie's lips, and she rested her chin on her right hand.

"You think I don't know you after more than a year? Go on, my love. Explain it all to me," Maggie said with an enticing tone.

"You're not going to like what you hear, but you should know that little John isn't to blame."

Maggie frowned. Why would she be upset with a three-year-old child? She was so curious she would have liked to shake Jason to make her spit it out, but she knew her husband well enough to realize she had to be patient.

"I'm waiting. I won't budge until you've said what you need to say."

"John is the natural son of your deceased husband."

Maggie felt like she might faint. Jason was instantly by her side, her arm around Maggie's shoulders.

"I had to tell you, Maggie, but I didn't want it to be such a shock." Jason caressed her cheek with such tenderness. "I'm sorry. Maybe I shouldn't have accepted…"

Maggie grabbed her husband's callused hand and kissed her palm before kissing her lips, stopping her from uttering more unnecessary apologies.

"You did the right thing. John's place is in Willowra. Not in an orphanage. I was just caught unprepared. I understand now why Aaron was constantly throwing in my face the fact that I couldn't have a child. I was so blind when it came to him. He had a child, a mistress, and I didn't suspect a thing. I was so naive…"

Tears silently ran down Maggie's cheeks, and Jason pulled her tightly against her. They stayed in each other's arms until Maggie calmed down.

"We have a son now, and you're a dad. How does it feel?' Maggie asked, finally overcoming her emotions.

"As long as he doesn't ask me how to use the implement I'm missing…"

"The time will come," Maggie said, while Jason blushed.

"Thank goodness I have a little while before that happens."

CHAPTER TWENTY-THREE

Kalgoorlie, Western Australia, 1925

Jason felt a furtive tug on her jacket, immediately bringing back a distant memory. Instinctively, and without taking the time to turn around, she threw her arm back and grabbed the stealthy hand that was busy picking her pocket. A sharp cry of pain. Jason didn't need to look. She could tell from the tiny hand and voice that the pickpocket was a child.

The youngster squirmed, trying to break free from the firm hold on its wrist and the punishment that would inevitably follow. He knew that every time he was caught, a shower of punches was waiting. But hunger was stronger than the fear of correction, and so he continued to plunder. Now the child knew it was over. The man's hold was too strong to escape, so he stopped fighting and stared the man directly in the eye, without pleading or whimpering.

Jason took a long, hard look at the ragamuffin standing in front of her. The urchin couldn't have been more than five or six. Dirty, with long strawberry-blond hair full of nasty tangles that were turning into dreadlocks, wearing tattered, torn clothing a few sizes too big and stiff with filth, the little one stared right back at Jason with its large blue eyes. Tears started to slowly form in the ragamuffin's eyes and run down its dirty cheeks, leaving furrows through the dirt. Gripping the overly thin arm, Jason perceived that it was trembling. She should have given it a good walloping, as was expected, but she hadn't forgotten about her own years of going on an empty stomach after her mother had died. She let go.

Eyes filled with bewilderment, the youngster took off as fast as his legs would allow, and once having reached the parked wagons, he turned around to observe the man who hadn't been violent. The man was staring back. *This is my lucky day,* the child thought before slipping between the wagons and wiping off the dirt from his cheeks.

"You shouldn't have let him go. He's just going to do it again. These little tramps never stop," a man who had watched the whole scene commented.

"And what would you have me do? Give him a thrashing? Drag him to the police?"

Jason's anger surprised the man, who felt these little pilferers who lived off honest people should be gotten rid of once and for all. No matter what means were used, they had to disappear. However, something in Jason's demeanour made him realise it was better to keep his thoughts to himself. He wordlessly disappeared into the crowd.

An hour later, Jason was leaning on a temporary counter with three acquaintances—Joe, Weasel, and Ted—peacefully sipping her beer, the incident already forgotten.

"How's family life treating you, Jason?" Joe, a swaggie whom Jason had met up with a number of times during her years as a swagman, asked.

Jason beamed. "I'm a happy man, Joe. Got a wonderful wife and the most beautiful son in the world. What else could I want? And if you come for shearing season, I'll introduce them all to you."

"You hiring?"

"Yep. For the whole shear. I pay twenty shillings per a hundred fleeces. I hire friends first. I've already seen you at work. You can shear what—150, 160 per day?"

Joe, holding his beer, smiled in agreement. He didn't dare tell him that since his back was hurting him, it would be a miracle if he could shear 140 in a day.

"And the food is excellent," Weasel added. "I told you, Joe. After Jason stopped swagging he didn't forget his friends. And then, if a woman like his made sheep eyes at me, I'd leave this dog's life behind in a jiffy."

"What kind of woman would be mad enough to kiss an old swine like you, Weasel?" Ted said, mocking him.

All of them started laughing, for even Weasel knew Ted was right. He was too old now. Since his wife's death, over thirty years ago, he'd lost interest in the fair sex. But that didn't stop him from being happy for Jason, who was a good bloke.

"I'll come back to see your family for the next shear, Jason. Send them my regards. A toast to your wife and son." Weasel raised his pint, followed by all the others.

Jason smiled, although all this attention made her a little uncomfortable.

"Are you sure you want to head back this afternoon, Jason? You could stay on a day or two more."

"I finished my business yesterday, Weasel, and if I hadn't promised to see you and your friends at noon, I would have left this morning. I have three days' travelling time, and Maggie will worry if I linger much longer."

"She keeps him on a tight leash, mate," Weasel replied, giving Jason a slap on the back. "But I understand you. Come on. I'll take you back to your wagon. You hiring for lambing season this year?"

Weasel and Jason took a dirt side street behind the houses to avoid the Main Street crowds, who were in town for the Kalgoorlie fair. Jason could have gone to a hotel, but habit and the wish to spend time with her swaggie friends had won over Maggie's recommendations.

"Yes, but only folk who aren't afraid of hard work. You interested?"

"Maybe, for the docking and branding, but I don't have enough teeth left to castrate properly."

Jason slowed for a moment. She didn't like castrating young lambs with her teeth. The smell of blood everywhere disgusted her. Luckily, it paid well, so it wasn't too difficult to find willing men for the job. "That works for me."

Muted noises and the sound of voices coming from a nearby alleyway attracted their attention. "What the…?"

"I don't know, but let's go see."

Jason agreed. Like Weasel, she remembered the misadventures that swagmen often suffered because people more fortunate than they considered themselves superior. On several occasions, she'd owed her life to a passerby who appeared suddenly, enabling her to flee. Some people saw swagmen as the dregs of society and didn't hesitate to treat them accordingly.

Three men were in the alleyway, but bizarrely, they didn't seem to be fighting. However, they sounded angry. It wasn't until one of the men strode over to the wall and kicked what looked like a pile of clothing that Jason understood. Grabbing Weasel by the arm, she approached them. "Come on. They're beating up a child!"

Weasel then saw what was happening. He grew so angry, despite his age, that he rushed the man who'd kicked the kid, while Jason ran between the youngster and the other men.

"You're up for a fight? Have the courage to face someone your own size—cowards!"

"He's just a petty thief," grumbled the man whom Weasel had thrown to the ground. "If nobody does anything, he's gonna grow up to become a murderer."

Although the light was dim, Jason recognised the man who'd criticised her for letting the child go. Doubt suddenly overcame Jason. Heart pounding, she turned to the shape hunched over against the wall and crouched. Carefully lowering the child's arms, she saw the bloodied face of the young pickpocket.

"You rotten scum!" she cried, standing back up and turning around toward the men. "I hope this happens to one of your children. Three adults against a five-year-old. That's nothing but pure cowardice!"

Jason clenched her fists and stared each man in the eye. "I'm ready. Who has the courage to face someone their size, someone who knows how to defend themself?"

The two men who hadn't moved since the beginning of the altercation exchanged a look and wordlessly started backing up. The other man, seeing his friends leave, lost his superior air. As Jason slowly walked toward him, the third man backed up as well. After a few more steps, he turned around and ran away.

Weasel spit in his direction. "Coward. He isn't worth the clothes on his back."

Jason didn't answer. She kneeled next to the motionless shape, caressing its dirty face before placing her finger on the side of its fragile neck.

"Did they kill him?"

"Not yet. But we have to find a doctor."

Jason, carrying the feather-light body in her arms, left the alleyway, followed by Weasel, heading for Main Street. After having asked several passersby, they found the office of the doctor, who immediately started taking care of the youngster while Jason and Weasel waited in the hallway.

"I don't know that we're doing this kid a favour," Weasel said.

"What do you mean by that?"

"If the doctor gets him back on his feet, he's going to return to the street and end up dead somewhere. You know it as well as I do."

"Not if I take him with me."

Surprised, Weasel stared at Jason. "You wanna take him back home?"

Jason thought for a moment about the words she'd just uttered. She and Maggie had spoken about adopting other children if they had the opportunity, so why not this one? It wouldn't be easy. The kid seemed to have one helluva personality; he was a fighter. Jason thought about little John. They were about the same age and could play together. And Maggie would love having another little one. Jason smiled. Yes. Maggie would love it.

"If he makes it, yes. I'm going to take him back to Willowra."

At that moment the office door opened, and the young doctor appeared. "A broken arm and countless bruises, but she'll survive."

"She?" Weasel asked.

"A little girl who would be quite pretty if she had someone to take care of her. Victoria is very intelligent. I suppose she was caught stealing again."

The doctor sighed when Jason nodded and said, "You know her?"

"Since her father died, I've been giving her something to eat every now and then. The pastor has tried to place her with a family, but she always runs away. Nobody in Kalgoorlie wants anything to do with her now."

"I can take her in. My wife and I have a sheep station three days from here. I came for the fair and am leaving today. Do you think Victoria can make the trip?"

The doctor observed Jason. A man in the prime of his life, robust, who wouldn't let anyone pull the wool over his eyes. One of his professors used to say that the eyes mirrored the soul, that you could read the truth in the eyes of a man if you knew how to. In the eyes of the man facing him, the doctor saw honesty and kindness. Yes, this man would take good care of Victoria.

"She can travel if you have a wagon."

"Then we can leave as soon as I've informed the person in charge that she's coming with me. Can you watch her in the meantime?"

"Go get your wagon, and I'll let the pastor know that you've taken her. Believe me, everyone here will be relieved, Mister...?"

"Jason McKellig. I live on the Willowra homestead, near Norseman...if somebody wants to check."

"No one's going to miss her. You can let me know how she's doing at the next fair. That's all I ask."

"No problem. I'll bring the wagon 'round in five minutes. The horses are already hitched."

❖

Jason once again glanced at the sleeping shape behind her. They were bound to arrive at the house later that morning. The child hadn't said a word during their entire three days of travelling. She seemed just happy to eat and sleep. Despite the shaky terrain as she rode in the back of the wagon, she hadn't even softly moaned. Victoria must have suffered, at least during the hardest jolts.

During the different breaks they had taken to eat, Jason had told her about Maggie, John, and the farm. Victoria had silently listened to everything, her huge blue eyes wide open. Jason knew it would take time and patience to entice this terrified but courageous little girl out of her shell. And it would also take a lot of love...but Jason trusted Maggie for that.

When Jason finally reached the familiar eucalyptus tree that marked the entrance to the property, she smiled. Home. Finally. She kept the horses from trotting, though, so the ride wouldn't be too bumpy and painful for Victoria. Jason would be in Maggie's arms in just a half hour. They had been separated for only ten days, but that was too many. The first year of their marriage, they had hired a roustabout to take care of things on the station so they could attend the fair together. But since John had come into their lives, that was no longer an option. Now that John had grown, perhaps next year they would attend the fair, all four of them, together.

When Jason stopped the wagon in front of the house, Maggie rushed into her arms. Jason lifted her from the ground as Maggie kissed her and started laughing.

"Papa, Papa!"

Jason put Maggie down and picked up little John. As she kissed him and swung him around, she was certain his joyful laughter was the greatest gift possible.

"Who's that?' John asked, pointing to the back of the wagon.

With her son in her arms, Jason walked over to the wagon and the child. Only the top of her body was higher than the side of the wagon. Maggie looked questioningly at her.

"May I introduce you to Victoria? Victoria, this is John and

Maggie. I spoke to you about them. Come on. Let's get down and say hello to your new family.

"I'll explain later," Jason whispered into Maggie's ear.

John wiggled in Jason's arms. He wanted to be set down on the ground to welcome this intruder. But once down, he immediately placed himself between his two parents to mark his territory.

Victoria climbed out of the wagon with some trouble. When Maggie saw her arm in a sling and her filthy disgusting clothing, she retched involuntarily and glanced accusingly at Jason.

"I decided to take her with me just when I was leaving, so I didn't have time to bathe her or get her clean clothing," Jason said apologetically.

Maggie glared meaningfully at Jason before approaching the little girl with a smile. "Young lady. I think a bath and clean clothes are in order. Then we can have something to eat."

Victoria didn't like baths. The cold water made her teeth chatter. And then you had to scrub your skin so hard it hurt. However, the idea of having something to eat made her happy. She could spend all day eating.

Maggie noticed the little girl's reaction and grinned more widely. "I figured Jason would be coming home soon, so I made a big leg of mutton with grilled potatoes and fresh bread. We have chocolate cake for dessert. John and Jason love chocolate. And you, Victoria. Do you like it?"

Chocolate cake? Victoria salivated nervously. She glanced at Jason, who was watching her. Contrary to what she'd expected, he hadn't hit her a single time during the entire ride.

"The cat got your tongue, Victoria? Don't you like chocolate cake?"

The woman was smiling kindly at her and didn't seem surprised or annoyed with her.

"Aye, ma'am. I do," Victoria whispered.

The woman's smile grew even brighter as she crouched down to face her.

"Since you're going to live with us, you can call me Maggie or Mummy, but not ma'am. Okay?"

Victoria couldn't understand what was happening, but she still nodded.

"Good. A bath then. John, can you go get us a towel and soap? John!"

John shook himself out of his reverie and hurried inside the house.

"There's hot water on the stove, Jason. It was for you. Would you pour it into the bathtub?"

Jason nodded with a complicit smile and winked at Maggie. "I'll wash up in the shed while you take care of her."

Maggie's eyes, filled with days of unquenched desire, immediately sparked a fire in Jason. She swallowed with difficulty, breathless. If the children hadn't been there, Jason would have taken Maggie straight to their bedroom. To hide her desire, Jason removed her hat and brushed her trembling fingers through her hair before straightening her shoulders. With a determined step, she walked to the kitchen as Maggie chuckled. God, she loved this woman! They didn't need words to understand one another.

CHAPTER TWENTY-FOUR

Willowra, Western Australia, 1926

John's brown eyes were brimming with frustration as he glared at his sister. He didn't dare try to grab back his toy because if they ended up fighting, Victoria would have the upper hand and get what she wanted—she always did. How he hated girls! Since she'd arrived, he'd had nothing but problems, but as Victoria was very sly, Maggie and Jason never saw a thing. John curled up his hands into fists as he tried to hold back his tears. First, because, well, he didn't understand why this girl never cried. Weren't girls supposed to cry all the time? He'd seen that when he lived with his mummy; girls were always whining about this and that. But not this one. John took a step forward, making another attempt to retrieve his toy.

"Give it back, Victoria!"

Victoria hardly deigned to glance at this silly baby, who wasn't even as big as she was, and continued to play with her stick and string. This game was stupid, but it was out of the question to give it back to John. She teased him mischievously.

"What will you give me if I give it back?"

John hesitated. The last time it had cost him his helping of cake. His lips started to tremble with despair. After all, he had been here long before this girl arrived. He had an idea.

"If you don't give me back my toy, I'll tell Pa."

"You're a tattletale," Victoria spit out as she walked up to John threateningly.

But John had seen a glimmer of fear in his sister's eyes. He smirked, realising he had the advantage. "First of all, if you aren't a good girl, Pa will take you back to where he found you and leave you there."

John didn't know he was tapping into Victoria's worst fears when he spoke these words. She liked it here and didn't want to leave. Feeling cornered, she reacted in the way the street had taught her. She caught John by the midriff and tackled him. The violence of the impact landed them both on the hard, red-dirt ground. Now having the physical advantage, Victoria sat on her brother's torso and showered him with punches. John attempted to protect himself and fight back, but Victoria was too strong for him and, unlike John, she had learned to brawl; she could give and receive blows.

"Take it back," she ordered as she continued to hit him.

She didn't hear Jason hurrying over to them and only noticed Maggie once she was high in the air, plucked off John like a feather. When she saw the anger on their faces, any impulse to continue to fight left her. Deep down she knew that, tomorrow, Jason and Maggie would get rid of her...as all the others had.

"Can somebody explain to me what's going on here?" Jason was scolding both of them.

As Maggie helped John back on his feet and wiped the blood flowing from his nose, Jason put Victoria down on the ground but didn't let go of her arm.

"I'm waiting," Jason kept insisting.

"I have to take care of his nose."

Just when Maggie was about to lead John to the house, Jason stopped them and grabbed the little boy's arm. "Not before I know who started this fight."

John threw a glance at Victoria, but she just pinched her thin lips tight and stared at the ground. Deep down, John was ashamed. And what if Jason really sent her back where she came from? She was just a girl, but all the same, he wouldn't like to have to go back to live with the reverend.

"If neither one of you explains, both of you will be punished."

Jason ignored Maggie's look of shock. She had noticed the rising tension between the two children these past months but didn't know how to appease it.

"All right then. Both of you to bed without supper, and no dessert for a whole week. Now go wash up!"

As soon as Jason let go of Victoria's arm, she rushed to the barn, while Maggie led John into the kitchen. Seeing Jason hesitate as to whether she should follow their daughter, Maggie suggested, "Let her calm down. We'll get to the bottom of things later."

Jason nodded before following her inside. In the kitchen, Maggie set John on the edge of the table and grabbed clean linens. After serving herself a strong cup of tea, Jason sat down on the bench.

"Okay, young man. Let's see about this nose." Maggie tenderly cleaned John's swollen face.

He winced every time the cloth went over the cut on his cheek. Incapable of looking Maggie in the eye, he focused on the stove top and the cooking utensils hanging over the sink. Little by little, tears welled up in his eyes and ran down his cheeks.

Maggie, seeing the child's distress, lifted his head by his chin and stared deeply into his eyes so he couldn't look away from her. "What is it, John?"

He hesitated. What if they abandoned him as well? Tears sprang up even more abundantly. He was afraid now. He had been mean. Maggie had made him understand quite clearly that she didn't like mean children when they had hurt a baby chick one day. He had received his first spanking for it.

As Jason was about to get up and approach them, Maggie signalled her not to move.

"John?"

"I…don't…want to leave here." John sobbed. "I didn't intend to be…mean…"

"Who's talking about leaving?" Maggie softly asked as she caressed John's brown hair.

Surprised, he opened his eyes wide. "You're not going to put me in an orphanage because I was bad?"

"Who gave you that idea? Of course not!"

Reassured as to his future, John murmured in a small voice, "I told Victoria you were going to abandon her because she was mean…that's why she beat me up."

Maggie didn't have time to answer before Jason was already heading for the kitchen door. She sighed. Raising children wasn't as simple as it seemed. Especially children with a past as difficult as Victoria's. Jason adored the child so much, at times her love was too visible. They would have to have a talk about it.

❖

"Victoria," Jason called softly.

Going from the harsh late-afternoon light into the dark barn blinded her momentarily. Jason waited a moment for her eyes to adjust before searching everywhere. After a while, she finally found Victoria huddled in the darkest corner of the barn. Jason got down on all fours to crawl under an old, abandoned, wagon flatbed, where Victoria was hiding.

The little girl didn't even look up. Her arms wrapped around her knees, she squeezed them tighter. Tenderly, Jason stroked her soft, strawberry-blond hair, but Victoria didn't respond.

"John was wrong to say we were going to abandon you, Victoria. It's not true. You are our daughter, and we don't abandon our children."

Needing to determine if her father was telling the truth, Victoria studied his face. How would she be able to tell? She had been lied to so often before. But Jason had never told her a lie. Ever.

"When I decided to bring you home with me, I didn't intend to give up at the slightest problem. It isn't easy for any of us. Neither for you, because you have to follow new rules, nor for us, as we have to figure out your personality and get to know you. But I want something to be very clear, Victoria. Maggie and I love you, and we will never, ever abandon you. Not now, and not ever."

The little ball of energy that threw herself into Jason's arms, clinging to her, nearly made Jason fall backward. It was the first time Victoria had sought comfort in her arms. Jason hugged her tightly to her. Little by little, she relaxed, letting the tension of the last half hour fade away. She savoured this rare moment.

"We're not punished then?" Victoria's little voice piped up in her ear.

Jason stopped herself from chuckling. Luckily, Victoria couldn't see the grin on her face when she answered. "You're still punished for having fought, and on top of that, you have to apologise to John for starting things."

Victoria stiffened against her torso. While she was pulling back from Jason's hold, Jason added, "And John will apologise for what he said."

Victoria nodded. A little smile brightened her expression, and she once again huddled in Jason's arms.

❖

When Jason walked into their bedroom, like most evenings, Maggie was already in bed waiting for her. And like every evening,

Jason had forced herself not to do a slapdash job checking on the animals before joining Maggie in the intimacy of their bedroom. Since the children had joined the family, they no longer could make love whenever they felt like it.

Maggie watched Jason remove her clothing, then the bandage that hid and flattened her breasts before she slipped on a large night shirt. Watching the transformation of the woman who shared her life usually turned Maggie on, but not tonight. This evening, the conversation was likely to be unpleasant. She sighed and then braced herself to get on with it. "We have to talk, Jason."

As she lifted the sheet to get in next to Maggie, Jason frowned and felt frightened. Maggie saw the distress in Jason's bright eyes and cursed her own lack of tact. To soften her sharp tone, she smiled and caressed Jason's cheek with her fingertips. She should have known by now that Jason, with her own past history, would be afraid of rejection.

"It's about the children. Nothing else. I love you."

Jason let out a sigh of relief before slipping under the sheets. "Should I turn out the light?"

"No. Just lower it. I want to see your face."

Jason slowly twisted the screw on the paraffin lamp to dim the flame. When she turned around, Maggie was lying on her side, watching her fix the sheet over herself. Now facing her, Jason smiled at the woman who was the sunshine of her existence. "I'm listening."

"You have to be careful not to favour Victoria over John. Otherwise, John will end up being jealous of her, especially given that they already have problems between them."

Jason opened her eyes wide in surprise. *Favour Victoria?* "I don't favour her."

"You pay more attention to her. You prefer her to John."

Jason would have liked to challenge her words. She opened her mouth to deny them, but then she stopped herself. If she looked at things coldly, she had to recognise that Maggie was right. She spent more time with Victoria.

"Is it because John is the son of my deceased husband?" Maggie softly asked.

"No! Of course not! You know that. It's just that…"

"That what?"

"Victoria is more difficult. She needs to be put on the right track. Also, she needs affection, she needs love."

"John too, you know. He needs his pa."

"What do you mean by that?"

"It's not a problem right now. But when they're older, don't forget that you are the man of the family, and others will consider it odd if you are too affectionate with your children. Certain people could take things the wrong way. I know you have as much maternal love to give as I do, Jason, but in our situation, you have to be very careful."

"Maggie, these children need so much. What you're asking me to do just breaks my heart. If only we could live together openly."

Seeing the depth of Jason's distress in the dim light, Maggie was afraid her heart would explode with all the love that rushed into it, all the love she felt for this sensitive woman. When just the two of them had lived at Willowra, Jason could reveal her feminine side, but since they'd adopted children and become a family, things had to be different.

"You once told me that no one should ever know…"

Jason pulled Maggie into her arms and hugged her with all her might to forget the sacrifice she knew she had to keep making, no matter how painful. Her face buried in Maggie's long, curly hair, she confirmed, in a voice husky with emotion, "Nobody can know."

❖

The horse and rider were one entity on this flat plain. Apart from a few trees here and there and the hills shrouded in the haze of the heat out on the horizon, they marked the highest point among the goosefoots and other bushes. From time to time, mobs of kangaroo hurried away in leaps to distance themselves from the horseman who ignored them. The horse progressed at a regular trot in this seemingly endless monotonous landscape.

Although sweat was trickling down her forehead, neck, and back, Jason didn't mind. She was used to it and focused on her objective. She was at the end of making her rounds of the two herds kept the farthest to the north, when the sight of flying vultures attracted her attention. Strange. Perhaps it was only a dead kangaroo, but as it wouldn't take her much out of her way, and considering the carrion feeders' strange behaviour, she decided to loop around and have a look-see.

Although in a hurry to return to Maggie and the children after a few days of separation, Jason didn't want to force her mount if she hoped to make it home by sundown. Maggie would be happy to know there were no problems with the sheep, or the shepherds, or the dogs. She'd been worried about the mulatto men Jason had hired for the work.

Jason had spent time with pure aboriginals and mulattos when she was a swaggie and so didn't make the same assumptions or have the same prejudices as other farmers. At least aboriginals weren't nostalgic for cities and had no problem with solitude, even if they were glad to see her when she came to restock them with tea, tobacco, and cartridges for their rifles.

As she approached the spot where the vultures were headed, Jason became more intrigued. A kangaroo wouldn't die beneath a tree. She realised that; unconsciously, this detail had convinced her to deviate from her route home.

Jason's thoughts wandered as she approached the site. Tom, one of the keepers, had told her that his dog was starting to show signs of fatigue. This Queensland Blue Heeler was getting old, and they'd have to start looking into replacing him. Maybe one of the Kelpie pups born last month? Maybe. If one of them showed signs of the required instinct. Jason sighed. She didn't like to kill pups that hadn't inherited the instinct to herd sheep. Maggie knew it and often saved her from having to perform this difficult task, which was, however, necessary, so idle animals wouldn't overrun the ranch.

Jason could now make out the shape of a body propped against the tree, so she spurred her horse on, and it immediately started to gallop. After she dismounted, she realised she was too late to be able to do anything for this aboriginal woman. The birds and various insects had already begun their work several hours earlier. This woman must have dragged herself to this mulga tree to lie down in its shade and die in the night or early morning. As Jason was about to get back on her horse, a small wail coming from the woman's bundle stopped her. Was her imagination playing tricks on her? That cry…

Placing her horse's reins over a bush, Jason walked around the corpse and opened the blanket covering the bundle. The sight of a newborn child wriggling about brought tears to her eyes. She delicately touched the child's silky skin with her callused hands, making sure she wasn't seeing a mirage. The little boy squealed again before flailing his frail members. Without a moment's hesitation, Jason wrapped the baby in the blanket and took it in her arms. The baby must be dehydrated. Milk? The nearest ewes were too far off, but they had cows at home. Water? It would be better than nothing.

Controlling her hurried movements, she grabbed her water flask to pour a few drops into the baby's mouth. The baby seemed to be swallowing them eagerly but started crying, as the water from the flask was getting him wet. Jason, completely panicked, stopped pouring it. She had never cared for a baby. It was easy with Victoria and John. They could speak and express themselves, but with a newborn baby, Jason felt out of her depth. Maggie would know what to do, she was sure. Without waiting a second longer, she secured the baby against her torso with a blanket, got on her horse, and took off at a gallop.

When she arrived at Willowra and rushed into the courtyard, the horse was bathed in sweat, snorting and breathing heavily. Although sore from several hours of a fast ride with the baby in her arms, she dismounted lithely.

Maggie, alerted by all the noise, rushed out of the house. Seeing the state the horse was in, she immediately knew something was amiss. Even the children, who had followed her out of the house, obviously knew something wasn't right.

"Jason?"

"I found him next to his mother's corpse. He's starved and dehydrated."

Without quite understanding what Jason meant, Maggie grabbed the bundle Jason was handing over to her. When she pushed the top of the blanket aside, she almost choked. "Oh, good Lord. A baby!"

Victoria yelled, "Can we see him?"

The two children, filled with curiosity, surrounded Maggie, trying to see the baby.

"Later," Jason said. "Take care of my horse, both of you."

Obviously a little disappointed but proud of the responsibility he'd been given, John grabbed the reins Jason held out to him and led the animal to the stables. Victoria hurried to follow him.

"And make sure you don't bungle it up, you two!" Jason yelled after them. "I'll be coming later to check on things."

When she turned back around to Maggie, she had already gone. It didn't take Jason long to find her in the kitchen with the baby in her arms and a baby bottle already in her hand. This tableau moved Jason. Even if at first the baby needed encouragement to drink the milk, little by little its strength came back, and he suckled with more vigour. Maggie seemed very excited.

"So?"

"I found him next to his mother's corpse at the foot of a mulga tree near Crazy-man's Stump. Nobody was around who could give me any indication of her tribe or where they came from."

"He's ours then?" Maggie asked softly, her eyes filled with hope.

Jason frowned. "I suppose so."

A contented smile spread across Maggie's lips.

"Maggie, he's black. An aboriginal," Jason softly whispered.

"So? You think I'm blind?"

"I thought you were prejudiced against the aboriginals."

"He's only a baby, Jason…our baby."

"People will talk."

Maggie's dagger-filled look ended the conversation. Jason sighed. Yes, people would talk, and so? Why did she bring the baby back if not to take care of it? Maggie's immediate acceptance and possessive attitude simply surprised Jason a little. She hadn't reacted that way with the two elder children. Exhausted from this long day on horseback, Jason gave up trying to understand.

"I'm going to wash up," she said, heading for the indoor bathroom they had recently installed.

❖

As Ann served tea, Mary couldn't keep her eyes off her friend holding her black baby. Maggie was glowing. If she thought about it, since she had married Jason, Mary hadn't heard a single complaint from Maggie's lips. A far cry from her days with Aaron. But really, an aboriginal baby…When Maggie had arrived at church with the baby in her arms, Jason and the children filing in behind her, Mary had thought Pastor Andrew would fall over from the surprise. Completely shaken, he gave the most incoherent sermon. She would bet everything she had that, next Sunday, the sermon would be about some aboriginal lost sheep.

"Are you really going to adopt him?" Nelly asked with a pinched face.

"Naturally. Jason already went to see your husband about the papers." Maggie looked up at her friends. "Have you ever seen such an adorable baby?"

None of the women answered. They loved Maggie, but going as far as adopting a baby from those naked savages…

Ann spoke for the others when she asked, "And Jason is going to give him his name?"

Maggie frowned. She seemed only at that moment to notice her friends' disconcerted and disapproving air.

"What a silly question! Of course Jason will give him his name, exactly like the others. We've decided to call him Robert McKellig. Just because he's black doesn't make him any less an innocent baby. Would it have suited you better if we'd left him to die in the desert?"

Mary cleared her throat. "No. Of course not. But you know the reputation of those people. The orphanages charitably take them in, but no one would ever consider adopting one."

"Well then, let me tell you something, Mary Taylor. Not only are we planning to adopt him, but Father Andrew is going to baptise him, and when he's old enough, we will home-school him like our other two. He'll learn how to work on the sheep farm, and when the time comes that he wants his share of the property, he will have it. And if one of you ever again criticises his presence among us, I regret to have to say this, but I swear before God, that will be the last time I set foot in this house."

Maggie's golden eyes sparkled with flames of anger. She hugged Robert against her and started to get up to leave.

"Stay, Maggie." Mary stopped her. "You're right. We haven't been very charitable. We're just concerned about you and your family. I hope the presence of this child won't ruin your happiness. Men, even the best of them, sometimes regret their actions."

Maggie got ahold of herself and scrutinised her friend's face. She seemed sincere.

"Jason isn't that type of man. He—"

At that moment the door opened, and Jason walked in with the two other children, whose eyes were instantly glued to the plate of cakes. Despite their clear longing to have one, neither child approached the plate. The only time they had done so, they'd both been deprived of dessert for a week. Victoria and John quietly waited for the mistress of the house to invite them to have one.

Mary waited for Maggie's discreet approval before holding out the plate to the children, who didn't have to be asked twice. Then Jason took one.

"May Robert also have a biscuit, Mummy?' John asked, his mouth full.

Before Maggie could answer, Jason reminded her son of his good manners. "Son, it's rude to speak with your mouth full."

John's big, dark eyes reflected his dismay. He had forgotten. Red-faced, he lowered his head.

"Babies don't eat biscuits," Maggie quietly answered.

Victoria conscientiously swallowed what she had in her mouth before she asked, "If Robert doesn't want his biscuit, can I have it?"

Maggie frowned, and Victoria corrected herself. "For John and me, course. We'll share it."

Her expression was so innocent that Maggie had to hold back a chuckle. From the corner of her eye, she saw her friends restraining their mirth with a sip of tea or by clearing their throats.

Maggie exchanged a look with Jason, who said, "All right, children. Say thank you and good-bye. I need you to help finish loading the wagon."

A bit of chaos fell upon the group as the children made their rounds to say good-bye. The silence that followed seemed unreal.

"Do you want me to take care of Robert so you can finish your tea?" Jason proposed.

Maggie hesitated. She didn't want to get rid of the baby just to make her friends happy, but she wanted to show her friends that Jason cherished Robert as much as she did. Making sure not to wake the infant, she handed him to Jason, whose face broke open into a beaming smile once she held the sleeping baby. She nodded good-bye to the others and left.

"Little Victoria has a sharp wit."

Maggie rolled her eyes at Nelly's comment. If only she could be a little less quick.

"She doesn't miss a beat. We always have to be very careful about what we say around her. Nothing escapes her."

"And how's John getting along?"

Maggie took a sip of tea to give herself a moment of reflection before answering. "Until last week I would have said things were difficult. But the situation seems to have changed, and several times this last week he and Victoria have joined forces and taken each other's side. I don't know whether we should be happy or worry about it."

Mary burst out in laughter. "It seems to me that you should worry, especially if Victoria is taking the lead. This young lady is going to be a handful, believe me."

"I'm afraid I do believe you, Mary, and that's what scares me."

CHAPTER TWENTY-FIVE

Norseman, Western Australia, 1930

Leaning on the hotel bar, Jason peacefully sipped her beer. Her calm demeanour hid her distress. What was she going to tell Maggie? The price of wool had dropped to only a quarter of what it had been the previous season, and their buyer wasn't even sure about taking their future stock. How had all this happened? Because on the other side of the world, in America, the stock market crashed? That's what she was told. That's what caused this disaster. But Jason didn't understand. What did America have to do with the price of wool?

"You don't look happy, mate."

Jason took a sip from her beer. True to form, Ben, the hotel owner, was standing behind the bar.

"Not a lot of customers today," Jason commented, pointing to the room.

Ben sighed. "You haven't been here much since you've had the kids. It's been this way for months. Prices have gone up and wages have gone down. A lot of people are making their own rotgut."

"How come your prices and the grocers' prices have gone up, but not wool?" Jason asked, bitterly. "What are we going to live on? With the prices I'm being offered for wool, I can't decently pay my shearers. Ben, no one's going to want to work for me."

Surprised, Ben stared at the man sitting at the bar. What planet was Jason living on? Hadn't he seen what had happened lately? He was about to answer sarcastically, but he remembered that Willowra was isolated, and if his information was correct, they still hadn't invested in a wireless. They weren't aware of anything.

"You won't have any problems hiring people for a quarter of your regular rate. I wouldn't be surprised if some of them agree to work just for food and board."

Jason raised a questioning eyebrow.

"Haven't you seen all the...vagrants? I won't say swaggie out of respect for you and your friends, Jason. We're in an economic crisis, mate. More people aren't dying of hunger because of the soup kitchens organized by churches everywhere. There's no work anymore, anywhere, no matter whether it's in Australia or Europe. Haven't you read the papers?"

Jason shook her head no. "Too much work prepping for shearing season. We did see more people come through than usual at Willowra, but apart from those of the old brigade, few people venture all the way out to Nullarbor."

"You're one of the lucky ones."

"Pardon me?" Jason almost choked.

"To have Willowra. At least you won't go starving."

Jason gasped. Slowly, the pieces of the puzzle started to come together in her mind. The vagrants with desperate looks on their faces, the sallow-looking women, the children...the price of wool, Pastor Andrew's sermon. How could she have been so self-centred and blind?

"You'll put the beer on my bill?"

Ben hesitated and cleared his throat. "I'm sorry, Jason, but I'd rather you paid...your whole bill..."

Without complaint, Jason did as he asked, refusing to think about the meagre amount of money she had left. She should have anticipated. How could she explain to Maggie that she had lacked good judgment, that she hadn't been a good husband and couldn't provide for her wife and children?

During the three-hour journey back to Willowra, Jason tried to find a solution. Sell a part of the livestock? For a miserly price? Never. Sell one of her most beautiful merino billy goats to O'Connor? He had offered a very good price last year, but now...No solution. She had to face Maggie.

"The children are asleep. Tell me what's going on."

Maggie, her hands on her hips, was standing next to Jason. That she came out to find her in the corral showed she meant business.

Since she had returned, Jason had avoided her eyes and given only one-word answers. Maggie had refrained from pushing her in front of the children, but now she had obviously had enough.

Jason placed one foot on the lower rung of the fence and her forearms on the top rail. Tears burned her eyes. Her stomach was knotted with worry. "I'm not a good husband, Maggie. I failed you. I swore to love and protect you until death do us part, and I'm not proving able to."

Maggie didn't understand. What was Jason talking about? Was there another woman? Maggie immediately dismissed this stupid thought. No, not Jason. Then what? Feeling her great distress, Maggie came behind Jason and wrapped her arms around her. She rested her cheek on her back. "Tell me."

"The price of wool has dropped to a quarter of what it was last season. We have almost no liquidity left, and stores in town no longer give credit. How are we going to live? I didn't see any of it coming... I'm sorry."

Maggie stayed a moment, holding Jason, who was shaking with sobs. "...you won't want me any longer..."

Jason's voice was so tenuous that Maggie wondered for a moment if she hadn't imagined the words. Without hesitating she turned Jason around and took her face in her hands.

"Never! You hear me? We are married for better and for worse, and we will face it all together. The situation seems difficult, but we will make it, and you know why?"

Jason shook her head no.

"Because we love each other, and we have three superb children who depend on us. John and Victoria will soon be ten. They can almost work like adults now. Even Robert, though he's only four, can help more than he already does. We're going to organise ourselves with a budget to spend as little as possible, and we will eat from what we can grow on our land. Prices will rise again one day. We just have to be patient, and with you by my side, I have all the patience in the world."

"Oh, Maggie. What would I become without you?"

Forgetting that she was "supposed" to be the strong one in the couple, Jason snuggled up against Maggie to be hugged and have her distress chased away by her tender care.

❖

As soon as John saw the dust in the distance, he spurred on his horse in the direction of the buggy that was quickly heading for Willowra. His father had given him the responsibility of surveying the pastures to the west of the house, but, despite his fear, he would have to find out who was on their property. When it had been decided to give Victoria and him the responsibility of tending to part of the station, each of them had also received a rifle. Times were hard, and disreputable people might end up on their property. Their duty was to protect Willowra and their family, whatever the cost, and John would not fail. It was out of the question to disappoint his father.

Pastor Andrew stopped in the middle of the dusty path as soon as he saw the horseman coming to meet him.

John arrived and touched the tip of this hat in greeting. "Reverend."

"G'day, John. How are you?"

"Good. Pa isn't home, if that's who you've come to see."

John examined the two children sitting next to the pastor and instinctively knew why Father Andrew was here. From atop his horse, and without taking his eyes off the children who were staring back at him, he leaned over to the reverend's ear. "We're hardly getting by as it is…"

Though Pastor Andrew seemed annoyed at being seen through so easily, he calmly replied, "It's up to your parents to decide. Giddyup. Off we go."

The horses immediately got on their way, and John watched them disappear in a cloud of dust. He wiped the sweat that, despite his hat, was running down his face. Should he escort them? His father had told him to make the rounds of the pastures and look out for strangers, not to stop the reverend from coming to Willowra. After glancing one last time at the cloud of dust, he headed in the opposite direction.

When Robert heard the cart, he hurried to warn his mother, who was cleaning the stables with a pitchfork. "Mama. We have visitors."

"Go get me the rifle."

Robert immediately complied, hurrying to the house to grab the rifle that was as tall as he was and carry it, without running, back to his mother. He didn't want to get scolded for having run with the rifle like he did last time.

As Maggie took it out of Robert's hands, she recognised the man who stopped his cart in the middle of the courtyard with two scrawny figures huddled together.

"You expecting trouble, Margaret?" the pastor asked, pointing to the rifle.

"These are difficult times…"

Maggie didn't need to finish her thought. They'd both heard about the incident on the Kilkoon homestead, located east of Willowra. One of the hands had been killed trying to fend off a horse thief. Since then, the watchword on every sheep station had been to shoot first and ask questions later.

"But what brings you all this way, Father?" she asked, trying to ignore the bright, big eyes riveted on her.

"Can we speak privately?"

Maggie and the pastor went inside the house into the kitchen.

"Robert, go take water to the two children who came with Pastor Andrew."

Without having to be asked twice, Robert took the water flask and left.

"Everything going well here? Jason? Victoria?"

Maggie nodded yes in answer to his questions. She already had an inkling why the pastor had come all this way, but she wasn't going to make the task any easier for him: her small personal revenge for various uncalled-for comments he had made over the years. Rather uncharitable, she knew, but so were his comments.

"I saw John on my way here. He's grown," the pastor said. "Maggie…"

"Father?"

"I need your help. You saw the children who were with me? Their parents abandoned them at the church, saying they'd come back to get them when they could feed them. We already have so many. The orphanages in Western Australia, in all of Australia for that matter, are overcrowded. I know Jason isn't here, but can you take care of them at least until their parents come back for them? Times are hard for everyone, but…"

"All right."

"You would be performing a charitable act…"

"Yes, Father."

The reverend fell silent, his mouth gaping open because Maggie had accepted so quickly.

"I'm going to tell them to get down from the buggy," he said.

The pastor was hurrying to the door when Maggie's voice stopped him.

"Father, we will take care of them, but I want you to swear before God that you will not bring us any more mouths to feed. I want to have at least enough food to sustain everyone in this family, and with more children, that will simply be impossible."

Father Andrew took his Bible out of his pocket and swore on it.

"Maggie, this is Audrey and Philip Mitchell. Children, you'll be good and behave until your parents return, won't you?"

Without waiting for an answer, the pastor jumped into his buggy and sped away from Willowra before Maggie could change her mind. His conscience wasn't exactly at peace, but he didn't have another solution. Should he have told Maggie that the mother was probably dead and that he was quite certain that the father who had left them there wouldn't soon, if ever, be ready to reclaim them? While snapping the reins to encourage the horses to go faster, he shook his head. God would forgive him this small omission that was for the sake of the children.

In the moonlight, Maggie, lying on her side, looked at the woman peacefully sleeping against her. She loved this woman a little more each day. No religion, no sermon could change her feelings. In this world turned upside down by hunger and madness, good people still existed. She held out her hand to caress a lock of Jason's short hair.

When she had accepted the burden Father Andrew had given her, Maggie had put more responsibility on Jason's shoulders. Yet Jason, once she was over her surprise, gave a great big smile as the two frightened children hid behind Maggie. Despite her fatigue, Jason had, with the greatest of patience, spent an hour successfully coaxing the children out of their shells and reassuring them. Now that she thought about it, Maggie couldn't think of a single time when Jason had lost her infinite patience with her or with their children. She was so happy. God had sent her the husband of her dreams.

❖

Willowra, 2006

As Victoria took a sip of her now-cold tea, no one around the table ventured a word. Victoria was such a riveting storyteller they all had the impression that Maggie, Jason, and their children were right there in Willowra with them.

"What happened to Audrey and Philip? Did their father come back for them?"

Tess's voice cut through the silence. She wasn't a member of the family, but she couldn't refrain from asking.

Victoria gave a sad smile. "No. He was never heard from again, not in Norseman or anywhere in the surrounding area. Jason officially adopted them in 1935. Philip died in '36, which greatly affected us all. Everyone was in tears at his grave…"

Victoria motioned in the direction of the little cemetery on the property. "Audrey is still alive. She lives in Norseman and comes to visit from time to time, but I think she never really accepted or forgave me for leaving in '42. She was only fourteen, and Elise's death, plus my departure, were too much for her to digest. When I returned in '50, she was married and already had a child. It took a very long time for us to reconnect."

Victoria didn't want to expand on Audrey's anger, or her accusations against her own lifestyle, or her harsh words about Ginger. Jason had thought that the loss of Elise had left Audrey "broken" somehow, and Audrey needed someone to blame. The feeling of being abandoned again just a few days after Elise's death was too strong for Audrey, and Victoria had made the ideal scapegoat.

"I didn't know you'd left Willowra for eight years. Where did you go?"

As the story unfolded, Gabrielle was experiencing one surprise after the other. She, who had been afraid of introducing her family to Tess, she who had fought in favour of same-sex families, was in fact a descendant of these exact families, necessarily hidden because of societal moral codes. Also, who was this Elise that Victoria was referring to?

A big smile came to Victoria's lips, and everyone stared at her.

Thomas grinned also. He already knew part of what was to follow. Over time he had stitched together different pieces of their family history without having ever heard the entire story. His sister, Simone, her arms crossed against her chest and sulking, also knew the answer, but she clearly didn't find this little game amusing at all.

"I joined the army and left to fight against the Japanese in New Guinea."

"What?" Gabrielle and Jeremy said in unison, and he sat up in his chair. "You fought the Japanese?"

He needed a confirmation. He wasn't sure he'd understood correctly. His grandmother? A soldier? He'd heard that the soldier in the photo in her room was really her, but he didn't think she'd actually fought.

"Sergeant Victor McKellig...wounded in Balikpapan on July 29th, 1945, during the Borneo campaign," Victoria said, appearing amused.

"Your limp..."

Gabrielle didn't need Victoria's confirmation. She could read it in the blue eyes that were staring at her.

"Tell us the story," Jeremy asked, still shocked.

As Victoria was about to speak, Aurore's gentle voice interrupted her. "After dinner, Victoria. It's already quite late, and we need to eat."

"Mum!"

"Jeremy..."

Aurore hadn't raised her voice, but to Tess's surprise, Jeremy obediently lowered his eyes.

Victoria laughed, quite amused. "You're absolutely right, Aurore. Let's eat first. My story and Ginger's can wait a bit longer."

PART IV: VICTORIA

CHAPTER TWENTY-SIX

Willowra, Western Australia, 1937

"Pa."

The hesitant voice coming from outside the stable's open door caught Jason's attention. She stopped what she was doing mid-gesture, letting the tines of her pitchfork rest on the ground, and turned to her son.

"Yes, John. Is there a problem?"

John slowly shook his head—so there wasn't one—but he nevertheless shifted his weight from one foot to another in the awkward way young men do when they don't know how to ask something that is important to them.

He looked at his father, who gave him an encouraging smile. During all those years, Jason had been unfailingly attentive to him and the other children. He knew Maggie and Jason had adopted them all, but that didn't change his love for them. To the contrary. However, the subject he wanted to broach with his father was delicate, and he had been hemming and hawing around the question for several days. He had spoken about it to some of his friends but wasn't sure whether he could trust their answers. John had waited patiently, observing his father as he cleaned the stables, not daring to interrupt him, but now that he had Jason's attention, as he was good-naturedly leaning on his pitchfork, he didn't have the courage to bring up the matter.

"Did you finish chopping the wood for your mother?"

"Yes, Pa."

Jason realised that what John wished to discuss embarrassed him. She set the pitchfork against the wall and walked over to him.

"What is it, son? You've been beating around the bush for several days now. I've noticed it, and so has your ma. You know you can ask us anything. We've never hidden anything from you. Let's go sit outside. It's too hot in here for talking."

Jason headed outside and sat on the bench set right up against the stable's south wall, protected by the shade of a large eucalyptus tree. They sat side by side—Jason leaning back comfortably with her legs stretched out, and John, fidgety, at the edge of the bench, with his hands between his knees, staring straight ahead.

Both lost in their thoughts, neither of them heard a furtive figure slip inside the stable and hide on the other side of its thin wall.

In fact, Victoria had noticed that her brother was up to something, but when she'd asked him about it, he'd said that it wasn't a girl's business. So when she'd seen him head for the stables, she'd left her chores to go spy on him. If John wanted to speak with their father, it meant the subject was important, and nothing would stop her from finding out what it was all about.

"Pa...what's it like with sheilas?' John murmured without daring to look at his father.

Jason glanced with surprise at him before blushing so violently she hoped he wouldn't turn and notice her. She'd known the question would come up one day or another, but she'd hoped to have a little more time to prepare. For the love of God, John was only seventeen. Taking a deep breath, she knew she shouldn't shy away from the inevitable conversation.

"Do you mean kissing, or something else?"

With an indignant expression, John finally turned to his father. "Pa! I'm not a baby. I know about kissing. It's the other stuff that..."

Jason opened her mouth then closed it, unable to utter a sound. After taking a deep breath, she finally found her voice. "I see. Young Maureen, right?"

John nodded. Despite his cheeks turning red, he no longer felt embarrassed. He waited with hope. His father had always known the answer to every question.

"I don't want you getting into trouble, John. I don't want things to turn out with Maureen in the family way. You've seen enough of the animals on the station to know the mechanics of it all."

"I don't want to get into trouble, Pa. I wanna marry her, and I don't want to mess up our honeymoon on our wedding night because I don't know how to go 'bout it."

"Oh. Pointless to tell you how then, 'cause I reckon you're both on the young side for getting married."

John shook his head.

Jason sighed. "I haven't been with a lot of lasses in my time, John, but one thing is certain. You have to be attentive and not hurry things if you want to…satisfy your woman. Sheilas…aren't like us. They need us to take good care of them before…the act."

Though John, listening intently, seemed fascinated, he apparently didn't notice Jason's growing discomfort. Only her imagination and swaggie stories allowed her to have an idea of what happened between a man and a woman.

"How do ya do that, Pa?"

At that moment, Jason understood that John didn't need an explanation of the act itself, but the preliminaries. Relieved, she sighed slightly. She knew this subject well.

"A woman needs for you to kiss her for a long time even before you touch her, son. You have to learn to kiss her well, both softly and with passion. Then you need to undress her slowly and caress her, to take her fears away. Only when she's ready can you engage in the act itself."

"But, Pa, I'll never be able to wait that long! Already after a kiss I'm…well, you know…"

Jason would have liked to burst out in laughter. This conversation was surreal.

"You're going to have to learn to control yourself. You'll see. Much of the pleasure is in the waiting."

John looked bluntly doubtful. He sighed.

"You have plenty of time, son. There's no reason to rush things."

"I've decided to ask Maureen's father for her hand in marriage next Sunday. I love her, Pa. I want to marry her, and she agrees."

"Does your ma know?" Jason asked to stall for time.

"Not yet, but I'm gonna speak to her before Sunday."

John put his hat back on and stood up. He was about to leave and go think over what his father had told him, but he hesitated and finally turned back to Jason. "Pa, I'd like to add a bedroom to the house for Maureen and me. Would you help?"

Jason looked at him and saw all his uncertainty. "Maureen is welcome. You know that. She's a charming young lass, but I think your future wife would prefer a home of her own. I'll discuss this situation with your mother as soon as you've told her of your wedding plans. We'll see if we can't build a small house just for you two someplace not too far from the homestead."

"Oh, Pa. That would be wonderful! I'm going straight in to speak to Ma!"

As Jason watched John head for the main house, she heard a slight noise on the other side of the wall. Silently, she stood and hid herself. With a smirk, she saw Victoria sneak out of the stable and head for the shearing shed. Nothing escaped Victoria, but it was so difficult to figure out what was going on behind her beautiful blue eyes. She'd become a young woman. Jason sighed.

Maggie had spoken to her so she wouldn't get into trouble with the local boys, and Victoria had laughed in her face, replying that all the boys around here were just silly kids who didn't interest her. Jason would have liked to speak to her about the risks she'd be taking if she opted for older men, but she didn't dare. She didn't know how she could advise her, as she had absolutely no experience in that domain.

Why had Victoria been eavesdropping on her conversation with John? Teenage curiosity? Oh, how Jason would have liked to better understand her. And now John was acting up. Thank goodness Robert and Audrey were still innocent little children. Otherwise, Jason's blond hair would have already gone grey.

CHAPTER TWENTY-SEVEN

At the sound of a galloping horse coming toward the house, Jason dropped her fork, glanced at Maggie, and sprang up from the table to go outside. A horseman in such a hurry could only mean one thing: bad news. She braced herself, hoping that nothing had happened to Victoria or one of the shepherds. Jason stepped outside, with Maggie just behind her. She had to squint in the late-afternoon sun to make out the horseman who was quickly approaching. It wasn't Victoria. That wasn't her way of riding. From afar, Jason could make out other men on horseback coming toward them as well.

"Get the rifle, Maggie. I don't like this."

The first horseman stopped right in front of Jason in a cloud of dust. Both the man and the animal were breathing noisily, but the rider jumped down from his horse without waiting to catch his breath. It wasn't until he was standing in front of her that Jason recognised the blacksmith from Norseman, Padaic O'Cleary. The look of rage on the man's face was such that Jason almost took a giant step back. Only once, a very long time ago, had she seen someone that enraged; and that was right before she'd received the biggest thrashing of her life.

"Where are they?" bellowed the man covered in dust and sweat.

"Padaic. What's going on?"

"Where's your bitch of a daughter, McKellig? I'm going to break her neck with my bare hands!"

Although her heart was pounding wildly, Jason forced herself not to move an inch. "Victoria left yesterday to check on the shepherds."

Jason's calm voice contrasted with Padaic's cavernous bellows. "No. She's led my daughter astray! Elise! Get over here!"

Padaic tried to force his way into the house as he screamed for his daughter. Jason stepped right in front of him, immediately receiving a punch to the chin, which sent her flying back onto the ground. While

Jason shook her head to gather herself, Padaic turned back, intent on entering the house. A rifle shot rang out.

"As surely as my name is Maggie McKellig, I swear that if you come any closer to this house, the next bullet is for you."

The man wasn't stupid. Despite his anger, he knew Maggie wouldn't hesitate to shoot. Outback women were tough, almost as tough as men. Padaic froze, while Jason got up with difficulty, rubbing her chin.

"Jason?"

"Don't worry, Maggie. I'll be all right."

"Where's my daughter?!" Padaic screamed.

Despite the dust caked on his face, the crimson flush of his anger was quite visible. Though still gesticulating, he was wise enough not to move any farther. Jason and Maggie, who still didn't understand what was going on, were relieved to see a policeman among the two other horsemen who'd stopped in front of the house.

"Maggie, Jason."

Chief Wilson tipped his hat to greet Maggie. "I don't think you'll be needing that rifle now."

Maggie gave the policeman a hard look before motioning to Padaic with her chin. "I know, but does he? He showed up at our homestead, punched my husband for no good reason, and then wanted to force his way into our house."

"O'Cleary'll behave," Wilson confirmed, placing his hand on the blacksmith's muscular shoulder.

"Pa," the young man accompanying the policeman said. "Elise isn't worth getting so worked up about."

"Stay out of it, Ken."

The young man jumped back at the sound of his pa's angry voice. His father had a quick temper with a heavy hand, and Ken didn't intend to pay for his sister's misdeeds.

"If you'd invite us in for some tea, we could talk about things," Wilson proposed. "It's still hot in the sun, and the ride from Norseman has left me parched."

"Maggie."

Jason called Maggie to her duties as a hostess. Hospitality was sacred in these parts. Finally lowering her rifle, she turned around and walked into the house.

Padaic took a step forward, but Wilson's voice stopped him before he could chance a second step. "O'Cleary! If you don't behave yourself,

I'll arrest you and lock you up. We're going in the house to drink some tea and talk things over. I very much doubt that Victoria and Elise are here. Jason?"

"Victoria left yesterday to check on the fences, and I haven't seen Elise for at least three months. Can someone tell me what this is about?"

Since they'd known one another, this was the first time Wilson had ever heard irritation in Jason's voice. He had always appreciated this quiet man, who did everything with moderation and could always be counted on. "Let's go inside, and we'll explain it all to you."

The relative dimness of the kitchen was a welcome respite from the hot outdoors, and the tea that Maggie served the parched horsemen put contented smiles on their faces. Even Padaic seemed to calm down, now that he had his cup in hand.

"I'm listening, Wilson," Jason said, to open the conversation.

"This early after—"

"Ma?"

Audrey walked in, interrupting the policeman. She had heard the outbursts of voices outside earlier but had hidden behind the woodpile during the altercation.

"You can take some tea and a biscuit, but go drink it outside, Audrey. This is grown-up talk."

The young girl took a long, hard look at each person in the kitchen with her deep-brown eyes before she took the teacup her mother held out to her and a biscuit from a plate in the larder. A glance from Jason sent her silently skedaddling out of the room.

"Your youngest? Boy, she's grown," Wilson commented. However, an insistent stare from Maggie made him continue his story. "Like I was saying, earlier this afternoon, Ken caught Victoria and Elise kissing behind the smithy. That right, Ken?"

"Yes, sir. They were kissing like I saw Ronald and Mary do," the young man said, blushing. "I told Pa straightaway."

Maggie and Jason exchanged a look. Padaic then slammed his hand flat on the table, making everybody start. "That little slut has depraved my girl. I'll teach her not to put perverted ideas in my Elise's head. And as for Elise, she'll be hearing from my belt."

"Let me make things perfectly clear, Padaic. You won't touch a hair on our daughter's head—or I'll have you thrown in jail. I'm the one who handles the problems in my family."

"Jason's right, O'Cleary. Your daughter is your business, but the young McKellig is not your concern."

"You're not gonna lock her up?" Padaic bellowed, half jumping to his feet.

"Sit down, O'Cleary. Put her in jail—for what crime? Kissing another girl? Come off it, Padaic. You know what young'uns are up to at that age. That's just experimenting. Maybe you'd like it better if Elise came back knocked up with a little brat?"

The dark glance Padaic threw Wilson let him know that his comment stung. He understood the man's anger, but the incident had to be put into perspective.

"Maybe it was just a little experimenting. In any case, they've run off somewhere," Padaic said.

Everybody in the room understood why and had to feel sorry for Elise.

"Did they take one of your horses, Padaic?"

"What?"

"Did Elise take a horse from your stable?" Jason asked again, slowly, as if addressing a three-year-old child.

"Nope. If that was the case, I would have reported a horse theft."

Wilson sighed but refrained from commenting.

"They're not here, Wilson. You have my word. Take Padaic and Ken back to Norseman, and I'll go see if I can find them. They can't have gone very far with only one horse. Seems to me they left because they were afraid of Padaic's reaction. They should turn up soon. We just have to wait."

"Wait? I—"

The police chief placed his hand on Padaic's shoulder. "What else do you want, O'Cleary? Go wandering yourself on this unfamiliar terrain to die from the heat and fatigue? You're right, Jason. See what you can do. Maggie."

After a polite nod, taking leave of the lady of the house, Wilson firmly pushed Padaic toward the door while Ken hurried to fetch the horses.

❖

Maggie and Jason stood side by side in the porch's shade, watching the three men ride away. They were barely out of earshot when Maggie asked, "Do you think that…"

"That Victoria's like me?"

Jason sighed. She turned to Maggie, her eyes filled with sadness.

"I've been such a fool, Maggie. I didn't see it. We thought she was interested in older men, when in fact she's attracted to women. My God. She must feel so alone and abandoned."

Maggie saw the anguish of the woman who was her soul mate. Although Jason had told her the story of her life, Maggie couldn't possibly fathom the depth of despair and solitude she must have felt after so much rejection. "Night's gonna fall soon. We can't do anything before dawn."

"I'm going to John's."

"You really think they went there? That would be risky."

"Not really. Only a handful of people know that since he married, John doesn't live at our place anymore, but two miles away. I think the girls are headed that way. Elise isn't accustomed to the bush, and Victoria would want to take good care of her. With just one horse, going the back way, I'd say they haven't made it yet. I'll get there before them if I leave now. Robert!"

His sister Audrey in tow, the eleven-year-old boy immediately arrived. The children hadn't missed a lick of what had just occurred, of course. In a place where nothing ever happened, the smallest event took on the grandest proportions.

"Robert, please saddle my horse."

"Yes, Pa."

The boy flashed a smile of perfectly white teeth that contrasted with his dark complexion. As though aware of his difference, Robert rarely showed himself when strangers came by. Today had been no exception. Jason saw him disappear inside the stables, with Audrey scurrying close behind him.

"I'll try to bring the girls back tonight, but don't wait up for me. At worst I'll spend the night at John's and let Maureen pamper me."

Maggie reached over, gently caressed Jason's soft hair, and whispered in her ear, "You devil. You can't help yourself when a pretty woman's around to feast your eyes on."

"The only woman I'll ever have eyes for is standing right in front of me, Maggie. You know that. Even if Maureen isn't unpleasant to look at," Jason added with a playful tone while brushing her lips against Maggie's.

"Here's your horse, Pa."

The children were smiling, their eyes shining with the joy of having surprised their parents in a sweet private moment. Not that those moments were rare, but the love between Maggie and Jason was like a great big blanket that reached out to protect and cradle them all, each and every moment of their lives.

After giving Maggie a last kiss, Jason got on her horse and rode off in a steady canter.

❖

When Jason reached the eucalyptus grove that protected John and Maureen's little house, the sun was just setting behind the small hills that bordered the property to the west. Despite the sun in her eyes, Jason tried to make out a horse with the riders coming toward her, but she couldn't see anything.

The minute he heard a horse, John came out of the house, accompanied by his wife. Their place was small, only two bedrooms, but John intended to expand it as his family grew. The only other building was the barn, which also served as a stable.

"Pa?"

"Have you seen your sister?" Jason asked before even getting off her horse.

John shook his head no. "I thought she was making the rounds of the herds."

"Me too, but it seems she wasn't," Jason calmly explained as she dismounted. "Hide my horse in the stables, and I'll explain it all. If they come here, as I think they will, Victoria mustn't see me before I get a chance to talk to her."

John didn't understand what this was all about, but being the good, obedient son he was, he didn't question his father's motives. Jason would eventually tell him all that was necessary. "Maureen, put the kettle on. Looks like it's gonna be a long night."

❖

A pinkish hue still glowed over the horizon when the familiar clip-clop of a horse's hooves reached the ears of the three people sitting at the kitchen table. Jason wordlessly opened the nearest bedroom door and slipped in to be out of sight as John walked out to welcome the new arrivals. He had promised his father to make sure that Victoria didn't run off before they could have a frank discussion.

"Victoria? Elise? What are you doing here at this late hour?"

"Help Elise get down instead of asking questions, brother."

John held his hand out to Elise, who slid down from her uncomfortable position behind the saddle. Visibly relieved to have finally arrived, Victoria dismounted.

"I'll put the horse in the stable," John told her. "Go on in. Maureen will fix you something."

Without waiting for an answer, John led Victoria's horse to the stables and then, following his father's instructions, unsaddled it.

"How are you, Maureen?' Victoria asked as she sat down on the bench next to Elise.

The fatigue on her beloved Elise's face worried her. Their little jaunt hadn't been planned, and during the entire journey, Victoria had racked her brains, trying to figure out how to get them out of this situation. If only Ken hadn't discovered them. But they had been powerless to do anything because Ken had instantly rushed off to his father to denounce them. Flight had been their only solution if they wanted to avoid a good hiding. Without really considering the consequences, both of them had chosen the less painful solution.

Lost in their thoughts and dazed by fatigue, neither of them noticed Maureen's silence or the way she frequently glanced at the bedroom door left ajar.

"All right, Victoria." John's voice cut through the silence. "What if you told me what brings you here, at this hour. What did you do this time?"

John crossed his arms over his chest, leaning back against the front door. He deeply loved his sister, and although he didn't know what his father was going to do, he nevertheless followed his instructions.

"John! It's just a misunderstanding with Elise's father, but we have to go...far. I'm gonna need money."

When Victoria saw her brother glance apprehensively at something behind her, she turned around and found herself face-to-face with her irate father. She held back a shudder as Elise, her forehead resting on the table, started crying. Victoria would have liked to take Elise in her arms and run off, but all the doors were blocked, and Elise was in no state to travel anywhere. Victoria looked at her father, then her brother, and with a defiant expression, she put a protective arm around Elise's shoulders, gently pulling her close.

"Don't cry, Elise."

"They're going to thrash us, Vic. I can't take it...no more..."

"I'll protect you. I promise."

Victoria clenched her fists and stared at her father with pride to prove she wasn't afraid. She could stand anything, but no one would touch even a hair on Elise's head while she was around.

Jason recognised that defiant look. It was the same one the five-year-old kid had given her the day she'd caught her picking her pockets.

Victoria's protective arm around Elise's shoulders would almost have made Jason smile if the situation hadn't been so serious. She calmly sat down facing them, nodding at her son to do the same, while Maureen dispassionately filled two plates with food.

"I thought you knew me better than that, Victoria." Jason sighed. "Have I ever beaten you or any of my children?"

Jason let the silence settle in until Victoria uttered "No" through pursed lips.

"Padaic showed up with Ken and Wilson this afternoon. Your mother and I had their version of events, and now I'd like to hear yours. But first you're going to eat and drink something."

Jason pushed the plates placed on the table by Maureen toward them and watched them silently, noticing how Victoria tried to get Elise to eat, as well as Elise's frequent glances toward Victoria for reassurance.

"Pa? Who did that to you?" John pointed to the bruise on Jason's cheek.

"A gift from Padaic before your mother got the rifle out to calm him down."

The clink of a fork on china. Elise was staring fixedly at Jason.

John coldly remarked, "O'Cleary did that? I'm going to kill him."

"I'll handle my own affairs, son. I forbid you to approach O'Cleary as long as this situation is unresolved. Understand?"

"Yes, Pa."

"As for you, young lasses, I'm waiting for your explanation."

"Mr. McKellig, everything is my fault," Elise dared to say. "We weren't doing anything wrong but…"

"I love her, Pa, and I'd marry her if I could."

Elise opened her mouth, but no sound came out. Time seemed frozen after Victoria's declaration. Jason saw the determination in her daughter's fierce eyes. Where did she get that courage? Jason envied her. If only she'd had this strength to fight for Kathryn. But no. She'd run off instead.

"Pa?" John didn't understand how his father could remain silent, faced with his sister's nonsense. Marry another woman? What a cockamamie idea.

"Stay out of this, John. Elise? I'd like to hear your opinion."

Though Jason's showed no anger, tears ran down Elise's cheeks, and fear knotted her stomach. She was old enough to know that the church didn't consider what she and Victoria were doing behind the smithy "moral," but she hadn't found the strength to resist her attraction to Victoria. Their time together was always too short; their stolen kisses had always left her frustrated. Without answering Jason, she jumped into Victoria's arms. "I don't want to leave you, Vic. I love you too much, but I'm so scared."

"Nothing will happen to you, El," Victoria promised, without taking her eyes off her father.

Jason brushed her hand against her own face, grimacing when her fingers touched the bruise. "All right. If you feel strong enough, we'll go home now. Maggie must be worried stiff about you, Victoria. John, can you saddle Victoria's horse and lend us one of yours? You can pick it up tomorrow. I'm counting on your and Maureen's silence. Maureen?"

"Of course, Jason. You know I'm not the gossiping kind."

"You can rely on me, Pa. I'll saddle the horses."

As Victoria was about to mount her horse, Jason took her to the side. "Don't do anything stupid, Victoria. I need to be able to trust you. Elise is in no state to gallop off into the night. If she's really dear to you, no stupid ideas."

Victoria pinched her lips together. Her teeth clenched, she gave in. "I won't do anything stupid, Pa."

How did Jason know what she'd been planning? However, once she glanced at Elise, who could barely sit up straight in her saddle, her shoulders slumped with fatigue, she understood that her father was right.

Jason put a reassuring hand on Victoria's shoulder. "I've never betrayed you, daughter, and I give you my word that your mother and I will do everything possible to ensure your happiness."

Victoria searched her father's blue eyes in the darkness and found sincerity and goodness in the face of the man who had taken her in twelve years before. An immense relief of not being alone filled her. These past hours the responsibility of her escape with Elise had been weighing heavily on her shoulders. In an uncustomary gesture, she threw herself into her father's arms, and Jason hugged her tightly against her.

"We should go," Jason said, breaking free from their embrace.

"I'll lead, and you bring up the end. And I'll take Elise's horse by the bridle. She's in no state to steer anything."

Less than a half hour later, the horses arrived in front of the Willowra homestead. Maggie was already standing outside by the time the three of them were getting off their mounts. "You found them, thank God. I was worried sick that they might be alone in the desert."

"Victoria, go take care of the horses," Jason said.

Victoria was about to protest. She wanted to take care of Elise, not the horses.

Jason and Maggie immediately sensed she was about to buck. "You are going to tend to the horses, like your father asked, while I help Elise take a bath. Then it will be your turn, young lady. You're not going to go to bed covered in sweat and dust, now are you?"

Rarely had Victoria heard her mother's tone so curt. She lowered her eyes to avoid the accusatory glare. After a long minute, clenching her teeth, she grabbed the horses' reins and went to the stables.

Her back now turned, she didn't notice the complicit glance her parents exchanged.

"Audrey and Robert?"

"They're in bed. Jason, can you go get the water I've been heating in the kitchen?"

Jason smiled, with an inquisitive look.

"I had a feeling you'd bring the girls back and that they'd need a good bath. You too, for that matter."

A small laugh rumbled in the back of Jason's throat. "I'll use the dormitory shower."

While Jason headed to the kitchen for the hot water, Maggie led Elise to the small room that served as their bathroom. She lit an oil lamp standing on a shelf. "Sit down here while Jason fills the tub. I'll get you a nightgown."

"Ma'am?"

"Call me Maggie. What is it, Elise?"

"You're not going to send me back to my father's…?"

The fear she saw in the young girl's eyes wrung Maggie's heart. "We're going to try to make sure that doesn't happen—but I can't promise you anything. It's—"

Just then Jason arrived with the hot water.

"I don't want to go back there," Elise murmured, tears streaming down her face. "He'll kill me. I want to stay with Victoria. Please don't force me to go back there. I'd rather die."

After having poured the hot water in the bathtub, Jason set down the empty bucket on the ground and kneeled on one knee, facing her. "Elise. I've promised I would do everything I can to help you two, and I'll keep my word. You won't go back to your father's if you don't want to. Trust me. Now, you're going to get washed up, have some tea, and off to bed. Tomorrow we'll take a look together at all the possible solutions. Okay?"

Wiping her tears off her cheeks with the back of her hand, Elise sat up. She wanted to believe this man whose face was so sincere. Slowly, she nodded in silence. Jason got back up and, as an aside to Maggie, said, "I'll leave you to help her."

"Where should she sleep?"

"In Victoria's room," Jason replied with a mischievous smile.

Maggie frowned. "And Victoria?" she asked suspiciously.

"In her room."

"You want the girls to sleep in the same room? In the same bed?" Maggie murmured, dumbfounded.

Jason slowly nodded.

"They're going to...they're likely to...under our roof?"

Jason nodded again, and Maggie glimpsed a tender look in Jason's eyes before she whispered, "Nothing will happen to them here. Nobody will strike them. No one will judge them."

"We need to talk."

"Later. When everyone's in bed."

"Where's Elise?" Victoria immediately asked as she walked into the house.

Maggie, her hip resting against the sink and a cup of tea in her hands, looked at her daughter. She was so young yet had already been through so much. Victoria had always been the sharpest and liveliest of all their adopted children, but she had also been the toughest and the most stubborn. Maggie gave a discreet sigh. No, Victoria would not give Elise up, despite the fear Maggie could see in her blue eyes, which, although darker, so much resembled Jason's.

"She just went to bed. She was exhausted. A good night's sleep will do her good...same for you."

"Where?"

"In your room. Go take a bath while the water's still hot."

In her room? Victoria didn't dare ask the question burning inside her because of Maggie's dark, slightly reproachful look. Without adding a word, she headed for the bathroom. Elise was in her room. Where was she supposed to sleep? Victoria sighed. In the empty dormitory, most likely.

When she came out of the bathroom in her nightgown, her father was waiting for her. He was manifestly on his way to bed too.

"Has Ma gone to bed?"

"Yes."

Victoria didn't know how to tell her father that she didn't want to sleep in the dormitory. She would rather unroll a swag and sleep on the kitchen floor to be closer to Elise.

"We'll speak about all this tomorrow. You and Elise start thinking about how you foresee things. I'm going to do the same with your mother."

"She's not happy about this, Pa. I can see it in her eyes."

"Your ma's afraid for you. Afraid this love will bring you great hardship. That's all, Victoria. She's not judging you. Believe me. Go on. Off to bed now."

Jason pointed to Victoria's room, and her eyes popped open wide. "In my room, Pa?"

"Where else?"

Victoria ran her tongue over her dry lips. "With Elise?"

Victoria's voice was a whisper, but Jason could hear the fear behind her strangled question.

"You overheard my conversation with John before he got married. The advice I gave him applies to you as well, Victoria, although seeing Elise's state of exhaustion, I'd advise you to let her sleep."

Victoria couldn't believe her ears, but the sympathetic glimmer in her father's eyes made her understand he wasn't joking.

"I never…I don't know if I would know how…Pa?"

"You're practical-minded, Victoria. I trust you'll figure things out. Just remember the walls are thin here."

A big smile lit up Victoria's face as she replied. "I know *that*, Pa. Don't forget that my room is right next to yours."

Jason tried to hide her blushing cheeks from Victoria, but the girl had already turned around and headed for her room. Jason imagined how nervous she must be. She remembered the first time she'd touched a woman. Kathryn. Such a long time ago. Another lifetime. At that moment, Jason vowed to do everything she could so her daughter could love without the fear she'd had to live with for so many years, until Maggie.

Returning to her room to find her beloved's arms, Jason thought about the first time she'd touched Maggie and her fear of being rejected.

❖

"Elise," Victoria softly whispered, getting under the covers next to the sleeping girl. "Elise…my beautiful Elise…"

Victoria would have liked to let Elise sleep, just to watch her in the faint glimmer of the oil lamp gently burning, but the temptation of finally being able to touch her was too great. After so many months of only being able to kiss her and touch her through her clothing behind that vile forge, Victoria couldn't resist discovering her soft, warm skin at last. Slowly, with the tips of her fingers, she caressed Elise's thigh, exploring the realm underneath her nightgown. Elise moaned in her sleep, and this sound, instead of stopping her, thrilled Victoria. She wanted to place her hand between Elise's silky thighs and stay there forever.

After many long, solitary nights, Victoria knew what provoked her own pleasure and supposed she would be able to satisfy Elise the same way. But what had her father told John? To take his time, to kiss and caress his wife at length. So, Victoria refrained from rushing things. She brushed her lips against Elise's cheek, making a trail of tiny kisses all the way to her mouth, which she took. Her heart leaped when Elise responded, and she clutched Victoria close against her. They then broke away, out of breath.

"What are you doing here?"

"My father told me to take care of you, so that's what I'm doing… if you want me to."

"It's probably not what he had in mind, but I do want you to."

Before Victoria could answer her, Elise's mouth sent her into a sweet, comforting bliss. No longer able to hold back, Victoria sat up and took off her nightshirt. Elise's eyes opened wide, gleaming with desire.

"You too," Victoria, hesitantly whispered. "And my father knew exactly what we were up to because he reminded me that the walls are thin."

Elise raised a questioning eyebrow, but she took off her nightgown as well. The sight of her milky skin almost undid Victoria with desire, making her fear that her heart might jump out of her chest.

"You're so beautiful," she said, slowly reaching out toward her beloved. "I love you, and I will never leave you."

❖

Maggie, snuggled in Jason's arms, raised her head to look at her life mate.

"What?"

"Do you really think it was reasonable to let them sleep together?"

Jason smiled. Then she made a face. "Reasonable? No. But they're going to love every moment."

Just as Maggie was about to argue with Jason, they heard a moan on the other side of the wall. Then another, much longer and more explicit.

"Jason!"

Jason laughed at Maggie, who was sitting straight up in bed. She understood Maggie's reluctance. Victoria was only seventeen, and Norseman was a very small town. "What will people say" weighed heavily on everyone's mind. Jason held out her arms toward Maggie to pull her closer, greatly relieved when Maggie gave in.

"I know she's young, Maggie, only seventeen, and life will be difficult for both of them. That's why we have to help. Who could be in a better position to understand them? At least here they're sheltered. Would you rather they explore their love for one another behind the forge, at the mercy of others and the risk of being exposed at any moment? I've been through that, Maggie, and I don't want Victoria to have to endure the same thing."

Maggie held this woman who was her husband close. All her friends had envied her, and still envied her, for having Jason. "Do you want to tell her about us?"

Jason immediately stiffened. "Absolutely not. Nobody can ever know. Not even her. One unfortunate slip-up and our life would become hell. Willowra, and the peaceful haven that it is to us, would come to an end."

A series of moans followed by a long, passionate groan brought them back to the present and the room on the other side of the wall.

"Obviously, it didn't take Victoria much time to find the right method," Jason commented. "I know two young women who are going to be tired in the morning."

A sigh escaped Maggie's lips. "We're not going to get much sleep either, you know."

"No. But I know quite a pleasant way to spend the time."

"Jason! You can't possibly be thinking of…"

Jason's hand reaching under Maggie's lacy, white nightgown cut short any vague protest from her.

❖

When Elise and Victoria stuck their heads in the kitchen at six thirty a.m., the circles under their eyes told the tale of an agitated night. Jason hid a grin while Maggie busied herself, pouring two cups of tea that she set down in front of the girls before joining them at the table.

"Robert and Audrey are feeding the animals, so we have a moment to talk. I don't suppose you've had the time to think things over."

Elise and Victoria blushed bright red, and Jason couldn't hold back a chuckle after Maggie remarked, "We'd like to be able to get a little sleep tonight."

Victoria bit her lower lip. She could have replied that she'd heard them too but didn't dare.

The look on her face, however, revealed what she was thinking. Maggie said, "Joking aside, the situation is serious. How old are you, Elise?"

"Twenty. I'll be twenty-one in four months."

"Her age doesn't matter, Maggie. You know very well that as long as she's not married, her father has all and any rights. The only thing we can do is convince Padaic to leave his daughter in peace."

"He'll never agree to such a thing," Elise murmured, tears in her eyes.

"In that case we'll leave the area," Victoria said, getting carried away.

"And what will you do?" Jason asked, annoyed. "How do you think two women living as a couple will be looked upon? Even if you're careful, you will eventually be found out and end up having to run, again. Is that the life you want for yourself? And for Elise?"

Victoria swallowed, her eyes gleaming with tears that she blinked away. Elise sought out her hand under the table and squeezed it.

"I can't leave her," Victoria mumbled, her shoulders drooping.

"I know, Vic. That's why I'm going to go speak to Padaic. And Maggie's going to take you by wagon with supplies to camp out at Camelback Spring. Whatever happens, I want you to stay there, even if you don't hear from us for several days. You'll have enough supplies for two weeks—just in case things get ugly with Padaic."

"I could go on horse…"

"No horses, Victoria. There's nothing for them to eat out there, and taking fodder would be a waste of time and energy. You won't need a horse because you won't be moving from there until Maggie or I come get you. Understood?"

Elise and Victoria nodded. Jason could read the frustration in her daughter's blue eyes.

"Listen to me, Victoria. If you have a future with Elise, it's here in Willowra. If I can convince Padaic, you'll be safe here."

"Listen to your father, Victoria. He's right."

CHAPTER TWENTY-EIGHT

Jason got down from her horse in front of the blacksmith's, where everyone in town was watching. She had been well aware of all the eyes upon her as soon as she arrived on Main Street. Naturally, the story had spread through the entire town and even farther in just a few short hours. She just hoped Padaic had calmed down and would listen to her before he started talking with his fists...and that a good soul would think to warn Chief Wilson.

Jason had barely stepped inside the smithy shop when the *clang, clang* noise stopped short. A cold sweat ran down her spine. Victoria was her daughter, and she had to find the courage she hadn't had for Kathryn and herself. Above all, she couldn't show the fear wrenching her guts. Like back when she was a swaggie, showing your fear meant you'd lost before things even started.

"I see you haven't brought my slut of a daughter back," a voice roared from the back of the forge.

Jason didn't move. She remained in the immense doorway, where everybody could see her. "Padaic, I've come to talk."

"I don't want your talk. I want to take my belt to that bitch, and you should do the same to yours. Where are the lil' wenches?"

Padaic, a heavy mass of iron in his hand, walked forward menacingly. Jason forced herself not to step back and especially not to think about the sledgehammer in the mastodon's hand.

She kept her eyes locked with his. "I don't know. Willowra is large, and Victoria knows it well. It's going to take some time to find them."

"Especially if they're being helped..."

Don't think about his right arm swinging with the weight of the hammer. Don't step back. Don't imagine the mass of metal in his hand.

Sweat formed an enormous spot on the back of Jason's shirt, chilling her.

"Especially if they're being helped," Jason confirmed.

"What do you want? What are you here for?"

"I told you. I want to talk."

A look of rage flashed across Padaic's face. Jason could tell he would have liked to beat her to pieces with his iron hammer, but the appearance of Wilson's figure and the sound of his throat being cleared in the background dissuaded him from doing so.

"I'm listening."

"Elise will be of age in four months."

"And?"

"Let's say she disappears during that time, and when she comes of age, you agree to leave her be."

Padaic threw back his head in a throaty laugh. "And why would I do anything of the sort? Hmm? When all I have to do is wait for Wilson to bring her back to me."

"To keep Willowra as your customer...along with the other breeders."

Padaic's smile immediately faded. He shook his head as if he hadn't understood. "And who will repair your machines? Or replace your horses' shoes?"

Jason pretended to think about it. "I can make do on my own, while waiting..."

"While waiting for what?"

Jason held back a smile. This was exactly where she wanted to lead Padiac. "While waiting for the arrival of a mechanic who knows how to work a forge. When I bought my truck last month, Rupett told me not to worry about repairs because he knows a guy who's planning to set up shop here. The only problem is, with so few vehicles in Norseman, he won't have enough work to live on unless he sets up a smithy shop with it. I could convince the other breeders that it would be a good idea to give him our business."

"My son is learning mechanics. He'll soon be able to repair anything," Padaic retorted. "No reason for a stranger to come all this way."

As he replied, Padaic realized the barely veiled threat in Jason's words. He was dumbfounded for a moment that this calm little bloke, who couldn't weigh more than 130 pounds soaking wet, would dare try to put him out of business. "Are you threatening me? Wilson! Did you hear that? Jason just dared to—"

"I didn't hear any threats, Padaic. Jason's just pointed out a problem that will get worse once everyone wants to buy a motorcar. Norseman's gonna need a good mechanic. Jason's right."

Wilson spit his chewing tobacco on the ground, showing Padaic he really wasn't concerned. He didn't like people who beat their children for the pleasure of showing who was boss, and it was only fair that the tables be turned for once on Padaic.

"What do I gotta do to ensure a future fer my boy?"

"Make sure he learns the trade and becomes the best mechanic there is. And come with me to see the judge, where you will officially hand over guardianship of Elise."

Padaic glanced at Wilson, who, as if by accident, was looking elsewhere. He clenched his fists. He didn't have a choice. He could survive without Willowra as a customer, but he couldn't afford to lose the other breeders. He might as well close up shop right away. Sweat beaded on his forehead. This little quiet-looking bloke had him backed into a corner.

"When?" Padaic growled.

"Why not right now? Seems like you don't have much else to do."

❖

"How about telling me what's on your mind before Nelly and Ann arrive."

Pretending to ignore Maggie's words, Mary closed the living-room door behind her. Between Pastor Andrew's sermon and all the gossip that had been circulating for the past three days, Mary no longer knew what to think. She was shocked by Elise and Victoria's behaviour, indignant over Padaic's attitude and her own husband's comments.

"How can you accept such perversion under your roof?" Mary finally asked her friend, standing up from the armchair where she'd just sat down.

Maggie raised her eyebrows and waited.

"After Robert, now Victoria..."

Maggie's brows shot up even higher. Silence.

"Are you just going to sit there and say nothing?" Mary was getting upset.

"What can I possibly say, since you've already made up your mind?" Maggie's voice was ice cold.

"You heard Pastor Andrew's sermon. It's against nature, and you and Jason, you accept it…"

"And what would you have us do? Hang them from the highest tree? Send them to a convent? Beat them senseless and throw them out? Come back to Willowra with me, and I'll give you a stick…"

The sarcasm in Maggie's voice contrasted with her harsh words. Mary squeezed her lips together in order not to scream out "yes" before collapsing into the closest armchair, her head in her hands. "Oh, forgive me, Maggie. I no longer know what to think. The pastor's sermon has me all turned around."

Mary was annoyed with herself for having acted like the others, treating Maggie and her family as if they had smallpox when they'd entered the church. Luckily, the absence of Elise and Victoria had prevented the situation from getting out of hand.

The door then abruptly opened on Nelly and Ann, who rushed into the room with a determined step.

Maggie sighed. She felt weary. She missed her husband's solid presence, but Jason had decided that a beer with John at the hotel bar was absolutely necessary. They'd discussed the situation late into the night, deciding whether to keep up their usual routine or stay in Willowra until things settled down. Jason had convinced Maggie that, if they wanted to live normally, confronting everyone head-on would be more beneficial to Elise and Victoria.

"How…?" Ann said.

"Stop!" Mary exclaimed, and the others, surprised, turned to look at her.

"Despite what happened, we are all friends. Let's not forget that," Mary calmly stated.

"And if we want it to stay that way, perhaps it would be better if we spoke about something else," Nelly added.

"Nelly!"

"She's right, Ann. After all, it's none of our business. If Padaic, Jason, and Maggie have nothing to say about it, who are we to cast the first stone?"

"Thanks, Mary," Maggie murmured, relieved that her best friend had changed her mind.

"Good. Now who would like some tea?"

❖

John had barely brought his horse to a stop when Victoria came running toward him. He stared at her, surprised to see her so soon.

"What are you doing here? I thought you were out at Camelback Spring?"

"I couldn't wait any longer to find out what happened, so I walked here."

"You walked here? And Elise?"

"She's still out there. Maureen told me about the agreement between Padaic and Pa. Don't you think he could have come by to tell us the good news?"

Without answering her, John turned to glance at his wife, who smiled apologetically at him, then got down from the wagon.

Impatient, Victoria grabbed her brother's arm. She was now looking into two dark, angry eyes. "What?"

"You send us up shit's creek, and you have the nerve to complain because Pa didn't run to tell you the latest development? Victoria, what if you took the time to think for five minutes before acting? Don't imagine that, because Padaic signed a piece of paper, you and Elise can now parade down Main Street. Pa and I heard every horrible insult under the sun when we went for a beer in town: 'perverts, sluts, depraved bitches.' Pick whichever one you like. And I'm being polite because Maureen's here."

Victoria swallowed, uneasy. She'd never seen John this angry.

"And you know what hurts the most? It's that Pa never weakened. He defended you steadfastly and ignored all the insults. He stopped me from punching their smug little faces. How could you do that to Pa and Ma after everything they've done for you?"

"I love Elise as much as you love Maureen," Victoria whispered simply, whirling around to leave.

Wiping her tears from her face with the back of her hand, she instinctively took the path to the house. She didn't want her parents to suffer because of her. She had made up her mind. She and Elise would leave. To go where? She still didn't know, but it didn't matter...some place far away.

The half-hour walk under the burning sun to the homestead hadn't been enough to calm her as she tromped up the porch steps to drink from the water bucket. The water that ran down her neck and torso was a delight.

"What on earth are you doing here? I told you not to leave Camelback!"

Without answering her father's question, Victoria clenched her teeth and stared straight into his eyes. "John told me what happened in town. We're going to leave. I don't want that because of me, they..."

Victoria lowered her eyes. She couldn't speak any longer for the lump in her throat. No one had the right to touch her father...nobody.

Jason took a step forward. The distress in her daughter's eyes was heartbreaking. She would so much have liked to tell her the truth, but the risk was far too great. Instead, she immediately put her muscular arms around Victoria's shoulders, a rare gesture, and hugged her tenderly.

"Victoria...it doesn't matter what people say. Your safety and happiness are the most important. If you leave, there will be no safe place for you, and your mother and I will constantly worry. Padaic signed the paperwork giving me custody of Elise. For the rest, it will take time. But you have to trust me. It will all turn out all right. Don't worry about us. Your mother and I have seen worse."

Her eyes brimming with tears, Victoria hugged her father as tightly as possible. She wanted to believe him. She did believe him. He had never lied to her.

CHAPTER TWENTY-NINE

Willowra, Western Australia, December 1941

John's horse stopped in a cloud of dust right in front of the Willowra homestead. Jason, surprised to see her son at such a late hour, got up from her armchair on the porch where she'd been sitting since the beginning of the evening.

Often, while Jason read or did their accounts, Maggie, sitting by her side, prepared the vegetables for the next day's meals. This had been their routine for years, and each in their separate activities cherished this calm moment of togetherness. At first, Jason used to help Maggie with the vegetables, but, when the children came, Maggie wanted their roles to be distinct and well-defined.

John jumped down from his horse and hurried up the wooden steps. "Pa, have you heard the news? The Japanese have bombed Pearl Harbour. The Americans have entered the war! Now Prime Minister Curtin has declared war on Japan as well!"

War had been raging in Europe, and it was the only thing people ever talked about in town. From the beginning, John, like all the young men, had been very excited, but not enough to join the regular army and leave to fight a war that wasn't theirs. Jason had been quick to remind her son of the Gallipoli campaign in 1915, where Australian and New Zealand troops served as cannon fodder on behalf of Britain.

John's age, as well as the fact that he was married, allowed him to avoid conscription, as well as the three months' training launched by the government when the British had joined the war. For several years, Australians had kept their worried eyes turned north, toward Japan. The invasion of China had shown the thirst of the Japanese for conquest, making the Australians fear they could be next.

"I'm signing up, Pa." John's eyes glistened with excitement.

Why did all these young men feel such an urge to go kill one another?

"You can't be serious, John." Maggie intervened. "You're not going to leave Maureen with two young children and a third on the way? You know as well as I do that your work here is necessary and will be even more crucial in order to provide our troops with wool and meat."

"Maybe, Ma, but with this drought, we have fewer sheep, and Robert and Audrey can lend a hand. Right, Pa?"

John was filled with hope as he looked at his father. Even if he was over twenty-one and didn't need his approval, he did need his father's blessing to leave with his mind at peace.

"Pa," he said. "I don't want to join the AIF. Just the militia, in case the Japanese come here. You know the militia can't be engaged in combat outside Australian territory. I won't be risking much, and I'll always be in touch with Maureen and the children, but at least I'll feel like I'm doing my duty. I don't want to be seen as a coward. All my friends are enlisting."

Jason sighed. She knew Maggie was against it. Was it better to oppose him, to please Maggie, knowing that John would do what he wanted no matter what, or allow him to leave with a light heart and the knowledge that his father approved of his decision?

"Okay, son. Just the militia, but promise me you won't take any unnecessary risks."

John broke out in a huge smile. It was almost Christmas, but his gift had come in advance.

"You know me, Pa, and that's not my way. I just want to serve my country. Thank you. Is Vic here?"

Jason shook his head no. "They should be arriving soon. They must have waited for the outside temperature to cool down a bit before returning from the southern enclosure. It's still at least ninety-five degrees out there, and the sun's just set. Wish we could get some rain. This drought has lasted long enough. I'll tell Victoria and Elise when they get home. Go back to your family."

Still smiling, John got on his horse and galloped off to his house.

Jason turned to Maggie, whose eyes were simmering with anger. "You don't approve, I know."

"How could you authorise him to go get himself killed?"

"The militia is the lesser evil. Did you see how his eyes were gleaming? He would have gone no matter what, Maggie. I didn't want him to leave with a heavy heart and feeling guilty. I've seen men die because they were eaten through with guilt and no longer had the strength to fight. John is a sensitive soul, and he should only have one thing on his mind when he goes: coming home."

Jason's eyes were brimming with emotion. Maggie, swallowing her anger, came over to her and rested her head on her shoulder while Jason's arms encircled her.

"John's not the only sensitive soul in this family," Maggie whispered as the distant sound of two galloping horses reached their ears.

CHAPTER THIRTY

Willowra, Western Australia, 1942

Maggie jumped to her feet when the kitchen door banged open. Anxious, she peered at the doorframe despite the hot desert dust swirling all around her. She'd seen many a storm in her day, but this one had come faster and stronger than most. In less than an hour the wind had started blowing fiercely, the sky was black, masking the sun's rays, and then the lightning started striking. A dry storm—the worst kind. With the last consecutive years' drought, they had a terribly high risk of fire.

A figure then quickly entered the house, immediately turning around to close the door and stop the sand from rushing in with the wind.

"Jason!"

Maggie rushed into Jason's arms. Audrey and Robert also came to hug her. Since they hadn't been far from the house, they'd ridden back as quickly as possible when they'd seen the sky darken on the horizon. As the hours went by, Maggie had become increasingly nervous. Despite the wind that made the roof shake, at the slightest noise, she would get up and check if someone was coming.

Jason removed her hat and hugged Maggie close. "It's been a long time since we've had to endure a storm like this one."

"Maureen?" Maggie enquired.

"I stopped by there on my way back. She wasn't very reassured, and the baby was screaming his lungs out, but they're okay. We need to invest in another wireless transmitter for situations like this."

Jason glanced around the room, noticing Robert's worried expression while Audrey was busy getting a cup of tea for her.

"Where are the girls?"

The anguish in Maggie's golden eyes gave her the answer. "They haven't returned…"

Jason slipped out of Maggie's arms before taking a few steps into the kitchen while rubbing the back of her neck. She absentmindedly grabbed the tea Audrey was holding out to her, sipped it, took a few more steps, then put the cup down on the big kitchen table with a resolute clink. She slapped her hat back on her head.

Before she made it to the door, Maggie, wrenched with worry, stopped her. "Where do you think you're going in this weather?"

"I have to find them."

"No. If they haven't returned, they've stopped to wait out the storm. A horse and rider are too easy a target for this lightning. But I don't need to tell you that. Victoria knows the property like her own shirt pocket. She'll take care of Elise."

Jason didn't answer. She looked at Maggie. The eastern pastures, where the girls had gone, were as flat as could be. There was no shelter. Nothing to stop the wind. A horseman would be overly exposed during such a storm.

Maggie knew she had to find the right argument to convince Jason to stay put. She didn't want to lose her. Just the thought made her want to cry.

"If something had happened, the horses would have returned on their own. Victoria knows what she's doing. She's used to these types of situations," Maggie insisted. "Jason, your daughter is an adult now. Trust her!"

Jason gave a deep sigh, took off her hat again, and sipped her tea—her throat now parched with fear. Maggie was right; Victoria was twenty-two and no longer a baby who needed to be protected.

"Pa, do you want something to eat?"

"Not right now, Audrey."

A little later, she asked, "Robert, did you have time to inspect the small enclosure?"

"Yes, Pa. It has a hole, but Audrey and I couldn't finish it before the storm came. We thought it wiser to come back here."

"Good decision, Robert. The hole will still be there tomorrow."

Maggie sat down next to Jason. Minutes felt like hours, and nobody would be able to sleep until their family was united.

Several hours later, everyone was sitting there silent when Robert looked up. "Pa?"

Jason squinted. The glimmer projected by the storm lamp in the middle of the table wasn't bright enough to make out Robert's expression.

"I heard a horse."

Maggie and Jason stared at him. How could he hear anything with that howling wind? Jason was often surprised by how their son could see, hear, or smell things better than anyone else. It was probably due to his aboriginal origin. Before Maggie could express her surprise, the door slammed open. She immediately recognised the figure in the doorway: Victoria!

Victoria walked in, and Jason helped her quickly shut the door. She leaned on Jason for a few long seconds, rubbing her dust-covered face, a slight smile on her lips. "What a storm!"

Before Victoria took another step, she noticed Jason's worried look. Slightly turning her head, her eyes met Maggie's, and what she saw alarmed her. She swept her gaze frantically around the kitchen and noticed the same tense expression in Audrey and Robert's eyes. She swallowed with difficulty.

"Where's Elise?"

"We thought she was with you," Jason murmured, obviously concerned.

"I sent her back when I saw the storm coming. Sweet Jesus. She should have been here hours ago."

Victoria's heart was pounding, anguish suddenly wrenching her stomach. Her beloved was somewhere outside in this storm! She had put her hand on the door handle and started turning it when Jason came and pushed the door shut, leaning on it with his full body weight.

"No. We have to wait until the bulk of the storm passes."

"She's outside, Pa. I have to find her!" Victoria shouted. "Let me go!"

Jason didn't answer her, but he didn't move away from the door either. Victoria tried once again to open it, but Jason was pushing against it with all his might.

Realising that Victoria was going to try to get out of the house whichever way she could, Maggie walked over to her. "You'll never find Elise in this storm. You'd only be putting your life in danger, as well as your brother and father's, who would never let you leave alone. As soon as the greater part of the danger has passed, we'll all go search for her."

"If she's fallen off her horse and is lying wounded somewhere…"

Victoria tried to hold back her tears. Maggie was slowly caressing her dust-covered cheek. Unable to contain her fear any longer, Victoria huddled up against her mother as a little girl would do.

Jason watched them. She had always envied Maggie because of the privileged relationship she had with their children. While Jason could take them in her arms when they were young, now, since they had grown, she had to hold back and force herself to remember to act like a father, who traditionally was less affectionate, less tender toward his children. Fathers possessed authority, not affection. So, with a heavy heart, she forbade herself almost all physical contact with her children other than an affectionate tap on the back with her son, or a hand on her daughters' shoulders.

Robert was silent. Just like his father, he knew that if Elise had fallen, her horse would have already returned. And if her horse hadn't returned, it hadn't been able to. He was pulled from his thoughts by someone sniffing at his side. Audrey was silently crying. His younger sister also knew that something serious had happened to Elise. Robert gently placed his arms around her shoulders and pulled her close.

Audrey had always adored Elise; from the beginning she would follow her everywhere. Robert had even been jealous at first, until his mother had explained that Audrey needed to have another girl to talk to now that she was becoming an adolescent and Victoria, although closer in age, was too much of a tomboy to share many things with her.

"Pa? I'm afraid," Victoria whispered, removing herself from Maggie's embrace. "She should be here already."

"I know, Victoria. The storm will soon pass, and we'll go search for her."

"The night…"

"We'll take the storm lamps, Victoria, and rifles. In fact, we can start right now getting everything we need. Robert, you take care of the rifles. Get a gun and a box of cartridges per person. Audrey, prepare something for us to eat. Victoria, the storm lamps, one for each of us, and matches. Maggie, flasks of hot tea. I'm going to saddle five horses."

❖

A hand shook Jason awake from the restless sleep into which she had fallen.

"Pa! Wake up, Pa!"

Victoria's voice brought Jason out of her torpor. Jason lifted her head and then realised she had fallen asleep sitting at the kitchen table. Silence. After many long hours of only hearing the wind howl, the silence was almost painful.

Victoria gave Jason a desperate look.

"What time is it?"

"A little past three. The storm has moved on."

"Wake the others."

"Ma and Audrey are changing. Robert is outside lighting the lamps."

Jason grabbed her hat from the table and put it on as Maggie and Audrey walked into the kitchen. Both of them wore breeches to be more comfortable while riding.

The group immediately joined Robert, who had brought 'round all the horses. Before getting on hers, Jason gave each person a task.

"Victoria and I will take the path Elise most likely chose. Maggie and Robert, you ride to the south. Audrey, go get Maureen, and both of you focus on the north. The first one to find her fires three rifle shots. Then one shot every ten minutes until the others arrive. Okay?"

Everybody nodded before mounting their horses and taking a lamp. They took off without hesitation, hurrying into the pitch-black darkness.

Although Jason wasn't a devout Christian, she did say a silent prayer that they would find Elise alive. She couldn't begin to imagine Victoria's reaction should something have happened to her.

Dawn was barely starting to break when Jason heard an unusual noise. She stopped her horse.

"Pa?"

"Shush!"

As Victoria was about to say something, they heard the noise again.

"What is it?"

"It's coming from over there. Let's go."

The morning sun made their obstacles more visible so they could pick up their pace to a trot in the direction of the noise. Jason hoped she was mistaken, that the noise wasn't what she thought it was. As they grew closer, it became more distinct.

"Neighing! Elise's horse!"

Victoria immediately kicked her horse into a canter.

"Victoria! Wait!"

Swearing under her breath, Jason galloped off after Victoria. She was afraid of what Victoria might find and wanted to get there first. The sound of a dying horse grew louder. Jason saw Victoria jump down from her horse before it had stopped, but the high grass prevented her from seeing where Victoria had gone.

A bloodcurdling howl that sounded like a wounded animal made Jason's blood run cold. Before she had reached Victoria, she knew the worst had happened. A few more metres...

Jason had to shut her eyes for a moment. Victoria was sitting on the ground with Elise's body in her arms, the horse lying not far from her with one of its legs skewed at a bizarre angle. As the sun rose, it gradually shed an eerie light on this morbid scene. Jason grabbed her rifle. She had to warn the others. Three shots. The first one put an end to the horse's suffering. The other two went into the air. It all felt like a living nightmare.

Setting the rifle down next to her, Jason kneeled in front of Victoria, whose her face was stricken by pain and tears.

"Victoria...Vic..."

"Why, Pa? Why?' Victoria screamed, before hysterically adding, "I should have stayed with her. It's all my fault."

Jason took her in her arms and clasped her as she sobbed. Although Elise was somewhat hidden by Victoria's arms, Jason could see that her face was peaceful. Apart from her messy hair, she looked as though she were sleeping.

"Come, Victoria. Get up."

"NO!"

"You don't want to leave her here. We have to take her back to Willowra."

But Victoria clung to Elise's lifeless body more determinedly. Jason stood, took her rifle, and gave another shot. From a distance she could make out two horsemen galloping toward her. Relieved, she recognised Maggie's riding style as one of the two.

Seeing the distress in Jason's eyes as she approached, Maggie understood the tragedy that had taken place even before hearing her daughter's sobs. She jumped immediately to the ground.

"Robert, go get the truck!' Jason ordered before Robert could dismount. "If you see Maureen and Audrey, make sure one of them sends a radio message to Norseman to ask Pastor Andrew to come."

Robert froze as he thought about Audrey. Oh, how Audrey would suffer when she learned the news.

"Robert!"

His father's voice brought him back from his thoughts. Digging his heels into the horse's flanks, he left again, galloping toward the homestead.

❖

Norseman, several weeks later

Removing herself from her mother's arms, Victoria turned slightly to face the man who had welcomed her into his home and heart when she was only a child. The emotion she saw in his eyes made her doubt her resolve to leave.

"Are you sure about your decision?"

"I can't stay, Pa. Everything reminds me of Elise."

Victoria held back a sob while pronouncing the name of the woman she had loved so much.

"Will you come back?" Jason asked, a knot in her throat.

"I don't know."

Jason, unable to utter another word, nodded. The tears that had been threatening to overwhelm her came dangerously close. Not caring what the others might think, she took Victoria in her arms and wept.

Victoria embraced this man she adored, the one person she had looked up to for so many years. The tears freely flowing down his craggy face showed the signs of time. She didn't know if she would ever return, but her love for him was eternal.

Victoria then stared into Maggie's golden eyes, full of tears.

Victoria hadn't wanted Audrey and Robert to come along to Norseman to see her off on the approaching bus that would take her to her destination. Although she'd remained vague when her parents asked her where she intended to go, she in fact knew exactly what she wanted to do: join the AWAS. Since John had left to serve his country, she had read everything she could about the war. As soon as she'd learned of the existence of the Australian Women's Army Service, she'd been fascinated. Only Elise's presence had stopped her from enlisting with these women who fought to keep the Japanese out of their country.

Jason delicately pushed her daughter away from their embrace, though it broke her heart to do so. "Go. The bus is waiting. But never forget that you will always be welcome at Willowra, alone or with someone." Victoria picked up her bag from the ground. And with a broken heart, she headed for the bus, taking a free seat at the back. She looked one last time at her parents before the bus took off, leaving her youth and her soul behind on the arid land she loved so much.

Jason wrapped her arm around Maggie's shoulders, pulling her close. "Do you think we'll ever see her again?"

"She'll come back, Jason. Willowra is in her blood. She just needs to lick her wounds."

"It's so hard to see our children leave."

"I know. And on top of it, you have to keep to your role as the father and remain stoic, although your maternal instinct is as strong as mine. Come. Let's go home. I asked Maureen to come live at the house while John is away. With two young children and a baby, she welcomed the offer. That'll keep us busy while we wait for our two eldest to return."

Maggie tugged Jason's arm.

She was still staring in the direction of the bus, but now the road was an empty expanse of settling dust.

CHAPTER THIRTY-ONE

Brisbane Line, Queensland, July 1942

John glanced back over his shoulder. Again. Either he was seeing things or someone was following him. Meandering with his buddies along the streets of Cairns, every time he looked back he saw the same soldier staring right at him. As far as he could tell, the man was wearing the uniform of the 7th Infantry Division. But why was he following him? The militia assigned to territorial defence didn't mix with soldiers from the regular army, no more here in Queensland than in his last posting, in Darwin.

Wanting to understand, John claimed he had to buy a gift for his children and left his friends to turn onto a deserted alley. Slowly walking up another street, he led his pursuer out of sight. He wasn't the kind to get into a brawl as some other men might, but if pushed...

When he reached the edge of a forest with its tall tropical trees, he stopped to see what the stranger would do once he realised John had spotted him. To his great surprise the soldier's face broke into a wide smile as he walked right up to him. Even if the man's attitude was in no way threatening, John stayed alert. As the distance between them diminished, the man's features began to seem familiar, but the brim of his hat still hid the top of his face, and John couldn't put a name to him. Only after the soldier was just a few yards away did he look up at John, whose jaw immediately dropped.

"Vic?" he stammered. "What? How on earth?"

"Hey, brother! I thought you might be taking us to see your sheila!" Victoria joked, beaming.

"What are you doing disguised in this get-up?"

Victoria pretended to be offended. "I'm not in disguise. You have, standing right before you, Private Victor McKellig, savouring his last hours of leave before shipping out to fight the Japanese in New Guinea."

The seriousness of Victoria's words silenced John. He checked her over. Indeed, if he hadn't known her personally, with her shaved head and flattened bustline, he would have thought she was a man. Victoria wasn't tall at five feet seven, but John knew she was solid muscle, and some men were even shorter than she was.

"Easy for the hair, but what about your chest…"

"Strategically placed compression bandages."

"That can't be very comfortable."

"I'll live."

"Why are you doing this, Vic? Ma and Maureen wrote me about what happened but—"

Victoria's grin vanished, and she raised her hand. "Please, John. I can't talk about it."

More than her words, her tone of voice and the look of distress in her eyes stopped John from continuing. "Why did you enlist?"

"I want to be useful. I thought about the AWAS, but in reality they only serve to replace the men who've gone to fight outside the country. Then once I got to Perth, I heard the 7th Division was recruiting…"

"Does Pa know?"

"No. Nobody knows except you, and I plan to keep it that way. Understood?"

"Okay, Vic. But if something should happen…"

"I want to be buried next to Elise…if anything's left of me."

John shifted his weight from one foot to the other. What his sister wasn't saying could be seen on her face, and it made him shiver. Victoria was going to war not intending to make it back alive. He wanted to convince her that she was making a mistake, that combat wasn't for women, but ever since they were little, he had never been able to make her change her mind once she'd made it up. How many times had he accused her of being as stubborn as a mule? No one was more obstinate than Victoria.

Victoria forced herself to smile. Seeing John reminded her of Elise. Although several months had gone by, her heart was still pierced with pain. Even the crazy training period she'd been through to bring the new 7th Division arrivals up to speed with the Sahara veterans hadn't helped alleviate her constant emotional anguish. Like everybody else in her platoon, she had suffered physically, but that was nothing compared to the crucifying pain she'd lived with since she held Elise's lifeless body in her arms. She forced herself to breathe calmly and chase away these dark thoughts, swallowing with difficulty.

"Look. Are you going to lecture me or offer me a beer?"

"When do you leave?"

Victoria looked at her watch. "I've got two hours. I'm expected at the base at eighteen hundred hours."

"Come on then. I'll buy you a beer."

John had started to put his arm around Victoria's shoulders when she took a step back. Surprised, he frowned.

She smirked. "Better watch your hands unless you want people to think you're a poofta."

John blushed and, setting out by her side, made sure not to walk too close to his sister.

CHAPTER THIRTY-TWO

Kokoda Trail, New Guinea, September 1942

Rain…the blasted rain never stopped. The rain was falling so hard the lush treetops that blocked the light no longer provided any shelter. Everything was soaked with water: the ground, the vegetation, their clothing. Nothing ever dried in the New Guinea jungle's never-ending rain, falling from a sky teeming with dark clouds and, in any case, barely visible from the dense forest.

It had been like this for weeks. Defend-retreat-counterattack. If they didn't hold their position, Port Moresby would fall into the hands of the Japanese, and that would leave them an open road to Australia. Staff Sergeant Potts had given the order to hold their ground, but they couldn't keep on eternally in these conditions when every day more men from their unit died in combat.

Crouching on their heels—it wasn't possible to sit on the rain-soaked ground—under the glistening trees leaves that gave a semblance of shelter, the exhausted, famished figures of their unit tried to rest. In order to sleep they would roll themselves up in their regulation oilskins, where they would soon awake suffocated by the heat and stewing in their own sweat. The oilskin was supposed to protect them from the rain during the day, but whoever supplied them hadn't realised that in eightyi-five degrees Fahrenheit heat, they became an actual steam bath. If they had to be soaked, the men preferred not to be smothered, so they let the rain stream down from their hat brims onto their backs and torsos, day after day, protecting only their ammunition, rifles, and cigarettes.

Night had already arrived, or was it just the rolling black clouds that gave that impression? No matter, the lieutenant had told them to rest and eat, so they rested and ate, silent figures difficult for the naked eye to distinguish amidst the lush vegetation.

Eating her cold ration straight from the can, Victoria tried to stop the water from her hat from channelling directly onto her food. Never ceasing, she restlessly scanned the tropical landscape, searching for danger of any kind. You had to be crazy to advance your troops in this weather, but the Japanese *were* crazy, so she was constantly on alert, even while sleeping. Those who got sloppy, if only for a moment, were no longer around to talk about it. How many of her comrades had she seen die from snipers' bullets or from setting off a booby-trapped branch or object?

She nervously glanced at the men grouped together under the leaves, her men...at least those who remained...between the Japs and malaria. They had all diligently swallowed those bloody Atabrine pills, but most of them had still caught the blasted parasite. Her last bout had occurred just last week, but she had refused to be evacuated, like Grayson, who had the shakes right now under his oilskin. They were all going to die like dogs here if reinforcements didn't come soon.

"Everything okay here, Corporal?"

Victoria barely looked at the man who crouched next to her. She had been expecting him. Every evening, Mac made the rounds of his men, at least those still "standing," to check on their morale.

"Perfect, Sarge. you've come just in time for a piece of grilled mutton."

Victoria pointed to the tin can where a few pieces of corned beef were swimming in rainwater. A few sniggers. Mac couldn't help but grin. Since McKellig had joined the 21st Brigade under his orders in '42, he'd faithfully proved to have a biting sense of humour, and nothing had changed over the past six months, except that now Mac knew him to be a superb soldier and leader of men. He had informed each new lieutenant that McKellig should be his potential successor in case something happened to him. Not that he intended to get himself killed, but he'd seen too many of his fellow soldiers die these last weeks and months not be completely clear-headed in that respect.

"I see all is fine here. Sorry I forgot the beers, mates, but I'm a bit distracted these days."

"What? No news from your wife?" Victoria teased him. "Don't tell me you've run out of paper. Hey! Does anyone have perfumed writing paper for the sergeant?"

A soldier posted not far from them joined in. "I've got some, Sarge, nicely perfumed in sweat, but a bit damp, I'm afraid. You see, we've had a bit of rain lately."

Hearty laughter. Mac laughed with them. He was reassured that they still had the strength to make jokes. He once again blessed the day McKellig had come under his command. Morale wasn't the same in the other platoons.

"How's the new lieutenant?" Victoria asked.

"Like an inexperienced young'un who's just cut his ma's apron strings. But at least he listens to us, not like the last one who strolled around the jungle like it was Buckingham Palace."

"Well, he wasn't in our way for long."

No more than two days, Mac thought, before stepping on a landmine on a path that Mac had warned him to avoid. The Japs had hidden mines on all the paths, and that idiot should have known better. Mac told himself he shouldn't let a simple corporal speak that way about an officer, but McKellig would have upped the ante if provoked, so he kept quiet.

"Gimme a smoke."

"And you nick my smokes on top of it," Victoria murmured as she grabbed the pack protected by a plastic case from her left shirt pocket.

She held one out to Mac and then took one for herself, lighting their cigarettes under the brim of their hats. They took drags in silence. At least you couldn't smell the smoke in this rain. Mac observed McKellig using the butt of his cigarette to burn leeches stuck to his forearm.

Might as well get them while you can, Mac thought, and did the same. With these disgusting creatures that constantly sucked their blood, did he have any left to run through his veins? They tended to hide in leaves, from which they'd let themselves fall onto the unsuspecting men, creeping into the slightest cracks. Even when they weren't fighting, their uniforms were covered in blood—their own blood. Mac would have preferred going back to battle the Germans in the Sahara Desert rather than rot away in this damn jungle, playing hide-and-seek with those blasted Japs, who never admitted defeat. He let out a heavy sigh.

"We move out early tomorrow morning. Headquarters wants us to counterattack."

Victoria winced before whispering her comment to Mac so the men wouldn't hear her.

"With what men, Sergeant? We're only a handful left. If reinforcements don't arrive soon, we'll all be dead. This jungle and the Japs will have our skin."

Although McKellig's defeatist comment surprised Mac, he understood. He too sometimes thought he would never see his wife, Meggan, or his son again. According to his calculations, they were down to about two hundred men from the fifteen hundred they'd started with. At that moment, Mac would have liked to fall to his knees and pray, but he couldn't allow himself to show the slightest weakness in front of his men. They were relying on him.

"One day at a time, Corporal. Get some rest."

CHAPTER THIRTY-THREE

Brisbane, Queensland, August 1945

Victoria opened her eyes with great difficulty. The scorching light shining through the window was too intense. She gradually became aware of the noises around her: hushed voices, clinking metal, a rolling trolley. The room was a faded, dirty white that had seen brighter days. Finally turning her head toward the window, she could see large leafy trees with bright-green foliage and a few white clouds in the blue sky. At long last, she could see the sky. If her right leg was actually in traction, the nightmare was over.

The last thing she could remember was an attack on a Japanese position during the Battle of Balikpapan: the deafening noise of an explosion, an intense pain in her lower belly, screams—probably hers—then nothing at all. She had been wounded and was apparently now at the hospital. But where? Since when?

Bracing her elbows on the mattress, she tried to sit up, but a blistering pain shot through her lower abdomen, radiating down her upper thigh. She saw stars. Victoria collapsed back onto the bed. Despite her clenched teeth, she couldn't hold back a squeal. Sweat beaded on her forehead as she took quick breaths to try to calm the burning pain in her leg that shot all the way up to her belly.

Someone placed a cool hand across her forehead. A comforting voice caressed her ears.

"Stay put, soldier. The doctor will be here soon."

"Thirsty," Victoria croaked.

A hand supported the nape of her neck, helping to prop her up while another one brought a glass of water to her lips. Victoria greedily gulped it down. "Where am I?"

The hand gently lowered her head back onto the pillow. "Brisbane."

"Since when?"

"You've been here two weeks. You had a concussion on top of your other wounds, but everything's going to be all right, now that you're awake and seem to be coherent."

Victoria opened her eyes to gaze upon the woman who was kindly answering her questions. She was young, with light-blue eyes and a lock of white-blond hair that had escaped out of her white headdress. Cute was the first word that came to Victoria's mind.

"Is it…"

Victoria's next thought made her hesitate. She saw that her leg was still there, but the gloomy prospect of having it amputated danced before her. She cleared her throat, forcing herself to utter the words. "My leg. Am I seriously wounded?"

"You have, among other things, a fractured femur, but nothing that would require an amputation. The doctor will explain it all to you in detail. You'll soon be back on your feet and hopping about like before."

Relieved and exhausted from these few moments of being awake, Victoria closed her eyes as the nurse watched her with a kind smile.

❖

Looking out the window, Victoria watched the clouds delicately float across the sky. She thought about the last battles, the soldiers who'd died, those who were wounded, the landing manoeuvres…and the fear. This terrible fear that never left her, the silent fear she could see in the eyes of all her comrades-in-arms. Would she ever manage to forget it? Could she learn how to live again? What for? And in any case, for whom?

"G'day, Sergeant. You're finally awake?"

Victoria jumped at the man's loud voice. Lost in her thoughts, she hadn't heard the door open. Standing next to the doctor, whose white lab coat sported captain's stripes, she recognised the nurse from before, who seemed minuscule in her white uniform compared to the man standing next to her. Victoria refocused on the smiling giant.

"Sir."

The doctor stared at her for a moment before grabbing her wrist to take her pulse.

"Stevenson. You're a lucky one, Sergeant, or should I say miss? If you had been a man, you would have been castrated. Might as well also admit that you gave quite a surprise to my colleague who first tended to you. Imagine it. He thought he was going to operate a patient having lost his manhood and ended up with a woman on the operating table. The story spread like wildfire in the 7th Division. Don't be surprised to see your superior officers coming to visit. I'm not sure they were particularly pleased with the news. They're going to try to hush up the affair."

The captain smiled. The situation seemed to amuse him. Victoria tried to move a little, but a piercing pain shot through her, making her grimace.

"I would advise against much moving around. On top of your abdominal wounds and a concussion, your pelvis and femur are fractured. You're not in too much pain right now because the morphine is still working, but we're going to gradually lower the doses. Let me check this wound, and I'll tell you where we stand."

The doctor lifted the bedsheet while the nurse came closer with a tray full of different objects, which Victoria couldn't make out clearly from her position. Did it matter anyway? Turning her face toward the window, she returned to contemplating the sky, wincing from time to time when the doctor's palpations touched more sensitive areas.

While attentive to the doctor's instructions, the nurse observed this sad-eyed woman. What was her story? Why had she disguised herself as a man to go fight in the depths of the jungle? Battle stories from this greenish hell were more horrible one than the other: a staggering number of dead, and the wounded…beyond all description. The look in this young woman's eyes was identical to that in other soldiers'—the look of someone who had seen far too much in their young life.

"Okay. That's enough for today. You'll walk again, even though it will take a bit of time and a great deal of physical therapy. Between the fractured pelvis and femur, you've a long healing period ahead. The surgeon who operated on you in the country hospital to stop the internal bleeding did a good job, and apparently the strong doses of penicillin you're getting have stopped the infection from spreading."

Now vaguely ill at ease, the doctor sighed. As a military doctor, he rarely treated women and didn't know how to announce the next bit of news. As quickly as possible was certainly the best way.

"The bad news is that you'll never have children. A piece of shrapnel did a lot of damage, and an emergency hysterectomy had to be performed."

Because of his patient's blank look, he explained in more simple terms. "They had to remove the uterus."

The doctor was surprised at how calmly his patient was taking the news. She appeared as if it didn't concern her. He exchanged a glance with the nurse before whispering a series of instructions to her.

As he was about to leave, Victoria stopped him. "Sir. How long before I can walk again?"

The doctor rubbed his forehead and took his time. "The femur has a clean fracture and shouldn't cause any problems. The various wounds due to the grenade fragments scattered throughout your body should heal without too much trouble, including the abdominal wound. However, the pelvic fracture will heal slowly. I'd say three months of immobilisation and then two months of physical therapy in a convalescent home. The length of time will depend for the most part on you and your willpower, but frankly, that's not something that worries me."

Victoria nodded in acknowledgment before looking out the window again.

"Mrs. Abbott, make sure to bring this young woman's file up to date while she's awake."

"Yes, sir."

Once the doctor had gone, Mrs. Abbott turned to her patient. She knew she would need to establish a relationship with this young woman to help her out of the depression looming over her head like a dark cloud. Walking around the bed to the window, she approached her patient, making sure not to block her view.

"Pretty day. Not many clouds. You'll see during hurricane season it's not at all like this. I'm Ginger Abbott, and you? Your file says your name is Victor McKellig."

An interminable silence. Ginger wondered how to get through to her.

"Can I have a cigarette, please?"

Although surprised, Ginger nodded before stepping out of the room to get a pack of cigarettes and matches. She quietly handed a cigarette to Victoria and then lit it. Time seemed to expand as she watched the young woman take drags from it, eyes locked on the view outside the window. Ginger sighed, feeling useless. How could she reach this woman...this soldier?

"Victoria. Victoria McKellig," Victoria finally answered. "The jungle was so dense we couldn't see the sky, and when we did, it was almost always filled with rain clouds. I never knew there could be so much rain."

A pair of blue eyes now stared into Ginger's. The sadness she saw in them broke her heart. Ginger forced herself to smile. "Where do you come from?"

"Western Australia. And you?"

"From here. Brisbane. I understand that you must miss the blue sky. It doesn't rain much over there toward Perth."

"My parents have a sheep farm on the outskirts of the Nullarbor Plain. It doesn't really rain much to begin with, but with the drought these last years…"

Victoria's voice dropped to a whisper. She would soon close her eyes and fall asleep. That's what would be best for her right now, to recover.

"Do you want me to contact your parents?"

No answer. Just two big blue eyes staring at the horizon before drooping shut. Frustrated without understanding why, Ginger grabbed the incandescent cigarette butt from Victoria's lax fingers and left the room to take care of her other patients.

❖

"How's our heroine doing?" Jane, Ginger's superior, asked.

They had been friends for years, having already worked together before the war. Jane, a big-boned woman whose figure seemed to take up the entire hallway, came over to Ginger. When patients were uncooperative, all it took was a visit from Jane, and the problems disappeared as if by magic.

"The doctor just saw her. It'll take time, but she's going to make it. By the way, her name is Victoria McKellig, and she comes from Western Australia."

"Not much to change in her file?"

Ginger shook her head no.

"Apart from her gender," Jane added with a wry smile. "I've always said women are just as able as men to do anything, Australian women in particular. And how is my favourite godson?"

"Thomas is fine. He took his first steps last Tuesday, and my mother thinks he's a gifted angel."

"Any news from Virgil?"

Again, Ginger shook her head no. Her husband was somewhere in the Pacific, and each day that passed with its share of dead and wounded made her dread bad news.

"Jane!" someone shrieked from the other end of the hall, interrupting them.

"Duty calls. See you later."

❖

Two knocks. Victoria watched the door handle turn and open. When she recognised the man at the threshold, she stretched her lips into a sincere smile. "Mac! Sergeant…"

Victoria held out her hand to shake Mac's, who crushed hers in his manly handshake and gave her a huge grin in return.

"McKellig! When I realised you were here too, I rushed over to see you. What good did it do to name you head of your section if you were going to get yourself wounded just a few days after me?! Nice room. Some of us have all the luck. How are you?"

"Better than ever. And you?"

Mac, an ironic pout on his face, gestured to his arm in a sling. "They told me I'd be rid of this contraption soon, but you know these doctors. They could lie through their teeth while swearing on their mother's grave. In any case, I'm done with the front and battles. I lost the mobility in my shoulder. Seems the nerve was hit. And you?"

"It's over for me too. Fractured pelvis, femur, and a bunch of other stuff I didn't quite understand. In short, several months of rehab in perspective for me. I'm happy to see you."

Mac lowered his eyes. McKellig's closely cropped hair, the strong handshake, everything indicated that his buddy, his comrade-in-arms and fellow-sufferer was right in front of him, wounded. How could what he'd been told be true? Dismissing the possibility of court-martial, he had accused the officers who'd come to question him about McKellig of being "liars" when they'd told him McKellig was a woman. A woman never would have fought so well.

"Got a smoke, Mac? They only hand them out in dribs and drabs."

Mac stuck a hand in his jacket pocket and pulled out a pack of cigarettes that he threw to Victoria. "Keep it."

"Thanks, Mac. Counting all the smokes you took from me, you can now be my official supplier," Victoria said as she lit one up, mocking him.

Mac chuckled at the familiarity of their exchange. Looking at his comrade-in-arms, he couldn't believe what he'd been told. At last, the words came out. "Is it true what they say? That you're a woman?"

"Yeah."

Mac sighed and stared at McKellig again to try to see the woman behind the familiar face. "Your name?"

"You can keep on calling me McKellig, or Vic. My given name is Victoria."

"Good God. I'd never have guessed it. You might be a slight fellow, but I'd never have imagined…I mean, you fought three months in my section. We faced military campaigns together…And besides, you saved my life."

Mac pointed to his shoulder. He had a debt to him…to her. Man or woman, it didn't matter. "If you hadn't bumped off that SOB as I was lying there bleeding like a pig, he'd have finished me off. Woman or not, you're my mate, and I'll do anything you ask of me!"

Ginger heard these last words as she entered the room, after having knocked at the door left ajar. She grinned at the athletic man, but she kept her brightest smile for her favourite patient. It had been ten days since Ginger had begun trying to pierce Victoria's armour to bring her back to the routine of the living. Ten long days spent trying to bring a sparkle to those blue eyes, with no luck. So, seeing the glimmer of joy in her patient's eyes in front of this man made Ginger very happy. Was Victoria in love with him? A knot formed in the pit of her stomach at the thought.

Victoria warmly introduced them. "Ginger, this is Mac, my sergeant."

"Madam. And on top of it, you're the lucky one, McKellig. How do you always figure out how to surround yourself with the prettiest ladies?' Mac asked, smiling at the beautiful nurse. "Mine had a hairy chin and ate onions for breakfast."

Victoria chuckled softly, holding her abdomen and taking care not to laugh too hard, since it was rather painful.

Ginger raised her eyebrows questioningly at Mac, who said, "I never saw a soldier as popular with the ladies. They all ran after 'him.' I understand now why they didn't interest you."

Victoria would have liked to explain that those women didn't interest her because her heart was taken by another, not because they were women. But what good would such a conversation serve when it could only hurt her mate?

"Were you also part of the 16th Battalion, Sergeant?"

"Yes, ma'am. The best battalion in the 7th Division. There aren't any better fighters, only solid men…" Mac glanced at Victoria and stammered, "Well, when I say men…naturally some were hairier than others."

"You know, I think I should have waited until that Jap finished you off," a smiling Victoria said.

"Had you fought together long?"

"I was in Tobrouk at first, but McKellig was among the new recruits who came to rally us when we were redeployed to New Guinea. She was assigned to my section. Since then, we've fought together from Kokoda to Shaggy Ridge and Gona. We had barely landed at Balikpapan when I was wounded. McKellig saved my life."

Ginger laughed. "I overheard the part about SO…uh, sergeant…"

Mac's face immediately turned red. He swiveled his head to stare right in Vic's eyes, complicit.

"Rotten luck they got you in turn, McKellig. Otherwise, you'd have finished this bloody war without a scratch."

"We're both very lucky, Mac, unlike most of our fellow soldiers."

"I'm happy you made it and that it's all over. Not a whole lot of us survived the Pacific campaign. Good thing the Yanks dropped their two bombs, or there'd be fewer of us."

Victoria nodded. For a few seconds she was overcome with sadness as her head filled with images of her fallen mates who hadn't been as lucky as they were. Tears glistened in Mac's eyes.

"Well, I'll be on my way and let you rest before your nurse kicks my butt out of here," Mac said, embarrassed by this display of weakness. "I jotted down my address in Sydney on this piece of paper. My wife decided to move there after her father died. Did I tell you he had a construction company? As soon as I'm discharged, I'm going to give it a try—see if I can manage it. If you ever come out that way, I'll introduce Meggan to you, and if you're looking for work, you can count on me."

"I won't hesitate, Mac. After everything I've heard, I sure want to meet that rare treasure of yours."

Victoria then added for Ginger's benefit, "Mac is the only man in the entire 7th Division who wrote at least a daily letter to his wife. You should see the number of photos of Meggan this mountain of muscle carries around with him. Who'd've guessed he'd have a young girl's heart?"

"McKellig! If you weren't a woman, I'd stuff your words right back down your throat. But I'll be gentlemanly today."

Ginger noticed Victoria's fantastic smile. It was the first time she'd ever seen it, and it gave her an undeniable charm. Ginger understood why all the women ran after her, but she didn't understand that nobody had realised she was a woman in the first place. Despite her crew cut, her features were definitely feminine. *People only see what they want to see.*

"If I could stand on my two feet, you wouldn't talk to me that way. I'm expecting you to drop by and visit. Don't you forget it." And then to Ginger, "Madam…"

"A charming man," Ginger commented as Mac's massive figure closed the door behind him.

"A better man doesn't exist. With someone like Mac by your side, you always have your back covered."

❖

"What's this?"

"Your Christmas present."

As Victoria took the package, she looked up at Ginger. She didn't understand. Christmas was in two months.

"The doctor's going to tell you when he makes his rounds later that tomorrow you'll be transferred to a convalescent home, so I'm giving you your gift now. No more days of lying about. From now on you'll be keeping your nose to the grindstone." Ginger was gently teasing.

The fingers busy opening the wrapping paper suddenly stopped moving. Victoria became filled with doubt. "You'll come see me?"

Ginger shook her head no, overcome with sadness. Her voice shook. Since she'd started taking care of Victoria three months earlier, they'd forged a strong friendship. It was hard to see her go. Who else could she confide in about her problems since Virgil's return home just after the armistice?

"You'll be flown to Melbourne to a physiotherapy centre that takes women."

Victoria didn't reply. Melbourne. Might as well be the other side of the world, given her physical state and Ginger's work. Over the course of the past weeks, the friendship between them had grown to the point that Victoria had started to hate Mondays, Ginger's day off. And Ginger came by several times a day during her breaks to chat with Victoria about everything and anything, but especially not about the war.

"Will you write me?"

Ginger hesitated before answering. "Of course."

While Victoria was more or less successfully using her crutches to walk across the patio, a surly voice called out to her. "Don't overdo it. It's a little early in the game for that."

Laboriously, Victoria positioned her crutches to turn around.

"You have a visitor. He says he's your brother, but he's an abo, and I don't—"

Victoria looked across the patio, behind the auxiliary nurse. An enormous smile broke across her face when she recognised her brother. "Robert!"

He hurried over to her and immediately held her against him. When John had written to Robert, asking him to go visit Victoria at this address, and told him why, he hadn't believed him. But he'd come as quickly as possible. It hadn't been easy for him to get inside the facility because of the colour of his skin. However, mentioning his sister's name was an open sesame.

"Vic. Look at you. If Ma and Pa saw you...You're thin as a waif!"

"I hope no one's told them what happened."

"Not that I know of. How are you?"

"Not bad at all, but I do need to sit down. Come on. These goddamn crutches are about as easy to handle as a wool press."

Victoria motioned with her chin to a few empty lawn chairs on the side of the patio, and as she headed over to them, she saw that the auxiliary nurse was still there. The disapproving look she cast at Robert angered Victoria.

"Can I help you?" she coldly asked the auxiliary.

"Your brother?" the woman replied, her face pinched and sceptical.

"Yes, my brother. You wanna see his birth certificate?"

Victoria's sarcastic tone and infuriated look stopped the woman from replying. She knew that Victoria had fought in the troops among men, as she had quite a reputation. The auxiliary nurse wouldn't have admitted it to anyone, but she was a little scared of this strangely silent woman who spent her days staring at the sky. She turned around without another word.

Once settled into her chair with Robert's help, Victoria contemplated the handsome chap sitting in front of her. "How old are you now? Nineteen?"

Robert nodded while scrutinising her. Already skinny to begin with, she'd withered down to nothing but skin and bones. When she'd left Willowra, her face had still been a little chubby, but now her cheeks were hollowed, hardened. Her bright eyes that had sparkled when Elise was still alive had lost their lustre. Robert forced himself to smile to hide his uneasiness.

Victoria observed Robert for a long moment and then whistled between her teeth.

"You've changed, little brother. Where's the scrawny teenager I used to carry on my back?"

Robert held up his arm to show off his biceps. "Gone," he replied, with a huge grin of flashing white teeth that contrasted with his dark skin. "Now I'm the one who'll carry you on my back."

"How's everybody? I got a letter from John last month, but fresh news is always better."

"Everybody's fine. I spent Christmas in Willowra. You should see Audrey now. She's a real lady."

"I knew she'd turn out to be a real sheila. What are you doing in Melbourne?"

"John didn't tell you?" Robert asked.

"What?"

"I'm a student at Adelaide University. John didn't want to leave Willowra and make the old folks suspicious, and since I'm geographically the closest, he asked me to come see you. Why don't you want them to know? They'll be fuming when they find out you've hidden this from them."

Victoria shrugged to chase away the idea and the guilt rising within her.

"Student in what?"

"Law."

"Law? You, a lawyer?"

"And why not?" Robert asked, seeming a bit piqued.

"You're right. Why not. Pa and Ma must be so proud. You're the first in the family to go to university. Tell me more about it."

Victoria listened to Robert talk about Adelaide, his studies, and his new friends. How eloquent he was, with his smooth, clipped accent and precise gestures. Instantly filled with pride, she beamed.

"And now it's your turn."

Victoria grew serious. "I don't have a whole lot to say. I got here almost two months ago and don't know when I'm getting out. It's a slow process. It took a month for me to be able to stand on my own, and they only just let me start walking alone last week."

Robert wanted to ask her about the war, ask her why she joined up, but only one question came to his lips. "Have you met anyone?" he asked.

Victoria's heart pinched as she shook her head no. "Nobody will ever replace Elise," she murmured, surprised by the tears welling up in her eyes after all that time.

"Ma puts flowers on her grave once a week, along with the ones for her parents, Aaron, and Philip."

"I don't want to talk about Elise, Robert."

He gave a sorrowful look before picking up again with a smile. "Do you know who's courting Audrey?"

"But she's just a baby!"

"She's eighteen, and she's talking about marrying the Norseman banker's son."

"A banker? But who's going to stay in Willowra to help Ma and Pa if she gets married? With you becoming a lawyer…our parents aren't getting any younger."

"John and his children. And you, if you wanted to. I know you love the station. You'll come home one day. I'm sure of it."

Victoria didn't answer. How could she ever return there without thinking constantly about Elise?

CHAPTER THIRTY-FOUR

Brisbane, Queensland, April 1948

Sitting on a low wall in the shade of a huge tree, a half-smoked cigarette dangling from her hand, Victoria waited, her eyes riveted on the hospital door. She was counting on Ginger to come out of this one. Hopefully she'd gotten the message. She hadn't been surprised when the people at the front desk had declined to give her Ginger's address. But why did they treat her with such disdain? Admittedly, she was dressed like a swagman, but so what? She had wordlessly swallowed her anger and walked out.

She'd been patiently waiting for two hours now. What else could she do? She couldn't find "Ginger Abbot" in the phone book, so she'd returned to the military hospital, where she learned that Ginger had changed hospitals at the end of the war and was working here now.

A short, slender figure stepped out of the huge hospital door and took a sweeping look around her, attracting Victoria's attention. It was Ginger, in her white nurse's uniform. Victoria quickly threw down her cigarette butt, jumped to her feet, and limped over to the small woman quickly walking toward her.

Ginger frowned for an instant when she noticed Victoria's limp, but she hastily recovered and enjoyed the pleasure of once again seeing her singular patient. She and Jane had often wondered what had become of her. Though Victoria stopped a yard in front of Ginger, the latter quickly closed the distance, taking Victoria into her arms.

Surprised at this gesture, but thrilled, Victoria wrapped her arms around Ginger. She fully savoured these precious moments of human warmth.

"I should give you a smack instead of hugging you," Ginger murmured, her voice full of emotion, then took a step back. "You were supposed to write. I had a letter ready, but I could never find out exactly where they'd sent you."

Victoria lowered her head. "I know." She was stammering. "But I didn't have the guts. It was…hard."

"I'm sure it was. We have so much to catch up on, but not now. I just finished my shift and have to get changed. When I saw your message, I couldn't help rushing out right away to make sure it was really you! Wait for me right here. I just need ten minutes."

As she hurried back inside the hospital, she couldn't resist turning around to make sure she hadn't been dreaming. It had been more than two and a half years since she'd had news from this woman whom she considered her friend, and then suddenly, she'd just reappeared.

Thinking of all the mistakes she'd made since they last met, she hoped Victoria wouldn't judge her too harshly. She didn't have to mention her ruined marriage, but if the subject came up, she wouldn't be able to lie. She was too honest. Everything in its own good time, a little voice murmured in her head. Surely Victoria was just passing through town and they wouldn't have enough time for her to reveal all her mistakes.

"Want to come to the house for tea?" Ginger proposed as soon as she came back out again. Victoria was still sitting on the low wall.

"Okay. How's Thomas?"

They walked toward the bus stop.

"Good. He'll be four soon. And Simone will be two in July."

"Simone?"

"My daughter."

A brief but uneasy feeling shot through Victoria without her knowing why. She fought against her disappointment; Virgil was still around. After hours and hours of conversation back when she was Ginger's patient, Victoria had had the impression that things weren't going well between Ginger and her husband. Victoria would have liked to ask her, but too many people were at the bus stop, and it wasn't the appropriate place. The old rickety bus that arrived put an end to their exchange.

Victoria had questions, but so did Ginger. Even if Victoria's blue eyes were brighter, Ginger could still glimpse signs of sadness or melancholy the moment she thought no one was watching.

The bus ride, although only twenty minutes long, seemed like an eternity. Ginger finally signalled that it was time to get off. Once out of the bus's stifling heat, Victoria followed Ginger along a small winding road leading to the heights of Brisbane.

Forcing herself to keep up with Ginger's brisk pace, Victoria winced with pain. The heavy sweat that ran down her back and face reminded her that she had returned to the tropics. She often had to force herself not to think about the claustrophobic jungle that invaded her nightmares. When Ginger finally stopped at the door of a tiny wooden house isolated from the others, Victoria was thoroughly relieved. As she caught her breath, she admired the carefully groomed garden and the wide, shaded veranda.

Ginger, who had stopped at her front door to wait for her friend, was now observing her. How did she perceive this house? She had tried to make it seem cosy, but she didn't like the place her husband had chosen for them: too close to the forest and its dangerous creatures for young children, and too small, while the land was too vast to maintain correctly. Ginger hadn't hidden her disapproval, but Virgil had just laughed at her…as he always did.

"Coming?"

Victoria turned to Ginger, who was waiting for her, and smiled. And she almost giggled when she heard a kookaburra's cry. She had always loved this bizarre bird's mocking laughter. Seeing Ginger grow impatient, Victoria hurried her step.

"Nice view," Victoria commented as soon as they were settled on the veranda with tea and biscuits.

Admiring the breadth of the ocean was still magical for Victoria. She had seen the sea for the very first time at Perth, about six years ago. Since then, she'd felt she would never grow tired of watching it.

"Yes. It is a nice view."

"But you don't like the house."

"No."

"Why? I've seen worse."

Ginger sighed. Indeed. How could she explain to Victoria what she felt without being judged? Was she ready to admit to her what she had been hiding from everyone? Against her better judgment, the words flowed freely from her mouth.

"Virgil chose it…without taking my opinion into account. He's never around, and I'm the one who has to take care of the garden and the house while working full-time. I didn't even choose the furniture. It's his parents'."

All of Ginger's resentment poured out. She glanced at Victoria, who, instead of judging her, was listening attentively. That was enough to bring tears to Ginger's eyes.

"Virgil is always away for work. And on top of it, I know he has other women in his life. I never should have married him."

This heartfelt statement broke the final barrier between them. Filled with regret and greatly distressed, Ginger sobbed quietly. Victoria placed a friendly hand on her shoulder, reminding her she had a guest. Ginger took a handkerchief from her skirt pocket and dabbed her eyes.

"I'm sorry, Victoria. I don't know what came over me."

"Sometimes you just have to let things out. I know something about that."

Victoria's soft, gentle voice, along with the warmth of her hand, helped soothe Ginger's emotions. Her tears gradually stopped coming, and she found the courage to look Victoria in the eye.

Victoria gave her an understanding smile and then took her hand away to go sit down. What else could she do?

Ginger took a sip of tea. The mix of tartness and sweetness instantly made her feel better. "And what have you been doing all this time? Did you go back to Willowra?"

Surprised by Ginger's memory, Victoria shook her head no. She didn't want to talk about Willowra. "Since my release from the physical-therapy facility, I've picked up work here and there. In Canberra, then in Sydney, for Mac—you remember Mac, my sergeant? With my handicap, it's not easy to find a job. Not to mention my also being a woman."

"Don't you receive a pension?" Ginger suddenly looked worried.

Victoria grinned. "They didn't want pay me one at first, but I threatened to disclose my story, so they are now. However, they refuse to make me eligible to receive veterans' aid."

Realising Victoria wasn't going to expand on the subject, Ginger asked, "Where are you staying?"

"For the moment, at a small hotel. If I find work, I'll try to move somewhere else."

Joy surged in Ginger's heart. Her friend wanted to remain in Brisbane. She would finally have someone she could talk to, but for the moment, her professionalism pushed her to ask questions she knew would upset Victoria.

"I've been watching you. You're in a lot of pain. Isn't that so?' Ginger pointed to Victoria's leg.

Victoria wasn't happy about the change in subject, but she supposed it was better to answer the question and get the conversation over with. Victoria let out a heavy sigh; she refused to hide the truth.

"Yes. They said the pain would subside over time, but there isn't any improvement. I suppose I'll be handicapped until the end of my days. In any case, it's my fault, right? I shouldn't have joined up. I just should have stayed put at home."

Seeing the defiance and anger in Victoria's eyes, Ginger kept quiet. Strangely, even the birds had gone quiet. Victoria turned her head to stare at the vast ocean stretched out to the horizon's edge. Without realising how bitter she sounded, she spat out, "I wanted to get killed, and here I am, nearly incapable of working. I'm not even sure I can get back on a horse one day. I can walk, but each step is sheer torture. Some would say it's God's punishment for all my sins. If I believed in God, I'd say so too. I don't want to go back to Willowra and see the pity on my parents' and siblings' faces. I left Sydney because Mac's wife was jealous of me. As if someone could be seriously interested in a cripple!"

When Victoria finally glanced at Ginger, she was surprised to see her face, which was usually so gentle, now red with anger.

"Are you done? Are you quite finished feeling sorry for yourself? I thought you were a fighter, but I can see I was mistaken."

The cutting remark made Victoria sit up in her seat, her nostrils flared, as anger rushed through her. "I'd like to see you—"

"Have you consulted a doctor? I'm sure you haven't. You revel in your misery. Since I first saw you in your hospital bed, I knew you were looking to get punished, that the pain was your punishment. For what crime? What did you do that was so horrible?"

Too surprised to realise that Ginger was right, Victoria opened her mouth, but nothing came out. A thousand things to say bumped about in her mind. She thought back upon the last years…the storm. Elise's death was an accident, an unfortunate accident. She wasn't responsible for her death.

"I didn't realise…you're right. I'm punishing myself for something I couldn't help. I'm going to see a doctor for my leg."

Swallowing her justified anger, Ginger sighed. "You won't tell me what happened, will you?"

"Maybe one day."

Knowing she wouldn't get any more out of her, Ginger said, "I know a good surgeon."

"Ah!" Slowly, a smirk crept up Victoria's lips. Ginger had just manipulated her. "I guess a nurse is well placed to suggest one. Who is it?"

"My boss."

❖

Ginger hurried over to Victoria, who was leaving the doctor's office. She had stayed late to wait for her at the end of her shift. "So?"

"I don't know. I didn't understand everything. On the X-ray he showed me a piece of shrapnel that was left in me. It's irritating the nerve that runs down the front of my thigh. How can such a tiny fragment in the lower stomach cause so much pain?"

"Curial neuralgia," Ginger mumbled. "I should have thought of it."

"What?"

"The technical term doesn't matter. You're lucky the presence of a foreign body didn't trigger an infection. It happens. I suppose as soon as the shrapnel is removed, you'll no longer be in pain. Is that what he said?"

"He said the pain should disappear, but I'll always have a slight limp because my pelvis is…isn't the way it should be."

"It's displaced. That happens after a fracture, but you won't suffer any longer, and that's what's most important. I knew he could do something for you."

Ginger put her arm around Victoria's shoulders in an affectionate victory gesture. "When will he operate?"

As Victoria didn't answer her, Ginger let go of her to look right in her face.

"Victoria?"

Victoria turned her head to escape her gaze.

"He's going to operate, isn't he? Look at me."

Finally, Victoria faced Ginger's questioning eyes. "I can't, Ginger. I don't have the money. I could pay for the operation with my savings, but spending several weeks without work when I have to pay for lodging, food, and physical therapy…I just can't afford it."

Ginger was overcome with anger. She forced herself to loosen her clenched jaw and shoulders before speaking. Victoria could be so stubborn sometimes!

"You can stay at my house. Room and board. I'll take care of the bandages myself, and that way you'll save money on nurse care."

"Your husband." Victoria tried to argue.

"That's my problem. And there won't be one," Ginger asserted with more certainty than she actually felt. "Now there's just the question of how to pay for your physical therapy. Your parents...?"

"No!"

"Victoria, you must immediately stop with this misplaced pride. You don't want to suffer for the rest of your life. Isn't that so?"

Ginger, hand on her hips, stopped suddenly when a slight smile came to Victoria's lips, and she looked at her, frowning.

"You often say 'isn't that so?'" Victoria explained, imitating Ginger's Queensland accent. "It's cute."

"Victoria!"

Ginger threw her hands up to the sky. This woman could be so frustrating. If she didn't control herself, she might strangle her.

"Okay." Victoria conceded in deference to Ginger's infuriated stare. "I'll ask John if he can send me some money. But you may end up regretting that you've invited me to stay at your place. I'm not an easy patient."

Ginger, whose anger had suddenly vanished, broke out in laughter. "You think I don't know that? Who took care of you last time? Me. Isn't that so?"

A grin wreathed Victoria's lips.

When Ginger realised why, she sighed and threw her hands up in the air once again without daring to say anything else.

❖

Victoria helplessly listened to the rising voices coming from the other side of the wall. If she'd been able to get up, she would have, but she was stuck in bed until the doctor gave her the authorisation to move around. He had been very clear on that account when he'd allowed her to leave the hospital earlier than expected. So Victoria clenched her teeth to hold back the cold rage growing in her heart. Virgil didn't deserve Ginger. Victoria had disliked him from the moment they met— too pretentious, too self-conceited and vain. The type of person who thought other people were always to blame and who managed to squirm out of everything unscathed. She had seen a number of men like that, hiding away while others were getting killed.

"How long's she gonna stay here?' he screamed.

"The time it takes. Victoria is my friend." Ginger sounded calm and steady.

Despite the situation, Victoria smiled. This tiny woman could make herself heard when it counted. How many times had she heard her raise her voice, though she'd never yell, at an uncooperative patient?

"You decided all this on your own!"

"You're never here, and Dr. Markham agreed to operate immediately. Why have her wait an extra day while she was suffering? Victoria was wounded in combat in Borneo. You can at least respect that fact!"

The sharp sound of a slap almost made Victoria jump out of her bed, but a blazing pain in her lower stomach instantly stopped her.

"I'm your husband, and I decide who we welcome into our home," Virgil screamed. "She's leaving immediately!"

"No!"

Her heart pounding, Victoria, powerless to do anything, heard several muffled sounds, then a few minutes later, a door slam and a car engine roar. Virgil had left the house. A moment of reprieve for Ginger. Victoria tried to unclench her fists, but she was overcome with worry for Ginger. Suddenly, the silence became oppressive.

"Ginger!"

No answer. The children were at their grandmother's. If Virgil had…No. Victoria didn't want to think the worst. Not yet. Suppressing her rising panic, she continued to shout, "Ginger! Ginger!"

No longer able to restrain herself, she threw back the bed sheet, ignoring the pain surging in her lower belly, and tried to sit at the edge of the bed.

"What do you think you're doing?" an anxious voice murmured from the doorway.

Victoria immediately froze and scanned for any sign of injury to Ginger, who came over to her, gently pushing her back onto her pillow. With expert hands she lifted the bandage to make sure her stitches were still in place. Seeming satisfied, she put the sheet back over Victoria.

"I heard…I was worried about you."

"You have no reason to be," Ginger replied, avoiding her eyes.

Victoria gently took Ginger's chin and turned her head to reveal the other side of her face, furious when she saw the reddish mark on her right cheek. "The bastard! If I weren't an invalid…One day he'll get what's coming to him."

Anger and indignation were flashing in Victoria's eyes, and Ginger's heart was aflutter for this woman and her chivalrous instincts. If only her husband were a bit like her.

"It's nothing," Ginger whispered, escaping Victoria's hand.

"Nothing?"

Ginger's silence suddenly made Victoria understand, and the certainty of her realization felt like a lead weight on her shoulders. She stammered as she asked, "That wasn't the first time, was it? He…he beats you? Why do you stay with him?"

Ginger sighed as she took a bedroom chair and pulled it over to sit down next to Victoria. It would provide welcome support for this conversation that she dreaded though needed to have. She didn't know what else to do.

"When he hit me the first time, just after our wedding, he was drunk and apologised the next day. I told myself the liquor was responsible, but the next time, he wasn't even drunk. I threatened to leave him, and he said he'd find me and kill me. Those weren't just words, Victoria."

"If you had told me, I wouldn't have accepted your invitation."

"I know. That's why I didn't say anything."

Victoria was about to say something but kept quiet. Who was she to judge other people's reasons for doing things? Ginger didn't want to be judged. She needed a friend.

"You can't let him continue."

"What else can I do? Divorce him and run away with the children to live in constant fear the rest of my life? I'm not the first woman this has happened to, and I won't be the last. At the hospital, I see women whose husbands beat them every day. Many husbands are far worse than Virgil. I often wonder whether all men beat their wives."

"Not all men. My father has never raised a hand to my mother, and if my brother John ever touched a hair on his wife's head, Pa would skin his hide. Not that he hit us often, only when we truly deserved it. But he warned John before he got married to always be kind to his wife if he wanted to preserve her love."

Despite her aching cheek, Ginger smiled. "How do you know that?" she asked, teasing. "Was it a family discussion, or were you eavesdropping?"

Red-cheeked, Victoria stirred slightly in her bed. Instantly a sharp pain distorted her features into a grimace.

"Something like that. John was seventeen and wanted to marry his sweetheart Maureen. I knew it, and I also knew he wanted to speak with our father, so I'd been watching them. I was curious. My father is a good man who never gets angry. He's a quiet, peaceful man. I've never seen him drunk."

"You admire him."

"I wish I were like him, but I'm much more impulsive. He often reprimanded me for that…"

Ginger raised her eyebrows. Victoria impulsive? She never would have guessed it.

"That's not the impression I have. Since we've met, you've been more quiet and taciturn than exuberant and talkative."

A look of doubt flashed across Victoria's eyes. She paused. "The war must have changed me and…the loss…of someone dear to me."

Victoria hung her head. Was she annoyed with herself for having said more than she intended?

"Ah! We've gotten onto uncomfortable ground. Isn't that so? I'm starting to pick up on your signals, Vic."

A wide grin from Vic gave Ginger the strength to get up from her chair. "You're making fun of my way of speaking again," she exclaimed, exasperated.

"No. Stay. I wasn't making fun of you. I smiled because I've never heard you call me Vic before. You took your time."

"I have to get tea ready for this evening before I fetch the children. Do you want a tamarind juice or something else before I start?"

"No. Water is just fine. Thanks. And Virgil?' Victoria asked shyly.

"He'll come back once he's calmed down. This evening, or next month, for all I care. It would suit me just fine if he never came back!"

Her back stiff with anger, Ginger briskly walked out of the bedroom, leaving Victoria alone with her thoughts: her father, Willowra. It was funny to realise that Jason had always counted more for her than Maggie had, while for John, Robert and Audrey, it was the opposite. Was it because she'd come to Willowra when she was already a little girl, while the others were babies or toddlers? Or perhaps because Jason had saved her from a certain death in that desolate street?

Was the love she felt for Jason only gratitude? She shook her head and smiled. Jason was the only man she had loved, and undoubtedly would love, her entire life. But not the same kind of love she'd felt for Elise. Her passionate Elise. Victoria sighed with melancholy before realising that for the first time she'd thought of Elise without tears instantly welling up in her eyes. An eerie feeling of loss, but without the pain. What had changed?

The sound of pots and pans clanking in the kitchen gave Victoria the answer. Ginger. *No, no, no*, she told herself. *I can't fall in love with her. She's married with two children!* But an insidious voice in her head whispered that Ginger didn't love her husband, and she had stood up to him so Victoria could stay. She wanted to fight these thoughts that foretold nothing good. What should she do? An ironic snort stuck in her throat. Nothing. She couldn't do anything as long as she was confined to bed.

❖

Ginger silently observed the figure sitting on the veranda. Every day when she came home from work, now that Victoria could get out of bed, she'd find Vic contemplating the ocean and the horizon. A few more physical-therapy sessions and she would no longer need the cane that now hung off the side of her armchair. Victoria would leave to go live elsewhere. Ginger didn't want to think about that fact, just as she didn't want to think about how embarrassed and sickened she'd felt the other day when Virgil had touched her while she knew Victoria was in the next room. Although Victoria hadn't said a word, she could see the reproach in her eyes.

Victoria brought a cigarette to her lips. Ginger smiled and shook her head. "That's a very bad habit for a young woman from a good family. What will the neighbours think?"

A smirk on her lips, Victoria turned to Ginger. And with the same light tone, she replied, "Just tell 'em I come from a sheep station in Western Australia, and that'll explain everything. After, I can dress and do as I like, and no one will have a word to say about it. Everybody knows that us people from the bush don't have no manners."

Ginger threw her head back to laugh. She loved it when Victoria laid on her back-country accent.

"Did physical therapy go well today?"

"Yes, and I found work."

So quickly...Ginger's spirit baulked. After a month, Victoria's presence had become indispensable. And the children adored her. She'd never met anyone with so much patience. Everyone would miss Victoria after she left.

"Where?" Ginger dared ask.

"I had a talk with Old Man Rodney when I went to see your mother and the children. He fired his delivery man for drunkenness, and I applied for the job. After swearing that I didn't drink—'everybody knows that women drink less than men'—and that I've been driving trucks since I was fifteen, he offered it to me. I start Monday."

And before Ginger could say a word, Victoria added, "They have a vacant room, so I'm moving there Sunday. That way you'll have your peace and quiet back."

Ginger swallowed. The news really wasn't that bad. Victoria wasn't going far; old Rodney's place was just two streets away.

"I'm going to miss you," she whispered, honestly.

Victoria didn't dare turn her head to Ginger, not wanting to betray her true feelings. She didn't want to go either, but hearing Ginger and Virgil make love in the next room was more than she could bear. It had taken every bit of self-control she had the other day not to intervene and throw Virgil out. How she had cried and cried tears of frustration.

"I won't be far. Don't worry. You're not getting rid of me that easily. I told your mother I would bring 'round her groceries every afternoon at the end of my day. That way I can see the children…if that's okay with you, of course."

Ginger gently laid her hand on Victoria's shoulder. Vic stifled the impulse to grab it and kiss Ginger's palm.

"The children adore you. Isn't that so? They're never better behaved than when you tell them stories about the bush."

"My father told me those stories when I was little. I loved them too."

"Mama! Vic! Grannie made a cake!"

Thomas, followed by his little sister, ran onto the veranda. A few seconds later, Ginger's mother appeared, holding a cake.

"You shouldn't have come all this way, Ma. You're going to tire yourself out." Ginger scolded her mother as she took the cake from her hands. "I would have come to get the kids within the next half hour. The doctor wants you to rest."

Ginger's mother, even shorter than her, paid no attention to Ginger's reprimands. "Victoria promised them a story when she came by earlier. They couldn't wait any longer."

When Ginger turned to Victoria, the two children were already comfortably seated in her lap as she started telling them the dromedary's tale.

"I can make tea in peace, from what I see," Ginger exclaimed, hands on her hips.

Victoria replied with a smile and a wink, making Ginger's heart flutter.

CHAPTER THIRTY-FIVE

Ginger took a good look at Victoria. She seemed different today. This generally silent but direct woman was hiding something—something Ginger wouldn't be happy about.

Victoria hadn't been herself since she had arrived earlier that evening. Over the past year, the two of them had established a comfortable routine: when Virgil was gone, Victoria came to the house after evening tea to say good night to the children and share a fresh fruit juice or hot drink with her.

But this evening seemed different. Victoria had of course helped put the children to bed. However, once the two of them were comfortably settled in on the veranda, she'd avoided Ginger's eyes and given only monosyllabic answers to Ginger's questions. Ginger couldn't hold back any longer. "Spit it out, Victoria!"

In the setting sun's faint light, Ginger saw Victoria's face change. Her nervousness had faded, but a deep, deep sadness remained.

"What makes you think I've got something to say?' Victoria asked, trying to put off the inevitable.

Ginger threw her a meaningful glance. No need for words. Their bond had only grown stronger with time. Victoria forced herself to utter what had been stuck in her throat. "I'm going to leave, Ginger. I'm leaving Brisbane."

Ginger drew a sharp breath. She had expected anything but that. Victoria wanted to leave? She couldn't wrap her head around it. She felt like screaming at Victoria that she couldn't abandon her, but she restrained herself.

Victoria lowered her head. Her resolve dissipated when she saw Ginger's features tensed. But what else could she do?

"When? Why? Where?"

"Tomorrow, I think. I'm returning to Willowra. It's time."

"Have you had news from there?"

Victoria shook her head.

"So why now? I thought Willowra was filled with bad memories, though you've never wanted to speak of it. Vic, I need you—here, with me."

Despite her pained heart, Victoria wanted to ignore her plea, but she couldn't.

"Willowra holds a lot of good memories, and one bad memory that I've tried to escape for years. My first love is buried there, and I just couldn't imagine a solitary life for myself…"

Even if they hadn't spoken about it, Ginger suspected something of the sort, which fitted well with Victoria's chivalrous personality. Her stomach was in knots. She had to find a way to keep Victoria with her.

"What's changed? If you go now, you'll still be alone."

Victoria leaned back into her armchair, closing her eyes. Ginger wouldn't be convinced without putting up a fight. She'd figured it out beforehand. What could she safely tell her without revealing too much?

"What's changed is that I know I'm finally able to love again. My heart will always be with my first love, but now I know I also have room for someone else."

"Are you in love?"

Ginger was surprised. But what surprised her even more was the jealousy rising within her. Imagining Victoria in love with a man, and her wanting to leave to be with this person…it was too much.

"Yes. An impossible love, but one that consumes me more and more each day. I have to leave to protect myself. I've fought it for a long time, tried to stop it from growing, but I can't any longer. Forgive me."

The distress on Victoria's face brought tears to Ginger's eyes. "Why didn't you confide in me sooner? We're friends. I could have helped you, made him change his mind if he doesn't want you."

Ginger already hated this man without even knowing him. She wanted to cry out, "Forget him and stay. I need you." Ginger had never really stopped to think about her feelings for Victoria, probably afraid of what she would find. Her pain at just the thought of never seeing her again was agonising.

Victoria opened her eyes and turned to Ginger, her heart wrenched by the tears she saw on the cheeks of the woman she loved. All she wanted to do was to take her in her arms, but she forced herself to remain seated and stay on the course she had set for herself—leaving

Brisbane. Yet within this insidious pain, which seemed like a slow death, Ginger's tears gave her a glimmer of hope. She had to kill this bud of hope in order to have no regrets. She had made up her mind and forced her sadness away.

Ginger noticed the change in the determined blue eyes that held her stare with great intensity.

"Not him. Her. I've never been in love with a man in my entire life, Ginger."

In a fraction of a second Ginger's stomach jumped. She swallowed several times to force herself to calm down. Jealousy instantly devoured her, and this unexpected feeling shocked her. The words stayed stuck in her throat while her heart screamed, "Who is this woman who has taken my place?" Yet her mind kept repeating, "This love isn't right. Victoria has to go."

"Who?" she whispered.

Seeing the gleam in Victoria's eyes, she immediately understood.

"You. I love you, Ginger, and not like a friend. Not being able to touch you, imagining your husband doing to you what I'd like to—then seeing the black and blue marks on your arms and not even having the right to defend you—it's all more than I can bear. I have to leave to avoid going mad with jealousy and ending up a bitter old spinster."

Ginger closed her eyes and instinctively wrapped her arms around herself, as if she could protect herself from the shock of the words. She took several deep breaths to calm her heartbeat. She had to give Victoria an answer, find the right words...but what were the right words? She opened her eyes and stared at Victoria, instantly understanding.

"You're expecting me to call you a pervert and chase you away. Isn't that so? That would make things easier for you. You could then leave, saying everything is my fault."

Spewing her anger, Ginger planted herself squarely in front of Victoria. She leaned over her, placing her hands on the armrests of Victoria's chair. "No, Victoria. You won't get away with this so easily."

With Ginger's face just a few inches from hers, Ginger's legs brushing against hers...Victoria's senses took over. Incapable of thinking, she reacted. Slipping her hand behind Ginger's head, she brushed her fingers through the silky hair she had dreamt so often about: the object of her fantasies. She slowly brought Ginger's head closer. The softness of Ginger's lips on hers made her senses soar. Everything else vanished around her. Her eyes closed. Lost in this world of sensation, she tasted the honey lips with the tip of her tongue, hesitantly at first, slowly penetrating the soft warmth of her mouth. A rush of blood surged when their tongues touched. One hand still stroking her soft hair, she slipped the other one down Ginger's shoulders to the tempting roundness before her.

When she felt Victoria caressing her breasts, Ginger instantly pulled away from her bewitching lips, pushing back on the armrests to distance herself from Victoria's chair. Standing in the middle of the veranda with her arms wrapped around her own waist, she closed her eyes. What had just happened? What she'd just felt threw her into a panic. She would have liked to chase away the intense pleasure that had filled her; forget the moistness between her legs, which made her red with shame. She had never before known such a feeling of utter voluptuousness, even with Virgil—particularly not with Virgil.

"Ginger," a gentle voice called out to her.

Keeping her eyes shut, Ginger raised her hand, ordering Victoria to keep quiet. A prolonged silence lingered until the voice, filled with sadness, started again. "I'm so sorry. I shouldn't have. I'll go now."

Ginger suddenly opened her eyes again. Surprised to see Victoria standing so near, she took a step back. Victoria turned away, avoiding her eyes.

Ginger then called out to her. "I would strongly advise you against running away, Victoria, not after what just happened. You have some explaining to do."

Victoria stopped and squared her shoulders back. She had faced death in the world's most dangerous jungle, and she wasn't going to wimp out now. Taking a deep breath, she turned around to confront Ginger. Although dusk blurred things, she could see the troubled look in her eyes, mirroring her own turmoil.

"Are you really sorry?" Ginger asked.

"No. I have long dreamt of that kiss—every evening before falling asleep these last months."

"Are you disappointed?"

A smile came to Victoria's lips as she shook her head. "Not at all. It was sweeter than I could ever have imagined."

Ginger was upset with herself for asking such questions. She should have chased Victoria away, told her to never return; but her senses betrayed her, and she wanted more. So, instead, she said, "That was the sweetest kiss of my entire life. My heart is still racing."

Surprised by her confession, Victoria didn't realise Ginger had come so close to her. When Ginger's hand hesitatingly rested on

Victoria's shoulder, all her muscles tensed at this oh-so-sweet touch. She took Ginger's hand, sliding it slowly down her own body to her breasts. Then she closed her eyes as Ginger started gently fondling her, opening them again when she felt Ginger press her entire body against hers. The soft lips she was offered were irresistible. Victoria lowered her head, brushing her lips against Ginger's before tasting them another time.

From soft and hesitant, the kiss grew warm and passionate. She wrapped her arms around Ginger, caressing her back and the nape of her neck, then stroking down to the soft round backside of this woman she so desired. Then she hugged Ginger against her with all her might without interrupting her kiss. Victoria wanted, she would have so much liked…but she didn't dare for fear of scaring her off. She practically shrieked in protest when Ginger removed her lips from hers.

Out of breath, Ginger snuggled up in Victoria's arms. Her legs shook so much she feared she wouldn't be able to stand. What Victoria made her feel was so new and strange, so different. For the first time in her life, she felt alive.

"Come," Ginger said, taking her hand.

Victoria didn't want to interrupt this divine moment. "Where?"

"To my room. I don't want to make a spectacle of myself on the veranda, and that's what's going to happen if we stay here."

Victoria hesitated. Ginger's room? With a bed? The temptation would be too strong.

"I'm not sure I'll be able to resist if we go to your room."

"Resist what?"

"Making love to you," Victoria whispered.

Ginger ran her tongue over her dry lips before answering hoarsely. "Who's asking you to resist?"

CHAPTER THIRTY-SIX

Victoria quickened her pace as she turned up the collar of her soaked leather jacket. She had forgotten that blasted umbrella—once again. Would she ever get used to having to drag it around with her everywhere she went during rainy season? At this time of year, Ginger never went anywhere without hers, but she was a local, and these tropical storms didn't faze her. If only a portion of this water could rain on Willowra, Jason and Maggie would be so pleased.

Readjusting her hat to keep the rain from running down her neck, Victoria continued to walk up the hill toward Ginger's house, smiling. They had been lovers for three months now, and Victoria had once again begun to enjoy life. The only shadow looming on their horizon was Virgil. They had decided to face him together the next time he returned from a trip. In fact, Victoria had made the decision. Ginger dreaded his reaction.

Although at least one more hour of daylight remained, the clouds were so dark and the rain pouring down so heavily that it was difficult for Victoria to avoid the rivulets streaming down the small road. What was the point of even trying when she was already soaked from head to toe? Ginger would certainly scold her and tell her to take off her clothes…the thought put another grin on Victoria's face. She loved for Ginger to help her get undressed. Only a few more yards and Ginger's warm, supple body would be welcoming her.

Just when Victoria was about to turn onto the small path that led to the house, her sixth sense kicked in. She looked toward the forest, where the path ended. A flash of lightning, immediately followed by a deafening thunderbolt, streaked across the sky. Once again plunged into darkness, she stopped dead-still. Her instinct, which had saved her so many times during the war, was on full alert. Had she imagined what she thought she saw during that fraction of a second?

Hadn't she spotted the reflection of a car's chromed features? Intrigued without really understanding why, she headed for the forest. Not until she was only two yards away could she make out the automobile parked behind the large bushes—Virgil's car! Her hair immediately stood on end. A thousand questions came to mind, but one topped all the others: why had he deliberately hidden his vehicle? He wasn't supposed to return until the following week. If he hadn't parked in the usual spot, it had to be to surprise Ginger. Did he suspect something?

Fear, similar to what she'd felt in New Guinea, assailed her, clenched her insides, and then, just as if she were on a perilous mission, a surge of calm and determination washed over her. Finding the stealthy agility that had more than once saved her life, she headed for Ginger's house, hiding herself as best she could. Between the darkness and the rain, it was highly improbable someone would see her, but at this moment, she needed to be even more cautious than urgent. Deep in her bones she believed Virgil had returned with bad intentions. The man was violent, unpredictable, and her gentle Ginger's life was in his claws. Every one of her cells told her to hurry, but her military training kept her step steady. Before the war, she would have rushed in without thinking, but life had taught her better; she'd grown far more mature.

Slowly, Victoria approached the side of the veranda, inching her way toward the door. The sound of the rain on the tin roof covered the noise of her steps on the wood-plank floor. But what hid her steps also hindered her ability to hear anything except the sound of the torrential rain beating on the roof. Taking care to avoid obstacles, she gradually made her way along the wooden walls to peek inside through the living-room window. What she saw made her blood frigid: Ginger, rolled into a ball, protecting herself from Virgil's relentless kicks. All reason instantly left Victoria. She dashed to the door, slamming it wide open, and rushed over to Virgil, who was screaming, "You disgusting slut. I'll teach you to cheat on me! Are you gonna tell me his name, or am I gonna have to kill you?! You stupid bitch! You dirty, ugly moll! You—"

Thrust forward over Ginger's body by a 120 pounds of pure fury, Virgil abruptly collapsed to the ground. He didn't have time to react: a hand had already grabbed his hair, forcing his head back and then violently slamming it against the floor...once...twice...His brain felt like it was rattling inside his skull. He tried to grab the individual who was keeping him pinned to the ground...three times...he could feel unconsciousness closing in...four...In a last life surge he pushed against the floor with all his might to unseat the individual on his back, but this move only allowed for his head to be thrust down more violently against the ground...five...Virgil suddenly collapsed...six... seven times...

Victoria had lost any notion of how long she'd been slamming the bastard's head against the ground; her right arm hurt. She gradually came to understand that the figure underneath her was no longer moving. Her arm, which had been robotically heaving up and down, slowed until it finally stopped. Out of breath, still tense with subsiding fury, she painstakingly released her grasp on his thick hair and snapped back to reality at the sound of a desperate moan. Recoiling from Virgil, she crawled over to the shaking figure entirely hunched up on its side: Ginger.

Taking her carefully in her arms, she kissed her forehead. "Ginger, Ginger...it's me, Vic. Talk to me, please! Ginger!"

Victoria tenderly rocked Ginger's warm body, tears running down her face. Not knowing how to help her, she kept Ginger in her arms, speaking softly, numb to the outside world, the raging storm, the rain coming through the still-open front door. Hours seemed to have passed.

In reality, if Victoria had looked at the clock, she would have realised that only ten minutes had elapsed between the moment she had entered the house and now, when Ginger was stroking her cheek.

"Victoria," Ginger murmured, trying to turn around in her beloved's arms. "What happened? Where's Virgil?"

"Ginger. Oh, Ginger! I thought I'd lost you!" Victoria buried her face in Ginger's neck and started to sob.

Ginger softly stroked Victoria's mussed-up hair with her fingers. Victoria's fear was still palpable. That this soldier who had seen everything could be frightened to this extent brought Ginger back to harsh reality. Despite the pain in her side and the weight of Victoria's body pressing against hers, she managed to sit up. Then, seeing Virgil limp on the floor right next to them gave her a shot of adrenaline that instantly cleared her head.

"Victoria! What happened?" she cried in a harsh tone.

Untangling herself from Victoria's arms, she looked up and wiped the tears from her face before taking a deep breath.

"He was kicking you, over and over. I saw red...I knocked him out."

Slowly, to avoid compounding her physical pain, Ginger made

her way over to Virgil. Years of habit and nursing experience took over instantly as she checked his vital signs. Stone-faced, she turned to Victoria. "He's dead."

"No!" Victoria opened her mouth, but nothing came out. She took a deep breath.

"I didn't mean to…I…he…I just wanted him to stop."

"He's stopped all right…for good. I'm going to call the police." Ginger got up with difficulty, leaning on the table for support.

"No! Not the police! If you call them, I'll end up in prison."

"I'll say he was going to kill me and you came to my defence."

Victoria jumped to her feet to take Ginger in her arms and looked her right in the eye.

"Think about it. With my being a soldier in the war and the neighbours' testimonies, the police will suspect our affair, and everything will be lost. I don't want to be separated from you."

"What do you propose then?"

Victoria took a moment to think. "His car is parked on the back road, hidden from sight. I almost didn't see it. Not a single person was out during the storm, so there's little chance anyone noticed Virgil was back. Help me put him in the car, and I'll get rid of the body."

"Nobody can ever find it. Go where the river flows into the ocean. It's filled with crocodiles. You have to dump it there."

Ginger interrupted herself. Now that she was freed from the person who had been the subject of her nightmares for so long, she was calculating rapidly. "I'll get an old blanket to wrap him in, just in case. We don't need the neighbours to see what we're carrying to the car."

Relieved, Victoria nodded while Ginger, despite the agonising pain in her side, headed for the bedroom. Scanning the room to make sure they hadn't left anything incriminating behind, she glimpsed two eyes watching her from the children's partially open bedroom door. Recognizing Thomas, she hurried over to him and crouched in front of him.

"You should be in bed," she said, forcing herself to remain calm and keep a steady tone.

"Is he dead?" the little boy asked in a small voice.

Victoria swallowed. What could she possibly say? If he told anyone what he'd seen, they were all lost. Her heart was wrenched with fear, but she stayed composed. "Yes. It was an accident. He wanted to hurt your mummy and—"

"He was mean! He hit Mummy all the time. He won't hurt her anymore, will he?"

"No, Thomas. He won't. I can promise you that."

Victoria hesitated to pressure the child, but she heard Ginger in the bedroom and knew she would soon be coming out.

"Go back to bed. We'll talk more tomorrow. But first promise me that you will never tell anyone. Not even your granny or your mummy, okay?"

Thomas nodded. He was very fond of Victoria. She never yelled at him, and his mummy often laughed when Victoria was there. Not like when she was with his father. He had often been awakened in the middle of the night by screaming. Powerless, hidden in the doorway, he had watched his father beat his mother many times. He hated the man lying on the floor.

"Okay. I promise."

Just like she would have with an adult, Victoria solemnly held out her hand to seal their pact. Thomas was surprised not to be treated like a baby; he filled with pride when he reached out to shake her hand.

"Go back to sleep now, quickly."

Victoria was closing the children's bedroom door as Ginger came out of her bedroom.

"What...?"

"I was just checking that the children were sound asleep."

This blatant lie made Victoria feel uncomfortable, but she didn't want to worry Ginger any more than she already had.

"A blanket and some rope."

"Help me cover him."

Ten minutes later, sitting at the wheel in Virgil's car, Victoria drove carefully down the flooded road toward the Brisbane River estuary. Even with the windshield wipers on full force, she could barely see because of the lightning and beating rain, but this deluge was in fact a blessing. No one was outside in this weather, and except for a few rare cars here and there, Victoria didn't encounter a living soul during the entire journey.

Cursing Virgil's heavy body, she quickly dragged it down the riverbank, cut the rope, unwrapped the blanket, and rolled him into the water. Hurrying away to avoid a surprise attack from a crocodile, she picked up the blanket and bits of rope, then quickly returned to the car. Ginger and Victoria had decided that she would leave the car near the docks to muddle their tracks. Victoria's only problem would be how to get back inside the house without anyone noticing, but with this heavy rain, the neighbour Rodney and his wife wouldn't hear a thing.

❖

The night's storm had given way to a bright-blue sky, which normally would have made Victoria smile as she began walking the path that led up to Ginger's mother's house. She had hurried her deliveries to free some time for herself at the end of the morning. *As long as Ginger agrees to stick with their decision and, above all, as long as Thomas doesn't say a word to anyone, we will all be safe. Talking to Ginger will have to wait for this evening, but speaking to Thomas…*Once again, when she saw the house, she wondered how to have a serious talk with a five-year-old. Would he understand? Would he reject her?

"Vic!"

Simone's shrill childlike voice welcomed Victoria as soon as she stepped into the garden. A little ball of energy jumped into her arms. Victoria smiled, listened, and answered the small girl's questions while seeking for Thomas. As soon as she saw him still standing next to his grandmother's armchair, she understood the anguish that had to be eating away at him. Without hesitating and still holding Simone in her arms, she walked over to them. Greetings were exchanged, as well as comments about the night's storm. Victoria spoke for several minutes with Ginger's mother, but she was focused on Thomas.

Putting Simone down, she held out her hand. "Come with me, Thomas. I want to show you something."

He simply gazed at her hand.

"He's been this way since Ginger dropped him off this morning," Ginger's mother said, as if to excuse him. "I wonder if he's coming down with something. Maybe I should take him to see the doctor?"

Victoria shook her head no, forcing herself to relax. "I promised you something yesterday evening. Do you want to come with me now?"

His eyes lit up with a bright expression that Victoria interpreted as hope.

Since Thomas had awoken that morning, the scene from the night before had kept playing again and again in his head. Deep down, he knew something bad had happened, and he was afraid. What if someone came to take his mummy or Vic away? What would happen to him?

Seeing Victoria now was reassuring. She hadn't gone. She held out her hand, and Thomas grabbed it.

"We'll be right back," Victoria told Ginger's mother. "I'll leave Simone here with you."

"I want to come too," the tiny girl immediately said.

Victoria kneeled to face her. "You're still too little. Stay with Granny."

Simone nearly stamped her feet with rage. She wanted to protest, but one look from Victoria calmed her. The last time she had thrown her toy in anger, Victoria had refused to tell her a bedtime story. So, her lips shaking, watching Victoria and Thomas walk away, she contained her anger at being left out.

"It's not fair..." she murmured under her breath, sniffling.

"Life isn't always fair, dear," her grandmother replied. "They'll be back soon. Don't worry."

At the end of the path, Victoria picked up Thomas to sit him down on a half-built wall partially covered with overgrown vegetation. Victoria had often wondered if the person who had started building the house had died in the war. Why else would someone start working on a project like this and not finish it?

She sat down next to Thomas and gazed at the horizon. She would never tire of it. The sea, the sky, an unobstructed view were the only things that chased away the years of nightmares of being in the jungle. That and Ginger's arms.

How could she speak to a five-year-old child about his father's murder? She took a few moments to think back to when she was only five: life in the streets, plundering, the hard knocks, being beaten, and then meeting Jason. She had been scared out of her wits when the strange man had put her in his wagon to take her back to that unknown place. However, every time she had looked into his gentle eyes, genuine warmth had filled her heart. "Jason never lied to you," a small voice inside her murmured.

"I never intended to kill your father, Thomas," Victoria said in a soft voice, noticing his big, innocent blue eyes. "I just tried to protect your mother. I love her so much, and he was hurting her...I...I lost control. I just wanted him to stop. I'm so sorry. I didn't want to take your pa away from you"

Surprised, Thomas looked up at Victoria, whose eyes were lost on the horizon. He had often seen her staring out into the distance this way, but he didn't understand what she saw there, apart from the sea and the trees. He gently tugged on the sleeve of Victoria's work shirt, his hand so small next to her big ones. She turned to look at him, staring into big blue innocent eyes.

"You won't leave?"

"Not if you want me to stay."

"Mummy won't either?"

"Never. She would never abandon her children. You and Simone are the people who mean the most to her."

"And you?"

Victoria frowned. What was he getting at?

"You, Simone, and your mummy are the people who mean the most in this world to me. The day you came into my life gave me reason to live again."

Victoria doubted that such a young boy could understand everything she was saying, but she did believe he would understand the feelings attached to these words. Moved by a sudden surge of emotion, she put her arm around his frail shoulders, and he threw himself into her arms.

"I thought you didn't love me anymore," Thomas sobbed.

Victoria gently ran her hand over his blond hair. "Why did you think that...son?"

Slowly, things started to fall into place in Victoria's mind. She no longer had a choice. She'd never really had a choice, but she hadn't realised it before. The moment she had returned to Brisbane, Ginger, Thomas, and Simone had become her family. Tears pervaded her eyes.

"You were mad at me last night."

"No. I was mad at myself. I was scared for your mum."

"But together we'll protect her. Isn't that so?"

Victoria smiled both at Thomas's comment as well as hearing him use his mother's "isn't that so."

"Yes. I will need your help, son. Women aren't always easy to understand."

Clearly confused, Thomas looked up at Victoria, who was a woman.

"Some of us are more women than others," she explained, truly smiling for the first time that morning. "But you'll understand when you're older."

CHAPTER THIRTY-SEVEN

Brisbane, Queensland, toward the end of 1950

As soon as Victoria heard the door open, despite the sadness she'd felt since she'd read the morning's mail, she smiled. Would she ever grow weary of seeing Ginger? She didn't think so.

"You're home! How did your shift go?"

"Okay. The children?"

"They're in bed. They wanted to wait for you, but I convinced them you wouldn't be happy if they stayed up too late."

Ginger planted a light kiss on Victoria's lips. Never had she imagined she could be so happy. Her children loved their second mother and only very rarely asked about their father. When she thought about it, she realised that Thomas had actually never asked about him—only Simone had. As Victoria handed her a glass of tamarind juice, Ginger noticed the sadness in her eyes.

"What happened?"

Victoria sighed. "I just got a letter from John. My mother is dying. The doctor says she has only a few months, maybe less."

"I'm so sorry," Ginger whispered, taking Victoria into her arms. They stayed that way for a few moments until Victoria stepped back to look at her.

"I have to go to Willowra. I want to see her before it's too late. And my father will need me."

Victoria hesitated. She had thought a great deal since she had read the letter on her way back from work. "Do you think you and the children would like to come with me? We could move there."

Faced with Ginger's silence, Victoria added, "You've been saying that the neighbours are starting to look at you funny, and you have the impression that people have been gossiping about us since your husband's car was found. It's the opportunity to leave everything behind us and turn over a new leaf in Willowra. No one will be there to watch us, except the sheep, maybe."

"I don't know." Ginger sighed, snuggling up in Victoria's reassuring arms.

"Nothing's keeping us here now that your mother has passed away. All we have to do is pack up what we want to take with us and sell the rest. In a week we could be in Western Australia, and to hell with the gossip!"

Ginger thought about it. Victoria was right. What better than a huge station to live this love that she still perceived as miraculous after eight months of sharing each other's lives? The children were young. They should be happy being able to frolic about freely in wide-open spaces. But what would Victoria's family make of them?

"Do you think your family would welcome us without any problems?"

"With open arms—sincerely."

"Then when are we leaving?" Ginger asked, hoping she would never have reason to regret her decision.

Joy exploded in Victoria's heart. She would have liked to jump into the air, but instead she simply hugged the woman who had given her so much to live for. "I'm going to telegraph John to warn them we're coming as quickly as possible. You'll adore Willowra—and my family."

Ginger beamed, chasing Victoria's fears away.

❖

When the train stopped in Norseman, Victoria, holding a suitcase in each hand, led her small family to the exit. She smiled at Thomas, who was using both hands to carry a suitcase nearly as big as he was, while Ginger had an oversized travel bag in one hand and held Simone's hand with the other. Victoria wanted to get them comfortably installed before taking care of the two trunks they were travelling with (their other belongings would arrive by freight train) and finding some way to transport them to Willowra.

When John's telegram had arrived three days after she had sent hers, with the words "waiting for you," her heart had started to beat wildly. She had waited until the day they got on the train to Sydney to send another telegram, saying "leaving today." So John knew they would be arriving at some point that week. Had he told their parents? Did he want to surprise them?

Stopping near a shaded bench right outside the train station, Victoria put the suitcases down on the dusty ground and indicated to the others to follow suit. "Wait for me here. I'm going to get the trunks."

"Vic?"

At the sound of her name softly being called, Victoria looked up. Ginger stood there with a questioning expression, staring at someone behind her. Victoria turned around and found herself looking right into her father's blue eyes. She just had time to notice that he had aged before feeling his strong arms around her.

"You've finally come home! We were starting to lose hope. Your ma will be so pleased."

Her father's voice. The familiar, almost forgotten smell of him. Victoria couldn't hold back her tears. "Pa. Oh, Pa!"

Not caring about how it looked, Jason cried with joy, feeling her daughter in her arms. When John had showed them the telegram, it was difficult to restrain her tears, though Maggie had freely expressed her emotions. Her daughter was finally coming home...with her family. Gently pushing Vic back just far enough to take a good look at her, Jason smiled before turning toward the little woman and the two small, wide-eyed children watching them.

"Pa, I want to introduce you to my family," Victoria murmured, her throat tight with emotion. "Ginger, my companion. Thomas and Simone."

Ginger ceremoniously held out her hand, while Jason spontaneously stepped forward and hugged the woman who had brought Victoria back home to her kin.

"Thank you for helping her come back to us, Ginger. And welcome to the family. You can call me Jason, or Pa, like everyone else."

Any fears Ginger might have had as to her being welcomed at Willowra immediately vanished because of this man's sincere words. When Victoria had described her father as a man without a mean bone in his body, who never lost his temper, Ginger had doubted someone like him could exist. But now that she was actually seeing him, she understood exactly what Victoria had meant. She watched him shake her six-year-old son's hand as if he were a teenager and call him "son," but what conquered Ginger once and for all was to watch this almost-sixty-year-old man get down on one knee with a great big grin to say hello to her daughter, who was hiding behind her skirts.

Still smiling, Jason got up and dusted off her pant leg before addressing Victoria. "I took the truck. It's less comfortable than the car, but I thought you might have a lot of luggage."

"Two trunks and the suitcases. The rest should arrive in about two weeks."

"Good. Help me get your little family settled, and then we'll take care of the trunks."

Jason grabbed two suitcases and walked toward the only truck parked out front. She put the suitcases in the back before taking one from Victoria's hand, along with the travelling bag.

"Thomas, I think you can travel in the back of the pickup with the baggage and let the women ride inside," Jason suggested.

Victoria winked at Ginger to reassure her, as a huge smile spread across Thomas's lips. "Oh, yes, sir!"

"Don't call me sir, son. You can call me Gramps or Jason. It's up to you, but sir is out of the question."

Jason helped Thomas climb in the back while Ginger lifted Simone up into the cab.

"I'm going to see about the trunks," Jason told Victoria.

"I'll go with you. How did you know we were arriving today?"

"I've come to meet every train since the beginning of the week. Not that we have many of them. You'll see that not a lot has changed out here."

As Victoria spoke, Jason observed her from the corner of her eye. Her face had lost the traces of childhood; her features were marked, her hair much shorter, just long enough to be held back in the short ponytail she'd gathered it into. Seeing Victoria limp caused Jason more sorrow than she could have imagined. That someone could have done harm to her baby filled her with rage. She knew she had to keep her mouth shut, but she'd had enough with all these years of silence and hiding her emotions. On top of it, since she had learned that Maggie…Jason took a deep breath. She didn't want to let her thoughts drift in that direction.

"You still have a limp," she said.

"I'll limp till my very last days, but it's much improved. At least I'm no longer in pain." Victoria stopped, surprised, and said, "You know? But John promised!"

"And he kept his promise. Robert let the cat out of the bag after he saw you at the rehabilitation centre in Melbourne in '46. He wrote us, and John finally explained it all. He's been keeping us up to date since."

Continuing to speak as if the subject weren't important, they headed for the unloading dock. Jason hid the disappointment she had felt at the time. Her daughter had suffered a serious injury yet hadn't wanted her by her side.

Jason forced herself to speak calmly. "You wanted to die, but you were wounded instead. Why didn't you tell us, Victoria? When your mother learned the truth, I almost had to chain her down to keep her from rushing to Melbourne."

Victoria winced and looked away. Her father's frank words caught her off guard. She knew she needed to explain, but not just yet, not so soon.

"It's these two here," she said, pointing to two trunks placed to the side. "How did you convince her not to go?"

"I told her that if you had wanted to see us, you would have written—that you probably weren't ready. I had a hard time convincing her. You know your mother."

"Meeting Ginger changed everything."

Jason smiled. "That's what I figured. A fine-looking woman, who seems to know her mind."

Surprised by her father's analysis, Victoria said, "Yes. She was my nurse in Brisbane when I was repatriated."

Seeing the question in her father's eyes, Victoria sighed. "It's a long story."

"It will be a pleasure for your mother and me to hear it. In the meantime, if you don't want your family cooked to a crisp by Western Australia's hot sun, I suggest we get a move on."

CHAPTER THIRTY-EIGHT

"You've reconfigured the paddocks."

"It was John's idea. The old ones were in bad shape, and not very practical. He was right. These make herding go faster."

Walking slowly, with Jason by her side, Victoria was looking out for changes. The truth was, few things had really been altered during the eight years she'd been gone. She was the one who was different.

Respecting her daughter's silence, Jason watched her from the corner of her eye. She seemed to have grown wiser, more reflective, but war had that effect on people. Jason would have liked to ask her many questions, but she couldn't utter them yet. Everything in its own good time.

"Ginger and the children won your mother over. They're such good kids."

"Pa…? About Ma…John wrote that she was dying."

Jason bit her lower lip. She refused to even think about the possibility of Maggie not recovering. "I don't want to talk about it," Jason said under her breath. "It's more than I can bear."

"I understand."

Seeing her father's glistening eyes, Victoria kept quiet. Tomorrow she would go see John and ask about Maggie's health. Silently, they returned to the house, walking past the stables. When she saw the bay mare, Victoria laughed. "You kept Betty?"

"Well, what did you want me to do with her? Turn her into glue?" Jason was joking to chase away her dark thoughts. "She's not as old as all that. She's just recently gotten this feeble. Anyway, I could never bring myself to get rid of her. Truth be told, having her gave me hope of seeing you again one day. And you know what? I was right."

"Oh, Pa…"

Victoria stepped forward and threw her arms around her, and Jason didn't resist. To hell with appearances. She hugged her back. Their embrace lingered, each of them holding back her tears and neither willing to break up this rare, fragile moment.

Finally, Victoria gently kissed her cheek before stepping back. Despite not wanting to, Jason let go. She had promised Maggie to fulfill her role, and she had and would keep her promise, no matter what.

"Pa…I didn't just do good things when I was away. You wouldn't be proud of me if you knew. I…"

Jason looked at her with an ocean of tenderness. Maggie was right: Victoria had always been and still was her favourite. She had always forgiven her everything. All those lost years.

"We've all done things we're not proud of one day or another, Victoria…myself included. I'm far from perfect."

Perceiving total acceptance and unconditional love in these few words, Victoria wiped away the tears running down her cheeks with the back of her hand. She needed to talk. Guilt had been choking her for so long.

"You don't understand, Pa. I killed Ginger's husband with my bare hands!"

Jason silently waited for her to explain, without expressing any judgment.

"He beat her, repeatedly, and I couldn't stand it. One evening when I went 'round there, he was beating her so hard I thought he would kill her. I jumped on him and slammed his head against the floor until he went limp. Every blow relieved me of my anger and frustration, as if I were doing for Ginger what I couldn't do for Elise…protect her…"

Victoria gazed out at the horizon as she relived the scene in her head. She protectively wrapped her arms around herself.

Jason softly brushed her callused fingers across Victoria's cheek, forcing her to look into her eyes. "Vic, a man has to do whatever it takes, whatever it costs, to protect his family. I was lucky I never had to kill for mine, but I would have if it had ever been necessary."

Surprise flashed through Victoria, like an electric shock. Her gentle, tolerant father not only wasn't judging her, but he gave her his blessing. Once again, Victoria flung herself into the arms of this man she loved so much.

❖

"Jason actually said that?"

Pinch-lipped and rigid-backed, Simone stared at this woman who had raised her alongside her mother. Victoria nodded in confirmation. You could have cut the silence around the table with a shearing knife.

"I can't believe that about Jason," Simone said. "He was too fine a man, uh, woman, I guess. Never...never would he...she have killed anyone."

She was burning with anger. If she could have struck Victoria down with lightning on the spot, she would have. How could she have killed her father? And with her mother's blessing? Simone shook her head, trying to refuse the reality of what Victoria had just revealed.

"I'm not surprised Jason felt that way," Thomas murmured.

All eyes turned to him, and Simone stared the hardest, widening her eyes with surprise, while his two children seemed to be dying to hear their father elaborate on his comment. Aurore gently pressed her husband's hand.

Only Tess kept her eyes on Victoria. Despite everyone's varied reactions, she greatly admired this woman whom she had been discovering as her story unfolded.

Thomas explained the situation. "I remember Jason well, even if I was only a child at the time. Growing up, I often spoke to John about his father. He described the gentle, hard-working man he was, but he also spoke about his determination. He would have done anything to protect what was most dear to him. Nothing in John's words ever led me to believe that Jason was really a woman. He spoke about Jason with respect and admiration, and of Maggie with great love. Now I understand better why."

"And you find Victoria's action excusable?" Simone almost screamed. "For heaven's sake, she killed our father and perverted our mother! She's the worst kind of criminal!"

Thomas calmly looked at his sister and thought back to that horrible period. "Victoria killed the man who regularly beat and abused our mother. I remember that night as clear as day, Simone, and all the nights before. I've never forgotten. Every time that monster returned, I would hear Ma's screams and shrieks of anguish, along with the sound of his punches and blows raining down on her. I'd clench my fists because I wanted to grow up faster to give him his due. Don't tell me you never heard anything, or that you've forgotten all the nights you came to huddle up in my arms shaking with fear."

Simone remained silent, lost in her memories. She vaguely

remembered upsetting moments, but did they have anything to do with this?

"Victoria," Thomas said, "was more of a father to us than our real one ever was…and a mother when Mum passed on. Whether you like it or not, she was always there when we needed her. Our mother loved her, and she loved our mother. And us—she loved us."

Simone wordlessly stood up and looked Victoria right in the eye. "I could go to the police and have you put in prison."

Victoria shook her head, feeling no remorse. Ginger and Thomas had forgiven her, and, more important, Jason had forgiven her.

"You could try, Simone, but the body disappeared long ago. Where's the proof? These are just a crazy old woman's stories."

Simone snarled and glanced at her brother, who shook his head. She wouldn't get any support from him, not any more than from anyone else, not even that Tess person. She refrained from screaming in vexation. She wasn't going to let them see her fall apart. Shrugging, she left the table. Just before leaving the room, she turned around, shooting a piercing look at Victoria. "I don't think I will ever be able to forgive you."

Victoria acquiesced with a pinch in her heart. She thought of Ginger, whom she had promised on her deathbed to watch over her children and grandchildren. At that moment, seeing Simone leave the room, she felt she had failed at her task. *One day children grow their own wings and decide for themselves.* Jason's words came back to her as she realised how right he'd been.

"So Ginger and you were a couple?" Gabrielle asked, to break the heavy silence that surrounded Simone's departure. "And our pa knew? What about you, Jeremy?"

"Of course not, Gab. I'm as shoc…surprised as you are."

Jeremy, despite his tan, seemed pale. He closed his eyes for a moment. How could he not have noticed that these two women he loved the most in the world were…different? How badly Victoria must think of him, knowing the comments he'd made about gays? And Gab? It was his fault his sister had left Willowra. Would they ever be able to forgive him?

The grandfather clock ticked the seconds away, and Victoria just smiled, taking a good look at her grandchildren. She could almost feel Ginger's presence by her side. There would be no more secrets in Willowra.

"What happened to Robert?" Tess asked, to lighten the atmosphere.

While Victoria gave her a grateful glance, Gab grabbed Tess's hand and squeezed it. A collective sigh of relief lifted the mood.

"He's still alive. I receive a few letters from him each year. After becoming a lawyer, he became active in the defence of aboriginal rights and took part in the negotiations to reclaim native lands. He's been living in Arnhem Land, rediscovering his native culture and militating against white prejudice. Jason would have been proud of his son."

"And not Maggie?" Tess asked.

"Maggie too."

Victoria hesitated and smiled apologetically before she continued.

"Jason always meant more to me than Maggie did. I tend to see everything through my father's eyes. I've often wondered if the love between us was more than filial. I wonder how I would have reacted if he'd revealed the truth to me much sooner."

A door slamming ended Victoria's speculations. Simone brought them back to the present.

"I guess I ought to take my sister to the train. She won't want to spend another night here." Thomas sighed.

Aurore placed her hand on Thomas's forearm to stop him from getting up. "I'll drive her. There's no sense in you having another fight."

Without any hesitation, Aurore walked away, grabbing her car keys.

"I'll come with you, Mum," Jeremy said, standing up. "Simone's suitcase feels like it's full of bricks."

Relief overwhelmed Thomas as he caught his son's eyes. They understood one another. Jeremy wouldn't let Simone spew her vile mood on his mother. Thomas suspected that his son also needed to talk. The car ride back would give them the perfect opportunity.

"You looked so handsome in your uniform," Gabrielle joked when only the four of them were left. "You must have been quite a hit with the sheilas."

Victoria chuckled, accentuating the wrinkles on her aged face. Her blue eyes glimmered mischievously. "If I hadn't been mourning Elise, I most certainly would have held the record for the 21st Brigade. Even though I wasn't interested, I had more than a few chances to look... and touch."

"Mum! I'm shocked. I've never heard you speak that way."

Victoria looked at him innocently. "What could I do? The sheilas would come over and sit right on my lap in the pubs. I wasn't about to push them away. Don't tell me you wouldn't have done the same."

Thomas's face turned bright red. Gabrielle heard Tess trying unsuccessfully to stifle her laughter and irresistibly started to laugh as well.

"Nan, you are incorrigible!" Gab commented while still laughing. "You'd get on famously with a friend of ours. You should come to Sydney so I can introduce you to her."

"With great pleasure, Gab. I've always wanted to go back to Sydney to see how it's changed. And my friend Mac would be happy to see me and meet my granddaughter and her partner."

"Mac, your commanding officer?" Tess asked.

"In the flesh."

"He'd be pleased to tell you all about their adventures in New Guinea," Thomas added with a grin.

Victoria winced. She remembered the evening at John's when Mac had come for a visit to Willowra. Luckily neither Aurore nor Jeremy had been there. Otherwise, Aurore would have turned beet red, and Jeremy would no longer have been able to look his nan in the face. It then crossed her mind that perhaps presenting Gab and Tess to Mac wasn't such a good idea after all.

"We'll think about it," Victoria said as she stood up. "You're not gone yet. Who's gonna help me get tea ready?"

Thomas excused himself. "I have to go look after the animals."

"I'll help you, Victoria," Tess offered.

Gab smiled at Tess before standing and heading out after her father. "I'll come with you, Pa. I could use a little exercise."

❖

"They're all buried there, and I'll be joining them soon," Victoria softly commented as she walked over to Tess, who was contemplating the area that composed the family's burial ground on the station. Victoria pointed to an opening between two tombstones slightly to the right.

"I'll be laid to rest between Elise and Ginger. My coffin and stone are ready."

"What a fine woman and incredible person," Tess commented, pointing to Jason's tomb in front of her. "Both stories, hers and yours, are fascinating."

Victoria laughed softly. With a naughty look on her face, she turned to Tess. "Thanks for the compliment, but without Jason, my story would have ended before it even had a chance to begin. I owe her everything. Not only for saving my life as a five-year-old child, but also for the love she and Maggie gave me and for protecting my right to love differently. Things have changed greatly since then. Just take you and Gabrielle, for example."

"Perhaps…She was still, however, very much afraid her family would reject her. We had a really good laugh when we went to bed last night."

"And you weren't just laughing…"

Frowning, Tess didn't seem to understand. Then, with a smile, Victoria said, "The walls are still just as thin as they were in Maggie and Jason's day…"

Tess blushed uncontrollably and had a tender thought for her air-conditioned home in Sydney.

Victoria gave a hearty laugh. "Believe it or not, I was thrilled to hear you. It took me back to my childhood. How did the thought never cross my mind that my parents were both women? It's a mystery to me, but it helps prove that you only see what you want to see."

Tess unconsciously caressed her slightly rounded tummy with her hand, and Victoria noticed.

"It's wonderful that you conceived a child together. You'll have to bring him or her as often as possible to Willowra and tell your little ones about their ancestors."

Tess hesitated. She didn't want to betray Gab, but she needed to confide in someone, vent her fears, even if things seemed to be going better between them the last few days.

"These last months, since the baby was conceived, Gab's been acting differently."

Victoria listened attentively. She had noticed Gabrielle steal glances here and there at Tess's belly but hadn't understood what it meant.

"Right before coming here, she admitted that she was afraid she couldn't rise to the task of being a parent; that maybe having the child was a mistake. I'm so afraid she's going to leave me. I love her, and I need her."

Victoria carefully wrapped her arm around Tess's shoulder. With her other hand she pointed to the tombstones before her.

"You don't think Jason was afraid when she told Maggie the truth? And when they opened their home to the children? That I wasn't afraid, faced with the responsibility of raising two children? I knew from the beginning that Ginger wouldn't be able to manage alone, and I can tell you I spent many a night doubting myself and my parenting abilities. Gabrielle was born and raised on Willowra. This is a harsh place. It requires uncommon strength of character. I trust she will face up to her responsibilities, because even though she doesn't have Jason's or my blood, our legacy runs through her veins. She clearly loves you, and she'll learn to calm her fears and love this child. Don't push her too much, and if she ever acts up, all you have to do is send her to me. I'll make it my job to remind her where she came from."

Touched, her eyes filled with tears, Tess swallowed.

"You're a beautiful woman, Tess, with a personality to match. If I was a few years younger," Victoria said, "Gabrielle would have some worries, 'cause I'd try to steal you from her."

Tess, despite the tears in her eyes, threw herself into Victoria's arms, whispering, "No doubt Gabrielle would have something to worry about if you were a few years younger. Thank you, Victoria."

❖

"What do you think they're talkin' about, Pa?' Gabrielle asked, sitting on the bench in the shade of the house.

Thomas looked out toward the cemetery and saw his mother wrap her arm around Tess's shoulders, then Tess throw herself into Victoria's arms. He raised an eyebrow. "No idea. Why don't you just ask them?"

Life was straightforward for Thomas, but when he turned to look at Gabrielle, the dark expression he saw in her eyes made him understand that he might be mistaken not to search further beneath the surface. Lucky for him, Aurore could always see things clearly. He smiled inside. Aurore never would have married him if she had seen only the tall, gangly, shy fella who could do nothing but blush when he spoke to her.

"Your grandmother's eighty-six. Don't go thinking that…"

Gabrielle sighed. She was stupid for feeling jealous. It was the first time in her life she'd felt that way…She slowly raked her fingers through her hair.

"I don't know. I really don't. Since Tess's been pregnant, I feel like I've been living outside myself. Victoria was so brave, determined, and I have the impression I'll never measure up, that Tess will realise I'm not as great as all that, with all my doubts and fears."

Surprised by this sudden confession, Thomas paused before answering. "Did you actually hear and understand the story your grandmother was telling us, Gab? Victoria had her share of doubts and fears. We all do...especially when a baby's on the way. Ask your mother how I behaved during her first pregnancy, or even her second. And then the baby arrives, and you no longer have the time to ask yourself all these questions. I immediately fell in love with each of you. You know, I respect Jason and Victoria enormously. They took responsibility for children who were already grown, with their flaws and qualities, and they loved them as they were. That wasn't an easy thing to do at all."

Gabrielle was so absorbed in reflecting upon her father's words that she barely heard the approaching steps on the veranda's floor. Suddenly, she realised that Tess was standing before her, blocking her view, her beautiful smile lighting up her face.

Immediately, Gab stood up and took Tess in her arms. Closing her eyes, she savoured the silence, the familiar contact, the smell of her. At that very moment, an absolute certainty washed over her, removing all her doubts. She would do everything in her power to protect Tess and the family they were building together.

About the Author

French author Kadyan (http://www.kadyan.fr/) has been living abroad for almost twenty years, especially in Asia and Oceania. With her spouse and her dog, she is now back in France as a full-time writer. Since 2003, she has published thirteen books in French, spanning genres from historical novels to thrillers to science fiction. In her free time, she loves to garden and to tinker, using all the cool tools.

Books Available From Bold Strokes Books

Can't Leave Love by Kimberly Cooper Griffin. Sophia and Pru have no intention of falling in love, but sometimes love happens when and where you least expect it. (978-1-636790041-1)

Free Fall at Angel Creek by Julie Tizard. Detective Dee Rawlings and aircraft accident investigator Dr. River Dawson use conflicting methods to find answers when a plane goes missing, while overcoming surprising threats and discovering an unlikely chance at love. (978-1-63555-884-5)

Love's Compromise by Cass Sellars. For Piper Holthaus and Brook Myers, will professional dreams and past baggage stop two hearts from realizing they are meant for each other? (978-1-63555-942-2)

Not All a Dream by Sophia Kell Hagin. Hester has lost the woman she loved, and the world has descended into relentless dark and cold. But giving up will have to wait when she stumbles upon people who help her survive. (978-1-63679-067-1)

Protecting the Lady by Amanda Radley. If Eve Webb had known she'd be protecting royalty, she'd never have taken the job as bodyguard, but as the threat to Lady Katherine's life draws closer, she'll do whatever it takes to save her, and may just lose her heart in the process. (978-1-63679-003-9)

The Secrets of Willowra by Kadyan. A family saga of three women, their homestead called Willowra in the Australian outback, and the secrets that link them all. (978-1-63679-064-0)

Trial by Fire by Carsen Taite. When prosecutor Lennox Roy and public defender Wren Bishop become fierce adversaries in a headline-grabbing arson case, their attraction ignites a passion that leads them both to question their assumptions about the law, the truth, and each other. (978-1-63555-860-9)

Turbulent Waves by Ali Vali. Kai Merlin and Vivien Palmer plan their future together as hostile forces make their own plans to destroy what they have, as well as all those they love. (978-1-63679-011-4)

Unbreakable by Cari Hunter. When Dr. Grace Kendal is forced at gunpoint to help an injured woman, she is dragged into a nightmare where nothing is quite as it seems, and their lives aren't the only ones on the line. (978-1-63555-961-3)

Veterinary Surgeon by Nancy Wheelton. When dangerous drugs are stolen from the veterinary clinic, Mitch investigates and Kay becomes a suspect. As pride and professions clash, love seems impossible. (978-1-63679-043-5)

All That Remains by Sheri Lewis Wohl. Johnnie and Shantel might have to risk their lives—and their love—to stop a werewolf intent on killing. (978-1-63555-949-1)

Beginner's Bet by Fiona Riley. Phenom luxury Realtor Ellison Gamble has everything, except a family to share it with, so when a mix-up brings youthful Katie Crawford into her life, she bets the house on love. (978-1-63555-733-6)

Dangerous Without You by Lexus Grey. Throughout their senior year in high school, Aspen, Remington, Denna, and Raleigh face challenges in life and romance that they never expect. (978-1-63555-947-7)

Desiring More by Raven Sky. In this collection of steamy stories, a rich variety of lovers find themselves desiring more: more from a lover, more from themselves, and more from life. (978-1-63679-037-4)

Jordan's Kiss by Nanisi Barrett D'Arnuck. After losing everything in a fire, Jordan Phelps joins a small lounge band and meets pianist Morgan Sparks, who lights another blaze—this time in Jordan's heart. (978-1-63555-980-4)

Late City Summer by Jeanette Bears. Forced together for her wedding, Emily Stanton and Kate Alessi navigate their lingering passion for one another against the backdrop of New York City and World War II, and a summer romance they left behind. (978-1-63555-968-2)

Love and Lotus Blossoms by Anne Shade. On her path to self-acceptance and true passion, Janesse will risk everything—and possibly everyone—she loves. (978-1-63555-985-9)